RAND: SON OF TALLAV

SONS OF TALLAV #3

CAILIN BRISTE

Rand: Son of Tallav

Copyright © July 2018 by Cailin Briste

eISBN 978-0-9989125-6-1

Published in the United States of America

Hot Sauce Publishing
PO Box 13508
Offutt AFB, NE 68113-0508

For all those struggling to find unconditional love.

ACKNOWLEDGMENT

To Sir for reading an early version of Rand with the eye of a sadist.

To Lea Scafer for her prowess as an editor.

To Samantha at Proofreading By the Page for picking out the nits that like to cling to the pages.

To my readers who encouraged me through the sometimes difficult journey of writing this book.

And not least, to my husband. Ever my first reader and number one fan; without his steady hand I'd be lost.

1

Briarcliff, Tallav

The slender slice of moon did little to light the edge of the cliff, over which the desperate bleating of a lamb sounded. Rhiannon, Tallav's second moon, had yet to rise and brighten the night sky. Why the gardener's boy sought Penny out on the patio rather than running to get the overseer, she didn't question. He was a child and probably ran for the nearest adult. Peering over, she could make out a patch of dirty white caught in a bush. At least the lamb had slid into the branches, it's fall blocked from the vertical plunge of the cliff to the river below.

How had it gotten here? The early lambs weren't old enough to be out of the lambing shed, which was nowhere near the cliff. She slid carefully down the slight grade of the rim and tried to calm the animal while she waited for help to arrive. She'd sent the boy on to the overseer with a request to bring rope.

Careful to stay out of range of the lamb's thrashing, she spoke to it in gentle, crooning tones. The animal quieted, no longer flailing but still bleating plaintively. The creamy tan color of the lamb's body was more difficult to see in the dark, but the face, white with black speckles, stood out. To her horror, she noticed one of those dark marks was in the shape of a heart. This was the orphan lamb the overseer had allowed Sophie to help feed. That lamb was bedded down every night by the overseer himself in the enclosure built next to his office in the main barn. Someone had to have brought this lamb out here. She'd damn well find out as soon as she rescued it from its precarious predicament.

Above her, loose rock skittered with the sound of someone descending. She tipped her head back and shouted, "Don't come down. Just drop the end of the rope."

"We won't need a rope."

The low, throaty words confused her. That wasn't the overseer. She lost sight of the darkened form above her when she sat up to roll over on the clumps of rock and grass beneath her to get a better look. A solid thud struck her back, sending pain lancing along her spine and around her rib cage. The lamb renewed its thrashing when she slid into it, knocking it backward. Squealing in terror, it tumbled out of view.

Heart pumping, Penny windmilled in a futile attempt to keep from falling forward. She straddled the bush with her legs, the sharp ends of broken stems lacerating her exposed face and hands, snagging in the long-sleeved pajamas she wore. For an instant, her momentum stopped. In desperation she clamped her fists onto the bush's base, ignoring the sting of abrasions.

A second strike from her assailant's booted foot hit her high to one side of her backbone.

Something snapped inside.

Pain flooded her shoulder.

Jarred forward, she began a slow-motion tumble headfirst over the bush.

Fingers and palms tore while branches slid through her grasp until the strain on her good shoulder from the somersault forced her to let go.

Oh God. I'm falling. Sophie. Oh God. I can't die and leave Sophie.

Her temple struck a jutting rock, and darkness claimed her.

Above, a figure scrambled to the top of the cliff, humming a cheery tune. The wordless melody stopped at the sound of someone rushing toward the precipice. By the time the overseer arrived, the spot was empty. No lamb. No Penny. Just moonlight casting the side of the cliff in shadow in the waning heat from a late summer day. With an exclamation of frustration and an oath that he'd see to that boy for pulling pranks, the overseer left.

It wasn't until the next day, when no one could find Penny, that the overseer mentioned his fruitless trip to the cliff edge. Her body lay on the rocks, half in and half out of the river. Officially she was a casualty of misadventure.

The Whip Hand, *Beta Tau*

Randolph stroked the disheveled softness of Eva's hair before firmly gripping the back of her neck. "You did very well, Eva." A shudder and sob were her only response. The time he'd spent with Eva over the last week had been a refreshing change from the business expansion consuming him for over a year. Although he might not have taken on Eva's remedial training if her master hadn't been a member of the Beta Tau board of directors.

Her body writhed when he drew a finger over the marks he'd left on her back. One or two spots were seeping blood. He swirled the tip in the fluid before scraping his nail across the abrasion. The sight of Eva, arms shackled above her head, undulating before him, sent a jolt of pleasure through him.

"Your master doesn't hurt you often, Eva. Perhaps that's why you believed you could manipulate him. He brought you to me to break that habit."

"Yes, Sir." A whimper escaped her lips.

Randolph threaded his fingers into her hair and pulled her head back, noting the tears inching down her cheek. "This is our last session before I return you to your master. The pain you've experienced was not a punishment. You've learned your lesson and learned it well." He brushed his finger through the damp trail on her face. "This was for me. Your tears are your gift to me. I'm a sadist, Eva. I enjoy hurting you. But I haven't taken you over the edge of what you could bear. If your master sends you again, I will break you. Do you understand?"

"Unnnhhh." The sound flew from her.

Randolph jostled her head. "Say you understand."

"I understand, Sir." The words came out with a squeak.

"Good," he said, unwinding his fingers from her hair. He allowed the chain attached to her shackles to lengthen with a flick of his wrist before again engaging the locking mechanism. Gripping both her hips, he pulled her back until she was bent before him. He smacked her bottom. "Do not come. Your orgasms belong to your master. Correct?"

"Yes, Sir."

"Say it," he ground out.

"My orgasms belong to my master."

Randolph stepped away, allowing her master to step forward and take over. He didn't watch the happy reunion when he exited the scene. He made his way to his office, brushing his fingertips through his neatly trimmed smoky brown hair. His cock had gone semihard, but Eva wasn't his type and she wasn't his. If she were, he would have taken her much deeper before fucking her.

His type. He had to smirk at that. His type hadn't really been doing it for him lately. Probably the stress, which in theory should be diminishing. The addition of a private play space to his new suite had been a gift to himself a long time in coming. He'd finally indulged himself. The combination of play space, office, and apartment allowed him a level of privacy he'd never had. Perfect on days like today when he was too tired to face the onslaught of those seeking a personal moment with the celebrity owner and top sadist of the Whip Hand. He rarely entered the main play floors anymore, so when he did, the clamor was more strident.

After keying open his office door, he strode to the bar and a bottle of high-priced bourbon, pouring himself two fingers. He settled into his desk chair, downed a swallow of the liquor, and set the glass on the black coaster that protected his expensive desk.

He leaned back, eyes closed, waiting for the ripples of the chair adjusting to end, and then tapped the button that started his personal massage program. Heat soothed his tired back before the chair switched to a gentle overall kneading. A wince tightened his face when it began pummeling the knots in his shoulders.

The yearlong renovation had included an upgrade to the Whip Hand's business offices. His new office was larger, including a sitting area and many other luxuries that put his old one with a desk and two chairs to shame. This desk was a work of art. The surface was black and white ebony inlay over black ebony. Its thick legs and panels were carved reliefs of tormented bodies struggling to free themselves from the wood. It made an impression on anyone who entered the room.

Yet he preferred his old office. Except for this chair. His old office with this chair would be just right, but the Whip Hand had evolved light-years beyond its original concept.

The expansion and renovation moved it well past its simpler days when he'd spent as much time on the floor as in his office. Now, a week could pass without him ever setting foot in any of the club's venues. He'd passed oversight of the club's subs to Tom. He was good at the job, but doing so still gave Randolph the sense that he'd allowed something to slip away.

As the chair resumed the previous gentle kneading, he realized what he missed: the immediacy. His own whip demos and playtime on the floor had evaporated, replaced by more and more meetings. Damn, he was a stodgy businessman now.

The chair's program ended. Randolph drained the glass of bourbon and was about to retire to his apartment, shower, and climb in bed. When he sat forward, the red light that signaled an emergency comm winked at him from the touch bar on his desk. He sighed and brought up the message viewer. His forehead creased when he noted the comm was from his mother. Tabbed open, the static image showed her, shoulders drooped, no makeup, face puffy, and eyes red.

Randolph's chest tightened. The last time he'd received a message with his mother looking this distraught was when she'd announced she was divorcing his father. He touched the start button.

"Randolph. I have bad news. Dear, I don't know how to say this, so I'll… Your sister died. She was trying to save a lamb. She fell from the cliff above the river." Tears streamed down her face. "It's awful, Rand. She lay there all night." She reached for a tissue offscreen and blew her nose. "Please come home as soon as you can. We've had her cremated. The memorial service will be held when you arrive." Pain was written in every line of her face. "Please, I need you here. I need you to stay."

Stunned, a lump forming in his throat, Randolph sat immobile, unable to assimilate what he had heard. Penny couldn't be dead. Both his beloved sister and nemesis, she, more than any other person, had driven him away from home, family… Tallav. How could the avenging angel, the destroyer of his life, be dead?

A replay of his mother's comm did little to answer the questions swirling in his mind. She fell from the cliff? A ripple of nausea hit him. Fuck all. Penny knew the cliffs along the river at Briarcliff too well to have fallen from them. Not until he'd replayed the message a third time did he apprehend his mother's last statement. Come? He would absolutely come. But stay? His mother just needed to get her feet under her. No way would he stay on Tallav longer than required to help her settle his sister's affairs.

His fingers drifted to rub the inscribed heart on the pewter bead tied to his wrist by a leather cord. Penny was dead. It wasn't possible. Someone so full of bullheaded life couldn't die. Not the sister he'd never stopped loving even through the slinging vitriol they'd both flung at each other over the last twenty-one years. The sister who clung to distorted facts. Refused to listen each and every time he'd tried to reconcile. She couldn't be gone. The hope he'd clung to that his big sister would once again be his best friend couldn't be shattered. Every bitter word he'd spoken to her in anger hammered at him. If only…

He dropped forward, head in his hands, while searing pain flooded his soul.

CAHERNAMON, *Tallav*

Jen O'Malley ran her sweaty palms over her navy slacks. Her morning had been spent vacillating between clothing options for this interview: formal business or kid friendly. She compromised and opted for casual business. But was that a mistake? O'Malleys expected formality. But this was the Meryons, not the O'Malleys. Stop second-guessing yourself.

If she were hired—and she needed to be—this would be the second job she'd ever held. Not that she'd had to apply for her first. Her appointment as third personal assistant to Lavinia O'Malley, grand-daughter of the O'Malley head of family, Cordelia O'Malley, had been granted when she completed school at age twenty-one. O'Malleys took care of their own. A mantra she'd heard many times, always followed by a but and the lapse that had her perched on the verge of being kicked to the curb.

In her prolific family, there were O'Malleys and then there were O'Malleys. She was one of the lesser, a mere third cousin twice removed of Lavinia's. Jen's branch on the family tree was so far from the main trunk as to make almost no difference whether it was attached. The sap flowed thin and only if you worked for it. It didn't anymore, and she didn't work for an O'Malley either.

Now poised for her first job interview at the age of twenty-five, her nerves were rioting. She needed to obtain this position before her recent indiscretion, as Lavinia had termed it, was whispered about. Not that the details would make their way into gossip. No, the family wouldn't brook that. The O'Malley name wasn't to be associated with such regressive actions. The whispers would be that much more damaging for lack of facts. It was up to the mind of the listener to decide what nefarious deed Jen had committed to get her booted from the family's affections. She brushed her hands down her slacks one more time before rapping on the door. A middle-aged woman dressed in dark gray slacks and a soft gray cable sweater answered.

She gave Jen an expectant look. "May I help you?"

Jen flexed her fingers. "Yes. I'm Jennifer O'Malley. I have an interview with Ms. Meryon."

The woman gave her a polite smile. "She's expecting you. Please follow me."

Jennifer glanced around at the apartment while she followed the woman. It wasn't what she'd expected. Lavinia O'Malley had followed in the O'Malley tradition of ostentatious antiquity in their furnishing choices. Ostentatious antiquity was a good way to describe everything about the O'Malley upper echelons. Although Lavinia would have taken exception to the term antiquity as it applied to her personally. She continually sought methods to retain the nubile perfection she'd had in her younger years.

This apartment was a complete contrast. From the color choices to the furniture and artwork, everything was understated. And none of it was cheap. The Meryons had money. And they were a first family, but not of the O'Malley stripe. No family could be as mired more deeply in traditional matriarchy than the O'Malleys. They would never have allowed the scandals that had struck the Meryons, divorce and a son who stood as the example used to scare young girls about what happened when men weren't kept in their place.

The woman leading her paused before a doorway. "Ms. Meryon, Ms. O'Malley is here."

"Send her in, Helen."

Ms. Meryon rose from an exquisite Carlton House inlaid desk. "Ms. O'Malley. I'm Claire Meryon." She extended an arm toward a love seat and chairs. "Please join me. Would you like tea or coffee?"

"No thank you." Jen took a seat on the cream brocade love seat. The room reflected a refined elegance that spoke to the gentility of the woman who sat opposite her. The rose silk blouse over dark gray slacks surprised her. This was a house in mourning, but the only outward signs that Jen could detect of the woman's recent tragedy were the shadows under her eyes and the overall sense of weariness she projected. "I'm so sorry for your loss."

Ms. Meryon lowered her gaze to the side for a moment before looking directly at Jen. "Thank you. It's been difficult."

An understatement. Losing your daughter must be devastating. Jen felt a pang in her chest.

Ms. Meryon let a pallid smile cross her lips. "And that is why we need you. You come highly recommended by Evaline Braddock. Tell me about yourself and why I should allow you to take care of my granddaughter."

Jen checked the instinct to wipe her sweaty palms on her slacks again by clasping them in her lap. "Well, I studied child development, but I can't say that much of that was of real-world value. It was academic. Lots of study and analysis. It's difficult to fit children into statistics. Each child is unique and shouldn't be limited by labels."

"Yes. Very interesting. But then what practical experience do you have?"

Jen flexed her fingers. "Well, I've always been the cousin that my family fobbed the children off on when all the cousins, aunts, and uncles gathered. Oh, not that I thought that way about it. No, they did. I loved it. Preferred it. I guess you could say I have a heart for children. And a knack for keeping them organized, well-behaved, and happy at the same time."

Ms. Meryon responded with a brighter smile and a nod. "You'll be attending to Sophie's academics, too. Do you think you can handle that?"

Jen took a quick breath and plunged ahead. "I also have an education certification. Now that was a practical, hands-on program."

"Really? I thought only men pursued education certification," Ms. Meryon said, her eyebrows rising slightly.

"Yes. It's part of a men's finishing school. But they allowed me to attend." Jen flicked a stray hair behind her ear. "I may have given the impression I was interested in studying men as primary educators of young children. Needed the firsthand experience of how they were trained." Jen bit the inside of her cheek. Maybe she shouldn't have said that.

Ms. Meryon's responding smile had a hint of amusement to it. "Sounds like you know what you want to do and don't let others stand in your way. That's very Tallavan of you."

"My mother calls it mulish."

"Ah." Her expression grew somber again. "Penny was like that. Stubborn as the day was long."

Jen hesitated, uncertain how best to respond.

Meryon sighed. "You seem like the perfect person for Sophie's nanny. Evaline gave you the terms of the position, didn't she?"

"Yes."

"Are they agreeable to you?"

Jen's stomach swirled. "Yes." Do I have the job?

"We'll need you starting the day of the memorial service. That hasn't been set yet. When it is, I'll let you know. Meanwhile, I'd like to introduce you to my granddaughter."

Jen rose with Ms. Meryon, twiddling her fingers instead of bouncing on her toes. She was hired! Her mother and Evaline Braddock had come through for her.

2

R andolph's gaze combed the spaceport pickup zone before spotting Maon waving at him. He grinned, jogging toward him and the huge Shirley family car. Maon Shirley was hard to miss in his bright orange shirt.

"You brought the land boat, I see." Randolph gestured at Maon's vehicle.

"Please. It's a luxury CMS." Maon's eyes twinkled, which meant there was a joke somewhere in that response.

Randolph grabbed him in a tight hug. "Luxury CMS?"

"Child moving system." Maon slapped Randolph's back. "Damn. It's been months. I'm sorry about your sister."

"Thanks. It still doesn't seem real."

"Climb in. I've got Petey and Drina with me." Maon pulled a Dairy Bar sack from the passenger seat. "Whoops. We stopped for a snack."

Randolph slid his six-foot frame into the car. "Selina lets you eat that stuff?"

"Of course not. We always eat healthy." Maon looked in the mirror at four-year-old Petey. "Don't we, Petey?"

Petey singsonged his reply. "We always eat healthy."

"Hi, Petey. Remember me?" Randolph asked.

Petey scrunched his four-year-old face.

Randolph laughed. "I'm Uncle Rand."

Petey dropped his gaze to the toy car he was holding and ignored Randolph.

"Who's this pretty girl? That can't be Drina." Randolph tweaked the toe of Drina's shoe.

"Hey!"

"She can talk!"

Maon glanced at Randolph while he worked his way through traffic to the throughway. "She is two."

"I two," Drina said, thrusting a fist with two fingers extended toward Randolph, who smiled and aimed two fingers back at her.

"You want me to drop you off at your mother's place?" Maon asked.

"Yeah. I might as well get it over with. My luggage is being sent on to the Wharton."

"Place to retreat?"

"Yeah. My mother's friends will be at the apartment. Which is wonderful, but I can only take so much of her set even when they're trying hard to be nice." If they tried to be nice. The probability wasn't high.

"Understood. You can always hide at our place. We're in town until after the memorial service. We're a whole different style of annoying though. Right, Petey?"

"We always eat healthy," Petey singsonged again.

Both men laughed.

A ten-minute drive later and they arrived at the building where Randolph's parents had kept an apartment since before he'd been born.

"Thanks for the ride."

Maon squinted at him. "Call me if you need me."

Lips pressed together, Randolph nodded. "Will do." He waved while Maon's car pulled away. Drina flapped a hand at him, but Petey just stared.

Randolph tugged on his shirt collar. A typical late summer day in Cahernamon, thunderheads promised rain in the near future. Used to the controlled climates of the domes on Beta Tau, Randolph regretted not wearing a jacket. The breeze pushed him along toward the entrance to his mother's apartment building, causing the back of his white silk button-down to cling to his spine. A middle-aged woman bustled toward the door carrying a bulky paperboard box. He sped up to reach the door first, opening it for her. She looked up to thank him and paused.

"Good, you're here. Your mother has been holding herself together, waiting for you to get here." An image of a general marshaling his troops came to mind when the woman squared her shoulders, pressed her lips in a tight line, and gave him a curt dip of her chin. Rigidly lacquered waves of brittle gray hair stood at attention in rows across the top of her head. She thrust her burden into his hands and marched into the apartment foyer.

"In case you don't remember, I'm Evaline Braddock." Randolph followed her into the lift and selected the proper floor. "Now that you're here, we can finalize the date and time of the memorial service." Her gaze drilled into him. "I assume your luggage is being delivered. You'll be in the room next to your mother's. Visitors are continuing to stop by. Please stay near your mother. However, it would be best if you remained in the background. They're not coming to visit you."

The lift pinged, and the door opened. Randolph shoved the bundle back to Evaline. "Madam, I thank you for your assistance to my mother. But I am perfectly capable of arranging my own accommodations. If I choose to greet visitors, I will do so at my mother's side. I loved my sister, and I feel her loss acutely. Black sheep I may be, but as the bereaved brother, I'm owed at least some measure of consolation."

Evaline's lips pursed, and her eyes glowered at him. He turned from her. Damned if he'd give this termagant another thought. When he reached the door to the apartment, he entered the security code, twisted the knob, and went straight in.

The apartment was quiet. A murmur of voices sent him toward the sitting room. He found his mother on a sofa reading a picture book to a little girl, the five-year-old niece he'd never met.

His mother glanced up. "Rand."

His niece regarded him with clear blue eyes. He stood motionless in the doorway while his mother whispered something in the girl's ear and then rose to greet to him, hands outstretched. Swept into her hug, Randolph closed his arms tightly around her.

When she pulled back to look at him, he asked, "Mother. Are you okay?"

She glanced to the side before returning her gaze to his. "Yes. I'm okay.

Come meet your niece." Taking his hand, she gave it a squeeze before urging him to follow her.

"Sophie. This is your Uncle Rand. Rand, Penny's daughter, Sophie."

The little girl had risen. "It's nice to meet you, Uncle Rand."

Randolph squatted before her. "It's nice to meet you too." Unable to resist, he brushed his finger along the strawberry-blonde curls at the side of her face. "You're as beautiful as your mother."

Her chin quivered and her voice was flat, but she responded. "Thank you, Uncle Rand."

"We were reading a book before Sophie takes a nap. Why don't you get yourself something to eat while we finish?" his mother said and gave him a pointed look. "Play nice with the ladies. Evaline and the others are my friends, and they've been a godsend. Evaline may be brusque, but she's got a good heart."

Randolph sighed. "Yes, Mother. I'll keep the peace."

When he glanced back at Sophie, she was peering at him, eyes filled with curiosity. He rose, placing a hand on her head, and said, "Rest sweet, Sophie." He watched while the pair settled on the couch with the book.

The gazes of the women sitting around the breakfast table chatting turned to fix on him when he entered the kitchen. The room had always been bright and inviting, with light lemon-yellow walls and white storage cupboards. When he was a child, it had seemed enormous to him. It could serve a full-course dinner to guests in the twenty-seat dining room. His best memories were of the warm, crumbly cookies his father had baked. On one dappled gray counter sat an array of platters with sandwiches, raw vegetables, and other finger foods. "Ladies, thank you for coming to be with my mother. What is the protocol? May I help myself to food anytime?"

Evaline tilted her chin high so she could look down her nose at him and turned away. The other ladies returned to chatting without responding, except for one kind soul. "Yes, help yourself." She continued despite Evaline's glare. "The plates and such are on the end. Would you like lemonade or tea? Both are in the cooler."

"Thank you, Ms. I'm sorry. I don't remember your name," Randolph said.

"Oh, I'm Ms. Reynolds...Kerry Reynolds. Claire's...your mother's downstairs neighbor. I don't think we've ever met."

The other ladies' conversation had grown louder until finally Evaline directed a question to Kerry. "Kerry, dear." Evaline pulled on her elbow, forcing her attention back to the group. "Which do you think is the more appropriate color? Blue or red?"

Randolph filled a plate and poured himself a glass of tea, ignoring the women. Before he headed to the sitting room to eat, he paused and directed a comment over his shoulder. "Thank you, ladies."

Finished eating, Randolph set his plate aside and sipped on his tea. The sweet berry taste reminded him of better times. Distant times, when his parents, sister, and he had been close, a tightly knit family. A pitcher of fruit tea had been a staple his father always kept in the cooler. The tea was a sweet reminder of a bitter truth. The possibility of being restored to his family, all taints of the past erased, was gone. In the year following his expulsion from the marshals for beating a child rapist he'd been sent to arrest and just after opening the Whip Hand, his mother had told him she was divorcing his father. That tear-soaked message had stripped away the last tenuous hope that if his sister would forgive him, he could go home. The divorce had shattered his family, and now his sister was lost forever. But it seemed his mother wanted him home.

He stirred from his reverie when his mother sat beside him, laying her head on his shoulder. He tipped his head against hers, her light brown curls soft against his cheek. Her fingers were cool to the touch when he shifted his hand from fiddling with the bead at his wrist to slide it over hers.

"Thank you for coming." His mother's voice was husky with the tears she was holding back.

"Of course." He brought his arm around her and clasped her close. When had she gotten so much smaller? She'd always been a presence in any room she entered, her charisma making her inches taller. "We'll get through this together."

~

RANDOLPH ADJUSTED the cuffs of his dark charcoal coat for the fifth time. He attributed his restlessness to the necessity of being polite to Evaline Braddock, who was managing the memorial service, managing his mother, and trying to manage him. If he admitted the truth, something an inner voice was demanding he do, he was fidgeting because he wasn't sure he could get through the memorial service without breaking down. Worse, he might reveal how angry his sister's death made him. Even a minor display of such wouldn't add another nail to his coffin. Polite society had long since buried him six-feet under. But it would justify their self-righteous dismissal of him. He'd be damned if he'd allow them the slightest bit of vindication.

Randolph shut his eyes, the breeze ruffling his hair, the midmorning sun warming his face and chasing the chill of early morning away. By afternoon it was forecast to be hot, the last hurrah of summer before the frigid autumn rains came to sweep them into winter. He let the chirp of a cricket, hidden in the bushes to his left, fill his mind, compartmentalizing his anger and burying it deep inside.

His upper arm was clasped by a large hand, and a masculine voice said, "Randolph. You okay, buddy."

Randolph recognized Shane. He paused another second before opening his eyes. Smiles weren't possible. Not here on this day. But he was pleased immeasurably that Shane had come and brought Adrianna with him.

"Shane. Dria. Thanks for coming." He clasped each of them in a tight hug. The softness of Adrianna's hand when she cupped his cheek after releasing him was almost more than he could take and maintain his composure. Her emerald-green eyes drilled into his as though she were mining his deepest, darkest secrets. Her empathic skills laid bare his emotions, good and bad.

"We're here for you. Whatever you need," she said.

"Thank you. I'm okay for now."

One finely arched eyebrow lifted in question.

Randolph acknowledged her disbelief with a quirk of his cheek. "If I boil over, a distraction might help."

"Distraction it is. I could always pretend to go into labor."

Randolph took in the sight of Adrianna's belly when she lowered her hand to rub it across the rounded expanse. He would believe it, even knowing she wasn't due for another two months.

"As long as I know it's not real, I'll play along," Shane said.

Randolph looked at his friend. "If you thought it was real, you'd make an even bigger distraction."

Adrianna laughed softly. "Too true." Her gaze focused over Randolph's shoulder. "Maon and Selina have arrived."

Randolph turned to acknowledge the tall blonde marshal and the tiny dark-headed woman with snapping topaz eyes he escorted. He greeted the couple with hugs. "Now that my support team is here, we should go in before Evaline Braddock comes and hauls me in by my ear."

"Gods. Don't tell me General Braddock is in charge," Maon said.

"Yeah. She assumed command before I got here."

Randolph found himself linked to Selina. Together they strode toward the open doors of the bereavement center. The sun's rays falling inside the doorway were held at bay by the hushed semidarkness of the center's foyer. Evaline Braddock stood at the entrance to the gathering room, the picture of solemn self-importance until she spotted Randolph and his entourage. Her face hardened, a sound of disgust her only response when Randolph nodded his head at her when they passed. The buzz of voices dropped away to silence when heads turned to note his arrival.

Selina's petite stature forced Randolph to shorten his stride. He looked down at her, gliding along the aisle between the rows of chairs filled with those come to mourn Penelope Renee Meryon. And those who had come to view the spectacle they hoped would ensue. Selina was serenity itself, acknowledging the stares of those they passed with the aplomb of a princess. If anyone wanted to tangle with Randolph, they'd have to get by the little fire Domme who'd put the room on notice that Randolph wasn't a pariah in her household. Add a tick in the positive column for those hoping for a show.

One seat remained in the front row. His. He'd been placed on the aisle next to his mother. Beside her sat Sophie, who held his mother's hand and the hand of the young woman who sat next to her. In the half a second his mind focused on the woman, he had an impression of youthful sweetness. *Who is she? Never mind.*

He bent, kissed his mother's cheek, and felt something furry shoved into his palm from behind. When he pulled it forward, he saw it was a teddy bear dressed in a fluttery pink dress. Bear clasped in his hand, he dropped to one knee before Sophie and offered her the stuffed animal.

"Sometimes it helps when you're sad to hug something soft."

Could a child be more solemn? He wanted to scoop her up and hold her until the world was right again. Her lips lifted in an almost smile before she took the bear from him and crushed it to her chest in a tight squeeze. He patted Sophie's knee and rose, his gaze meeting that of the young woman seated next to the little girl. Eyes full of rain and swirling clouds stared at him. His first impression of sweetness remained, but those stormy eyes told another story. Selina placed her palm on his back. He turned, embraced her, and sat. She gripped his shoulder in reassurance before she made her way back along the aisle with Maon.

WHEN THE ROOM WENT SILENT, Jen turned to discover what had drawn their rapt attention. It was him. Randolph Meryon, Sophie's Uncle Rand. Sophisticated, dangerous, masculine were all appellations that flitted through her head. Jen's heart fluttered. On his arm was a strikingly beautiful woman. *A date? For a memorial service? No. That's Selina Shirley.* Her husband trailed them. For an instant Randolph Meryon focused on Jen, his shiny chocolate eyes like the hard candy shell on an ice cream cone. She shivered inside, unable to decide what affected her most, the sinister nature she'd been told he hid behind that shielded gaze or the virility pulsing from him.

Evaline Braddock had recommended Jen for the position of Sophie's nanny. It was a favor Jen had desperately needed, with the added benefit to Evaline, who now had an informant in the enemy camp. Not that Jen thought of the Meryon estate as the enemy camp, nor did Evaline. The enemy was Randolph Meryon. Evaline had filled Jen in on the facts, rumors, and innuendo that would have made a fat dossier on Randolph Meryon if it were compiled into a single file. Her advice had been to keep Sophie as far away from her Uncle Rand as possible in the short time he'd be on Tallav. She'd been certain he'd return as soon as he could to his den of iniquity, the place where he brutalized women for his own sadistic pleasure, the club he owned on Beta Tau.

It was hard to reconcile the stories Evaline had told her with the man who had just kissed his mother and was now kneeling, offering Sophie a teddy bear and speaking softly to the little girl. That was a kindness whether it had been his idea or Selina Shirley's. In the short time Jen had spent with Sophie, the child had been reticent. When confronted with adults expressing their condolences to her, she had politely replied with brief answers. Her eyes were too wide, darting about while she tried to make sense of this adult event, a memorial service. The hug she gave the teddy bear was the first time she had accepted comfort from anyone save her grandmother.

No, this man didn't seem dangerous. And then he looked at her. The muscles of her throat tightened as her breath caught. Shiny chocolate eyes had become deep pools of muddy brown that darkened toward the center so that no line marked the boundary of pupil and iris. She was drawn to him even as a insistent voice inside her warned her to pull away before he sucked her under. Then he broke contact, and she struggled to regain her equilibrium.

The lay priest stood to begin the service, somber in her cadet blue gown, a stole, black with gold crosses on each end, placed around her neck. Behind her a large vidscreen was filled with an image of Penny holding Sophie on her lap, smiling, and pointing to something out of the frame. After a brief look of benevolent sympathy to Sophie's grandmother, the priest began with a prayer to the Holy One and words of comfort before summarizing Penny's life and accomplishments. Finally she said, "I've described the public life of Penny Meryon, but those of you who knew her as mother, daughter, sister, friend might want to share more intimate memories with us. I invite you to come forward and stand here so that all may hear."

The priest seated herself on the front row on the opposite side of the aisle. A few minutes passed before the first person rose. After six or seven women had offered their remembrances of Penny, another pause ensued. Jen heard Randolph Meryon clear his throat. All eyes focused on him when he rose from his seat, walked forward, and turned to face the assembled crowd.

"For those of you who don't know, I am Randolph Meryon. Penny's brother. Little brother." He cleared his throat again. "My sister and I have not spoken for many years." His eyes, which had been dark and shielded while his gaze roamed the room, softened to deep pools of sadness when he anchored his focus on Sophie. *My God, what he could do with those eyes.*

"It was an estrangement I didn't want and didn't know how to fix." He pressed his lips together, his chest visibly rising and falling while he took several breaths. "My sister was my champion when I was a child." His voice broke, and he paused to recover. "She was four years older and could have used that as an excuse to ignore me. She didn't. She included me in all her grand adventures. Taught me how to climb trees and showed me the best ones for spying on people." He managed a tentative smile.

Jen fought to keep the tears that were tickling the back of her eyes from falling. Next to her, Sophie was riveted on her uncle, bear held tight against her.

"We had lots of special places at Briarcliff. I promise to show you every single one, Sophie. In the spring we'll sleep on the dock at the pond and listen to the peepers. We'll build snow forts like the one your mother and I built the year we had three hundred inches of snow. There's a spot where the sun doesn't hit, and the fort will last almost forever. I'll take you to our secret cave."

"I know where that is!" Sophie's soprano voice rang out clear and sweet.

Randolph brought a hand up, covering his mouth for a moment before wiping a knuckle across his eye. "Do you now? Well, we'll sneak cookies out of the kitchen, and you can take me there and show me the cave painting you made with your mother."

Sophie nodded.

His gaze returned to roaming the room, his jaw squared. "I loved my sister. I hate that she died so young. She had so much to offer her daughter, Tallav."

His focus dropped to the floor for a moment. When they rose, they were filled with something indefinable. Something that would have riveted his audience even though the room lay thick with a heavy silence and every soul already sat entranced at the spectacle of Randolph Meryon eulogizing his sister. It drew everyone to wait in anticipation for what he would say next. Jen had been told of his charisma, and now it was on display before her.

In firm, level tones he said, "Even if she never spoke to me again, I'd much rather it was because she chose not to than the impossibility her death has made it. She was proud, stubborn, kind, and full of life. She was my sister, and I miss her."

With that, he sat, taking his mother's hand and bending his head to listen to the words she whispered into his ear. A rush of sighs rustled through the room, as though everyone had been holding their breath and released it at the same time. No one else came forward, so the priest rose again and concluded the service with more expressions of comfort and a closing prayer.

The family, along with Jen, were ushered to a spacious parlor, lined with sofas and chairs where those in attendance could speak with them briefly. Jen stood behind Sophie while people spoke a few words to the little girl before moving off to chat. Sophie had once again encased herself in a shell of polite distance. Most kept their words of sympathy brief. Randolph was treated with consideration, which might not have happened. But even Evaline Braddock had apparently been moved by Randolph's eulogy. She'd frowned at him and spoken two words.

"My condolences."

To his credit Randolph didn't treat it as a victory.

andolph looked out the shuttle window at the ocean below. From this height it was an unending expanse of blues and grays with a slightly rippled texture. This far north the water would be cold. Most would experience hypothermia within an hour of unprotected exposure if the waves didn't exhaust you first. Briarcliff was located on Rathlin Island, a chunk broken off from the main mass of the Great North Island. Its 352 square miles were owned by his mother, passed down from the founding member of the Meryon family that had chosen this bit of Tallav as their demesne.

The land was largely dedicated to apple orchards tended by tenant farmers. Sheep and goats were pastured on the upper slopes of the Giant's Tit, or the Tit, as the mountain at the center of the island was called. It had garnered its name from the shape of its top, bare of trees and curved to a central knobby peak, at least on the side that faced the harbor with Rathlin Island's only seaport. The back side looked as though someone had taken a sledgehammer to it, breaking it up into long runs of tumbled stone. The wild ruin was difficult to traverse, much less viably farm. Amid the slurry of rock, feral goats grazed. Their numbers were kept in check by the brutality of the winter winds that struck full force against the north face of the mountain while the island's wiser residents stayed snug in their well-heated homes on the other.

His mother returned from the bench seat at the back of the shuttle that doubled as a narrow bed for Sophie. The little girl had fallen asleep within the first hour of the trip and had yet to awaken. After she sat, his mother closed her eyes, leaning against the suede burgundy fabric of the headrest. Randolph studied the dark circles under his mother's eyes. She showed no signs of the aging that occurred after the point of decline, an unavoidable reality for those that lived to be one hundred, but that was thirty years away for his mother. Still, that future was visible in the exhausted sadness of her face. He took her hand with its long, slender fingers into his, allowing the warmth of his to lessen the papery dry chill of hers.

She squeezed and opened eyes the duplicate shade of brown as his. The color was inherited from Granddad Meryon, who was spending his waning years in a cottage near the ocean, fishing with his caregiver. Penny's had been a cornflower blue and her hair a strawberry blonde, the look of a traditional Meryon and their father. That had been about all there was of traditional Meryon to Penny.

"What happens after the interment ceremony?" Randolph asked.

Her gaze dropped to their clasped hands. "There'll be some legal matters. The will to be read and probated." She returned her gaze to him, looking deep into his eyes before she continued. "Guardianship of Sophie to be established."

"That shouldn't take long. I assume Penny made you Sophie's guardian."

"I don't know. She didn't tell me, and I never saw her will." The old do-as-I-say charisma flared in his mother's face. "I want you to be Sophie's guardian, or at least a co-guardian with me."

Randolph's eyes widened, his thoughts arrested, momentarily stunned by his mother's statement. "That would be a bad idea, Mother. No court on Tallav would make me Sophie's guardian."

His mother's fingers tightened. "Sole guardian perhaps. But co-guardian might be managed."

Randolph narrowed his eyes, his head shaking in protest, while he stared out the window. "You don't really want to dig up all the old scandal? Do you, Mother?"

"Maybe it's time. Time to set things straight."

Without looking, Randolph knew his mother's chin had done that rigid thing that declared she was digging in for a fight. "It's been twenty-one years since my reputation began its downhill plunge. And since Penny isn't here to recant, no one will believe the truth now. It will be seen as a crass attempt to rehabilitate me after her death. Her friends won't allow it. They'll take up the hue and cry in her name, and you know it."

"For Sophie's sake, we should try."

"Huh." When Randolph once again looked at her, a glint of determination and something else…need burned in her eyes. He'd seen that look before whenever his mother went to battle for him. She'd been the only family member who had eventually truly believed him. His staunch champion. He would do just about anything for her, even face the pain of old wounds being ripped open, scabs he'd been picking at since his mother had told him of Penny's death.

"All right." He would capitulate that far, but he would not return to live at Briarcliff permanently. He had a business to run.

"Thank you."

"But first let's see what her will says."

"Yes."

They sat in silence, Randolph staring out the shuttle window, his mother resting. His mind skittered from past to present and back while he contemplated the ocean. Finally he broke free of the mental swirl. He realized he was still holding his mother's hand and squeezed it.

"Mom."

She opened her eyes. "Yes, dear?"

"Where did the nanny come from? Jen? Right?"

"Jennifer O'Malley. Evaline arranged for her to be Sophie's nanny. At least for the next six months."

Randolph looked over his shoulder at the young woman sitting in the seat closest to the back bench where Sophie slept. Her black hair was swept in a ponytail. Slate-gray eyes were focused on her tablet. What was she reading? While he watched, she scooped her hand up her forehead and over the top of her head, rumpling her bangs.

"The O'Malleys? How did we rate an O'Malley?" he asked and returned his attention to his mother.

"She's got the bloodline but is far enough removed from the main branch there's probably little to no stipend. She's credentialed for child development and education."

"Doesn't look that old."

"She's twenty-five."

Randolph twisted to study her. Jennifer O'Malley was the picture of innocent sweetness. At twenty-five she was too old to be innocent. But sweet was perhaps what Sophie needed. He hadn't been with someone sweet for a very long time. Sweet women ran scared from him. As battered as he felt, sweetness might be what he needed, too. But Sophie's need supplanted his. He didn't want the woman to quit because she feared his advances. When he brought his gaze back to his mother's face, he caught an odd look he couldn't quantify.

"I'm sure Evaline gave her the full scoop," he said.

"Now Rand. She seems like a thoughtful girl, well able to make up her own mind about people."

"Hmm. If she can't handle my reputation, we'll have to find someone who can."

His mother pointed out the window. "We're almost home."

Randolph spotted the southern coast of the Great North Island. Within the hour they would be over Rathlin Island and landing at Briarcliff. Home.

The estate was built into a curve of the land along the island's largest river and facing the pristine beauty of Lough Gur. The original Meryons had been stout believers in the Druidic mysteries. Near the lake, they'd constructed a stone circle and dolmen. The dolmen was the location where the ashes of generations of Meryons were buried. It now stood unused after, three generations back, the Meryon heir broke with tradition and returned to Reformed Catholicism during the Great Catholic Reawakening. Since that time the family had remained nominally Reformed Catholic, although Penny had announced at sixteen that she was an atheist. At that age she had made many pronouncements she seldom stuck to for long, so his mother hadn't worried about her lack of Catholic fervor. Randolph assumed Penny's tenacious atheism had persisted through her death. He had wondered at the Lay Priest officiating at the memorial service. That wouldn't have been Penny's choice.

If she'd remained in the Catholic fold, would she have forgiven him? Who knew? She hadn't, and home had become a place where his family lived and he visited.

He could count on one hand plus a few extra fingers the number of times he'd been to Briarcliff since the day his parents packed him off to boarding school. It had never been the same, and it wouldn't be this time.

WHEN JEN STEPPED from the vehicle that had taken the family from the shuttle pad to their home, she came to an abrupt halt. Her focus in the car had been on Sophie. The first sight of the place where she'd be living for the next six months hit her all at once. Perhaps it was the time of day, early evening. Perhaps she was tired. It was probably the thoughts of death that made her shiver. Briarcliff was an imposing pile of gray stone. A castle built to appear old when it was new, and now, hundreds of years later, it was properly aged. All it lacked was a ghostly apparition on the parapet to complete the gothic-novel atmosphere.

Beside her Randolph said, "Don't worry. There's only one ghost."

Jen's cheeks heated. She continued to survey the castle as though she were completely at ease, noting a section that looked fallen in. "Just one?" She hated how her voice sounded thin to her own ears.

"Granny Meryon. She'll love you. You're an O'Malley."

His tone was sardonic. *Score one for the family name.* She winced. He moved toward the door where the butler stood awaiting their approach, and with another shiver she followed him.

Claire Meryon, Sophie holding tight to her hand, was speaking to an older woman when Jen entered the foyer. When Randolph reached his mother's side, she introduced him to the assembled staff. They acknowledged him with courteous nods, except for the older woman, who beamed at him.

"Welcome home, Mr. Meryon."

Randolph grasped her by the shoulders and kissed her on the cheek. "It's good to be home, Mrs. Polgrey. And it's Rand to you."

Her cheeks flushed pink. "I made sure Cook baked your favorite cookies. There'll be a plate of them waiting for you in your mother's sitting room."

Claire turned and motioned Jen forward.

"Mrs. Polgrey, this is Jen O'Malley, Sophie's new nanny. Jen, our house-keeper, Mrs. Polgrey. Polgrey, will you see that Jen is shown the nursery and send a maid to help her settle in?"

"Yes, ma'am. I've her room prepared, and I'm sure Sophie will want to give her a tour of the nursery." She beamed at Sophie, who gave Jen a nod.

"Nice to meet you, Mrs. Polgrey." Jen liked the woman, whose smile was a bright flood of sunshine.

Claire swung her granddaughter's hand. "Sophie, why don't you take Jen to the nursery now."

Sophie released her grandmother and took Jen's hand. "That will be fun." A shy smile flitted over her lips.

Walking with Sophie to the gray stone staircase that loomed in an upward sweep of weighty shadow, Jen heard Claire say, "Is Father James here? We asked him to meet us to take Penny's ashes to the chapel."

"No, ma'am. He commed to say one of the lay priests had been delayed. They should arrive shortly."

Jen wished she could stay and meet this Father James. The things she'd been told about priests couldn't be true. They'd all be locked up. But the supposed condescension with which they treated women was something she wanted to see for herself. Curiosity would have to wait.

The nursery turned out to be a suite of rooms built for more than a single child. Children's bedrooms lined one side of a hall, with the nanny's bedroom in the center. Doors on the other side of the nursery corridor opened to a large bathroom, a playroom, and a quiet study room that doubled as a dining space. The atmosphere in the rooms was the opposite of the gloomy outer impression of the castle. These rooms were bright with plenty of little girl pinks and purples, decorated with Sophie in mind.

Sophie settled on Jen's bed once Mrs. Polgrey left. The room was comfortable, including a small en suite bathroom, but it was bland, with light blue walls, a dark blue coverlet, and a throw rug on the hardwood floor. The walls were empty of pictures. The desk held nothing but a vidscreen. She'd packed personal items to brighten it up, but that could wait. Mrs. Polgrey had said supper would be brought up to them in a few minutes. "Let's get ready for supper."

By the time they'd washed their hands and taken their seats in the quiet room, the food arrived. The meal brimmed with Cook's special comfort foods, which Sophie wolfed down. She was coming out of the shell she'd hidden inside at the memorial service. Rather than make her sleepy, the full tummy seemed to energize Sophie. She had had a long nap on the shuttle.

Dragged to the playroom by an eager Sophie, Jen was soon the center of the little girl's frenetic need to show her the best, the prettiest, the loudest, and the most wonderful of her things.

"This is Bunnzy. He lost his ear, but Grandma has it and says it can be fixed." The stuffed bunny was shoved to the side before Jen could examine it, and a doll was thrust in her hands. "This is Milly. She's my favorite doll because she has green eyes. I wish my eyes were green. She also has five dresses, including an evening gown. Yellow with little flowers." The dress was thrust forward for inspection.

Tucking the doll under one arm, Sophie pulled Jen toward a shelf and a large wooden dollhouse.

"Watch. The lights turn on." She flicked the knocker on the door. "And the knocker really knocks. Listen." It made a respectable *tap, tap*. "This is the way I like the furniture. There are people too." She pulled the figures from the different rooms. "This is Mommy. Grandma. And Polgrey." She pulled a male figure out, glancing up at Jen with an anxious expression. "This is Uncle Rand, but I never told Mommy that. She was mad at him, but not Grandma."

"It's nice you included him."

Sophie's face eased at Jen's comment. "I like to make up stories for them." Her face crumpled, and she twisted the figure of Uncle Rand in her fingers. "Can I still make up stories about Mommy? Even though she's gone to heaven, and I won't see her anymore?"

Jen knelt and put an arm around Sophie. "Of course you can. Your mommy may be in heaven, but she still loves you. She's a part of you that will never go away."

Sophie gave her head a decisive nod.

"How about we play a game? What's your favorite?"

"Jumble Bears. I'm really good at it." Sophie dashed to where boxes of games and puzzles were shelved.

After several rounds of Jumble Bears and three picture books, Jen caught Sophie yawning.

"Time for bed."

Decked out in pink pajamas dotted with little yellow ducks, Sophie announced night-night visits were the next order of business. After requisite hugs and kisses from her grandmother and uncle, Sophie had insisted they say good night to the staff. Several were in their lounge, and they made a fuss over Sophie noisy enough to draw the cook from her bedroom.

Cook insisted that Sophie have warm milk and a cookie, bustling off and back in minutes from the employee kitchen. The staff chatted with Sophie while she ate her cookie and drank her milk. A footman announced that a new batch of kittens had been born in the lambing barn. Jen learned from a maid that a nightly visit to the staff lounge was a regular event. It certainly had a calming effect on Sophie tonight.

Bedtime snack finished, Jen told Sophie to say her good nights. This took an extra ten minutes, but it was well worth it to see Sophie relaxed and smiling, finagling to extend her bedtime.

Jen's research said there was usually a stiffness when a new nanny was introduced into a family before the children became comfortable. But Sophie was dealing with more than a new nanny. Jen was her first nanny. Penny had assumed primary care of her daughter even though it wasn't the norm to do so. It made Jen's position that much more difficult, but she was determined to help Sophie as best she could.

In her own room Jen saw that the maid had unpacked her clothes. After putting on her own nightgown, she shut off the light and opened the door a crack. If Sophie woke in the night, she wanted to be able to hear her. Then she crawled underneath the dark blue coverlet, felt the mattress ease under her, and waited for sleep to overtake her. When it didn't, her wandering mind eventually strayed to Randolph Meryon, Uncle Rand. He was an enigma. Not the villain she had pictured from Evaline Braddock's portrayal.

Jen had found her gaze drawn to him all too frequently. It was something about the way he held himself, the way he moved. And those brown eyes weren't just brown. They were expressions of the emotions he felt, intense expressions that reached out and compelled those they caught to fall in line. And yet most of the time his eyes were like a shell or a shield he used to hide his true thoughts. His eulogy to his sister had been touching, but even then she suspected he was holding back, letting his sadness cover a darker side to his grief.

If Jen were to describe him, she'd have to say he was good-looking but not overly handsome. He was of average height and build, but strong, lifting her trunk from the shuttle with an ease the porter hadn't shown. Nondescript brown hair, brown eyes, and—mesmerizing. His body language told the whole story. It said, *if I want you, I can have you, and you will do everything I command you to do.* He generated a longing in her to touch him that was as potent as the overpowering sense that to do so would lead to intense pleasure and, if the gossip was reliable, the sting of pain. Still, if he twitched a come-to-me finger at her, there was no doubt she'd go straight to him, a willing victim.

He'd use a whip. She'd done an ident search on him and followed it up by combing through newsie stories. His favorite instrument of torture was a bullwhip unless space was limited, and then he'd use smaller whips. Vids showed he was a master, skilled at the precise placement of each strike. In one vid he'd drawn a pink circle on a woman's bottom with carefully aimed snaps of his whip. Beyond the pain he inflicted, he mentally tormented his victims, cracking the whip without coming near to tender skin, mixing pain, anticipation, and dread.

At some point known only to him, he would smooth a hand over the damage he'd wrought, wrap an arm around the woman he was playing with, and speak into her ear. Whatever he said, at that moment his partner would melt into him. He'd jerk open his black leather pants, pull out his erection, and fuck the woman hard and fast. His body was packed with muscles that flowed beneath his skin in masculine grace. His nipples were two darker circles that peaked into hard nubs when he was aroused, perfect for licking. And his cock was a work of art. A little longer than average, and definitely bigger around, it rose straight and true, the plump purplish head ready to penetrate wherever it aimed.

Jen pushed her hand down under the covers and into her panties. Randolph Meryon bent her over, thrusting into her, growling savage, erotic words into her ear. He was rubbing her clit, stroking her to release, sucking on her neck and shoulder, and pounding her pussy. Gods, she wanted to come all over his cock. Her orgasm struck with blinding force. Every muscle in her body contracted, squeezing intense pleasure from her until she was limp and sated. She lay panting, wishing her fantasy could be reality, but as her body calmed, her mind did too. Randolph Meryon wasn't someone you dallied with. He was a risk she needed to avoid for obvious physical reasons—that damn whip—and to remain a marketable commodity as a nanny or tutor among the aristocracy.

Best to keep her distance as Evaline had advised. He didn't seem to like O'Malleys, so that should be easy. She had overheard his conversation about guardianship of Sophie. It didn't look as though he wanted to stay. Exasperated with herself, she rolled over, punched her pillow, and snuggled back down. No more thinking about Randolph Meryon. Instead she went over the schedule for the funeral mass and committal tomorrow and drifted off to sleep.

4

andolph rose early, wanting to visit the estate chapel before it filled with people from all over the island coming to share the family's grief. When he stepped into the vestibule, the quiet peace of the building covered him like a mantle. Time seemed to have stood still here. It was as he remembered from his boyhood, from the lemon-soaked scent of the polished wooden screen that separated the vestibule from the nave, to the click of his shoes on the tile floor.

When he opened the door into the nave, early morning sunshine streamed through the rose window, creating a brilliant pattern of colors dappling the altar. Beeswax, incense, and more of the lemon polish combined their scents to trigger a memory of the tension before confession. He'd laid aside all religious sentiment long ago, but whether from disused habit or something else, he dipped into the holy water, bent a knee, and crossed himself. He made his way along the side aisle to the arched opening leading to the sacristy, surprised to find its door standing open.

His footsteps echoed around him while he descended into the flickering dark where the ashes of his family found their final resting place. Someone had lit the fat candles that served as the only light down below.

A reedy baritone voice rose to meet him. "Hello. Who's there?"

"It's Randolph Meryon."

A sandy-haired, freckle-faced man stepped into the pool of light at the base of the stairs, pale blue eyes peering up at Randolph. "Oh. Hello. I'm Father James." Shadows accentuated his furrowed expression. "My condolences for your loss." He turned his head to look toward the family crypt, pressed his lips into a tight line, and looked at Randolph with a wince. "I was on my way to speak with your mother, but since you're here, we won't have to involve her."

Even in the poor light it was evident to Randolph the man was disturbed. The priest motioned with his hand. "Come. I have something to show you."

Randolph clattered down the final steps and followed the priest to the large stone crypt. Additional candles brought the reliefs carved into the sides of the elevated crypt into sharp contrast. On this side the Good Shepherd carried a lamb in his arms, a stream flowing behind him. The scene, meant to bring comfort, struggled against the cold hard marble and the chill of the room. Something obscured the Meryon family crest etched into the covering stone.

"I regret that someone has desecrated your family's crypt. At any time it would be reprehensible, but now…and so clearly aimed at Penny." The priest shook his head, holding his fist to his mouth.

Randolph stepped closer. On top of the nubby wool of a lambskin lay the broken pieces of a doll, a fashion doll, its torso snapped in half, legs and arms akimbo. Despite his lack of knowledge of the details of Penny's death, it was obvious the doll was a crude representation of his sister.

Randolph scowled. "Do you have any idea who could have done this?"

The priest dropped his hand. "No. I don't. It was a shocking thing to find."

"My mother doesn't need to know." Randolph pointed at the nasty effigy. "Have you touched it?"

"No. No, I haven't laid a finger on it."

"I'll deal with it. Please keep this to yourself." Randolph grimaced. *Fuck all! Who in the hell would do something so malicious?* He'd find out. "Do you have a seal sack handy, Father?"

"Let me check upstairs. I'll be right back."

The rapid plod of the priest's footsteps reverberated through the chamber. Randolph studied the broken doll. With any luck, fingerprints and

DNA would be found. But the point of such a malicious act? Was this a threat? He and his mother had both been consumed with questioning why Penny would have let herself get into a position to fall from the cliff to the river. Murder hadn't entered his mind, but it did now. Was this token meant to imply someone was planning to murder another member of his family? Had other nasty expressions of hate been left for them to find?

He touched the polished marble of the covering stone, chilled fingers meeting solid cold. Secured beneath were the ashes of three generations of Meryons. Now the remains of the first of the fifth would be added. Penny. Too early. The possibility that the timing had been accelerated by a murdering son of a bitch crawled under his skin. He'd damn well find out.

At the sound of feet returning, he looked up. Father James rushed to him, holding out the sack. "I think this will be big enough." When their eyes met, the priest's bushy brows drew together.

The expression on the priest's face made Randolph realize that his body had gone nearly rigid. He let the tension ebb away with the skill of a man used to masking his emotions. "Thank you, Father. You needn't stay. You have preparations to finish."

The opening of the seal sack was wide, allowing Randolph to slide the doll and lambskin inside.

"If you'd like to talk? I have time. I know your grief is complicated with other issues…"

"Thank you, Father. I appreciate the offer, but I'm not a particularly religious man." He zipped the closure shut on the bag.

"What I have to offer isn't particularly religious. A man-to-man conversation. Your sister and I had grown closer over the last year. There are things she'd want me to share with you. Please find time to meet with me. I believe it will ease your mind."

Randolph had been edging away, his attention already moving on when what the priest had said penetrated. "You were close with my sister?"

The priest pursed his lips. "I like to think I became a kind of sounding board for her. She was going through a philosophical upheaval, a crisis of faith, if one can ascribe such to an atheist."

The familiar sense of despondency that visited Randolph whenever he thought of his sister flooded through him. "I didn't know."

"No, of course not. But I believe she might very well have reconciled with you given a little more time."

Dizziness struck, and Randolph tensed in a moment of disorientation. Reconcile? That was...impossible. The overpowering need to escape, to clear his head rushed over him. "I'm sorry, Father. I-I need to go. We'll speak again later." He turned and strode to the nave door.

"Yes. Whenever you wish," the priest called after him.

RANDOLPH LET his eyes wander over Penny's office. The request to deal with it had come from his mother. Something he would get to, but for now he made space on his sister's cluttered desk so he could sync his tablet to her vidscreen and work. On one corner lay the bag containing the broken doll and scrap of fleece that had been left on the family crypt, its noxious contents muffled by their plastic covering. A call to the local garda station had garnered a promise from the sergeant to collect the bag for DNA testing and to take a report. She'd meet him after the Funeral Mass and interment. By the end of the day he should know who was disturbed enough to leave something like that for the family to find.

The Mass was scheduled for ten. Soon he'd need to dress. From the desk chair, sized for Penny's smaller frame, he studied the room. As an adult Penny hadn't outgrown her habit for leaving any space she occupied a mess. He was certain the maids kept her bedroom and closet straight, but she wouldn't have allowed them in her inner sanctum. He pressed his thumb into the inscribed heart bead on his wrist, then brought it up to stare at the impression. Penny had given him the bracelet when he was nine, saying he was to wear it always to remind him they would love each other forever. He'd never taken it off, despite the war she had launched against him five years later.

Somewhere in this mess was Penny's diary. She'd started the habit of writing her thoughts in a bound book at an early age. She'd probably filled several dozen over the years if she'd continued at the rate she'd scribbled through them in her teens. He'd found a pile of older journals on one shelf but nothing current. It wouldn't be easy reading, but it might explain the woman Penny had become and tell him if she truly had been considering a reconciliation between them. He gave a frustrated tick of his tongue. He'd start with the oldest one he'd pulled from the stack and work his way forward.

A *click* drew his attention to the door when the handle moved. A woman with a short bob of sleek blonde hair appeared.

"Oh. I wasn't expecting anyone to be here."

"And you are?"

She moved inside, shut the door behind her, and rushed toward him, offering her hand across the desk to Randolph.

"Lanny. Lanny Conyer. I'm Penny's assistant."

Randolph took her hand and gave it a brief shake. "Don't you mean you were Penny's assistant?"

The woman flushed, withdrawing, and crossed her arms over her chest. "Well, yes. That's true. Isn't it?" Her shoulders slumped, and she pulled a tissue from her pocket, bringing it to her nose. "I'm going to miss her so much. She was a mentor and, I like to think, a friend."

"She'll be missed by many people." Randolph watched her.

"Yes." She dabbed and put the tissue back into her pocket. "Did you need something? I feel I owe it to Penny to finish the projects she was working on and help the family sort through this mess." She swept her arm out to encompass the room and its stacks of books, papers, and junk of all sorts. "Penny had an antiquarian nature. She couldn't organize all the jumble that created."

"She was the messy Meryon. Speaking of antiquarian, do you know where she kept her diary?" Randolph asked.

Lanny ran a hand over her hair, smoothing it, although she hadn't a strand out of place. "It should be in the top left desk drawer. But it's locked. I got the key from your mother." She offered it to Randolph.

He tried the drawer. "Yeah, it's locked." The key turned easily, and the drawer slid open. "It's not here."

She leaned forward, checking for herself. "That's a surprise. She always kept it there. I was hoping to use it to help with a couple of things she left unfinished."

"Hmm. For now you should put that on hold. I'll be handling this part of her affairs. You'll continue to be paid, but consider this a vacation while I orient myself."

Lanny scowled. "She was working on a book that would be a major triumph. It should be published." She thrust a finger at him. "She wouldn't want you to block it because you disagree with its substance."

"Since I haven't read it, I wouldn't know whether I would agree with it. But its publication is not for you to decide. My mother and I will take care of any posthumous works by my sister."

Her aggressive posture melted away. "Naturally. I apologize for over-stepping. She was passionate about the book, and I suppose some of that has rubbed off on me. If I can be of any assistance, please call on me."

Randolph eyed her. Something about the sudden shift of tone wasn't right. Others had tried to placate him in the past. Lanny wasn't good at it or at hiding her feelings. Probably thought he'd burn all of Penny's things.

"I'll do that."

Lanny nodded and smiled tenuously. "I'd like that. I'll go see if your mother needs any help. Call me when you're ready to work on the office."

"Thank you." Randolph studied the door after she left, stood, walked to it, and stretched a hand to the frame above it. The key he expected to find was there. He scanned the room one more time before leaving, locking the door and dropping the key into his pocket.

JEN HAD NEVER ATTENDED a Reformed Catholic Mass before. Lavinia would be appalled at an O'Malley involving themselves in such patriarchal heresy, but Jen was off her good list anyway. Ritualized cannibalism was the nicest description she'd heard of Catholic rites while growing up. Her family had led the unsuccessful attempt to make Catholicism illegal on Tallav. In the end it had been declared as much of a viable Irish tradition as the goddess worship of Tallav's state religion, a decision O'Malleys to this day wanted reversed. Jen had already proven she wasn't a typical O'Malley.

Her stomach fluttered while she straightened the collar on Sophie's navy swing coat. The reserve Sophie had displayed prior to arriving at Briarcliff had returned. The bear Uncle Rand had given her was clutched tight in one arm. After the Mass and interment, Jen had been instructed to return Sophie home to the nursery. The other members of the family and the staff would walk to the village on the edge of the estate where a luncheon would be served at the community center.

Randolph strode into the foyer, accompanied by Mrs. Polgrey. "Please make sure."

"Yes, sir."

Heat flushed through Jen's body. The dark charcoal suit Randolph wore was perfectly fitted to his toned physique. He was the picture of a sophisticated, aristocratic son of Tallav. She turned her face toward the stairs, hoping the craving he inspired in her wasn't apparent to anyone else. Somehow she had to put an end to the physical reaction she had any time Randolph Meryon came anywhere near her. Back on Beta Tau, where his reputation didn't matter—or more precisely, his reputation increased his allure—he must have scads of women falling at his feet. She didn't need to be one of them. Add in that she was an O'Malley and his employee...her heart palpitations were pointless.

"I'll lock this door once the family has left and the staff exit when we leave." Mrs. Polgrey said. "All the other doors are already locked. I've given Miss Jen the pass code, so she and Sophie can get in when they return."

"Thank you. I don't expect anything to happen, but a funeral is the perfect time for thieves."

"Och. Anyone who would do such should be strung up."

At that moment Claire stepped down the broad stone stairs that led to the upper floors, flinging a black cape around her shoulders. "Everyone is here? Good. Granddad Meryon will meet us at the chapel. Has the car arrived?"

Randolph opened the massive iron-studded wooden door. Finely balanced, it swung with ease. "The car's here." He offered an arm to his mother.

She took it with a deep sigh. Lips pressed firm, she gave a tight nod and proceeded outside.

Once they were seated in the car, Sophie with her grandmother and Randolph with Jen on facing bench seats, Claire clasped Sophie's hand and kissed the top of her head. In a soft voice, she sang.

"I see the moons, the moons see me;
God bless the moons and God bless me:

There's grace in the cottage and grace in the hall;
And the grace of God is over us all."

Sophie tipped her head, strawberry-blonde curls tumbling back, and looked at her grandmother. "Mommy's song. She's in heaven with God."

"Yes, *alanna.* She is."

"Can she see me like the moons?"

"I believe she can. And every day she asks God to bless you. Today we say our last goodbye to her here on Tallav, but we'll see her again in heaven."

The response seemed to touch something inside Sophie. She settled back, contented. A moment later her brow furrowed. "I wish she could have waited. I miss her."

"Me too, *alanna.*"

The car stopped in the drive that circled in front of the chapel. The stone walls of the building rose to a bright red peaked roof. It was too small to accommodate everyone, so the walkways and grassy areas surrounding it were thick with overflow mourners. The crowd grew quiet with respect for the family. The chapel's double doors were perfectly matched in color to the roof. A path cleared when the chauffeur came around to assist the family from the vehicle. No one approached or spoke while Claire, Randolph, Sophie, and Jen made their way to the open doors at the top of three wide flagstone steps.

Randolph escorted his mother, and Jen held Sophie's hand, following behind. Sophie's fingers tightened when they arrived atop the final and broadest step. A plump middle-aged woman dressed in a flowing sage caftan offered a sprig of green plant to Claire and Randolph.

"To ward you."

Randolph brushed the woman's arm away. "No thank you." He steered his mother toward the door with one hand while extending his other arm to Jen and Sophie to conduct them past the woman.

She approached Jen, fingers extended from a belled sleeve stitched with ancient Celtic designs. Jen heard tinkling and flicked a glance at the round pendant that overlapped the embroidered split collar of the woman's kaftan. The woman pushed the leafy stem closer. "For the little one. It's a sprig of thyme. To keep negative emotions from overtaking her."

Jen shifted Sophie into the circle of her arm and pressed past to

Randolph. It was clear the Meryons didn't welcome the pagan gift. Why would anyone think they would at a Catholic funeral Mass?

Once they'd made their way through the vestibule and into the nave, Jen scanned the worship center. Not a worship center, a chapel. This differed from the gatherings she had attended growing up where the Great Mother was reverenced and peace and harmony celebrated. She'd done research so she wouldn't embarrass herself or the Meryons. Each of the Meryons dipped a finger in a font filled with holy water, bent a knee, and made the sign of the cross before entering the nave. Wooden benches filled with people lined either side of the main aisle of the chapel proper. Ahead, to the left, stood a statue of a woman with arms spread open: Mary, Mother of God. The statue on the right was a man holding a child. Candles glimmered in a room hushed except for the stirring of bodies and a cough, whisper or shushing noise from time to time.

Randolph stopped when they reached the front pew, allowing his mother to greet her father, before he motioned for Sophie to sit next to his mother. He sat on Sophie's right, which put Jen on his right. The pew, meant for four adults, was snug with the addition of Sophie. Jen was mortified that sitting next to Randolph caused her breathing to quicken. He smelled of earthy narcotic herbs with undertones of dirty, musky leather. If only she could nuzzle into his neck and let his scent engulf her senses. *Not appropriate. Not appropriate. What is wrong with you?*

When Randolph handed her a small booklet, the warmth of his fingers infused her own chilly digits. "Are you cold?"

"No, just my hands. They're always cold."

His mouth quirked, and he stared at her for a moment that lasted an eternity until he finally said, "This is the order of the liturgy. You need not kneel with the others or pray. I won't be. If you get lost, follow what I do."

After a pause in which her vocal cords refused to work, she croaked, "Thank you."

His lips quirked higher. She stifled the need to release a whoosh of breath when he looked away, slowly easing the air trapped in her lungs a bit at a time. She was grateful when the Mass began a few minutes later. Soon she was caught in the words of the scripture readings, the music, and the prayers. She missed nothing from her front-row seat, including the priest's statement when he offered communion to each recipient. "The body of Christ." This was the cannibalism her family accused Catholics of committing? What a ridiculous claim. But not a surprise. O'Malley's believed all kinds of nonsense.

Something about this service was comforting. Perhaps it was sitting close to Randolph. His was a commanding, solid presence. The emotion he'd displayed in his eulogy for his sister was hidden. It wasn't until near the end of the Mass and the final commendation that he faltered. When the priest said, "Eternal rest grant unto her, O Lord, and let perpetual light shine upon her," those in attendance were to respond, "Receive her soul and present her to God the Most High." A barely audible sound of utter anguish welled from deep within him. Jen's instant response was to place her hand in his and hold it while the priest prayed. When he finished, the priest asked that all nonfamily members make their way to the vestibule to allow the family privacy during the committal.

Randolph squeezed her hand and looked at her with eyes that roiled with emotion. "Thank you."

Heat rose in her cheeks at the intensity of his gaze. "I'm very sorry for your loss."

His lips pressed together, his eyes growing distant as though he beheld sights lost in the past. Then he snapped back to the present. "Please wait here with Granddad Meryon. He isn't steady enough to traverse the steps down to the crypt. Mother and I will bring Sophie to you afterward."

Jen nodded. "Yes, sir."

5

J en rose to move along the pew to introduce herself and sit next to Granddad Meryon. Before she could scoot to her left, the sound of a dispute brought her attention to the door of the sacristy where the priest, Randolph, and the woman who'd offered them a sprig of thyme at the chapel door were heatedly, if quietly, discussing something. Clutched in her hands was a wreath. Jen recognized the marigolds in its design. The woman's voice rose.

"But this is Mary's own flower. The incarnation of the goddess your own faith attests to. There's evil surrounds your sister's death. You all must turn back to the goddess before another of you is struck down."

Randolph's face was suffused with fury. To the priest he said, "Get. Her. Out of here." Then he strode through the sacristy door.

The woman attempted to follow Randolph, but the priest clasped her shoulders and stopped her. Jen could not hear what he said to her, but the woman's pleading became more distraught.

"Please. I must. There's evil here. I can feel it. It's watching us all. It wrestled with Miss Penny and destroyed her. I was there. I saw a figure shrouded in darkness. It was the *aos sí* that dwells in the Giant's Tit come to seek retribution on the Meryons for abandoning the Goddess and her people. I heard the melody she wove when her revenge was achieved."

The priest gestured to the end of a pew and steadily moved the woman toward it until at last she sat. Fingers molded around the wreath, she was visibly trembling. The priest turned and went through the sacristy door, closing it behind him.

The room was silent. Over her shoulder Jen saw that not all of those in attendance had left as suggested. Those that remained were all staring at the woman and, when it became clear the drama was over, began whispering to each other. She looked back at the woman, who lifted her face, pale in a frame of wavy red hair, to gaze at Jen from anguish-filled light green eyes.

"They should never have abandoned the Goddess."

Jen smiled slightly and nodded. Maybe the woman was trying to do good. But couldn't she see that angering the family on this of all days, just before they said their final farewell to Penny, was an atrocious breach of common decency? Apparently not. Jen hadn't detected even a hint of lunacy in the woman's eyes, although her statements could be interpreted as fanatical. She was glad Sophie hadn't been witness to the woman's near hysteria.

Jen turned and moved down to stand by Granddad Meryon. "Sir. I'm Jen O'Malley, Sophie's new nanny. May I sit with you while we wait?"

He waved his hand toward the spot beside him. "Please do. I wondered who the pretty girl next to Rand was. So you're the nanny?"

"Yes, sir."

He heaved a sigh. "If I was steady enough for the steps, I'd visit Martha. Haven't been down to see her for three years. Damned decline. Now Penny's there too."

"I'm sorry for your loss."

"Yes. Well." He brushed his hand over his nose. "It is what it is."

He looked past her for a moment and then bent closer. "So what was that"—he lifted his eyebrows and tipped his head toward the woman with the wreath—"all about?"

Jen hesitated. It wasn't proper to gossip about what she'd overheard, but surely he deserved to know what was happening in his family.

"She wanted to place a wreath on the tomb, I think. Mr. Meryon refused to allow it."

He gave a short nod. "Humph. Genevieve's as batty as the day is long, but it's usually best to let her do as she pleases. True believer in her herbs and spells. Not many follow the old beliefs on Rathlin. But some do. Most don't give a fig one way or another. The Father will take care of her."

"I hope he can calm Mr. Meryon. He was furious." Jen glanced toward the sacristy door.

Granddad Meryon patted her hand. "Not to worry. It looks like he's learned control at last. His temper has gotten him into trouble in the past. Don't know where it came from. We Meryons aren't a particularly choleric lot. Violence isn't our way. Never understood the boy." Lips pressed together, he shook his head and looked at the floor.

"Mr. Meryon seems kind and thoughtful," Jen said.

Granddad Meryon brought his gaze up to pierce her with an inquisitive look. "You think so? It's good to know a pretty girl sees something besides the hoopla he surrounds himself with."

Jen smiled. "I haven't witnessed the hoopla, so I can't be a judge of that."

"Maybe you won't. Maybe he's ready to settle down. He needs a wife, especially if he becomes Sophie's guardian as his mother wishes. A woman could do worse than marrying my grandson." He cocked an eyebrow at her.

Jen dropped her eyes to her lap, certain her cheeks had flushed. The soft *squeak* of the sacristy door opening eliminated her need to respond. "That didn't take long."

The priest was the first to reenter the nave, moving directly toward the woman with the wreath, making sure she remained seated until the family left. Claire followed, holding Sophie's hand, and Randolph brought up the rear. They ignored the woman, except for Sophie, who darted several glances in her direction.

Claire bent to kiss her father's cheek. "If you're ready to leave, Father, I'll have Brian fetch your chair."

"Yes. I'm ready," he said.

"Mother, I'll meet you and Granddad in the village. I'll see Sophie and Jen off," Randolph said.

"Thank you, dear." His mother kissed Randolph. She waved at a young man standing in the back of the room. "Brian's coming, Father."

Once Granddad Meryon was seated comfortably, he navigated the aisle to the doors using the chair's controls. Claire and Brian followed. Jen eased out of the row and took Sophie's hand. Randolph motioned them to precede him.

Outside Jen stopped and drew in a deep breath. The air was sharp with the tang of autumn. The trees here were already wearing hints of their fall colors. A scent of wood smoke floated on the slight breeze. It was a perfect day for a walk. Most of those attending the funeral had waited for the family to appear before starting the trek to the village.

Randolph stopped next to her. She tipped her head toward the road leading down the hill and asked, "How far to the village?"

"Over a mile. In the city that would seem a good distance, but here on Rathlin it's right next door."

"Hmmm."

Sophie pulled out of Jen's grasp and stared up at Randolph. "Uncle Rand? Will you walk home with us?" Sophie asked.

"No, pumpkin. I have to speak with someone." To Jen he asked, "You remember the way back?"

"Yes. It's not far."

"Good. We'll see you later then. Probably two hours at least."

Jen looked up at him. She wanted to smooth the creases in his forehead. After a slight roll of her shoulders, she said, "We'll be fine."

Randolph gave a distracted nod.

Okay. He's got other things on his mind. "Come on, Sophie. Mrs. Polgrey said she was leaving us a treat for lunch."

"Do I have to hold your hand?"

Jen smiled. "Not if you stay close by."

Sophie's initial response was a hidden grin. "Deal."

RANDOLPH WATCHED as Sophie and Jen set off. He was baffled. Jen didn't act like any O'Malley he'd ever heard of. For one thing, she was nice. If anyone had told him an O'Malley would offer him comfort at his sister's funeral mass, he would have laughed at the joke. Not likely. But she had. She was a puzzle. Why was she here working for his family? Was she here to safeguard the daughter of one of the conservative movement's heroines?

Penny had been in lockstep with most of their beliefs, at least so far as men were concerned. A gifted speaker and writer, she'd been a leading advocate of their cause to keep men in their place. Jen O'Malley was a mystery, and he would figure her out, for Sophie's sake if nothing else.

"Mr. Meryon?"

Randolph broke from his reverie to see a well-dressed woman approaching. In her hand she held the seal sack with the broken doll and lamb's wool found on the family tomb.

"You must be Lt. Sanders," he said.

Sanders nodded, dropping her eyes to the bag she carried. "Yes, sir. Your foreman gave me the package. I have a few questions." She pasted on a smile and returned her gaze to him.

Randolph scrutinized the woman. She'd opted for civilian clothes rather than her uniform in deference to the funeral. Past middle age, hair in a tight bun, she looked eager to be of service with enough spit and shine to show that details were important but didn't overwhelm her. "Allow me to tell you what I know, and then you can ask any questions that remain."

A hint of pink tinted her cheeks. "Yes, sir."

Her display of nerves was nothing new to him. At least it was better than the hostility he expected on Tallav. "The bag's contents were discovered this morning by Father James on our family's tomb below the sacristy. No one has touched the items. They were placed in the seal sack as found. Both the Father and I believe the broken doll is an effigy of my sister. The wool represents the lamb that led to her death." He stepped forward, looking down at the sergeant, who was six inches shorter than he. "Check for fingerprints and DNA. I want to know who would act in such a reprehensible way. And why."

The sergeant's shoulders pushed back and her jaw set. "Yes, sir. I'll make that a priority. If I may, one question. Who else knows about this?"

Randolph grimaced. "Myself, the Father, and our foreman, Jim. I've asked Jim if there was anyone he knew who would do this. He was stumped."

The sergeant nodded, her expression thoughtful. "I don't think we'll have to question anyone at this point. The forensic evidence will tell us what we need. This isn't something a knowledgeable criminal is likely to have done. Amateurs rarely fool us."

Randolph narrowed his eyes and frowned. "That was my assumption. Whoever did this, I want to know if it was inspired by petty malice or if something darker is happening."

The sergeant looked at the bag in her hand, drawing a finger along one of the doll's legs. "You're not thinking political motivation, are you?"

Randolph rocked on his feet, considering the question. "I don't know. Anything is possible. Mother and I are both having trouble believing that Penny would put herself in a position to fall from that cliff. How in-depth was the investigation into her death?"

She jerked her head up, looking as though she wanted to step back, but she held her ground. "I was in charge. We followed standard procedure for a reported accidental death."

Randolph widened his stance. "And that entailed?"

Before answering, she cleared her throat. "We took images and vids of the accident location. When we arrived, the body had already been removed from the scene. Your foreman had taken an air cart down the ridge and brought your sister up to the castle's back lawn. I would have preferred that they'd left her there, but your mother was distraught and wanted her daughter out of the water."

"So the scene was completely compromised."

"Yes. Even so, all evidence pointed to a mishap. Witnesses all believed it was an accident."

He folded his hands with an outward display of composure. "Was there an autopsy?"

"Yes. Dr. Tomlinson conducted a primescan autopsy. After an informal inquest, she brought a verdict of death by misadventure."

What the fuck! He'd strived to stay calm, but he couldn't keep the challenge from his voice. "Informal?"

She flinched in an abbreviated move away from him but then squared her shoulders before answering. "Yes, sir. Most inquests are informal. It means Tomlinson used the documents from the garda's investigation and her own autopsy to reach her decision rather than hold a hearing. The result would have been the same."

Back off. You're intimidating her. Not helpful. Randolph drew in a slow breath. "I apologize for seeming to doubt your ability to investigate my sister's accident. I'm not at my best. Both you and the coroner found nothing that would indicate foul play. My mother and I will have to accept that my sister's death was a senseless mishap."

Her expression softened. "I'm sorry. If you would like to review the documentation, you may."

Fatigue washed over him. "Yes. I would. And the autopsy records?"

"Address an official application to the coroner. I don't see why she would refuse if your mother made the request."

He scrubbed a hand over his face. "Thank you. I'd appreciate you sending all the information you gathered, including images and vids, to Briarcliff's main comm."

"Certainly." She gave him a weak smile. "If there is anything else I can do to assist you or your mother, please let me know. Everyone on the island holds your family in deepest sympathy. It's come as a real blow to many of us, considering how much in the last year your sister has taken an interest in island affairs. It finally felt like she was one of us, placing Rathlin ahead of her Tallavan political beliefs."

"Really? I didn't know."

Her eyes brightened. "Oh, yes. In particular child welfare, parenting, and infertility work. Your sister was such a lovely young woman."

This was the second person that had spoken of a change in Penny over the last year. A change he would never witness. "Thank you. I appreciate… I'll pass your sentiments on to my mother."

She acknowledged him with a bob of her head. "I'll get the process started on this"—she brought the packet up—"before heading to the community center."

6

I f Mrs. Polgrey hadn't shown her, Jen would have had no idea how to open the front door to Briarcliff. It was made of solid oak planks with vertical and horizontal oak pieces attached with iron studs to create decorative rows of tall rectangles. The top row was curved to match the arch of the recessed enclosure where the door hung. It looked ancient and massive. She grasped the iron knocker and gave it a firm twist. The panel connected to it turned with ease. Beneath, she found the keypad and entered the pass code she'd been given. A clunk sounded, followed by a metallic *kachung*. Jen slipped the knocker back in place and felt the door move inward. She pushed it, and it opened soundlessly.

Sunlight streamed inside, brightening a patch of the interior gloom. More light shone through high mullioned windows onto the second-floor platform of the massive staircase that connected the foyer to the upper floors of the castle. The steps made a right-angle turn, advancing up into deepening shadow.

Sophie scooted past Jen, vanishing down a hallway. An unsettled feeling had taken residence in Jen's stomach. Being alone in this place was spooky. Not that she believed in ghosts. Tales of ancestral specters were just that, stories made up to add to the ancient Celtic atmosphere of Briarcliff. She jumped when the sound of a door opening and banging against a wall reverberated from the hall where Sophie had disappeared.

Jen looked about for a means to turn on a light before shutting the front door. She didn't want to search for it with only the haze of sunshine from the windows high above. Their little patch of light didn't illuminate the dim shadows of the first floor. Briarcliff's architect had purposefully forgone a few modern conveniences. The lack of automatic lighting was one feature Jen would have preferred. A bank of switches was located to the left of the entrance. She quickly toggled them all on, shut the door, and attempted to use her pass code to lock it. Silence. If it clunked when it opened, shouldn't it do the same when it was locked? And the keypad didn't produce a locked notification, so she wasn't sure she'd bolted the door. She dropped her shoulders and sighed.

"Sophie?" No response. *Great.* How was she going to find the child if Sophie hid? Jen's anchor point was the nursery. From there it might be possible to locate the rooms she'd been to in the castle, but with all the matching wood plank doors and dark paneled hallways, it would be easy to get lost.

She strode to the end of the corridor. Dim passages diverged at right angles to her present track. A little farther to the left a door, recessed in a stone arch, stood open with light shining from it. Two suits of armor with lethal looking swords pointing down before them, stood guarding the doorway.

"Sophie!" No response. "Sophie!"

The little girl's voice chimed from inside the lit room. "Come see, Miss Jen."

Upon entering, the first thing that drew Jen's gaze was a life-size replica of a horse and rider, both in full medieval armor. One hoof was lifted as though the black horse was taking a step toward her. A crimson plume flowed from the top of the knight's silver helmet. Exhibit cases and free-standing pieces filled the room with every type of weaponry.

"Look."

Jen stepped to where Sophie stood pointing at a case with more armor on display. "This was Mommy's favorite."

The little girl's face was pensive. Behind the glass, a lifelike male mannequin that bore a slight resemblance to Rand was outfitted with a combination of a long chain mail shirt, a leather breastplate with a pair of metal plates attached, a plate helmet with a raised visor worn over a chain mail mantle that covered the figure's throat and shoulders, and separate plate armor on the legs and arms. A large sword was buckled around the torso in a leather sheath with another attached to it for a long dagger. The figure held a spear in his right hand.

"His equipment isn't as beautiful as the armor of the man on the horse, but he seems more fearsome," Jen said. She noticed that a plaque stated this was a replica of Anglo-Irish armor worn in the fifteenth and sixteenth centuries in Ireland.

Sophie pursed her lips. "It's Great-Great-Great-Great-Granddad Meryon dressed in armor. Four greats."

"What did your mother like about it?" Jen kept her gaze fixed on the display after asking her question.

"She said they didn't wear shiny armor 'cause they didn't fight big battles. Just skirdmishes. Little ones. And they couldn't kick the bad people out." She flung her arm up from her side, flopping her hand out at the wrist. "But the bad people were too afraid to go out of the bucket."

Jen withheld the laugh that bubbled up inside her. "You mean the pale?"

"Oh. Yeah. The pale. She said if they tried to be like the bad people, they would've lost. So always do what's best for you no matter what other people do."

"That sounds like good advice," Jen responded.

Sophie nodded. "Yeah. Mommy was smart. She wrote things in books." She glared at Jen. "I'm going to read them all." Then she spun around and threw her arms out. "There's loads of stuff in here. Knives, bows and arrows, daggers, swords, axes, head bashers. Really old guns. Really old. Not like ours. They shoot metal bullets. If bad people come here, I'll get a weapon and fight them off. I know how. I have my own wooden sword."

Sophie swung an imaginary sword in imitation of a doughty warrior.

Jen was surprised at the fierce grimace Sophie made while wielding her pretend blade. Sophie's personality was nothing like the sad, quiet little girl Jen had first met. Meryons were fighters. Sophie's mother had been, although she'd fought with words. Penny Meryon's essays and books had been required reading in the O'Malley family. Jen had heard several of

Penny's lectures. She'd been a fiery speaker but never a strident one. Jen was glad Sophie had her mother's scrap, but she was still a child who needed boundaries to protect her from her superhero self-confidence.

"How about you first run and find an adult, and if they say you need a weapon, then you can come get one?"

Sophie cast a scowl in Jen's direction. "You're not my mommy. I don't have to do what you say."

Oh gods. Here it comes. Jen knelt before Sophie. "No, I'm not your mommy. No one can take her place, and I would never try to. But I am your nanny, and that means when I tell you to do something, you have to do it. I won't be mean about it. Part of my job is to keep you safe."

Her lips smushed in disapproval, Sophie studied Jen. When she spoke, her voice dripped with reluctance. "Okay."

"Let's go get lunch. You'll have to show me how to get to the kitchen from here."

Mollified by Jen's need for help, Sophie grabbed Jen's hand and pulled her toward the door. "This way. I know a shortcut."

Sophie tugged Jen along the corridor to the right. When she stopped unexpectedly to face one of the panels lining the hall, Jen almost ran into her.

"This one. It's the middle one." Sophie reached out and touched a spot a little higher than where a doorknob would be. The panel swung inward to reveal a narrow, murky passageway. "I don't have my hand light, so it's gonna be dark." Sophie yanked on Jen and plunged inside. "Shut the door."

Jen reached back and pushed the panel closed, plunging them into complete darkness. Unnerved, Jen gripped Sophie's hand tighter.

"Don't worry. I can find my way even in the dark." Sophie walked at a brisk pace. "There's shortcuts all over. The servants use them to get places fast. I know all of them. Even the secret one."

"The secret one?" Jen asked.

"Yeah. Behind my bedroom. I wasn't supposed to know about it. Mommy used it one night when I was pretending to be asleep." Sophie giggled. "I saw her."

"Really?"

"Yeah. But there's no door in your room, just the kid's rooms. It goes all the way to Mommy's and Grandma's room, but not Uncle Rand's. That's 'cause he's on the other side. I'll show it to you."

"First, lunch."

"Yep."

The passageway brightened when Sophie opened the panel at its end. Jen recognized the corridor they entered as the one that led to the main kitchen, but they hadn't come out where she had expected from the map of Briarcliff that had been forming in her mind. She needed to ask for one.

Jen found the lunch the cook had left for them in the cooler. "Shall we take this upstairs to the nursery or eat here?"

"Upstairs. Then I can show you the secret passage."

Jen handed Sophie two glasses of sweet cider, picked up their plates, and followed Sophie to the back staircase and up. When they'd finished their turkey sandwiches, veggie sticks, and frosted sugar cookies made to look like autumn leaves, Jen suggested they wash. Sophie splashed her hands under the water for a few seconds and then grabbed a towel.

"Sophie, wash properly."

The little girl's face set in a stubborn expression. "I did."

"No, you didn't. Wash again."

Sophie squinted, dropped her shoulders, and returned to the sink. After she'd finished washing and drying her hands, she asked, "Can I show you the secret passage behind my room now?"

"Sure."

Sophie bounced on her feet and grabbed Jen's arm. "Let's go."

Jen allowed Sophie to drag her off. Sophie was a bundle of raw energy. Was she always this way, almost frenetic? *I'll have to ask her grandmother if this is normal behavior or if it might be a reaction to her mother's death.*

Sophie drew Jen to the back wall of her room. Over her shoulder Sophie said, "This one's trickier." She pressed a series of three flowers on the wall covering, and a panel popped open. "It's so kids can't accidently open it. Come on. Oh, wait; let me get my hand light." She dashed to her bedside table and pulled it from the drawer.

She flashed Jen a big grin and tugged her through the opening. "Okay. If we go that way"—she pointed the light to the left—"we can get to the other bedrooms in the nursery. If we go this way"—the glow of the hand light aimed right—"we go past your room and the other kid's rooms. Come on."

Sophie halted before one of the children's secret doors. "There's peepholes. You have to uncover them. I can't reach them, but the servants use them all the time, 'specially the dining room one." She pointed to a round, flat cover that had a hook on one side resting in a catch. "You slide it up."

Jen did and placed her eye to the hole that was revealed. Sure enough, she could see into an unused nursery bedroom. She slid the covering back in place just as Sophie grabbed her hand and pulled.

"Let's go to Grandma's and Mommy's rooms. But we have to be quiet. This is secret."

Jen smiled to herself. They moved along the passage, past the empty family bedrooms that lay between the nursery and where they were headed, the glow of Sophie's hand light illuminating their path before the distance faded into gloom. Finally Sophie stopped. "This is Mommy's room," she whispered and pointed to the covering attached to the wall at Jen's eye level.

Jen responded in a quiet voice, "Yes."

"You can look." Sophie's eyes were wide and unblinking in the shadows cast by her hand light. Two hectic red spots colored her cheeks. Jen's scalp prickled. *Sophie's just overwrought with everything that's happened today. This wasn't a good idea. One quick peek and then it's quiet time for both of us.*

Jen slipped the covering up and put her eye to the hole. *Oh!* Inside the room, a woman was riffling through Penny Meryon's things. *No one's supposed to be here. What should I do?*

She rotated the cover back in place. "Okay. I've seen it. Now let's go back." She placed a finger to her lips. "Quietly."

Sophie grinned and copied Jen. She slipped past and led the way along the passage.

Once they were inside Sophie's bedroom again, Jen announced nap time and got Sophie settled. She kept her demeanor calm for Sophie's sake, but it was difficult. Who was the woman in Penny's bedroom? Was she a thief? If so, why was she in Penny's room when valuable items were in easy reach on the ground floor? The house was supposed to be empty. Would staff have already returned? No. They should be gone for at least another hour. But maybe someone had come home early to steal something from Penny's room.

Jen shut Sophie's door with a soft *snick* and quietly walked down the corridor to the nursery entrance. The hallway that accessed the family bedrooms was empty. With as much stealth as she could manage, Jen padded along the ornate carpet runner that ran the length of the hall, counting the doors as she went to be certain she opened Penny's first. But it was already slightly open. Inside, a drawer scraped and someone cursed softly.

It's probably a maid sent to find something for Ms. Meryon. You're letting your imagination run wild. Stop it. She brought her head closer to the gap and listened intently. There were no more sounds. *Just go in. All right. Okay.*

Jen burst through the door to find the woman she'd seen before on her knees, peering under the bed.

She looked up, her eyes wide, and squealed. "Oh. You scared me."

"Hello. I'm sorry I startled you. I wasn't expecting anyone to be at home. At least I was told no one would be. So when I heard a noise coming from this room, I thought I should check. Maybe a dog got locked in or a mouse or a burglar. But you're not. Are you?"

The woman blinked and swiped a hand through her short blonde hair. "I'm not…?"

"A burglar. Oh, excuse me, I'm running daffy. I'm Jen O'Malley, the new nanny. And you are?"

"Lanny…" The woman rose, brushing her hands over her slacks. "Lanny Conyer. I was Penny's assistant, and I'm helping go through her papers and finalize her work."

"Oh my goodness." Jen covered her face with one hand. "I don't know what to say." She curled her fingers and pressed her knuckles to her lips. "It must be the spooky atmosphere of this place. I let my imagination run away with me. You're so obviously not a burglar."

A loud *clunk* broke into the women's conversation when a bottle fell from the highboy, and they both jumped. Lanny made a face halfway between a grin and grimace. "Easy to do. It's pretty gothic."

"Gods isn't it. I just put Sophie down for a nap. Is there anything I can help you do?"

Lanny winced and shook her head, avoiding gazing directly at Jen.

"No. I've looked in every drawer and cupboard in here and haven't found what I'm searching for."

"Which is?"

Lanny hesitated. "Penny Meryon's diary."

"Oh." Why would Lanny need Penny's diary? Lavinia had never let Jen near anything personal. And to look for it while everyone was out of the house was…odd.

The smile Lanny directed at Jen didn't reach her eyes. "Let's get out of here and grab a cup of tea."

"Can we do that in the nursery? I really don't want to stray too far from Sophie."

"Sure." Lanny smoothed her hair in place and stepped through the bedroom door when Jen extended a hand, motioning Lanny to go first.

Jen followed her. "What's important about the diary?"

"Nothing probably. But it's gone missing, as have the data cubes for the book Penny was working on. I wanted to get things in order as much as possible so that if the book were nearly complete, it could be finished and published."

Lanny's explanation filled the time it took to arrive at the nursery and enter the study room. Jen pointed at a table with chairs sized to be comfortable to adults and said, "Have a seat."

Then she went to the corner where the tea supplies were stored. "Earl Grey, green tea, or chai?"

"Green tea," Lanny said.

"Plain?"

"Yes, please."

Jen placed two insta-tea containers, two teacups, spoons, and covered bowls of dry creamer and sweetener on a tray. After setting the load on the table, she offered Lanny the green tea and a cup, punching the heating nubs for her. Jen then heated her own tea, poured it into a cup, and added creamer and sweetener. She took a sip and sighed.

"What was Penny's new book about?"

Lanny set her cup down. "It was a history of the matriarchist families of Tallav. Penny did extensive research. I helped her with that, but she allowed no one, not even me, to see the manuscript. She said she wanted it complete before others read it."

"Hmm. It doesn't sound like her usual book. Didn't she write political treatises?"

"Yes." A gleam came into Lanny's eyes. "Penny was the voice of her generation for traditional values and policies." Lanny reached inside her blouse and pulled out a necklace. "She gave me this." The shiny, round, silver pendant was inscribed with an ornate *M*. A tiny grass-green stone glimmered on one side. "*M* for matriarchist. But you probably know as much as I do about preserving our foundational way of life since you're an O'Malley. It must be amazing to have Cordelia O'Malley as head of your family."

I'll never get away from the O'Malley name, at least not while I'm on Tallav. "There's no one quite like her."

Lanny tipped her chin higher and lifted her lips in a smile of satisfaction. "No, indeed. She's a staunch champion of matriarchist rule. Is that why you're here? Did the matriarchists arrange to have you care for Sophie?"

Jen was speared by Lanny's intent focus. "Umm."

"I know Penny was worried about who would be guardian for her daughter if she passed away suddenly. She remade her will to change the designee. I think she changed it from her mother to someone who fell more in line with her beliefs."

Jen wasn't sure how to respond. She'd wanted to get Lanny to open up about what she'd been doing in Penny's room. Maybe if she were vague... "I don't know about that. When I worked for Lavinia O'Malley, Cordelia's granddaughter, I attended many of Penny's lectures. I'm not political though. Too much arguing, debate and such."

Jen resisted the urge to sigh when Lanny gave her a conspiratorial look. "No, we all can't take up the sword and defend our matriarchal rights, but you're still doing your part for the cause."

"Hmmm."

Head cocked to one side, Lanny said, "There is another way you can be helpful."

"Really." In the past, helpful had meant working at rallies, soliciting donations, and chauffeuring party movers and shakers around Cahernamon.

Lanny leaned in. "Yes. Keep track of Randolph Meryon. If he finds

Penny's diary and data cubes, he'll destroy them. He's always opposed Penny's political viewpoints."

Interesting. Maybe she could get answers to questions Evaline had been unwilling to answer about the man. "Is that what caused the rift between them? I mean, I know there was some kind of scandal. Something he did that brought shame on his family, but the details were never made explicit, at least not in the book Penny wrote about her conversion to the matri-archist party. The people who knew or acted like they knew all treated it like a big secret they kept mum for Penny's sake."

"It's depraved. I didn't find out until I worked for Penny. She told me late one night. When her brother was just fourteen, Penny caught him in a sexual situation. And he was beating an estate worker with a riding crop."

"Sweet mother!"

Lanny dipped her chin primly. "He claims she ruined his life. So you can understand why he'd want to destroy her work, and why she'd worry about who became Sophie's guardian."

"I do."

"Keep an eye on him for me. If you find out he has the data cubes or diary, let me know. If you can get your hands on them, bring them to me. Whatever you do, don't let Meryon mesmerize you. Women who fall for him get the crap beaten out of them."

Jen's nodded response was distracted. It was the same advice she'd received from Evaline. One question consumed her thoughts. What caused a fourteen-year-old boy to become a sadist?

"I should probably get going. My car's in the drive by the servants' entrance." Lanny rose. "It was nice meeting you."

"Oh. Yes. You too."

"And please, keep my visit today to yourself. Don't misunderstand. I'm not hiding what I'm doing. But Mr. Meryon might not like me being here by myself."

"Right. May I walk you out? I'm trying to learn the layout of the castle. I'm not sure where the servant's entrance is."

"I'd be happy to show you."

7

The servant's entrance turned out to be near the main kitchen. Several cars were parked in the small, graveled car park, including Lanny's light gray sedan. A row of garages built to resemble stables lined the far side. Bright red tomatoes, yellow squash, and orange pumpkins nestled in the lush, green foliage of the kitchen garden on one end of the parking area. The midafternoon sun warmed Jen's skin.

When Lanny drove away, Jen turned to go back inside. Next to the step into the building, the stub of a burned candle rested atop a small mound of a deep brown substance. Jen plucked the stump from its resting place and brought it to her nose. Plain white paraffin and something spicy. Dark grains stuck to the wax and now clung to her fingertips. Cloves. Why would someone burn a candle in a pile of cloves by an entrance to Briarcliff?

Jen's mother had renounced the practice of magic that pervaded some sects that worshipped the First Mother, claiming it was all superstitious nonsense. Lavinia professed that aligning one's mind and heart with the goddess was the primary focus of a true worshipper, but she dabbled in spells and kept a wise woman on staff. That's where Jen had learned cloves were useful for protection, as were white candles. Someone had set a spell of protection here. But why? Had they done it at every door?

The layout of the ground floor was shaping itself in her mind with greater accuracy. At least she remembered the path from the main kitchen to the corridor that bisected the castle into two halves. Someday she would explore everywhere. She wanted to visit the library to see the rare print books it contained.

If she followed the corridor, it would take her to the front foyer and the main entrance. Stillness settled on her. She took slow, cautious footsteps as though any sound she made might disturb… something. *You're such an idiot.* Idiot or not, the paneled hall with its medieval arched doors and dim lighting was eerie. It wouldn't surprise her to find a ghost gliding along, moaning or whatever ghosts did. *Even if they are real, they can't hurt you. They're incorporeal.*

She'd nearly convinced herself that she had nothing to fear when, stepping around the corner into the front hall, she stopped dead. An apparition, filmy white, floated in the foyer before Briarcliff's front entrance. The hair on the back of Jen's neck and along her arms lifted. Her leg muscles tightened. Poised on the edge of running to hide, she noted one disparate detail. The ghost had hands, raised as though in supplication. They weren't ghostly. They looked like a real person's, down to the bright pink fingernails. And the specter wasn't floating. The sound of shoes scraped on the tile floor.

Too involved in its dance or ritual, the ghost didn't notice Jen's approach until she spoke. "What are you doing?"

It dropped its arms and turned. The white flowing dress and veils that covered it from head to toe made it impossible to tell who it was. The figure ran to the front door, sweeping past a circle of lit candles laid out in what looked to be more ground cloves. It flung the entrance open, dashed the veils back, revealing long red hair, and sprinted away.

Jen reached the entry, running into Randolph's solid body. He gripped her shoulders, and she latched her arms around his waist, burying her face in his white shirt. His jacket and the top buttons on the shirt were undone. Her cheek pressed into his warm skin.

"What is going on?" His voice was gruff.

"It was a ghost. No, not a ghost." Despite her answer being muffled, she didn't want to pull back. Then she'd have to look at him. She wasn't sure why she'd fastened herself to him. For some crazy reason it reassured her.

His hands tightened, and he pried her away from him. "Where's Sophie?"

Waves of irritation rolled off him. She was caught in his glaring gaze, unable to respond.

His eyes narrowed a fraction. "Is Sophie okay?"

"Y-yes. Sophie's in her room, taking a nap. She's fine."

His fingers bit into her upper arms. "And you're okay?"

"It's been a rather busy afternoon, but I think my heart has stopped beating a mile a minute."

He hauled her against him, enfolded her, and stroked her hair, murmuring soothing words. Once again she hugged him tight. He was so warm, and whatever scent he wore smelled sinfully good, wild and masculine. If she turned her head, she could kiss the vee of tanned skin that his open collar exposed. His heartbeat was a strong, steady rhythm where her ear lay against him. Solid. He was so damned solid. And then she realized that another portion of his anatomy was also firm against her abdomen. Her stomach dropped, and her ears went hot. At almost the same moment, they both pulled apart.

Jen gave a shaky laugh and brushed her bangs back from her forehead. "I should go check on Sophie. I've been away from the nursery about fifteen minutes."

Heat sparked in his eyes. "I'll come with you."

"S-sure."

Upstairs she found everything in order. Sophie was still sleeping peacefully.

Outside Sophie's bedroom door, Randolph placed a hand on her upper arm. "We need to talk."

Jen suggested the same spot where she'd taken tea with Lanny. "Do you want something to drink? Tea?"

He settled in a chair, his forearm resting on the edge of the table. "No. I've had enough tea to float a boat today."

"Okay. I'll just make one for me." Her back to him, she took her time heating the beverage, pouring it into a cup, and adding sweetener and cream. She tried to steady herself while she did. *What the hell is wrong with you? You were clinging to your boss. Who by the by is considered to be a dangerous man. You will not screw this job up by falling for someone you shouldn't even be thinking about in that way.* Tea prepared, she had no other reason to avoid facing him.

A wisp of steam rose from the cup she'd placed firmly on the table before her. She kept her gaze on it, one finger stroking the handle. She crossed her legs. Her heart fluttered when she inadvertently nudged his knee doing so.

Randolph took no notice. "Why was Genevieve Kavan running out of Briarcliff?"

So that's who it was. Genevieve Kavan. That makes sense.

"Did you let her in?"

Whatever previous sympathy Randolph had held for Jen had disappeared.

A glimpse proved she hadn't mistaken his tone of voice. His face was stern. "I didn't let her in. But I may have left the door unlocked. The pass code didn't work. Sophie had run off, and I had to find her. It slipped my mind after that."

"Humph. We need to do a better job of orienting you to Briarcliff. My apologies for leaving you on your own. Do you have an idea what the woman was about?"

"I believe she was setting a spell of protection over Briarcliff." She sneaked another peek at him, and he quirked an eyebrow at her.

She brushed her bangs back from her forehead. "There's a pile of ground cloves with the stub of a candle at the servant's entrance. She must have tried the main door and, when it opened, decided to set her spell in the entry. When I came into the front hall, I thought she was a ghost. She was dressed all in white fluttery fabric and was dancing with her hands raised."

"Ghosts aren't real."

Jen brought her gaze up. "Of course not. I was startled for a moment. And it was dark. When I realized it was a woman, I asked her what she was doing. She ran out of the door. And then you were there."

"Yes." His eyes glittered with something Jen couldn't interpret but which her body responded to with a flood of heat.

Jen returned her gaze to her teacup. "Did you see the circle of white candles set in ground cloves when you came in?"

"I did, but I didn't know the brown stuff was cloves."

"Both are used for protection among those who practice goddess magic."

"At the service entrance too?"

"Uh-huh. Outside."

"Jen. Look at me."

Jen raised her gaze. She hadn't taken a sip of her tea. The cup had been more of a prop to give her fingers something to hold on to and still their restlessness. She was suddenly thirsty. Lifting it to drink would create a shield between them, but Jen couldn't bring herself to try. She was pinned in place.

"Why did you go out the servant's entrance?"

"I-I was saying goodbye to Lanny."

"Lanny was here?"

She hesitated. She didn't owe Lanny anything. The woman was sneaking around behind the Meryon's backs. "Yes. She was looking for Penny's diary. In your sister's bedroom."

Randolph's brow furrowed. "Maybe you should tell me everything that happened this afternoon from the beginning."

Jen gave a full account, including the adventure Sophie had taken her on through the secret passage and Lanny's request to keep her visit from Randolph. "That's why I came to the front entrance and caught Genevieve setting another protection spell."

Now that she'd spilled her story, Jen felt lighter. It would be the perfect time for Randolph to take her in his arms again and tell her... What would he tell her? *Get serious. He's your boss. He's not interested in you. So he got an erection. He had to peel himself away from you. And you're forgetting he's a sadist who started inflicting pain on his victims at an early age.*

One hand rubbing his forehead, Randolph pursed his lips. When he lowered his arm to the table, his brows drew down. "Thank you for telling me about Lanny. I'm sure it was a struggle against your matriarchist principles."

Jen glared at him. "Hardly. Being an O'Malley doesn't automatically make me a matriarchist. I'd appreciate not having O'Malley baggage loaded on my back. I've enough burdens of my own."

Randolph's eyebrows rose. "So you're not an undercover matriarchist spy?"

"Good gods no!"

He cocked his head to the side and squinted. "Huh." The spark returned to his eyes, and he straightened and leaned in toward her. "I'll remember that."

She jumped when he slapped the table.

"Thank you, Ms. O'Malley. You've exceeded expectations. I'll leave you to your duties." On his way to the door he turned. "Tomorrow afternoon the lawyers will be here to read Penny's will. Please keep Sophie in the nursery."

"Yes, sir."

He nodded and departed.

Jen blew a long stream of air out when he was gone. Six months being around that man would be hard. Maybe he would leave soon like Evaline expected. But if he didn't…

RANDOLPH DRAGGED a hand down his face and took another sip of whiskey. Tomorrow he needed to deal with the problem of Darrin Kavan, Genevieve Kavan's son. What the fuck was wrong with that family? Hadn't they done enough in the past? The mother kept intruding on the Meryons with her spells and wreaths, even entering Briarcliff uninvited. And now Darrin was established as the culprit behind the broken doll left on the Meryon family crypt. The kid was just fourteen years old, so Randolph had told Lt. Sanders he wouldn't pursue charges but handle the matter personally. Maybe Darrin was acting out because of Genevieve, but it was more likely he held a grudge against the Meryons. Something Randolph could understand, but he couldn't allow the boy to continue down the path he was on. A heart-to-heart ought to clear things up. Preferably without the mother present.

Clearly Genevieve had scared Jen O'Malley. The atmosphere at Briarcliff could induce a case of the creeping horrors all on its own without the addition of the sudden appearance of a ghostly draped Genevieve Kavan. As kids he and Penny had spent one night in the attics, moving from room to room, attempting to find the ghost of Grandma Meryon. Penny had claimed she'd seen it flit past a doorway. That had been all Randolph had needed to demand they leave. He'd ended up in Penny's bed that night and for about a week after. His father had wanted to know why. When Randolph refused to betray Penny, she'd been lectured anyway.

Genevieve Kavan's invasion had frightened Jen. Why else would she plaster herself against him when he'd arrived back at Briarcliff? Her softness in all the right places had stirred his libido, something which had been decidedly inactive since his return to Tallav. If he spent more time on Tallav than expected, she might be the distraction he needed. A fresh-faced, vanilla girl would be a nice change of pace now she'd declared herself a nontraditional O'Malley. *Good gods no, she was not a matriarchist spy!* He chuckled. Get her beneath him and he was sure he could discover all her secrets. Whip not required. She was attracted to him. Her reactions during their chat this afternoon had proven that. If he were careful, he could play with her without causing her to quit her nanny position. In correct circles one didn't dally with the staff, but he didn't have a proper bone in his body, and the temptation was powerful.

"Here you are," his mother said.

"Sorry, I didn't realize you were looking for me. May I pour you a drink?"

Claire sat on the arm of Randolph's chair. "No, thank you. The lawyers will be here tomorrow."

"Yes. And?"

"Have you come to a decision about the guardianship of Sophie?" She rested a hand on his shoulder.

"No. Let's find out what's in Penny's will. I'm sure she has Sophie's future all planned out."

"Naturally. But I want to be prepared to circumvent her wishes if she's chosen someone outside the family to care for Sophie."

"Do you expect that?"

"I would have, but with the changes in Penny over the last year, I'm no longer certain. It will depend on when she last updated her will."

"The lawyers will give us guidance whatever arises. The logical person to assume Sophie's guardianship is you."

"We'll see."

Randolph shook his head. His mother was adamant he become Sophie's guardian. It made no sense except as a means to force him to come home to Tallav. He couldn't do that. Mother and Sophie would get along fine without him. He had a business to run, a growing BDSM empire.

Claire stroked his hair. "Are you okay?"

"I'm fine." The smile he'd intended to reassure her was hard to maintain. "I missed out on so much of Penny's life. She's a stranger to me."

"I wish..."

"No, Mother." He took her hand. "We can't undo the past."

She squeezed his fingers. "We can do better in the future."

"Yes." His response would upset her, but he didn't look forward to tomorrow or the days to come. They seemed full of responsibilities that would crush him under their weight unless he decided to cut and run. His mother would still speak to him, but her disappointment would damage their relationship.

He swallowed the last of his drink, allowing the burn to dissipate into the mellow flavor of the whiskey. "One step at a time, Mother. That's all any of us can do."

She kissed the top of his head. "And if that includes stepping back from operating the Whip Hand?"

"Don't push, Mother."

"Mother's prerogative." She rose from beside him and patted his shoulder. "Get some rest, darling. The problems and decisions will be here tomorrow."

Randolph grunted. *That they will. That they will.*

8

Randolph halted outside Genevieve Kavan's home, a modest cottage located on the Meryon estate just off the path to the village. Another building stood to the left, doing double duty as a workspace and a retail outlet. When he'd stuck his head into the entrance, Randolph had seen drying plants hanging from the rafters and a display rack with packets, but no Genevieve. Behind both buildings were the large gardens and greenhouse where the herbs she sold for a living grew. His knock on the cottage door was answered by Darrin, who stiffened when he recognized Randolph.

"What do you want?" Darrin asked, his jaw jutting out.

The gangly youth looked nothing like his mother. But he was somehow familiar. The obvious struck Randolph. Darrin had Randolph's father's eyes and chin. Sufficient proof for his father's betrayal if the DNA tests hadn't proven it long ago. "I need to speak with your mother."

Darrin brought his arms up as though he would cross them over his chest but instead lowered them to his sides. "She's not here."

"Will she be back soon?" Randolph kept his gaze leveled on the boy until Darrin dropped his own.

"She's in the greenhouse." The words were mumbled.

"Would you fetch her for me?"

Nostrils flaring, Darrin raised his chin, his eyes cold. "Right away, sir. Nothing I'm doing is more important than making sure your every need is met." He brushed past Randolph and stalked away, leaving the door standing open.

That kid has a giant chip on his shoulder. I suppose I did at his age too.

The sound of Genevieve Kavan fussing at her son arrived before she did. "Did you invite him inside? Tell him how lovely it was to see him? He's a Meryon. You didn't leave him waiting on the doorstep." She bustled around the corner of the house, holding her hands out as she approached. "Mr. Meryon. It's so lovely of you to drop by."

Randolph pulled his hands back, avoiding her grasp.

She brushed her palms on her skirt. "I'm so sorry. I was potting settings. Just a little soil." She gestured to the entrance. "Please come in. I'll make tea. I have a de-stressing mix that is quite lovely."

The inside of the Kavan's home was dim and reeked of incense and burned herbs. The small windows didn't allow much light to filter through. The front room contained several shelves crammed with jars of feathers, jumbles of ribbon, and other odds and ends. An old wooden desk held a pile of ogham divination sticks. The far end had been transformed into a pagan oratory with an altar, candles, and a flat stone that held ashes.

"Follow me." Genevieve beckoned him through the kitchen to a much brighter room in the back of the house. Large windows lined one wall. A ledge ran the length at sill height. Potted plants of every description from bushy to spiky succulents fought for their share of the sun. "Please have a seat. It's so lovely to have you in our home."

Randolph sat on the edge of the sofa, ignoring the stain on the worn cover.

"I'll go make the tea," she said, fluttering her fingers.

"That won't be necessary."

"Oh. Well if you're certain. It's quite lovely."

"I'm sure."

She perched on the edge of an armchair, wringing her hands. Randolph attempted to catch her gaze, but she never looked directly at him.

"Ms. Kavan. I'm here for two reasons. First, to insist that you never enter Briarcliff without invitation again. You frightened my niece's nanny."

She covered her mouth. "Oh my. That was not my intention."

"I'm certain it wasn't, or I'd have asked the local garda to take up the matter."

"Oh my. Oh, thank you. That's so lovely of you. I didn't know what else to do. No one will listen to me. I went to the garda to explain, but they said the case was closed." Her gaze lifted, eyes filled with terror finally rose to meet his. "Something must be done. The danger—"

"If you're referring to the *aos sí* seeking retribution against my family—"

She shook her head. "No, no. At first I thought it was the *aos sí*, but I've reconsidered. The voice wasn't of the faerie world. It was a person. A living person. Someone murdered your sister. I'm so afraid they will do it again."

Randolph narrowed his eyes. "Tell me what you saw and heard that night."

Once again fluttering her hands, she said, "I know I'm fanciful at times, but I did see someone in the dark, walking away from the cliff and—"

"What were you doing there?"

"Oh, well, I had gone down to the riverbank to gather marshmallow root. It's quite useful for combating a cough, especially when gathered in the light of a full moon. Although the moon wasn't full that night, but it was waxing—"

Randolph's jaw tightened. "You can't get to the river from the spot where my sister fell."

"Oh no. No. Of course not. I'd seen mistletoe in a tree along that part of the cliffs and thought to collect some on my way to the trail that leads down to the riverbank. It's such a long walk, but with the marshmallow, the mistletoe, and whatever else I found, it was well worth it. There's special magic in moonlight."

"I see. Can you describe the person?"

"They were quite a way off when I noticed them. I was squatted down burying a bit of bread at the roots of a hawthorn. Such lovely fat red berries. I heard the singing first. Well, not singing, humming. It was such a jaunty tune. Lovely. Gave a lift to my spirit to hear someone else enjoying a moonlit walk. But when I'd got to my feet, they were disappearing. Where the land takes that dip. Right out of view, so I turned about and headed downriver, never knowing something terrible had just happened."

"Was it a man? A woman?"

"I couldn't say for certain. Not from that distance. But I think a woman."

"And when you returned, you saw nothing else?"

"Oh. I'm so sorry. I didn't go back that way. I crossed to the road and followed it. Easier on my feet. If I'd only known." Face turned down, she shook her head.

Randolph reined in the urge to offer brusque thanks and leave. He still needed to deal with Darrin. "I need to speak with your son."

Genevieve lifted a wide-eyed gaze to him. "He had nothing to do with your sister's death. He wasn't there that night."

"I apologize. This isn't about that. Did you know your son left a surprise on our family crypt the day of my sister's internment?"

"A surprise. No. What kind of surprise? Not a wreath—"

"A broken doll on a lamb's wool."

Her expression was puzzled. "Why ever—"

The woman has no idea what her son gets up to. "It represented my sister's body and the sheep she tried to save."

Genevieve reared back, throwing her hands up in front of her chest. "Oh. How ugly."

Randolph grimaced. "Indeed."

As quickly as she had pulled away, Genevieve pressed toward him, waving. "But Darrin wouldn't do such a thing. He's a good boy."

"The garda has verified it."

Her face sagged, and Randolph realized that she looked older than she should. She must rely on herbals rather than the standard nanite treatments that fended off old age. "Oh. Oh my. I..."

"May I speak with him?"

She'd been fingering her hair, but now she clutched at Randolph. "You won't hurt him, will you?"

Gently Randolph pulled from her grip. "I have no intention of harming Darrin. Whatever is at the root of his malice needs to be dealt with. I remember what it's like to be fourteen and confused."

"Yes. Well then...okay. Shall I call him in?"

"Do. I think we'll take a walk together."

When she left the room, Randolph stood and paced. If Genevieve had only told someone what she'd actually seen and heard instead of fashioning it into a supernatural tale that no one would believe, maybe the garda would have handled the investigation of his sister's fall with greater care. Perhaps all she'd seen was the boy going to fetch the overseer. But why would the boy be humming a cheery tune?

Who would want to harm his sister? The only person he knew bore Penny ill will was Darrin. Genevieve ought to have been able to recognize her own son humming. But maybe she was shielding him. Why then stir things up by claiming to see and hear someone at the cliff edge? The investigation had determined it was an accident. Darrin wouldn't have been in any danger. No, it didn't seem likely that the boy had been involved despite the nasty calling card he'd left for the grieving Meryons to discover. But if Genevieve was telling the truth and not fabricating the story, then perhaps Penny didn't fall from that cliff. She might have been pushed. Who could or would murder her? Why? He might learn the answers to these questions if he could find Penny's diary.

Genevieve returned. "He's waiting for you in the yard, Mr. Meryon. Please be kind? He's made a mistake, but he doesn't deserve—"

"I have no intention of harming Darrin physically or otherwise. You have my word." Randolph brushed past her, through the front room, and out the door.

Darrin stood outside, body taut, arms crossed over his chest, and his expression sullen. It was obvious Genevieve had told the boy what Randolph wanted to speak to him about, and Darrin was preparing himself for an attack. It was a stark reminder. *I was this raw, this angrily defensive when I was caught. The same age too.*

"Walk with me, Darrin."

"Why?"

"Because this is between you and me. Your mother doesn't need to be involved." He waited. Patience in this instance was a definite virtue. His reward was a slight nod. Randolph strolled out to the road with his hands in his pockets, Darrin tagging along beside and a little behind him.

"Let's head toward the village." This time he didn't await a response, turning to his left and continuing to walk, his pace slow and leisurely.

"Tell me why. And don't bother to deny it. The garda verified you handled the doll."

A long verbal silence followed during which Randolph kept his gaze on the path ahead. Beside him Darrin strode, legs stiff, blowing out a series of noisy breaths. When he finally spoke, his voice was hard. "I was mad. Still am."

"What about?"

Darrin stopped, planted his feet, and fisted his hands. "As if you don't know. You're one of them. The sainted Meryons who everyone bows down to. Who never deign to acknowledge someone's existence unless they're telling you how to run your life. Why couldn't you keep on ignoring us? Isn't it bad enough that I'm the son of a rapist? No, your sister has to bring it all back up, but this time claiming my mother wasn't raped. Saying the truth would be revealed when she got all the evidence. Making my mother even crazier." His voice had grown louder as he spoke until the bitter tumble of words ended, and Darrin stood quivering, arms locked, and knuckles white.

"I understand your anger—"

"You can't." His chin jutting out, Darrin challenged Randolph.

Randolph rooted himself in front of Darrin with one quick step and grasped his shoulders, thwarting Darrin's attempt to retreat. "Who do you think you're talking to? I'm not only the black sheep of the Meryon family, I'm a pariah on all of Tallav. Even here on Rathlin, disgust underlies much of the courtesy I'm afforded. I was fourteen when something I did made my parents send me away from home."

The boy trembled beneath Randolph's fingers.

"I won't let that happen to you." He gave Darrin a shake and then released him. "I'm not going to hurt you. We're brothers, and it's high time we got to know one another as such."

Darrin regarded him with narrowed eyes. "Why now?"

"Because I'm here now. I've spent most of my life away from family, and my sister's death made it clear I can't wait forever to make things right. I could have used a brother when I was fourteen. I didn't have one, but you do. And I intend to be there for you."

"All right, but stay away from my mother. She didn't do anything wrong." His voice grew harsh. "Our father is to blame. He's the one who raped her and denied doing it until DNA evidence proved he was lying. After your sister threatened to expose my mother as a fraud, Mom got even worse, going out late at night to conduct rituals at the stone circle, spending more time on incantations than minding her herb business. She spends all our credits on 'ancient' herb lore and magic books. Hundreds for stuff that anyone can see is fake. She's…" He threw up his hands. "I've heard her crying and praying that the goddess will forgive her for bringing harm to your sister. She thinks her spells caused the accident. I don't think she can take much more."

"I'm sorry your mother is so distressed. She told me today she thinks she saw and heard someone on the cliff the night Penny died, someone she believes killed our sister."

"Your sister."

"You may be angry at her, but she's still your sister too. I never knew her as an adult, but you would have liked her when she was younger."

Darrin scowled, not yet ready to change his opinion.

Can't blame the kid. Penny probably rode in on her high horse. No one could beat her at displaying righteous indignation. "I intend to investigate what happened to Penny, but I'll try not to involve your mother any more than I have to."

His response was clipped as though Darrin begrudged the word. "Thanks."

At least he has proper manners beneath his load of grievance. "Have you done anything else I need to be aware of?"

Gaze cast down, Darrin said, "I rode my bicycle through a deep puddle and splashed muddy water all over your niece."

Randolph fought the urge to cuff him. "That was unkind. She's a little girl."

"I know." His expression pinched, he looked up at Randolph. "I felt bad about it later."

Randolph patted his shoulder. "Come on. Let's head to Flanagan's Cafe. We can get some pie à la mode and talk more."

"Sure."

~

AFTER A STILTED CONVERSATION with Darrin at Flanagan's, Randolph had sent him home. It would take time to develop any rapport with the boy.

Now he scanned the length of the village's main street. Well-maintained, quaint buildings meant to replicate the High Street of an old Earth Irish hamlet looked much the same as when he'd been a boy. Mullins Greengrocer, Anne's Bakery, and the Drunken Apple Pub still offered fruit, vegetables, baked goods, and hard cider. He eyed the pub sign with its image of a winking apple.

Why not? Maybe good old-fashioned gossip will help. He strolled across the street and through the pub's bright red door. It took a moment for his eyesight to adapt from the sunshine to the tavern's dim interior. A bar with dark red leather stools lined one wall and matching booths the other, with tables filling most of the remaining space except for a small raised platform in one corner meant for musicians. A few old-timers were seated at the far end of the bar. They nodded toward Randolph when he settled onto a stool. The couple buried in the far booth didn't look up.

The bartender moved from where he'd been chatting with his customers. "Afternoon, sir. What'll it be?"

Randolph detected neither animosity nor a fawning attitude in the man. His solid slab of a face was hard to read. "A pint of Rathlin's best."

"That'd be Tillie's Select." The barman pulled a bottle from a cooler below the bar. "Won the hard cider competition at the festival last year."

The smooth, slightly sweet taste with a crisp apple bite was delicious. "Amazing. Tillie is still brewing?"

"She and her daughters. They'll not let anyone take the crown without a fight."

"A good tradition."

"I was sorry about what happened to your sister. She was coming round to being a real blessing to Rathlin."

"Thank you. It was a tragedy for more than my family."

One man at the end of the bar said, "We were all proud of that girl, the way she pitched in with helping the less well-to-do families."

A grizzle-haired woman added, "Not a stuck-up bone in her body."

Brow furrowed, Randolph asked, "So she was well liked on Rathlin?"

The woman nodded her head vigorously. "It took us a bit to warm up to her, but in the end I don't think anyone had a bad word to say about her."

"Genevieve Kavan thinks she was murdered. Pushed off the cliff."

The bartender snorted. "What Genevieve believes and what's true wouldn't fit in a thimble."

"She's been blabbing that nonsense everywhere since the garda told her to leave off." The woman jerked her thumb over her shoulder at the pair in the far corner. "Jemmy said she's been in three times, changing her story."

At the sound of his name, Jemmy raised his head, and Randolph saw that he was a local garda constable. "Come on, luv. I need to get back."

The woman rose with him. Lanny Conyer. On their way past Randolph, Jemmy paused. "You'd do best to ignore Genevieve Kavan. Last month she proclaimed a plague was going to strike this year's apple crop. Harvest is just around the corner, and the plague never appeared. Of course now she claims she averted it with her spells and prayers to the Mother Goddess. She's full of claptrap."

"My mother and I are having a hard time believing Penny would be careless enough to fall from that cliff. Perhaps we're grasping at straws, but I don't want to stop short of discovering everything I can about that night."

Lips pressed together, Jemmy glanced at Lanny, who closed her eyes slowly and gave a tiny shake of her head.

Randolph clenched his jaw. *Damn fools. Made their minds up and can't be bothered to consider alternatives. Genevieve Kavan was there, and she saw and heard something.* He glared at the garda constable. "I was planning to stop by the station and request my sister's final EBC download. I wasn't sure if I should ask you or the doctor who did her autopsy. We'd like to have a copy of everything she had stored."

While Randolph was speaking, Jemmy glanced at the door three times, not bothering to hide his desire to end the conversation. "I'll look into it for you. We don't have many murders on Rathlin. Usually the mortuary takes care of that, but I'm sure the coroner would have accessed it."

"Thank you. I don't know if my sister was in the habit of storing lots of data to her internal server, but my mother would like to have whatever was saved."

"Yes, sir." Jemmy took Lanny's elbow, but Randolph wasn't finished.

He turned his gaze on Lanny. "Afternoon, Ms. Conyer. I'll want to begin on my sister's office at the start of next week."

"Yes, sir. I'll be there. If there's anything I can do in the meantime…"

"Nothing urgent."

She smiled and allowed Jemmy to push her toward the pub's entrance.

When the door closed behind them, Randolph turned back to the people sitting at the bar. "How long have they been seeing one another?"

The bartender shrugged. "Not long. I think it was a few days before your sister's wake."

The woman at the end piped up. "Jemmy's usually too shy to get himself a girlfriend. That Conyer woman bowled him over. Decided she wanted him and went after him. We all figure she'll dump him when she's had her fun. He's not a proper match for the likes of her."

"Poor sod thinks he's finally made it," said the other man. "You aren't planning to keep her on at the big house, are you?"

"Once my sister's affairs are settled, there won't be reason to."

"Can't be too soon to see the back side of that one. Died in the wool, man-hating aristo." The man dipped his head to Randolph. "Begging your pardon."

"We're in perfect agreement on Lanny Conyer." Randolph drained the rest of his hard cider and plunked the empty glass down with a sigh of appreciation. "I'm going to invest in some cases of this at the next festival."

The bartender grunted. "Harvest is early this year. Tillie'll have a batch or two ready by festival. But you'll want to get your order in early. She only makes so much."

"That I will." Randolph stood. "Thank you all for the conversation."

"Look forward to seeing more of you," the woman said.

Randolph nodded even though the chance was slim that he'd be back to the pub often. Once things were settled, he'd return to the Whip Hand.

The early fall sunshine was bright against a cerulean sky when Randolph stepped out on the cobbled sidewalk. Along the curb a weed poked its head from a crack. *Never see that on Beta Tau. Everything is manicured to perfection.* Tallav had its own level of constructed environment. But nature had charted its own course, sending weed seeds to sprout and add to the picturesque charm. He'd always considered Tallav to be a false utopia, a planet that controlled every aspect of society to preserve an imposed bias. Maybe the weeds brought a little reality.

He chuckled to himself. Randolph Meryon. Philosopher. Time to walk back to Briarcliff. The exercise and fresh air stimulated his appetite. *Wonder what Cook's making for supper. I hope it's chicken pot pie.* No one had ever made as flaky a crust as Cook. He ambled along the road, sticking his hands into his pockets and whistling an off-key tune.

9

R andolph spent the next morning on Whip Hand business, dealing with all the fiddly fart minutiae that kept the club open and functioning properly. Some of it he'd handed off to his staff, but he'd intended that to be temporary for the duration of the renovation. Even if he didn't take those tasks back on, he still oversaw all financial ledgers and accounts as well as making the purchasing decisions. In the beginning micromanaging all the details had consumed him. He'd wanted the club to be perfect. But as it had grown, all the minor issues had become a heavy burden. He should hand off more of the workload, especially if he wanted to spend more time on Tallav. *How does Selina keep up with her sector-wide business?* Life spent comming wasn't something he would enjoy.

He leaned back in the padded reading chair he'd occupied since coming to the library. The room was a bastion of quiet, an excellent place to sit and think. And sip fine whiskey. He stretched his arm out to snag the glass on the end table next to him. He rolled the drink in his mouth, enjoying its mellow plummy sweetness with hints of cinnamon and dark chocolate, crowned with a note of barley in the finish. Nothing was quite like a really good sipping whiskey.

After the reading of the will, he should be able to leave for Beta Tau soon. His mother's nonsense about Randolph becoming Sophie's guardian was absurd. Penny wouldn't appoint him because she'd never want him near her daughter. His mother would become Sophie's guardian, and he would return to life as usual at the Whip Hand.

That should please him, and it did, but an undercurrent of discontent stirred eddies deep inside him, disturbing things settled long ago. A wife, children, family. All had been expunged from his plans for his future. Even Shane's recent lapse into marriage and fatherhood hadn't fazed Randolph. In Adrianna, Shane had found his perfect partner. The chance of finding Randolph's own ideal mate was statistically impossible. Not worth the mental and emotional angst pursuit would elicit. No woman had ever gained his complete confidence. And he'd always claimed he'd never tie himself to someone he didn't absolutely trust. Women were unreliable. This truth had been brought home to him at a young age. His sister had denounced him, made him the center of her anti-male rhetoric. Even his mother had allowed him to be dumped out of sight at boarding school a year earlier than most boys.

For lack of a wife, he lost all hope of having a family of his own. At least on Tallav. Despite his own aversion to Tallavan aristocratic society, he loved Briarcliff. It was the ideal place to raise children. As guardian to Sophie, he had his only chance at becoming a father. But what did he really have to offer her? She was better off with an Uncle Rand who dropped in from time to time to provide a little adventure like climbing the back of the Giant's Tit.

Footsteps announced others entering the library. "Good. Randolph is already here."

Randolph rose and turned to greet his mother.

"Edward, Stephen, this is my son Randolph Meryon. Randolph, Edward is the family lawyer, and Stephen is the lawyer Penny used to make her will."

Randolph shook both men's hands with all the appropriate acknowledgments. Why had Penny chosen to have her will drawn up by a legal firm other than the family solicitors? Keeping secrets?

"Gentlemen, let's sit here." She waved a hand at two chairs positioned opposite a love seat. Randolph sat next to his mother.

"Ms. Meryon," Stephen said, "your daughter's will is straightforward. Rather than read it in its entirety, I would suggest I offer the general points now. You may examine it at your leisure. I have copies for you and Mr. Meryon, and a printed copy of the will and the data cube needed to execute the will for your counsel, Edward."

Randolph took the sheaf of paper he was handed and scanned the first page, standard legalese.

Stephen continued. "Penny left everything, save for a few small bequests, to her daughter, Sophie Meryon. She has named you, Ms. Meryon, as her executor. Since Sophie is underage, Penny has also named the person she wishes to assume Sophie's guardianship. That would be you, Mr. Meryon."

Randolph's jaw dropped. "Me."

"Yes. She changed that provision in her will three weeks before her death. Please don't take this personally, but I advised her not to do so. The courts are not given to appointing men as the legal guardians of first family heirs. But Penny was insistent."

Randolph was nonplussed. Penny had insisted?

"I have a sealed letter she wrote explaining her reasons." Stephen handed an envelope to Randolph.

Randolph studied it. His name was written on it in Penny's unmistakable scrawl. Inevitable. Fucking inevitable if he opened it and read Penny's words. His life would change irrevocably. But it could also contain a small measure of the reconciliation he'd longed for with his sister. Would she convince him to honor her last wish, to seize the opportunity she offered?

He let the letter fall to his lap, closed his eyes, and rubbed the center of his forehead. "Mother, did you know Penny was naming me guardian? Is that why you've been insisting on it yourself?" He opened his eyes and leveled his gaze on his mother.

"No, dear. I didn't. Your sister and I discussed many things, but this was not one of them. I had no idea she had changed her will until Edward informed me he was not in possession of it."

Randolph nodded. "I see." He fingered the bead at his wrist.

"Probate should be quick and simple. The only true issue is Sophie's guardianship. If you, Ms. Meryon, are satisfied with your daughter's recommendation, and Mr. Meryon accepts the duty, no one should stand in the way of completing the legal requirements for making Mr. Meryon Sophie's guardian," Edward said. "However, there always exists the possibility that the case will be brought before a judge opposed to granting men exclusive guardianship rights. In that event, a woman will have to act as co-guardian."

"We'll cross that bridge when and if we come to it," his mother said. "For now, Rand needs time to read Penny's letter and absorb what it says."

Both Stephen and Edward rose, offering to assist as needed. Randolph stood and shook hands, but he was distracted, his mind whirling. When the lawyers were gone, his mother touched his arm.

"Dear, read what Penny has to say. We can talk when you feel ready."

"Thank you, Mother. I'm a little at sea. People have told me they saw changes in Penny, but I..."

"Read the letter, dear. It should hold answers to at least some of your questions."

"You're right. Thank you." He kissed her cheek.

The door clicked shut behind her. Randolph picked up his glass and refilled it from the whiskey bottle he'd left sitting out atop the satinwood cellarette. He let the fruity aroma tease his nose before he took a sip. Penny's letter had been laid aside on an end table. He brushed a finger over his name before plucking it up and moving to the chair he'd occupied previously. He deposited his drink on a side table. A wave of apprehension inundated him, making his chest tighten and his fingers grow cold. Staring at the envelope would get him nowhere. He sat and tore it open. The paper rustled as he opened the single sheet of fine linen stationery.

Dear Rand,

You're probably in shock right now. Pour yourself a whiskey if you haven't already.

I was wrong. You above all people know how hard it is for me to admit that, but it would be an injustice to you not to do so. I hope these words are only a reminder of a conversation we have had in person. If not, I'm sorry you will never see the true regret and sadness I feel for the damage I've done to our relationship. I took far too long stubbornly refusing to hear your side of things. My journey toward the truth is contained in my diaries. You'll find them stacked on my office shelf. The most recent is in the locked drawer of my desk. They'll answer the why better than I can in this brief letter. It started with discovering the truth about what broke Mother and Father apart. I haven't shared that with Mother as of this writing, but I intend to request you visit us, so I can tell you both together. Maybe that's already happened, but if not, it's just as important as my discoveries about you.

Mother tried to tell me your side of things from that terrible night, but I refused to listen. My reading list at the time was heavy on the political and cultural foundations of the matriarchy. I imagined myself carrying the torch of traditionalism for my generation, full of myself, all ego and no brain. Leaving Briarcliff for school was a relief. My beliefs and opinions weren't constantly assailed. I buried myself in the noble fight to stand against those that would take my rights as a woman and future mother from me and my heirs, and I stayed away for years, rarely returning home for visits. When Sophie turned four, I realized that she needed to live at Briarcliff, to learn to love it, the island, and its people. City life wasn't an adequate replacement for the joys you and I shared growing up at the castle.

Perhaps I grew up over the intervening time, but somehow my mind went down new pathways, often surprising ones. I've rejoined the Reformed Catholic Church. Shocked you, haven't I? I was drawn by the need for forgiveness, not least for the hurt I caused you. And I did cause you real harm. You wouldn't have had to leave Tallav if I hadn't made you a public pariah, parading dirty family laundry for the world to see. Even now I find that apologizing isn't sufficient. I must do my best to restore what I've broken.

To that end, I've been working on a book that will disclose the truth of what happened twenty-one years ago and how I wrongly vilified you. You were fourteen. The woman was thirty-two. That alone should have given me pause, but that and so many other facts never made it past the filters I'd put between me and those who could have enlightened me. You watched her from the loft in the stable having sex with another man. If I'd been up in that loft, I'd have settled in for the show with you. She claimed you were jealous and had snatched a riding crop and turned it on her. I know now this wasn't true. You intervened in something beyond your understanding, and your anger got away from you. Rumor hinted that sado-masochism had been involved, but you weren't thrashing that woman for sexually perverse thrills as I came to believe.

You know these facts. I'm stating them to make it clear I know them now too, and I intend to set the record straight. I can think of no better way to announce my renewed trust in you than to make you Sophie's guardian should I die. Sophie is all the world to me. She needs someone who will show her what it means to be a Meryon, to teach her about our legacy, to help her understand that as a first family *we have a duty to care for those who live and work under us. I've read about you and the Whip Hand. How you've grown it from a small start because of your attention to detail and commitment to open, honest relationships with your staff and customers. You have many admirers in the sector, and no few on Tallav. Selina Shirley sings your praises to the press frequently. You deserve to come home.*

So I'm asking you. Return to Briarcliff. Be Sophie's guardian. Stand in for me as no one else can. Find a woman to love. Get married. Have children. Cling to your family because they are a part of you that you cannot ever eliminate.

I love you brother.

Forgive me.

Take care of Sophie.

Your sister,

Penny

〜

Raindrops pattered and streamed down the window where Randolph stood in his bedroom. The storm had come quickly, as they so often did this time of year, and would move off with equivalent speed after providing the necessary water to the apple groves that covered Rathlin Island. Too much or too little and the crop would be affected. But Rathlin was situated for near perfect growing conditions. With the harvest would come the traditional celebrations, the annual festival with its cook-off and apple queen, the harvest dance, and applejack and fine brandy tastings. He remembered his first drink of applejack when he was ten years old. His father had allowed him a swallow, but only one. The taste was misleading as to the true alcoholic content of the smooth, fruity liquor.

It was a remembrance from the before side of the division that cleaved the timeline of his life. Happy times came after too, but most didn't involve his family. He'd spent so much time living with the difficult after memories that he rarely reminisced about the good from before. Until now, when he really didn't want to be flooded with anything from the past.

Fuck. Focus. He was uncertain what to do about Sophie. The decision was daunting. If he made a mistake… No, he had to stop himself from thinking in those terms. The future was yet to be determined. It couldn't be predicted. What-ifs were just that, what-ifs. What was best for Sophie right now? He needed to figure that out.

It was three hours before midnight, so Sophie had been in bed for over an hour. Still, something compelled him to visit her. Yes. He would look in on her. Putting thought to action, he strode from his room, down the hall, and through the nursery entrance.

Before knocking on Jen's bedroom door, he popped his head into each of the main rooms and discovered Jen seated at her desk in the quiet room. Her vidscreen was on, displaying information on Rathlin Island.

"Jen."

She jumped. "Oh my gods. You startled me." Her cheeks flushed.

"Sorry. I wanted to tell you I was going to look in on Sophie."

"She's asleep."

"I won't wake her."

Her eyebrows rose. "No. Of course not. I wasn't trying to stop you."

"You were correct to remind me. I'll only stay a few minutes."

Outside his niece's room, Randolph paused and took a deep breath. Then he silently turned the knob and slipped the door open. A night-light brightened the space, enough for him to see a boudoir fit for a young princess. The heart-shaped, white filigree headboard of Sophie's bed was set against the far wall. Shelves holding an entire zoo of stuffed animals stood along one side of the bed. A wall-mounted mister spritzed a delicate floral scent into the air. Sophie's strawberry-blonde curls, sweet face, and the head of a rabbit missing one ear poked out of a nest of lace-trimmed lavender bedding.

Randolph picked up the child-sized, satin-covered stool from the dressing table. He rested his arms on his knees as he sat looking at her. Peaceful. Innocent. Defenseless. Protecting her was a father's duty. Could he be that man? Whoever the sperm donor had been, the burden couldn't be shifted to him. Randolph's own father was out of the picture. His mother would never allow her ex-husband, Conlin Meryon, into Sophie's life.

But Sophie had never had a father. Would she miss one now? She would feel the loss of her mother. A succession of nannies couldn't come close to filling that void. Neither could he, but he could provide continuity.

He reached out carefully to brush a stray hair from Sophie's forehead. Her nose twitched, her eyelids scrunched, and then she blinked twice before opening her eyes wide, lifting her head, and beaming at him with a sleepy smile.

"Uncle Rand."

"Hi, pumpkin."

"Did you come through the secret passage?" She clasped a hand over her mouth. "Oh. I wasn't going to tell."

"No worries. I already know about it. But I didn't use it."

Sophie yawned. "If you want to, I don't mind."

"Sure thing." Randolph stood and bent over her. "Sleep sweet, pump-kin." He kissed her forehead.

"Sleep sweet, Uncle Rand." She rolled over, snuggling into her lavender bedding.

Randolph smiled to himself. Keeping his hand on her back, he moni-tored the steady rise and fall as her breathing deepened. She trusted him. Completely. Something in his chest swelled tight. Could he prove worthy of that trust? He wanted to try. There was an element of *I'll show the world I can*, but that was a minor part of this growing drive. If he became her guardian, he would do it for her, for Sophie.

He carefully lifted his hand, returned the stool, and went to the door. Before closing it behind him, he stood for a moment, watching as Sophie burrowed farther into the covers. He shut the door and found Jen observing him.

"Sorry. I woke her up."

"It sounds like she's settling back down fine."

"Yes." Randolph hesitated and then asked, "May I speak with you? About Sophie."

"Sure. Are you still waterlogged with tea, or would you like a cup?"

"No, thank you."

"Let's go sit in the playroom then. The chairs are more comfortable."

Jen's bottom drew his gaze as he followed her. Soft and sweet. The kind of woman you wanted to stay in bed with, to wrap yourself around while you slept. He snorted softly. Like Sophie with her bunny. But much better.

There was a lot to find agreeable about this unpretentious female walking barefoot before him. He would have to be careful, but it was now definite. Seducing her would be his reward for staying on Tallav longer to figure out what he would do about Sophie.

JEN'S HEART FLUTTERED. It was such a daddy thing to do, looking in on a sleeping child. Her own father was a sperm donor, a number in the system that tracked consanguinity and potential defects by DNA analysis but removed all other identifying information. O'Malleys didn't need daddies. So she'd done without and envied the other children who had them. Most matriarchists didn't eliminate men from family life as thoroughly as the O'Malleys. Sons were rare in the O'Malley clan, medically eliminated during the process of in vitro fertilization. The occasional love match sometimes resulted in the birth of males, but it was scandalous.

Randolph prowled restlessly around the playroom, selecting toys to inspect and then replacing them. When he reached Sophie's dollhouse, he squatted, examining the rooms.

"Three female figures. One male figure. Who do you imagine she thinks they represent?"

Jen moved to stand beside him. "Your mother, Penny, Mrs. Polgrey, and you."

He tilted his head to look at her. "Me!"

"Yes, she thought her mother was mad at you, so Sophie never told Penny that the male figure was you."

Randolph picked it up and rubbed his thumb over it. "Huh." He replaced it in the dollhouse's nursery.

When he rose, he moved toward Jen. Too close. She stepped backward onto a stray bildiblock and then lurched forward.

"Ow!"

Randolph caught her by her forearms. "Steady."

A rush of heat flooded Jen. Disconcerted, she let him guide her to an easy chair.

"Sit here."

She complied, mortified when he dropped to the floor and took hold of her foot. *Randolph Meryon is giving me a foot massage. And he's good at it.*

"Settle back. Relax. You need this after the day you've had." His smile was devastating.

Damn, my ears must be flaming red. Oh so obvious with her hair tied in a ponytail. Why did she have to have ears that flushed crimson whenever she felt strong emotions? She looked away.

"You have lovely feet."

He was still smiling. She was certain. You could hear it in his voice.

"Very pretty."

She bit her bottom lip and brought her gaze back to him. The color of his eyes had turned to melted dark chocolate. Their intensity made the seed of desire take root. She breathed a response. "Thank you."

"You're welcome." His lips remained slightly parted. So sensual. Kissable. But for this man, his fingers, hands, lips, teeth, and tongue were weapons he wielded for his sadistic pleasure. If she allowed him to use his personal arsenal on her, would he rip her to pieces? Would he discard her once she was spent? Was it worth finding out? The tingles that ran up her leg encouraged an affirmative answer.

He gently set her foot down, scooped up the heel of her other, and quirked an eyebrow. "I think this one looks neglected."

A groan escaped her lips. Yes. He was kneading the spot on her arch that often hurt, but it had never felt this good when her mother had given her foot rubs. Her eyelids drooped. "That's perfect."

He purred his response as though he were the one being stroked. "Yes. It is."

Not satisfied with tending her feet, he moved his hands higher. All resistance to his magic fingers vanishing, she slumped into the chair cushion when he dug into her calves. How much better would this feel if there were nothing between him and her skin? She peeked at him through her lashes, watching as he pushed the leg of her slacks up. And then he kissed her on her inner knee.

"Oh gods!"

A wicked grin broke across his face. "No. Mere mortal."

In the next instant he had nudged her legs apart and slid up her body, placing his hands on either arm of the chair. She leaned toward him, her heart pounding, waiting for the touch of his lips.

"If I kiss you, kitten, I'm going to want more."

"More. Yes."

"Are you sure you can handle it?"

"No." The idea thrilled her, but another, maybe a greater part of her wanted to run from the trap she feared he was setting for her. "We shouldn't be doing this."

"I won't tell if you don't." His voice throbbed with undisguised hunger.

"D-didn't you want to talk about Sophie?"

"You're very distracting." His breath caressed her with each word.

"Sorry."

A smile flitted across his lips. "Don't be. We'll discuss Sophie later."

The kiss she expected never came. Instead he gathered her into his arms and carried her to her bedroom. Jen turned the handle, and he kicked the door closed behind them. Then, finally, he kissed her.

That's what it was called, a kiss. But it went so far beyond any she'd ever received. He took her mouth, claiming her, compelling her to acknowledge she was his to do with as he pleased. Escape was unthinkable. She moaned, entreating him to make good on the implied promise of passionate indulgence.

What had started as a tender brush of his lips deepened until the stroking of his tongue enticed her to her own exploration. The tentative hesitation of her initial probe was overcome by the erotic power of his tongue twining with hers. She savored his taste with its hint of whiskey. All her innate respectability fled, leaving her open and available, longing to discover all that this man could show her. He nipped at her lower lip before he drew away.

"I've been craving something sweet all day." His eyes blazed with a heat that would caramelize sugar. "Do you taste as delectable everywhere else?"

"You'll have to find out."

In an automatic response she raised her arms when he pulled the top of her shirt up. He trailed one fingertip over the rounded crest of her breast and along the lacy edge of her white bra.

"Very demure." He lowered his head to run his tongue over the same path.

Demure... What was she thinking? This was insane. She was letting

Randolph Meryon have his way with her. Why not? The shameless side of her refused to give back the ground his kisses had gained. This was the most erotic experience she'd ever had or was likely to have. And she had yearned to touch his supple skin, stroke the chiseled muscles of his abdomen, and wriggle her fingers through his hair. Oh yes. Her body was fully on board. But a niggle of doubt remained.

"Are you going to hurt me?"

He lifted his head, his face serious except for a telltale quirk of his lips. "Do I look like I'm going to hurt you?"

"No…"

"There's nothing to fear." He tapped the tip of her nose. "If you die, it will be from pleasure." Then he flashed that wicked, devastating smile, and she was lost. Even the nice girl wanted to know what it would be like to expire from perfect bliss in Randolph Meryon's arms. The ache was demanding. *Find out.*

"Okay."

He delved a hand inside her bra and pinched her nipple.

"Yes." The sibilant ending of the word became a hiss.

The rest of her clothing fell away as though by magic. But Randolph wasn't a sorcerer casting an enchantment. His wizardry came from experience. Bucketloads. And all of it was focused on her. Jen O'Malley. The black sheep of the O'Malley family, now allowing the blackest sheep on Tallav to suck her breasts. *Oh gods yes.*

The tip of his tongue swirled. "Sweet here too." His voice rasped, low and husky.

He bit and, when she jerked in reaction, gripped her sides and flung her onto the bed, landing on top of her. The instant after her shoulder blades hit the mattress, her arms splayed out, and he hauled her tightly against him. A shudder ran through her. The hard column of his cock was jammed into her thigh. With effort she overcame the haze of arousal that was immobilizing her. She moved her hand, her fingers crawling along the coverlet and wriggling between their bodies.

"No." He snatched her wrist and placed it over her head, then brought the other up beside it. "No touching until I say so. Keep your hands here." His eyes fixed on hers, compelling obedience. She dipped her chin in agreement. The cold smile he flourished made her stomach churn. But then he nuzzled her neck and scraped his teeth down to her shoulder.

A sharp intake of breath filled her lungs, followed by an openmouthed slow exhale as his intense onslaught continued. He found erogenous zones she didn't know she had. Insistent hands compelled her to shift positions, turning her over so he could assail new places—her spine, the spot where her bottom curved to meet her thigh, and the back of her knees.

"Please."

He smoothed a calloused palm over one cheek of her ass, drawing his fingertips along her cleft. "Please?"

Gods-forsaken man knows what I want!

He gave a dry chuckle, moving his fingers closer to where she ached for his touch. "Have I forgotten something, kitten?"

"Please."

He rumbled his amusement. Without a hint of warning, he pried her cheeks apart, forced his face between them, and flicked his tongue over her anus. Her legs slammed shut in an involuntary response, but his hold on her thwarted the action. His breath puffed against her backside. "Relax. I'm not fucking you here." He bit her. "Yet."

If he thought that would ease her mind... Then he released her and smoothed his hands along her sides, down to her thighs, and back. Slowly the tension in her muscles ebbed. When his lips found her rear again, they were tender. She shook her head and moaned.

"You've got a sweet ass, kitten."

He gradually pulled her checks apart and licked until he was tonguing the star of her anus. This time she was prepared. She'd heard that some men enjoyed doing this. Why was beyond her. It was a different sensation. Dampness in a spot where moisture was usually problematic. She wasn't crazy about it, but she didn't hate it either. By the sounds of his murmuring appreciation, he was enjoying himself. So she'd go along, but taking her up her bum... no.

The urgent demand of her arousal had tapered off until he flipped her over in an effortless show of strength. Desire returned in a rush of liquid warmth. He was fulfilling her most cherished fantasy to be taken by a powerful man who sated his lust for her with unrelenting passion, not like the compliant males she'd bedded before who put her needs before their own, asking permission before trying anything that even hinted at wild abandon. Randolph wasn't a supplicant. He did as he pleased. And it was perfect.

He rubbed her pussy lips, his fingers splayed and thumbs extended. Her clit pulsed with each stroke. "Oh gods." Climax was near, just out of reach.

"Say my name."

She shuddered. "Randolph." If he would… she didn't know what.

"Call me Master."

"Master." A whimper escaped.

"Who am I?"

"Master."

"Master who?"

"Master Randolph."

"That's right." Then he lowered his mouth to her pussy and applied his tongue to bring her to the cusp of ecstasy. He scraped his teeth over her clit, and she was beyond the pinnacle, soaring in a wave of bright sensation, losing all sense of place and time. Her body trembled with the aftershocks.

"Now you know what it's like to die from pleasure. But it's my turn." He shoved himself off her and stood. She watched as he stripped, her eyes hooded. He wasn't tall. Maybe six foot. Nor was he big. But he was all compact hard muscle and perfectly proportioned wild grace. A panther about to spring. On her. A poet would use lyrical words to describe him. To her he was stunning. And when he shed his slacks and underwear, that was the single word that reverberated through her mind. Stunning.

His wicked grin had returned. He sauntered toward the bed, rolling his hips in the way men confident of their desirability did. Oh gods, he looked good enough to eat.

RANDOLPH CONTEMPLATED JEN, splayed before him like a thoroughly pleasured wanton. He hadn't been sure how his sweet kitten would respond. Better than he'd expected. She was submissive, and whether she acknowledged it, she liked at least some pain. A small percentage of his wannabe subs at the Whip Hand had cut and run when the biting started.

Jen had jerked when he used his teeth on her nipple, but her hips had thrust toward him rather than pulling away. She'd startled when he'd tongued her anus but let him get his fill on his second attempt. Startling a sub was one of the simple diversions of life. Jen would be a lot of fun to teach the joys of pain-laced submission. But not tonight.

He'd promised her only pleasurable pain. If he were ever to have her under his whip, patience now was required. This wasn't a woman who came preprogrammed to want hard-core kink. Even if she'd researched him and the term *sadist*, he doubted she truly understood what she was letting herself in for with him. They'd have to talk, but his cock needed to fill the tempting pussy available to him.

Randolph stroked his erection, studying her. Beneath heavy lids, rain clouds scudded across her eyes. Her ears were red. Was she aroused or embarrassed? The tip of her tongue darted out in a quick swipe. Aroused it was.

"Do you like what you see?"

"Yes." She licked her lips again. *Fuck.* He could almost feel her lapping his balls. He suppressed a groan.

"Yes what?"

Her eyebrows squeezed together.

"No second thoughts. Yes, Master."

Mouth set in a firm line, she clenched and released her hands. "Why?"

He narrowed his eyes and sternly said, "Because it pleases me to hear you call me Master."

"I-I don't know."

"Yes, you do. Say it. Now."

"Y-yes, Master."

He smiled in approval. "That's my sweet kitten." Throughout this exchange, he'd continued to caress his erection. Her gaze returned to it, and her pupils dilated.

"Suck it, sugar puss." *Hurry,* he wanted to add when her tongue brushed across her lower lip.

"Yes, Master." The edge of the bed dipped when she shifted closer. She rolled to her stomach, propped herself on her elbows, and took him in her mouth.

Someone had given her lessons, or she'd incorporated techniques he'd used on her, because this was one of the better blow jobs he'd ever received. *Imagine that.* If he had her at the Whip Hand, she'd be on a leash, available to drop to her knees whenever it pleased him.

"Fuck, that's amazing." He would come if he didn't stop her. "That'll do, kitten."

She lightly scored the top and bottom of his cock with her teeth as she slid him from her mouth. When the tip remained, she bit hard enough he jerked. Fortunately she released him, smacking her lips and grinning at him with feline satisfaction.

He seized her ponytail, twisting, forcing her to roll to her back. The mattress gave as he sprang atop her, pinning her beneath his body and trapping her head between his hands, fingers splayed around the curve of her skull, thumbs caressing the corners of her mouth.

"Biting is not sucking. You were told to suck."

Bangs partially hid her raised eyebrows. "Sauce for the goose."

"It's dangerous to play rough with me. Naughty kittens get disciplined."

Trepidation flickered in her eyes. Her breathing quickened, rhythmically pressing her breasts against his chest. She wasn't totally domesticated. No way he'd declaw her. The right amount of fight in a woman was all to the good. He rubbed her lower lip with one thumb, and then whipped his hand down, grabbed her below her left calf, and bent her leg up to her chin.

"Hold your knee."

Wide-eyed, she complied. Then he smacked the exposed curve of her rump.

She jumped beneath him. "Oh!"

He continued to spank her until her face crumpled. But no tears came. Enough. She'd cry for him eventually.

"You may put your leg back down."

Her eyes were thunderclouds under glowering brows. "You said you wouldn't hurt me."

He raised one eyebrow. "I didn't. That wasn't painful. If it had been, you'd have begged me to stop. It's your pride that was bruised."

"I…" Her lips pinched tight.

"Nothing to say? I thought not." He stroked her cheek with his thumb.

"No more biting my cock. Or my balls. Use your teeth and claws on less sensitive areas. All right?"

She refused to answer for another moment and then said, "All right, Master."

He beamed at her. "Very good, kitten!"

She stuck her bottom lip out in an adorable pout he promptly nipped. His patience was at an end though. It was past time to be deep inside her.

He brought her hands over her head, wrapping a one-handed grip around her wrists. To reacquaint himself with her texture and taste, he swept her jawline with his lips and tongue, moving to graze the salty sweetness where sweat had dried on her neck. Her sugary scent filled his nostrils. He explored the curves and planes of her body with his free hand, caressing with long strokes down her hip, squeezing the soft handhold at the dip of her waist, returning to cup her breast.

The surging pressure as she undulated against him made his cock throb with each roll of her hips. The sound of her gasps and whimpers amped up his craving to plunge into her, a tension that would dissolve when he found his release. But an agitation foreign to him also speared through him, disturbing the emotional distance that was his standard operating procedure in any sexual situation. *Fuck.* His hands were on the verge of shaking. *It's been a while. That's all.* Once he got off, he'd be fine.

He pushed his hand from her belly to her crotch, running fingers through the moisture coating her. *Definitely ready.* He released her wrists, resettled himself so his cock now pressed at her entrance, and clutched her bottom. "Let your wildcat loose, kitten."

In immediate response her legs sprang up, wrapping him in a tight embrace while her arms did the same around his shoulders. Fingernails sheathed themselves in his skin. The arch and release of her torso pushed against the tip of his erection, which had swollen taut and was weeping pre-cum. One thrust and he lost himself to the sensation of snug, wet heat burnishing his cock. He drove himself with ruthless stabs until a shining bright ball of energy ignited in his groin and he exploded in ecstatic fulfillment. He came, driving into her, his balls releasing streams of cum in five heaving eruptions.

Spent, he collapsed onto her. The rasping sound of his panting and the thunder of his pulse filled his ears. That was the best sex he'd had in...

forever. He rolled off her and snugged her in close to his side, her head resting on his shoulder. A soft, womanly body to hold was a pleasure in itself. The scent of warm vanilla soothed him. That was the aroma. In the throes of sexual abandon his brain had registered sweet. But now he detected the vanilla and a hint of cinnamon. He grinned. She smelled like a cinnamon sugar cookie. And tasted better.

It had been a long time since he'd seduced a woman, gone slow and made things good for her. Shackle, whip, and fuck had been his routine after turning sub training over to Tom. In the early years of the club, he'd kept a personal submissive, but rarely for more than a few months before moving on to another. Somehow he had forgotten the benefits of forging a deeper connection with a partner. If he stayed on Tallav, he could do that with Jen.

She was playing with the hair on his chest, sliding her fingers through it.

"We should talk, kitten."

"Mmm. Sophie."

He tipped her chin up so he could look into her face. Her soft gray eyes were like a bank of concealing fog. "Yes. But first about what just happened. I'm not through with you."

The fog dissolved into a silvery sheen, and the soothing strokes on his chest became fidgeting tugs. "You're not?"

"No. I want to teach you things about your body you've never imagined. And to discover what other surprises you're hiding beneath that thick layer of wholesome sweetness you're wrapped in."

She blinked three times in rapid succession. "Surprises? I'm...just...me."

"You bite every man's cock you suck?"

"N-no." Her lips pursed, and she ducked her chin. "You're the first."

The hair tie holding her ponytail had slipped. Randolph pulled it out and ran his fingers through her rumpled locks. "You claw your lovers' backs?"

She sighed. "No. Just yours."

"See what I mean?"

"Hmm."

"It's time you found out more about that wildcat."

Jen squirmed against his side.

"I won't let it interfere with your job or flaunt what we're up to and ruin your reputation. When either one of us wants to quit, we'll stop. Are you in?"

"Isn't there supposed to be some kind of negotiation, rules or something?"

"Yes. We'll settle that before we play again. If you don't want to go farther than we went today, I'll accept that for now."

She lifted her chin and studied him seriously. "Okay."

He pulled her tight against his body in a one-armed hug. "Excellent." Jen's bedroom was too small and way too close to Sophie's room. Some other location would need to be arranged, someplace with sufficient space. Maybe he should check out the dungeon Great-Uncle Axton had decorated with gothic implements of torture.

"And Sophie?"

The question broke into his reverie. Sophie. That's who he'd come to Jen to discuss. "Do you think Sophie needs me? Me in particular? Penny named me Sophie's guardian, but I can't believe it's a good idea. I'm not daddy-substitute material."

Jen scooted, sat up, and regarded him. "Children need both maternal and paternal figures in their lives. She hasn't had a father. You're probably the only person who can fulfill that role in her life."

"Perhaps, but that doesn't make me suitable."

"I think you might surprise yourself. Maybe it's hiding inside you."

He grunted. "Turnabout's fair play, huh?" More to consider. Staying meant he'd have a minimum of six months with this luscious woman. He pulled her on top of him and fervently kissed her.

10

Randolph raised his arms over his head and stretched his full length under the striped sheet. This was the first morning since his sister's death that he had woken refreshed. His erection twitched, a physical reminder of why his body crackled with life. Jen O'Malley had been the perfect antidote to what ailed him. If she weren't busy with Sophie, he'd find her and let her mouth take care of the throbbing between his legs. He threw the sheet back and reached for his shaft. Images of her lips surrounding his cock and her cheeks moving as she sucked him brought him close to the edge, but then he remembered the nip she'd given the tip of his penis.

His wild kitten. He'd disciplined her for that, and she'd taken it. And then taken him, giving as good with her claws as she did with her teeth. He thrust into his fist, imagining her pussy was clutching him, tight and wet. He came with a groan, his cum splattering across his stomach and chest.

Holy fuck! He'd had two orgasms in one eight-hour period. That hadn't happened in months. Gods, he'd actually gone more than five days without having sex multiple times in the last half year. Proof that life as an infamous sadist and owner of a pleasure planet BDSM club wasn't all kinky sex. The club had taken over his free time as it had expanded. This break was what he needed, and Jen O'Malley was the intriguing woman he would teach the joys of submitting to the painful delights he could give her. Tonight she was coming to his room, away from Sophie and the need to be silent.

He smeared his fingers though his cum, slicking it over his skin. Today would be full. A shower was the first order of business and then breakfast. He rose from the bed and strolled into the en suite bathroom. After indulging in a long, hot shower, he dressed in a flannel shirt and denims, finger combing his hair rather than taking the time he'd normally spend on his appearance. When he entered the dining room, he found his mother finishing her toast and coffee.

"Rand, there's something important we need to discuss."

Randolph nodded his head and helped himself to a pastry. "All right. What about?" A maid brought him a cup of coffee, black as he preferred it. "Thanks."

When the maid had left, his mother took a moment to study him as though she were deciding the best way to tell him something he wouldn't like.

"How bad is it?" he asked.

She pursed her lips. "Not bad at all. I think it's more than past time that you should take this step."

He closed his eyes. Gods. She was going to bring up marriage again. That topic was supposed to be relegated to the trash heap.

"Rand."

Frustration filled her tone but also worry. He sighed and opened his eyes. "Just say it."

"I've had discussions with our lawyers about Sophie's guardianship. They have found a liberal judge willing to accept you based on Penny's wishes, but she insists on one provision. You must marry an acceptable Tallavan woman."

Rand grimaced. "And what are the parameters of acceptability? How long would the marriage have to last? Does the judge have suggestions?" He couldn't keep the sarcasm out of the question.

"Now Rand."

"Don't 'now Rand' me, Mother. You know I do not intend to marry, especially a Tallavan woman."

His mother, her expression stern, said, "Please, lower your voice, dear."

"My apologies. Assuming the responsibility for Sophie would upend my life enough without adding the distraction of a new wife. Where are we supposed to find anyone willing to marry me and then disappear from our lives until it's time for me to divorce her? We'd have to pay that person a substantial amount of credit to even listen to such a crazy idea. Tallavan women have never wooed me for reasons we both comprehend."

"I believe we can find someone acceptable. And I don't agree that we'd have to bribe her to do it."

His mother exuded confidence. She'd already made plans. "You have someone in mind?"

"I do. Jen O'Malley."

Randolph's eyes widened. *Jen O'Malley.* A knot tightened in his chest. "You think she'd agree?"

"She's had a falling out with her family. They've renounced her. She hasn't much more than the clothes on her back. Yes, I believe she'd accept whatever terms we offered her."

From diversion to wife was a significant leap in status. Jen was sexually malleable, but once he'd married her, would she comply as easily outside the bedroom? "The lawyers would draw up a contract that would keep her out of my business? If she agrees and later changes her mind, I don't want her to have any legal right to claiming even a sliver of the Whip Hand."

"I've already discussed this with Edward. A standard prenuptial agreement tilted in your favor instead of the wife's will suffice."

Randolph grimaced, lowered his head, and gave it a slight shake.

"Will you consider this?"

He raised his chin and leveled his gaze at his mother. "I will. But I need time."

"I'm sorry to push you, but the Social Welfare Department has sent us notice that guardianship must be settled in the next thirty days. She's my heir, and the First Family Compact requires underage heirs be fully protected from exploitation. Normally this wouldn't be a problem, but it limits how long you have to decide. The hearing is set for a week from today. If your answer is no, Edward will need time to prepare the documents to contest Penny's stipulation that you become Sophie's guardian and to assign her guardianship to me."

His voice flat, Randolph said, "Perhaps that would be best."

"You know it wouldn't. Penny wanted this. Whatever her reasons, it was clear in the months leading to her death that she was searching for answers. Her focus had turned from politics to family. She brought Sophie home. She was helping young women have babies and start their own families."

Randolph furrowed his brow. "Her letter explained all that."

"Did it explain the long conversations we had about you? She wanted to reconcile with you, to bring you back, and restore our family. Tell me you haven't wished for the same over the years. Please don't refuse this opportunity."

"I said I would consider it. And I will. But I won't be rushed. This isn't about you, me, and Sophie alone. Another person is involved in this plan. I need to weigh what is best for her too. Give me three days. I'll have a decision for you then."

His mother rose from her seat, stepped around the table, and laid a hand on his arm. "Take the time you need. But please. Let the past die. Don't carry it into the future and allow it to continue to harm this family." She placed a kiss on the top of his head.

"I'll try, Mother."

After his mother left, he stared at the half-eaten pastry on his plate. His appetite had fled, and his mind was a jumble of images. Sophie sleeping peacefully in her lavender-decked bed. Penny pulling him up by the arm to sit beside her in the leafy green of the huge tree next to the lambing barn. The haze of arousal in Jen's eyes. A stab of pain shot through his chest. A stable, a taunting woman, a riding crop, burning anger, and stark humiliation.

He lunged to his feet. That was the past. If he were going to make a sound decision, he needed to learn what had changed Penny's mind. Her diaries were waiting in her office. He'd spend the morning reading.

RANDOLPH MERYON HAD LEFT Jen's bed sometime after she had fallen asleep, but not before he had stripped away her sense of who she was. Shy, retiring, and introvert were all labels she'd claimed to describe why she'd allowed herself to be relegated to the background within her family. How many times had she been told she was a follower rather than a leader? She'd always told herself there was nothing wrong with that. The universe needs followers. Being one doesn't make you a patsy. Unless your decisions about whom to support are bad. Many reasons exist why people concede leadership to others. Inertia being a prime example.

She'd resisted the assumption that she was blindly obedient. Whether her family accounted it as assertive or not, she'd managed to obtain the education she wanted. Still she had never openly questioned family dogma to their faces, never been the spirited cousin who openly wrestled with her elders, forcing them to take her on her own terms. She was a follower, and that was okay.

But last night she'd learned she was more than someone as benign as a follower. Randolph Meryon had exposed the hidden depths of her nature, revealing a part of her fundamental character she had never dared consciously examine. She was a submissive.

Yes, she'd balked at calling him master when the throes of sexual desire weren't clouding her mind. But then she'd acceded to his request. No, his command. *Say it. Now.* He'd said it would please him. The statement had plucked a taut cord of need, rusty from neglect. But O'Malleys weren't submissive. She'd struggled against that imposed tenet her whole life, never measuring up, derisively relegated to become a low-level underling, treated with barely disguised contempt. She took orders. Didn't argue. That wasn't what Randolph offered her. Acquiescence to him didn't bring scorn but approval. Sweet kitten. He'd called her his sweet kitten.

And then he'd spanked her. It was appalling, an offense against the name of O'Malley. Which was ridiculous. She, an outcast O'Malley, who hated everything the family held most dear, shouldn't hold a trace of pride in who she was. But Randolph had slipped the cover off that little surprise too. That revelation had overshadowed another aspect of their interaction. She'd wanted him to put her in her place. Stinging swats to her rump weren't what she'd expected, but now she hoped he'd spank her again. In doing so Randolph had released her inner brat, her wildcat as he termed it. Why had she reacted that way? How could she be both a submissive and a wildcat at the same time? Both questions needed further consideration, but

Sophie had completed her numeracy studies for the day. Jen had promised her a trip outdoors when she finished.

"Miss Jen. Miss Jen. Can we ask Uncle Rand if he'll go with us to the secret cave? He said he would." Sophie bounced in place next to Jen's desk.

Jen took Sophie's hand. "We can try, but your uncle has a lot on his mind, so don't be disappointed if he can't go today."

"Yeah!" Sophie dashed away.

"Hold on. Put your hikers on and get a rough-and-tumble. It's a little chilly. I need to put on my boots and get a jacket too. Don't leave the nursery without me."

Sophie ran to her room. When Jen exited her bedroom, Sophie was standing, hopping from one foot to the other, at the door leading from the nursery. Jen had barely spoken the words *let's go* before Sophie shot into the hall and headed toward the main staircase.

Jen allowed Sophie to lead the hunt for Uncle Rand. They found him in Penny Meryon's office, ensconced in a feminine side chair, reading.

"Uncle Rand!" Sophie burst through the door. "Go with us to the cave. Please. Can you? Now?"

"Good morning, pumpkin." He set the bound paper book to the side and glanced out the window. "Looks like a perfect day to explore the cave."

Sophie jumped into his lap, threw her arms around Randolph's neck, and said, "Thank you. Thank you. Thank you." She pulled out of his embrace and stood. "Let's go."

Randolph chuckled. "Impatient." He dropped his gaze to his feet. "I'm not prepared for outdoor adventures." He wiggled the ends of his slippers. "Let me change. I'll meet you at the servant's entrance. You and Jen can beg for cookies in the kitchen."

"Right." Sophie twirled and grabbed Jen's hand. "Come on."

Over her shoulder Jen grinned at Randolph. "Apparently I'm no longer in charge."

Randolph's eyes sparked. "But isn't that how you prefer it?"

A flame of arousal lit inside her. She didn't respond, allowing Sophie to drag her from the room. "Slow down, sugar pop. You're going to wear me out before we step a foot outdoors."

Sophie's pace decreased a fraction, but more because she was once again traversing a hidden passage without light than that she was heeding Jen. Since they were on the opposite side of the castle, it was logical a servant's hallway would provide discreet access to this section of Briarcliff. When they arrived at the kitchen, the cook was making pastry for fruit tarts. Her staff were kneading dough for the oatmeal bread they baked every other day and working on lunch preparations.

When Sophie burst into the room, everyone turned to smile at their favorite disruptor. "We need cookies. We're going to the cave. Me and Jen and Uncle Rand. And he said to get cookies."

The cook rinsed her hands and wiped them dry. "Cookies it is." She pulled a small soft-side cool box from a cupboard and filled it with the treats, water cartons, and a freshening cloth pack. Sophie bounced on her toes while she waited.

"Here you are, Miss Sophie. I've put in chocolate chip for you, oatmeal raisin for Miss Jen, and cinnamon sugar for your Uncle Rand. He always loved my cinnamon sugar cookies when he was a boy." The cook beamed with satisfaction.

Sophie tossed the long handle of the cool box over her shoulder and sped toward the door.

"Sophie. What do you say?"

Sophie twisted toward the cook, mischief illuminating her face. "Thank you." Then she resumed her race out the door.

The cook threw her hands in the air and laughed. "Reminds me of her mother. God rest her soul."

"Thank you," Jen said. "I better hurry. I'm getting left behind."

Randolph was striding along the hall toward Jen when she exited the kitchen. He'd changed into worn denim pants that conformed to his hips and thighs and an off-white, expensive, Aran sweater. Gods. He was pure relaxed sensuality. She couldn't keep from grinning.

Sophie was impatiently bobbing by the servant's entrance. When Jen and Randolph reached her, he scooped the cool box from Sophie's shoulder and slung it over his own. "Let me carry that, pumpkin."

Outside they headed through the car park toward woods that sloped to an open expanse and the lake Jen had seen from the shuttle.

"I brought my hand light, Uncle Rand." Sophie waved the gadget she'd pulled from her pocket.

"Excellent. I have one too."

Jen slowed. "Is the cave dark?"

"Have you ever been in one before?" Randolph asked.

"No. Will there be animals in it?" Why hadn't she considered the possibility before blithely agreeing to this expedition? *It can't be all that bad. A five-year-old's been there.*

He squinted at her, mischief twinkling in his eyes. "The cave we're visiting is hidden in a thick bank of trees and scrub, so not a lot of light gets inside. Small animals do nest there, but nothing terrifying. Sophie and I will protect you."

Her smile less than confident, Jen said, "With two such doughty warriors, I'm sure I'll be safe."

Sophie tugged on Randolph's hand. "I showed Jen the armory."

"Did you?"

"Yes. Miss Jen, you don't have to worry. Mommy said she's only ever seen shrewmice. And they're very sweet."

The woods thickened, so Randolph took the lead with Sophie behind him and Jen taking the rear. They meandered through trees that were showing the first signs of changing color. Bright cornflower-blue patches of sky were visible when they crossed an occasional glade. Their path led them steadily down until Rand arrived at a drop-off and stopped.

Jen cast a glance at the steeper slope, imagining herself losing her footing, rolling, smacking into rocks and underbrush.

"Our cave is just five feet below. There's a ledge free of scrub that we'll climb to." He eyed Jen. "You up for this."

"Absolutely." She shot him another bright smile.

Sophie patted Jen's arm. "It's easy. I was afraid the first time I did it too. But even though you can't see it from here, you won't fall. Even if you slide, you land on the ledge."

"I'll go first and then Sophie. I promise to catch you," Randolph said.

Jen ignored the smirk he directed at her. "I'll be fine."

After finding the first foothold, Randolph said, "Here goes nothing." He never went out of sight. The top of his head was still visible when he called to them. "I'm on the ledge. Sophie, you can start."

The little girl dropped to her hands and knees, scrambling as quick as the tree squirrels that inhabited the woods. "Your turn, Miss Jen."

Jen steeled her nerves and released the branch she'd been holding. Her heart beat faster as she searched for the first foothold, but once she'd found it and then the second, Randolph's hands touched her ankle and tension melted from her. Another step and he clasped her hips. When she was standing on the ledge, he encircled her with his arms and held her, making her pulse race for an entirely different reason.

"Well done." He nuzzled her ear and whispered, "To be with me, you have to be brave."

A shiver ran through Jen. "I'm not brave."

His hand slid to cup her breast. "I beg to differ."

To their right Sophie popped out of a dark, slanting hole in the side of the hill. "Come on." Then she disappeared in the gloom of the cave.

Randolph pushed her to walk in front of him. A curtain of trees ran the length of the ledge, making it seem like they were tucked into their own little world. Jen ducked her head, peering into the mouth. The glow of Sophie's hand light brightened the wall about twelve feet farther. It dipped to illuminate a large metal chest. Inside the floor was rough, the footing uneven and difficult to distinguish. Jen nudged her way forward with the toe of her shoe. When Rand entered behind her, he shined his hand light at the floor, allowing them to pick a path toward Sophie, who was attempting to lift the chest's lid.

"Let me do that." Once the top was open and propped against the rock wall, Randolph lifted out a portable lantern, flicked it on, and hung it from a hook dangling from a chain over their heads. Most of the cave was now visible except for nooks and crannies in the back. A broad, flat area that slanted up the side to the rounded ceiling held the paintings Randolph had described in his eulogy.

Sophie clasped Jen's hand. "Come see my cave painting." She pointed high on the wall. "Mommy held me up, so I could paint it above hers. That one is Grandma's, and that one is Uncle Rand's."

"Very nice. Is that a picture of you?"

"Yep. Me and Mommy. Uncle Rand painted a lamb." In an audible whisper she added, "Mommy had to tell me because it doesn't look like one."

From behind Jen, Randolph said, "I think it's a fine lamb."

Sophie giggled. "Great-Great-Great-Great-Granddad Meryon, the four greats one, painted a knight on a horse, and it really does look like one."

"His passion was Irish medieval armor," Randolph said.

"I've seen him in the armory," Jen said.

"That's right. They made a mannequin resemble him." He moved over to the chest, rummaged inside, and returned with a can of paint markers of varying widths. Holding the container out to Jen, he said, "Your turn."

She furrowed her brow. "Oh. I shouldn't—"

He pushed the can into her hand. "On anyone's first visit to our secret cave, they make a painting."

"But I'm not family."

"You're an initiate into the Society of the Meryon Cave. You know the secret now, so you must seal your pledge to never disclose it by creating your own artwork here."

She narrowed her eyes. "Is that a real thing?"

"It is now. We only use white paint, so your choice is in how thick you want your lines."

"Okay. Maybe something small. And easy."

"While you paint, Sophie and I will look through our treasure boxes."

Jen nibbled on her lower lip, examining the wall for a likely spot. She was no artist, so it would have to be simple. An empty square amid a cluster of other paintings caught her eye. Perfect. After selecting one of the smaller markers, she drew the first arc of her design. Behind her, she heard Randolph ask Sophie a question.

"Did you bring anything to add to your treasure box?"

Sophie's voice was filled with reverence. "I brought the pink quartz Mommy and I found on our last hike."

"I'm sure your mother would approve adding it." Randolph sounded wistful.

Jen looked over her shoulder. Sophie lifted the hinged lid of her box and placed the rock inside. When she closed it, the top, inlaid with tiles that spelled *Sophie Meryon*, was visible. Once he put Sophie's box in the chest, he asked, "Do you want to see what's in mine?"

Jen turned back to her painting, quickly adding the second and third strokes that completed it. The pen capped, she went to the pile of rocks where Randolph had brought his box and sat to show the contents to Sophie. She knelt beside him as he pushed a finger through the items.

"This is the first quartz rock I ever found." He plucked it out and placed it in Sophie's open palm. "It's not pink like yours."

"But it's still pretty." Sophie examined every side before handing it carefully back to her uncle.

He drew out a leather lanyard. "I made this at overnight camp when I was nine." Sophie scrutinized each object as Randolph withdrew them from the box, offering comments on each. Jen remained as still and quiet as possible. This was too precious a moment for outside interference. When all had been given proper scrutiny, Randolph closed the lid.

"I'd like to look inside at your mother's treasures, if you don't mind, Sophie."

"I don't," Sophie said softly. "Mommy said we must never open some-one's box who was still alive. So it's okay." Her voice hitched. "I never knew the other dead people. Now Mommy's in heaven like them. She must be sad to leave her treasures behind."

Randolph drew Sophie into a long hug. "I'm sure she is, but the things in her box are earthly treasures. She has heavenly ones now that are much better. The treasure she must miss most is you, Sophie, but she knows that one day you'll be in heaven too. People are the only treasures we can have on earth and in heaven."

Sophie sniffled. "She's my treasure in heaven."

Unable to speak for a moment, Randolph cleared his throat. "Yes, she is, pumpkin." He held Sophie for a few moments longer. "You can tell me what she added to her box since the last time I came to the cave."

"Okay. She told me about all of them."

He patted Jen on her shoulder. "But first let's check out Jen's painting."

"Oh yes!" Sophie tugged on Jen's wrist while Randolph held her elbow to assist her to rise. "Show us."

At first Sophie couldn't find the sketch Jen had made. "Where is it?"

"Between the house, the sun symbol, and the waterfall."

"I see it. It's a knot."

Jen nodded her head. "That's right. A triquetra or trinity knot."

"Very Irish," Randolph said. "But you have to put your initials and the date." He pulled a marker from the can Jen still held and handed it to her.

She added the date and her initials with a flourish. "There."

Randolph took the container from her, stepped to the chest, and placed it inside. He withdrew a box made of blonde wood. Painted pictographs covered every surface, and it appeared to be solid without an obvious lid.

Sophie reached for it. "Can I open it? Mommy showed me how."

"Sure." He allowed her to take it and watched as she pressed individual images in a set order. The top opened when she finished.

"It's a puzzle box," Sophie explained. She moved to the stones to sit. Jen and Randolph joined her. One by one she removed items from the box, retelling the stories as she'd heard them from her mother. After Randolph and Jen had been allowed to inspect each treasure, she placed them on the rock beside her. Her expression grew puzzled when she pulled out a data cube. "This wasn't in here before."

Shining the beam of his hand light on it, Randolph examined it closely. "It's not labeled. I wonder what's on it."

"Why did Penny bring it here?" Jen asked.

Randolph shook his head. "I'm going to take it back to the house and find out. Is that okay, Sophie? I promise to return it."

"It's okay." She put the other items into the box. When she finished and had resealed it, she handed it to Randolph.

Once it was back in the chest, he said, "It's time for cookies. Do we want to eat them here or out on the ledge?"

"I vote the ledge," Jen said.

"Me too," Sophie said.

"It's settled then. We'll eat on the ledge. Sophie, why don't you go with Jen. I'll turn off the lantern once you're outside, pack the chest, and follow you."

When Jen reached the mouth of the cave, Randolph was holding Penny's treasure box, rubbing a finger over the top. He was gazing ahead at the rock wall. He shook himself and looked at her. The smile he sent her was strained. Moments like this underscored how wrong people were to call him a heartless bastard.

11

R andolph sat in an armchair in Penny's bedroom. The needlepoint seat was exquisite but hard. He hadn't come to make himself comfortable. The diary he hoped to find wasn't here. It had been a half hope. Penny's assistant, Lanny, had already searched and apparently hadn't found it. But what he had come across might shed light on Penny's accusation against Genevieve Kavan.

He looked at the slip of paper in his hand. Genevieve's name and a comm address were written on it. He accessed Comm Finder through his internal data link (EBC) and discovered it was for a fertility clinic on North Island. Penny had claimed she had proof that Genevieve hadn't been raped. Was this clinic where she got her evidence?

His father, Conlin, had always denied the rape allegations, said he'd never touched the woman or spoken more than a few words to her in polite greeting at festival time. Once the DNA evidence had proved that Darrin was his and Genevieve's genetic son, no one believed him. No charges were brought because Genevieve hadn't wished to press the matter and said Conlin had been drinking. But Claire Meryon had severed their marriage. Conlin had moved to Cahernamon, and Randolph had never spoken to his father again.

Their relationship had been uneasy since the day his father insisted

Randolph be sent to boarding school a year early. Mother hadn't wanted to let him go, but his father had persuaded her it was the best thing to do. When Randolph learned that Conlin had betrayed his mother, his enmity toward his father had been sealed. But what if he hadn't been lying? What if he hadn't slept with Genevieve? *What if! What if! How do you explain the DNA evidence then?*

If I could get my hands on the damn diary, all this would be explained. Reading Penny's earlier diaries had shown him his sister was a detailed chronicler. Anything she found important went into her diary. *So where the hell is the thing?* Maybe the data cube they'd discovered in her treasure chest would give him a clue. Although it was much more likely to be a stash of family images or something similar.

He pushed to his feet, placing the slip of paper into his pocket, and went to his own bedroom. The cube was where he'd left it, under his socks in the dresser. The vidscreen in this room was hidden behind a panel. He verbally commanded it to open and slid the cube into the screen's data bay. Seated on the bed, he scanned the table of contents. It looked to be a series of text files labeled "chapterone" through "chaptertwentyfour."

The "chapterone" file began with the title *Our Mothers: A History of Conservative First Family Misandry.* A flush of adrenaline tingled through his body. He read the chapter, a smile building on his face as he did. He fell back on the bed when he finished.

Misandry. His sister had written a book about misandry among the conservative matriarchs. For the darling of the old-line man-haters to call them on their prejudice...it would create a social and political earthquake. No wonder she'd kept the book's contents secret. She hadn't even shared them with her assistant. But she wouldn't. Lanny Conyer was a dyed-in-the-wool supporter of matriarchal rights. Why then hadn't Penny hired a new assistant? Unless she was afraid it would incite the wrong kind of curiosity before the book was published.

Gods! What happened to you, Penny? Why did you change your mind so completely? Nothing he'd read in her diaries had hinted at such a profound alteration in her beliefs. He slammed a fist into the bedspread. *Back to that gods-be-damned missing diary. I've got to find the latest one. So many questions would be answered if I could get my hands on it. Maybe Mother knows.*

He checked the time. Supper was twenty minutes away. He sent the contents of the data cube to his personal server on Beta Tau and then placed it in his dresser. After a quick change of clothes into something less casual, he went to the nursery to find Sophie and Jen. Two female voices, one younger, came from the playroom.

"Do you like the leaf I drew?"

"Very nice. I like the way you made the tip curl."

Randolph stood quietly in the doorway. Sophie was holding a large journal in front of Jen.

Sophie nodded her head. "That was hard to do."

"As you practice, you'll find it gets easier." Jen continued cutting something from red paper when Sophie returned to her seat. Both were engrossed in their work.

All the tension that had been building in him over the mysteries surrounding his sister eased as he watched the pair engaged in purely domestic pursuits. Domesticity. Was that what his life lacked? He hadn't missed it until now. Or perhaps it was nostalgia. No, that didn't describe what he felt toward Jen O'Malley. He liked her. Liked that she was sweet, tenderhearted. Maybe that's what he needed. A little TLC. Someone who recognized when he was hurting and held his hand.

Plus, they were physically compatible. She was naturally submissive and hadn't protested when he'd been rough with her. Not that he'd gone far. He'd yet to introduce her to a whip. But even if her limits blocked him from his usual play, he could forego his needs while he was on Tallav. At least half of his time would still be spent on Beta Tau. Probably more. Family man on Tallav. Sexual sadist on Beta Tau.

It could work. He'd make it work. Not that they'd have a traditional Tallavan marriage. For one thing he would be the one proposing. And working outside the home. No hint of stay-at-home dad existed in him. He was the property owner, not the woman, although not on Tallav. His business on Beta Tau had made him wealthy. Jen had nothing. The whole situation was topsy-turvy for Tallavan aristocrats. He grinned. One more opportunity to spit in the eye of the staunch martiarchists of Tallav. With an O'Malley at that.

Jen and Sophie hadn't noticed him until he cleared his throat. "What are two of my favorite ladies up to?"

Without looking at him Sophie said, "I'm drawing leaves."

He walked to her side. "I have a favor to ask, Sophie."

The little girl's hand stilled, and she peered at him.

"Would you be willing to eat here instead of in the dining room with Grandma, Jen, and I? I need to discuss adult things with them."

A scowl was Sophie's initial response. "I guess so." Then she brightened. "Could I go to the kitchen and have supper with the staff when they eat?"

"That's fine with me if it's fine with them."

"It will be."

Jen said, "Maybe we should ask first."

"Okay. I'll go ask. If they don't want me, which I know they will, Mary or Anna will come eat with me here." Sophie scampered toward the door.

"Pick up first!" Jen said.

Pencils and journal were swiftly cleared, and Sophie flitted away. "See you later, Miss Jen."

"I wish she was that quick at cleaning all the time," Jen said.

Randolph laughed. "Then she wouldn't need a nanny."

"True." Jen swept stray bits of paper and placed them in the trash. "I'll finish this when I return."

Before Jen could step past him, Randolph pulled her into his arms. He'd meant to give her the semi-platonic hug and kiss he'd seen his parents give one another growing up. Once he'd touched her, that idea was obliterated by the sensation of soft curves molding to him. He grasped the back of her head, using her ponytail to position her. Reveling in her acceptance of all he had to give, he ravished her mouth. That she returned his passion with equal ferocity was still a welcome surprise. Jen O'Malley was so much more than a quiet nanny who wore a ponytail as though she were a naive girl. Yet nothing about the way the woman kissed was innocent.

When he released her hair and pulled his head back, panting for the air he hadn't wanted a moment ago, he locked his gaze on her. "There are so many layers to you. I want to peel each away and learn everything about you."

A tiny furrow appeared between her eyes. He stroked a finger over it. "Not all at once. I think you'd be surprised at what I might discover. You have a boldness inside you. I feel it when you kiss me."

Her gaze dropped, and she bowed her head. Lips pressed to her hairline, he murmured, "You're a beautiful mystery, Jen O'Malley."

Randolph let the moment linger, soaking in the peace that flooded him while holding this gentle yet passionate woman. When the five-minute supper bell sounded, he was loath to relinquish his embrace, but the next step to making this relationship permanent awaited.

"Time to go." He escorted her downstairs to the dining room where his mother was already seated. His decision had been made. A sense of calm pervaded him.

When they entered the dining room, Jen had been reluctant to release Randolph's hand. Their connection was so new and, in her mind, tenuous.

"Sophie is eating with the staff tonight," Claire said.

"Yes. I asked her to," Randolph said while assisting Jen to take her place.

"I see. Have you come to a decision then?"

"I have." He took his own chair.

Addressing the butler, Claire said, "We'll eat family style tonight."

"Yes, ma'am."

Once the food had been brought in and each of their glasses had been filled, the butler asked, "Will there be anything else?"

"That will be all." Claire waited until the door closed before glancing at Randolph. "What have you decided?"

Jen studiously observed her plate, taking each dish as Randolph handed it to her without looking at him.

"I'm accepting Penny's request that I become Sophie's guardian."

The announcement startled Jen. They'd discussed it, but it had seemed like he was seeking reasons to offset the significant grounds that suggested he decline. He was such an enigmatic man, offering no hint of his decision when they'd been upstairs.

His mother clapped her hands together and then reached for Randolph. He grasped her fingers and brought them to his lips for a kiss. "I'm so pleased. And the other?"

"Yes. That too."

His mother smiled widely. "Oh, Randolph. You have made me so happy."

"I think we should let Jen know what we're talking about." He directed his gaze at Jen. "I'm sure you've heard some of this via the staff. It's hard to keep a secret in a place like Briarcliff. I've discussed with you that Penny wanted me to be Sophie's guardian. That request stunned me. We hadn't been on speaking terms. The letter Penny left for me made it clear she intended to repair our relationship. Unfortunately she didn't have the time to do so." He dropped his gaze to his food and must have realized he had yet to eat a bite. He scooped a spoonful of mashed potatoes.

The need to comfort him was blocked by the presence of his mother. It wasn't Jen's place. She sampled the roast and pushed peas across her plate while chewing. Randolph continued.

"Penny didn't put any strings on me, but the court has. The judge who is overseeing the case will agree to making me Sophie's guardian if I marry and my wife becomes co-guardian." Jen let her fork drop, placed her hands in her lap, and stared at Randolph.

Claire said, "The problem being that this marriage must happen very quickly. Within a matter of days. The woman must be Tallavan and of good family, which further limits the candidates."

Were they suggesting that she might be the person they were looking for? She fit both parameters by virtue of being born in a Tallavan first family. Plus Sophie had already accepted her.

His expression gave nothing away. "I've asked my mother to make a list of Tallavan women who might agree to harness themselves to me."

Jen's chest tightened. "I see. I hope you'll be able to work things to your advantage." She picked up her fork in a tight grip and took a bite of food. The roast was tasteless. Any appetite she'd had before supper was long gone.

"My dear, we thought—"

Randolph interrupted his mother, squeezing her hand and communicating something wordlessly.

After a tiny nod Claire continued. "We thought you'd accompany us to Cahernamon for the court appearance. The judge may wish to speak with Sophie, although the arrangements have already been made through the

Child Protective Services. The hearing will be the final stamp of approval of what has been negotiated and decided."

That settles it. Randolph doesn't want to marry me. I'm an O'Malley. Why would he? Besides it's much too sudden. He's looking for a contracted marriage. The woman would probably not even live at Briarcliff, not someone who was already enmeshing herself in his family. She gave one long blink and then attempted to smile. "Of course. I'd be happy to." She couldn't resist a glance at Randolph before dropping her gaze to her plate to continue eating the flavorless meal.

His expression showed concern. How nice. He was concerned for her. Concerned. After all, she was the nanny. A post the aristocracy would never take. She'd become part of the serving class, perfect to have a fling with but nothing else. He wanted a Tallavan aristocrat who would accept his money and never involve herself in his or Sophie's life. Everything would be the same as now, with herself available for his physical needs when he visited Briarcliff.

After she'd spent a reasonable amount of time pushing the food around her plate, she said, "I'd better see to Sophie. Please excuse me." She rose from her chair. The warm smile Claire directed at her didn't lessen the stab of pain her next words brought.

"You've done wonders with her. I can't thank you enough for the care you've given her."

Jen bit her lip. Yes. To the Meryons she was firmly planted in the serving class. "Sophie is an easy child to love." Jen rushed to the doorway in an attempt to avoid further conversation.

THE PLAY OF emotions across Jen's face when his mother spoke of marriage candidates had acted like a splash of frigid water to Randolph. He'd been trying to keep Jen's perspective in mind, but his good intentions had gone astray. He hadn't been able to offer her marriage in a cold, clinical manner at the dinner table with his mother looking on. But his hesitance had obviously led Jen to believe he didn't want her as a wife and that she was nothing more than a handy lover. He'd have to wait until Sophie was in bed to dispel that notion.

"She's upset. Why didn't you tell her you hoped she'd agree to the proposition?" Claire asked.

"Because I don't want her to think of it as a proposition. Jen's sensitive. She wants to be wanted, not simply needed. Would you have asked Father to become your husband so you could breed a daughter?"

"Of course not. I take your meaning. But this isn't a love match. It's a marriage of necessity."

"It doesn't have to be."

Claire's eyebrows rose. "Really! Are you infatuated with the girl?"

"Mother, please."

"You are. Well, that does color things differently. I was always afraid you would never find love. I've never quite given that dream up. And I admit to hoping that Jen might be the one. I have something for you."

When the butler responded to her comm message holding a small box, she thanked him and handed the package to Randolph.

Inside two rings lay nestled on a bed of satin. "They are your great-grandfather and grandmother's rings. Typically the woman provides them, but since we're far outside the bounds of normal Tallavan etiquette…"

"Thank you. This will be perfect."

"If romance now means grandchildren in the future, I'm only too happy to assist."

Randolph smirked. "One step at a time."

He placed the box on the table and took his mother's hand. "I do have something else I need to discuss with you. Do you know where Penny's diary is? I haven't been able to find it."

"No, I don't. Did you ask Lanny? I gave her the key to the drawer Penny kept it in."

"Lanny can't find it either. It wasn't in Penny's desk. Lanny's still looking for it. Jen caught her going through Penny's bedroom the day of the internment."

Claire's voice was curt. "Lanny's been helping me finalize Penny's business accounts and asked to look in Penny's room for data cubes that might contain her latest book. I told the woman I would do it. She shouldn't have been in there. I was planning on letting her go in a few weeks, but I believe I'll move that date up."

"I think that would be best. Sophie, Jen, and I took a trip to the secret cave. I found a data cube with Penny's book on it in her treasure box."

Claire pressed a hand to the table. "Oh, thank heaven. I was beginning to fear we'd never find it. Penny was so secretive about it. She didn't even allow Lanny to read it, and the woman was her research assistant."

"She kept it hidden for a reason. It's a complete about-face from her previous work." He paused a moment before dropping the bombshell. "She titled it *Our Mothers: A History of Conservative First Family Misandry*."

One hand to her chest, Claire leaned back. "Oh my goodness. I knew she'd begun to doubt her convictions, but I had no idea she was taking such a drastic step."

"Did she talk to you about it?"

"The book, no. But we did have conversations about Sophie. Penny decided she'd been wrong denying Sophie a father. Part of the reason she came home to Briarcliff was to give Sophie a connection to her family. She didn't want her growing up in Cahernamon, worrying Sophie wouldn't love Briarcliff without childhood memories of it."

That can't be all there is to it. "What made her change her mind? She was always committed to matriarchal values."

Her gaze distant, Claire said, "She didn't confide in me. But Father James might be able to help you understand. Penny spent time with him every week. She began going to mass regularly, taking communion and going to confession. She seemed more at peace with herself."

Rubbing the heart bead at his wrist, Randolph said, "Me too. Being here."

Claire's lips curved in a loving expression. "You're back now, and you're going to raise Sophie. At least some of the fractures in this family have been mended."

The smile Randolph attempted to give his mother faded quickly. If he could discover the evidence Penny claimed to have about Genevieve Kavan, perhaps that other rent in the fabric of their family could be repaired. "Did Penny talk to you about a fertility clinic on North Island?"

"The Mother and Child Clinic? Yes, she did. She conceived Sophie there through anonymous sperm donation. It's one of the best on Tallav. Here on Rathlin she was gaining a reputation for her work on child welfare and parenting. She negotiated a discount for the women living on Rathlin who couldn't afford the clinic. The injustice of a system that required medical treatments for fertility issues be provided by expensive specialty clinics was a hot-button issue for her. I've never seen her angrier than when she was discussing how this priced simple medical procedures out of the working class's ability to pay."

Randolph took his mother's hand. "I found a slip of paper in Penny's room. It had the clinic's comm number on it along with a name, Genevieve Kavan. Did Penny ever discuss Genevieve with you?"

Beneath his fingers, Claire's hand tightened. Her shoulders slumped. "We didn't discuss Genevieve or your father, but perhaps we should have. Penny was angry at him with an intensity I couldn't handle. I didn't hate your father. I loved him. Still do, or the man I always imagined him to be. If he had just admitted to what he'd done, given an explanation, I would have been able to forgive him. But he denied it completely in the face of irrefutable proof."

"Penny believed she'd found evidence to support Father's claim that he didn't rape Genevieve."

Claire sat forward. "What! Evidence? Do you have it?"

"No. I don't. But I think it must have something to do with the Mother and Child Clinic. If we could find Penny's diary, I'm sure she'd have written about her suspicions and theories."

Her brow furrowed. "Then we need to find that diary. I needed to speak with the clinic director about continuing Penny's legacy with the discount and a memorial fund to help poor women access the clinic's services. I will try to discover what ties Genevieve Kavan to the clinic."

"I'll keep looking for the diary. You should know that I've spent time with Darrin Kavan. I intend to develop our relationship."

Claire lifted her chin, her gaze steady. "That's good of you. I did what I could to help Genevieve out, deeded over the property where she lives and has her business. At first the pain was too difficult for me to have anything to do with her or the child. It became the norm to treat her as a distant acquaintance. But I'm glad you'll be involved in the boy's life." After a pause she added, "Genevieve isn't altogether stable."

A rap sounded on the door, and Jen stuck her head in. "Sophie's here for her good-night hugs."

12

Randolph had accompanied Jen and Sophie to the nursery. Before leaving, he had whispered to Jen, "Come to me. I have something important to ask you." Now he waited for her. He had no doubt she'd obey him. Her lips had parted, and she'd gasped, the tiniest of inhalations that proved she desired him. She'd followed that with a scowl and a nod, after which she'd pasted on a cheery smile and started Sophie's bedtime routine.

The implements he planned to use on her were laid out on the bedside table. He hadn't brought his toy bag to Tallav, so he'd been forced to improvise. Jen needed to get the full picture of what she'd be letting herself in for if she agreed to marry him. Not that she couldn't opt out of the marriage bed, but the physical attraction between them hadn't been dimmed by their first encounter. He didn't want to take the time to seduce her slowly into becoming masochist to his sadist. She would accept him as he was or not at all. No waiting to find out after the marriage that she could't handle his sexual sadism.

After depositing the ring box in the drawer of an end table, he settled into the dark brown leather chair next to it. He steepled his fingers, closed his eyes, and attempted to relax. He was on the verge of committing himself to an action he'd long since decided he'd never agree to. Prior to his sister's death, marriage had been a hard limit for him. Each step toward overcoming that rule had been taken with due consideration, each logically and rationally arrived at. Marrying Jen was the right thing to do even though he struggled to find the balance he was used to. The fulcrum had moved, but he would adjust and make this new life work for all of them.

A knock sounded. "Come in."

Jen hesitated after entering, her hand on the doorknob as though she were ready to flee.

"Shut the door behind you." Randolph gave her a reassuring smile. The virginal nightgown she wore with its long sleeves, high collar, and the suggestion of creamy, unmarked flesh underneath was more erotic than any negligee. His groin tightened. "We need to talk."

She gave him a slight nod, her mouth pressed into a line, and closed the door. "I'm not sure we should continue this. Wives don't like their husband's sleeping with the nanny."

"The wife I have in mind won't mind me sleeping with you."

She narrowed her eyes, not responding.

"Kitten, let me explain, please. Lock the door."

When she turned after flipping the heavy bolt, she ducked her head, but she didn't move forward.

Randolph reached a hand to her. "Come sit on my lap. I won't bite. Yet."

"I don't think that's a good idea either." She turned toward the door. "I shouldn't have come."

He jumped to his feet, rushed toward her, and held his hand out. "Don't go. Please. I have something important to ask you."

Her hand went to her throat. Eyes locked to hers, he awaited her decision, knowing he was being weighed in the balance. His tension eased slightly when she placed her fingers in his palm and allowed him to draw her back to the chair he'd been sitting in. He pulled her down, hoping she wouldn't balk, and positioned her sideways, placing his arm around her, his hand flattened against her stomach. She held herself stiff. That wouldn't do. He nuzzled her hair. "I'm sorry I upset you. It wasn't my intention." The scent of warm vanilla enticed him to nibble her earlobe, continuing along her jawline. Her rigidity eased some. Groaning, he drew back. "I promised not to bite, but you're so irresistible."

"Am I?" Her words sounded soft, with an aching note of pain. She fingered a button on his shirt and then abruptly dropped her hand to her lap.

He took hold of it. "Very much so."

How did he go about asking a woman to marry him? He should have planned this part. Most of his adult life he'd been able to point at a female and tell her what he wanted her to do to receive an immediate, affirmative response. This was different. No courtship period allowed them to get to know each other. He'd jumped into a physical relationship because he'd thought of Jen as a fling. But marriage was akin to a Dom collaring a submissive. Something he'd never done, never come close to considering. It required a rapport that they hadn't developed. Nothing for it but to play this as straightforward as he could.

"When Mother told me that as a condition to becoming Sophie's guardian, I would need to marry, she suggested that you were perfect to fulfill the role."

Jen stiffened again in his embrace. To soothe her, he rubbed the back of her hand with his thumb. "At that time I wasn't ready to agree to take on that responsibility, much less acquire a wife." He dropped her hand to brush his fingers through his hair. "This has all happened so quickly, and yet I've come to believe that becoming Sophie's guardian is the right thing to do. The obvious correlation being that I must marry. You were the first person, the only person, Mother suggested."

A furrow appeared between Jen's eyebrows.

Is that a positive or a negative sign?

"I am not a typical Tallavan aristocrat, and marriage to me would be far from normal. My business on Beta Tau has made me financially secure. I'll never be dependent on a woman. My home is an apartment inside a BDSM club. It's no place for a child to grow up, nor is Beta Tau the ideal planet to raise a family. That would mean I would be away from Briarcliff much of the time. Until we were told the judge was insisting I marry, I'd thought that my mother and you, or someone else we hired to be Sophie's nanny, could manage the day-to-day child-rearing. I realize that sounds harsh, that I'd be skirting my responsibilities, but as I said, this has been a shock. I was trying to cobble together a plan that would make everybody happy.

And now, it would seem I'm substituting the nanny for a wife. It makes me look even worse."

He paused pressing his lips together before continuing. "One thing I can offer is a steady income, allowance, whatever you want to call it and a home for as long as the marriage lasts. Our lawyer believes that after three years the court might allow a divorce if Sophie is stable and happy. If that should happen, I'd settle a sizable amount of credits on my wife, enough to keep her for the rest of her life.

"I've probably made the case for why any woman, let alone a Tallavan woman, would refuse to marry me." For the first time in a very long while his confidence deserted him. He broke eye contact to look away and rubbed the back of his neck. Jen laid her head on his shoulder and placed her hand over his heart. The gesture soothed the turmoil that quivered inside him. He placed a kiss on her hair, taking a deep breath of her sugar-cookie fragrance.

"Look at me, Jen."

She straightened and met his eyes. The lack of disgust in her expression was in his favor, but the way her hands tightened into fists when she said, "Rand—" was unsettling.

He placed a finger on her lips. "Don't answer yet. You need to contemplate this thoroughly. Call a family member or a friend for advice."

She pushed his finger away. "Are you asking me to marry you? Because if you are, you haven't actually done that."

His eyes went wide. *Damn. She's right. I didn't ask her.* He took a deep breath and released it. "Will you marry me, Jen O'Malley?"

"Thank you for the proposal. If it weren't for Sophie, my answer would be an immediate no."

His chest tightened. "That's not a no, but its not a yes either."

She banged her fist on her thigh. "I don't understand what you want from me. You speak of marriage in businesslike terms, but I'm sitting on your lap. If you had a hundred candidates ready, willing, and available, would you still choose me? I need to know I'm more than just an interchangeable part to you."

"Fuck." He brushed a hand through his hair. "I've really screwed this up." He stroked his thumb over her cheek. "If it were any other woman, I'd never have contemplated this. I'd be on my way to Beta Tau after refusing to become Sophie's guardian. You make this possible. Who you are. I…"

He brought his lips to hers and kissed her tenderly. "I wanted you to know that if you say yes to this insane proposal, I'll always take care of you. I know that you should turn me down. There are many reasons why this would be a mistake for you. Not least of which is the darkness inside me that I express through my sexuality."

Jen's brows knit together, and she shook her head. "You're not evil no matter what people say about you. The man I've seen over the last days is kind. He cares about his family, protects them. You didn't do anything in bed that I didn't enjoy. Now that I've discovered it, I want to explore that part of myself, and you're the only person I know who could make that possible."

"Please understand. I've been on a leash."

To his surprise she looked intrigued. "Really?"

"Would you like me to show you? I think it's only fair you get a better taste of what you're getting into with me."

A spark came into her eyes, a slight smile to her lips. Gaze riveted to his, she nodded. The fire he'd kept banked flared inside him, and the expression a long-ago sub had dubbed Happy Mr. Evil spread across his face.

"Normally I'd tell you to strip, but I'm going to have fun removing that nightgown. Tell me, Miss Modest, are you a naughty girl? Do you want me to do wicked things to you?"

Her cheeks flushed, and her ears reddened. "Yes, Sir."

Gripping her chin, he kissed her roughly, thrusting his tongue into her mouth, relishing the taste and feel of her. When she moaned and sucked on him, he broke away. His whole body ached to be inside her, but this was meant to be more than a good fuck.

"Your safe word is 'red.' Use it if I go too far. I'll stop, do what's necessary to make things better, and leave you for the night. If you need to ask a question or if you are uncomfortable with something I'm doing, you will say 'yellow.' We'll discuss things and then continue. Do you understand?"

"Yes, Sir."

"Good. Unless I ask you a question, you will not speak except to use your safe words. Can you do this for me?"

"Yes, I will."

He lifted her from his lap to stand between his knees. "Put your hands behind your head."

Arms wrapped around her, he clamped his palms to her bottom, squeezing hard enough to leave bruises if she were easily marked. The tips of her nipples were visible against the fabric of her nightgown. Her body quivered when he stroked one with his tongue, then took it into his mouth and sucked. When he bit down on it, she gasped but didn't pull away.

"You like when I do that, don't you?"

"Yes, Sir."

It pleased him that she'd naturally begun to call him *sir*. Slowly he pulled the nightgown up her hips while tonguing her other nipple. He delved underneath, finding silky, unmarred skin. Tonight he would leave his mark on her, multiple times if she allowed him. He bit again, and this time she groaned. Miss Modesty liked it dirty, and he planned to push her to her limit.

"This needs to be off. Step back."

He stood, pulled her nightgown over her head, and cast it aside. Her body was as lovely as he remembered, pale ivory skin flushed with health and curves that fit his hands perfectly. Cupping her breasts, he muttered, "Yes, perfect." For a moment he thumbed both nipples and then pinched them. "I have decorations for these."

When he scooped her into his arms, she offered no resistance but trembled against him. "Are you afraid?"

"No. Yes. A little."

Confusion shown in her eyes when he gently placed her crossways on the bed. Creating a dichotomy in his behavior, randomly switching from tender care to inflicting fierce pain, was his preferred method of overwhelming a sexual partner's equilibrium. "It's okay to be afraid. Your fear arouses me. Don't hide it."

From the nightstand he selected a pair of nipple clamps. "Put your knees together." He straddled her legs. Pulling and twisting one nipple, he said, "These will hurt. I need you to bear the pain for me. Will you do that?"

Pupils dilated, she was panting. "Yes, Sir."

She didn't flinch when he attached the clamp, so he tightened it until she hissed and then took it one twist further. Moisture glistened along her lower eyelids, but she didn't cry. The second clamp received a similar response.

"Come." He helped her to her feet. "I want you to see how lovely you look in these."

Her face scrunched into a wince as she took the few short steps to the mirror. Each clamp was weighted with a sparkling blue gemstone that intensified the tug on her nipples with every movement she made.

He led her in front of the mirror and stood behind her, giving her a moment to study her reflection. "Much better. Do you like them?"

The pain must have receded because her face had relaxed. "Yes, Sir. I do."

"I don't have my toy bag with me." He chuckled to himself. "I wasn't expecting to find such a delectable play partner at Briarcliff. These were in my attaché case, a sample someone tried to sell the club."

He reached around and tapped the dangles, making them sway. Her body tensed, and she leaned toward him, releasing puffs of air.

"Perhaps I'll invest in some. They're good beginner clamps." When her eyes widened, he laughed out loud. "I have so much more fun to introduce you to."

He had her right where he wanted her. It hadn't escaped his notice that she had spotted the items he'd laid on the nightstand. The knife stood out with its promise of blood play. But the things he'd gathered from the armory were equally alarming if you knew what they were for. She must have seen him glance in the mirror at the nightstand, because a shudder ran through her.

"Is that fear, sweetheart? Or do you want more?"

Her gaze fixed on the floor, she said, "More please, Sir."

He turned her, inhaling the thick scent of vanilla and aroused woman, surprised the combination was so erotic. "Look me in the eyes." Her pupils were blown wide with just a rim of shadowy gray ringing them. Through parted lips the tip of her tongue slipped out and swiped a lick. His heart rate kicked up a notch as exhilaration flooded him. He was more aware of her than he'd ever been before. This was the high he loved to ride, found only with a woman who matched his need to give pain with her desire to receive it. How much Jen would accept was yet to be determined, but she liked it when he hurt her. If he swept a finger through her folds, they'd come back wet. He smirked, took her hand, and led her to the bed. "Lie facedown. Hips on the edge."

When she'd complied, he grabbed her ankles and yanked her toward him.

"Aaahh!"

Her reaction was due to the clamps tugging hard on her nipples as he dragged her over the bedspread. She blew air from her mouth in a long stream.

The bed shook when he threw himself beside her. He shoved her head against the spread, pressing down, controlling her, bringing his gaze in line with hers, face-to-face, not quite touching. "You're doing very well. I'm so turned on, I could strip your panties off and fuck you right now. But I won't. I want to see how much I can force you to endure, to make you cry and sob and moan. I won't stop unless you use your safe word. Do you remember it?"

"Yes, Sir. Red, Sir."

"Very good." Her breath was warm against his lips. Her tongue glided out in another lick. He'd told her not to speak, but perhaps that had been a mistake. "I've changed my mind. Make as much noise as you like. You won't be heard. Stone walls. Solid oak door. I could kill you in here and no one would know."

Her eyes widened, and his cock grew harder. "Do you trust me?"

Her voice quavered. "Yes, Sir."

He let the wicked grin that was an essential element of his sexually sadistic personality rise inside him to spread across his face. "Good. You'll have to if you want to please me. You can curse me, scream at me, extol my godlike abilities, but above all I want to hear you beg me for more. Beg me to do every evil thing my mind can invent. And then take it and thank me for it. Do that and I'll fuck you so hard you won't know if you'll live through your orgasm."

Hand still clamping her head to the bed, he rubbed a thumb along her cheek. "I have so many plans. I want to mark you. Leave you a souvenir of tonight. A little scar. Someplace visible that others can see. They'll ask you what happened, and you won't be able to tell them. Perhaps you'll blush when you remember that you begged me to do it. I'm going to make you plead with me to cut you."

The trembling had started slowly, but with his last words she was shaking. "Does that scare you?"

"Yes, Sir."

"Do you want me to stop?"

"No." She hesitated. "Please don't stop."

He covered her mouth in an avaricious kiss, plunging his tongue inside, savoring her flavor and filling her with his own. Her moan of appreciation was all the encouragement he required to prolong it until only the need for air forced him to break away. He released her head and dragged his hand down her back, giving her bottom a sharp pop.

Her nostrils flared. "More, please. Sir."

"Like that, do you?" He sat up.

"I discovered that the last time."

Chuckling, he smoothed his palm across each of her cheeks. "I can make it hurt more."

"I'll bet you can." Lifting her fingers to cover her mouth, she squeaked. "I'm sorry. I didn't mean that like it sounded."

"Yes, you did." He slapped her backside hard, receiving the *oof* he expected. "But I like saucy Jen. She's fun to play with. Don't hold her back, sweetheart." One hand placed across her lower spine, he applied himself to spanking her, working at a stinging pace until she colored to a bright shade of pink.

After each smack Jen wriggled and lifted her bottom, seeking the next slap. But he had yet to make her writhe in agony. He snatched the manacles he'd found in the armory. Authentic replicas, they would keep her hands restrained overhead and away from her butt. Shaking the cuffs above her face, he said, "I'm going to shackle you. You're too new to this for me to trust you'll keep your hands out of the way. Your tush can take what I intend to do, but I could crack a bone in your hand if I couldn't pull back before striking you."

He eased her arms up and attached the manacles onto her wrists, screwing the key until they'd closed tight enough so she wouldn't slip free. "This isn't punishment. It's for your protection. Understand, I rarely use pain to punish those I play with. A masochist would enjoy it too much.

And you, sweetheart, are a masochist. To what degree, I'm about to find out." Assured she was adequately yet comfortably restrained, to the extent possible with metal cuffs, he selected the broad-backed wooden hairbrush he'd found in a guest bedroom.

It fit his hand perfectly. After two swings through the air to stretch his muscles, he brought it down with a hard smack.

"Ouch!"

In rapid succession he hit her three more times at separate spots on one cheek. Jen's breathing had grown heavy, and she made pained exclamations, settling on the word "shit" when he treated the other half of her bottom to a series of sharp, thudding swats. The skin grew red but not the purplish-red that denoted a new bruise forming. He continued spanking, stopping to soothe her heated ass from time to time. "How are you doing?"

"I'm fine, Sir. Thank you for asking."

He chuckled. "Do you remember your safe word?" Before she could answer, he thwacked her again. Punctuating the phrases of his next question, he struck her three more times. "Do you…want to…use it?"

Grunts followed each hit. "No, Sir. Please don't stop."

Gratification filled him, making his chest lighten. Imagine finding a masochist at Briarcliff. Taking a wife was turning out to be just what he needed. Someone to nurture and care for his niece, to soothe him from the cares of the world, and to fulfill him in bed. She had admitted to being afraid, but she'd placed her trust in him. He studied her for a moment. An inordinate amount of trust. He'd expected her to balk, but she'd acquiesced to everything he asked of her. Most novices would be disturbed by their reaction to his sadism, especially those that had no idea masochistic desires were buried inside them.

Abruptly he flipped her and straddled her. "Why do you trust me?"

Her eyes widened, and a furrow appeared between her eyebrows. "I…" She winced.

Gripping her pliant shoulders, he dug his fingers into her flesh and shook her. "Why?"

"I…" She gulped. "I want to find myself."

What does that have to do with allowing me to hurt her? He narrowed his eyes, willing her to continue.

"I've always been what other people wanted me to be, but you've revealed something about me that's been hidden, that's the real me. I like the pain. It's more than being compliant. I'm sick of being good little Jen who does as she's told. For once in my life, I feel like I'm in control. You want things from me, but I'm the one who determines how much I give. It's not do it or else. It's can you give me more. You make me feel free."

"That's the way it's supposed to be between sadist and masochist, but you didn't answer my question. Why do you trust me? You're Tallavan. You can't have missed my reputation for savagery."

A smile bloomed on her face. "I've seen your heart. I've watched your kindness to Sophie, seen you protect your family, and treat others with respect. You didn't fling me against the ground, beat me, and rape me like some predatory fiend. You seduced me into bed and made plain your predilections and the measures you take to safeguard me. And I've seen you in pain. No man who mourns his sister as you do can be evil. Wicked perhaps, but not evil."

He slammed his mouth to hers, kissing her with an aggressive clash of teeth and tongue, biting her lower lip as he pulled away. He held himself with one arm above her, smoothing her hair back from her face. "You are beautiful, Jen O'Malley. Ebony tresses. Skin like pearls. Bloodred lips." He nipped at them again. "You're my own Snow White, escaped from the malevolent O'Malley witches."

"Are you my handsome prince, Sir?"

"No." He leered at her. "I'm your wicked prince. And I haven't finished with that very fine ass of yours."

Jen cried out when he flipped her to her stomach. Wielding the brush, Randolph built a steady rhythm of hits: five smacks, then a pause for her to process the pain. Her curses turned to shrieks and then to whimpering as she writhed beneath the palm he held firmly against her back. When the signs of bruising began to appear, he threw the brush aside and rubbed her heated backside, pinching a few of the least vivid spots, enjoying her squawks.

When he rolled her over, her eyes were hazy and watery from tears. "I feel… Hmmm."

"Are you floating?"

"Yeah. Kinda floaty…" A contented smile fluttered onto her face. "I like it."

Randolph brushed a finger across her lips. What a woman. At her center was a core of courage. He could hardly believe she was letting herself go like this—and with him, of all people. Strength, hidden inside her, allowed her to embrace new sensations and novel ideas about herself.

He wanted to plunge into her, fuck her until she screamed his name, but first she had some begging to do. Few play partners agreed to let him cut them, to make them bleed. Even though the damage was fleeting, easily fixed with a dose of the proper nanites. Still most people were squeamish about blood sport. The whip he usually used wasn't as intimate as what he planned for Jen. How far would his kitten allow him to go? The idea sent flaming heat through him.

After helping her to her feet, he grabbed a length of rope and led her to the closet, opening the door. He tied one end to the chain that connected her shackles, backed her against one side of the door, and threw the rope over to the other side. He tugged her hands over her head, keeping the rope from sliding off the top, and then tied it down tight to the knob and shut the door. Before him, Jen stood open and available. He could do whatever he wanted to her.

The fog of subspace had dissipated some. Her gaze followed him as he slowly removed his clothing. When his cock sprang free, her eyes widened. Gods, she was fun to play with. "Like what you see?"

She shook her head. "No."

Hands on his hips, he cocked an eyebrow at her.

She smirked. "I love what I see."

"Little tease." He went to the nightstand, picked up the remaining items, examining them so she could observe each of them before selecting the knife and the sharpening steel.

His heart rate ticked up another notch, sending more blood to his throbbing groin. That ache would have to wait. He slid the knife along the steel in long, even strokes. It didn't need to be sharpened but doing so allowed him to ratchet higher the tension Jen was already feeling.

She closed her eyes and sucked in a deep breath.

"Keep your eyes open."

Her eyelids flicked up, and she blinked at him. The playfulness was gone from her expression. A tiny crease had appeared between her eyebrows. "Yes, Sir."

The moment she shifted her weight from one foot to the other, he threw the steel to the side and drew the blade along his thumb. A line of bright red liquid welled.

"Lick."

Her tongue slipped out, the tip swiping the blood. He groaned and pushed it into her mouth.

"Suck."

Images of his cock thrusting between her lips left him spellbound for long moments. When he pulled his thumb out, a pop sounded. "Your turn."

She stiffened but, in a show of bravado, said, "Whatever you want."

"This is not about what I want. It's about you. By the time I'm through with you, you're going to plead with me to cut you." To satisfy his growing desire, he pressed himself to her, wrapping a hand around her nape, whispering in her ear. "Are you terrified yet?"

Sweat sprang up between them. Whether it was his, hers, or theirs was impossible to tell. It trickled down his abdomen when he released her, staring into her eyes, awaiting her response.

Her voice rough, she said, "Yes, Sir."

"Good. You should be. Give me your fear and pain, and I will make something glorious with it." He chuckled, low and wicked. "It's what I'm known for."

She shuddered when he brought the knife into her line of vision. "Don't move." He waited for her to regain control, one finger stroking her cheek. Then he slid the dull side of the blade along her shoulder and down her arm. Her whimper was like a balm to the part of him that lusted after darkness, but she held still. He did the same to the other side, holding her wrist to be sure she wouldn't jerk.

Each puff of sound from her panting was sweet to his ears. It took all his concentration to keep his hand steady while he brushed the flat of the blade over the top swell of each breast, ending with taps to her nipples. A tear slid down her cheek. Time to get on with it before she fell apart. He braced his forearm against her torso and drew a line between her breasts to her abdomen with the knife tip. Not deep enough to make her bleed, but a pale pink streak appeared.

"Oh gods." She lowered her chin, trying to see the cut. "Is it deep? It isn't bleeding."

"I didn't press hard enough to draw blood. Yet. Ask me to." He gripped her jaw. "Now."

Beneath his fingers she trembled and hesitated before finally speaking. "Please cut me. Please make me bleed for you."

In a voice that growled with displeasure, he said, "Not good enough."

Her breath came in bursts, in and out. "Please, Sir. I feel like I'm on the cusp of something. An unknown that only you can show me. Let me loose, and I'll get on my knees to you. You said I'd beg, and I am. I want to do this for both of us. Please." Tears began to slide down her cheeks.

"Very well." He picked up the black scarf he'd placed at the end of the bed. "I'm going to blindfold you now. It will keep you from jumping for the next few cuts. I wouldn't want to injure you too badly."

JEN CLOSED HER EYES, gasping when Randolph tugged the scarf tight. She heard him moving about the room, and then he was before her, the heat of his body radiating from him, countering the wave of cold that was washing through her.

His voice a fervent whisper, he said, "Hold completely still."

She froze. Sharp and hard, the knife blade sliced the skin on her chest. She hissed. Warm, wet blood welled and trickled. *He's doing it. He's cutting me, marking me.* The knife lifted, and she shivered.

"I said hold still." His voice was gruff, commanding.

"Yes, Sir."

Three times more he carved strokes that ran with her blood. *Is he drawing a picture? The letter M?* The pain that accompanied each slice was nearly imperceptible she was so giddy from fear, excitement, and the passion roiling within her.

"One more cut and we're finished. I want others to see this whenever they look at you. This one is dangerous. If you don't remain motionless, we'll be making a trip to the med bed. Understand?"

In a quavering voice she managed to say, "Yes, Sir."

"Do you want to use your safe word?"

"No, Sir."

Leaving her no time to brace herself, he slashed the blade across her throat. She went rigid, a scream building inside her. Seconds later it ripped from her, cutting through the silence in one long, shuddering shriek that stopped only when she ran out of breath.

What the fuck? What the fuck? He slit my throat. She shook uncontrollably, wrestling against the cuffs at her wrists. Then his arms were around her, and he was nuzzling her hair.

"All done. My brave darling. You did very well."

"I-I...bl-bleeding." *Why isn't he doing something? Cutting me down? Getting me to a med bed? What kind of monster is he? He's letting me die.*

"No, kitten." He pulled the scarf away from her eyes and rubbed a towel over her neck, showing her it was unstained. "No blood."

Oh gods. He... What?

A finger slid between her folds, rubbing her clit. He flicked his tongue along the curve of her ear and nibbled the side of her neck. His erection pulsed against her stomach. "That was perfect. You make me so fucking hard. You're everything I need."

Her mind was numb, unable to sort through the emotions flooding her —anger, betrayal, shock, and pleasure. Pleasure at what his finger was doing, and pleasure at his words. *Gods, say it again. Say I'm perfect for you. Tell me you need me.* As fervently as she desired him to voice his approval, her body ached for him, blossomed with the rapacious need to have him plunging inside her. She wanted the bastard despite what he'd just done.

He continued to stimulate her nub, both torment and ecstasy, until she bucked against his hand. He yanked both her legs off the floor, positioning her thighs at his hips. The brush of flesh against flesh was delicious, eliciting a groan of impatience from deep inside her. *Now. Take me now. Make me yours.*

When the tip of his cock was centered, he plunged inside her, sliding into her pussy, filling her, his own moan matching hers. Hands clutching her ass, he thrust with a ferocity she'd never experienced with any other man.

Twined with him in a desperate spiral toward a point just out of reach yet so far away, approval roared through her. She had more than whet his appetite. She'd inflamed him to the point where nothing could stop him from quenching the blazing need to explode. Her own raspy sighs filled her ears while the mingled fragrance of sex and Rand's dirty-leather scent invaded her nose. Soon all else faded until the singular awareness of touch remained, focused on his cock plunging into her. And then she was squeezing his erection, coming around him in a long, clenching orgasm. Release struck him, in what must have been a similarly staggering detonation of bliss and primal gratification because his whole body went hard, his grip on her bruising.

Their heated joining had melded them. If he were to disentangle himself from her now, it would be like ripping away a part of her. Thank whatever deities were looking down on them, he continued to cling to her, his chest heaving. She hummed soft sounds of satisfaction while kissing his shoulder.

"That was beyond...beyond." His expression dazed, he gave a brief grunt of a laugh. Then he must have realized he was pressing her into the door. He blew out a puff of air and broke his hold, pushing back. She scrunched her face and mewled in protest.

"You can't stay tied to the door forever, kitten."

Releasing her turned out to be far more difficult than tying her had been. Her legs were wobbly. He untied the rope that anchored her in place, caught her, and lifted her in his arms, carrying her to the bed, where he removed the shackles. *Gods, I really am a masochist.* The mix of pain and pleasure while he rubbed the muscles of her arms and shoulders made her smile. The expression evaporated when he released each nipple clamp in turn. "Shit, shit, shit."

He stopped her curses with a languid kiss, broke it, and pulled back to stroke her forehead with his fingers, staring into her eyes. "That's the best sex I've had in a very long time, maybe ever. Where have you been my whole life?"

She winced. "Someplace you would never have thought to look for me."

"Thank the deity of your choice you escaped." He gave her a more perfunctory kiss and rose from the bed, picking up the towel he'd used in the scene. While he was wiping the sweat from her face and neck, she reached for her throat, remembering the horror of the knife slashing her. "You didn't cut me."

"No, I didn't cut you." His smile was cocky.

She snatched the towel from him, rubbed it against her chest while peering down at her skin. "No blood at all. But I felt it. The knife cutting. Blood running down my chest. How did you—"

"Ruler. Warm water. Your mind did the rest."

Her expression changed from puzzled to provoked. "Why didn't you? You said you were going to mark me." Fingers running over her chest where he'd supposedly carved a square, her eyes flashed. "What the…"

"Mind fuck." He pulled the towel from between them and gently kissed her. "If you want me to mark you, I can do that. But not under these conditions and certainly not while you're tied upright to a door. Anything permanent I give you must be perfect."

The scowl didn't leave her face. "Okay. But no more mind fucks."

He kissed her again, biting her lower lip before pulling away. "Sweetheart, I am the master of mind fucks. It's who I am and what I do. That's something I'll never give up. Non-negotiable."

"Hmmm."

"Spread your legs."

Her eyebrows lifted. When he waggled the towel in front of her, she complied, allowing him to clean between her thighs. Finished, he sent it sailing across the room and pulled her in tight against his body.

Nestled in his arms, a sense of safety and security filtered through her. Her life had taken a bizarre turn, one she couldn't be sure would lead to better things. But in the embrace of her lover, the sadist who had skillfully released her masochistic nature from its hiding place, retreat wasn't possible. She was falling for this man. Her heart told her that wasn't as foolish a thing as it sounded. She brushed doubt away. He may be a sadist and a reluctant husband, but he was a tender sadist and that boded well for him being a tender husband too.

13

The room was dark when Jen awoke. Next to her Randolph was deep in sleep, his face relaxed from the cares of the world. He seemed at peace, but that was far from true. The wounds he nursed had never been allowed to heal. How could they when they'd been ripped open repeatedly, even by family? Life had shown her a thing or two about kin, and none of it was particularly good.

The man was a contradiction, a tenderhearted sadist. If she'd been asked if that were possible before getting to know Randolph Meryon, before becoming the recipient of his sexual sadism, she'd have said absolutely not. What a revelation that had been, a sea change to her self-understanding.

When he'd attached clamps to her nipples, every movement had brought searing pain, yet she'd longed for him to tap the dangling jewels again. His eyes had darkened and the bulge in his slacks had grown harder against her bottom when he'd stood behind her, his gaze reflected in the mirror as he watched her reaction to the clamps. She had fulfilled the erotic fantasies of this man. Somewhere hidden inside her was this wanton who wanted him to do nasty dirty things to her. Was it perverse to desire that he hurt her? If it was, she was lost. How he went about it didn't matter as long as he accepted the offering of her body to be used as he willed.

She had proven to him that she was worthy of him, worthy of the infamous sadist, Randolph Meryon. She ought to be shocked that in only a few days she'd allowed her primal urges to overtake all rational thought. He'd said it himself. This man was the exact opposite of a proper Tallavan husband. He'd asked her to marry him and proposed it as more than a contractual arrangement to gain custody of Sophie. Then he'd shown her what that more entailed, and she'd loved it, would beg for more.

She was about to cast the last of her upbringing to the winds. It hadn't been a slippery slope but an icy cliff she'd found herself on when she first caught sight of him. Before she'd known what was happening, she was already falling. It was his eyes that moved her. When they lost that dark chocolate candy-shell look and became pits of emotion, she wanted to reach out and soothe him. He needed her as much as Sophie did, and truthfully, he was just the man to bring about her own personal transformation. The time she spent with him produced within her a greater confidence. Together they could build something that could lead to mutual happiness and maybe, someday, love.

"Good morning, sweetheart." Randolph observed her, his eyes a soft brown and hazed from sleep. He smoothed a hand down her hip and then pulled her to him.

"Morning." Any other words she might have said were consumed by his kiss. *Gods, the man even woke up intensely passionate.* And all that ferocious sexuality was directed at her. *Lucky me.* Before he took her so deep she couldn't remember her own name, she thumped him on the chest repeatedly until he acknowledged her.

His response came out with a growl. "Yes?"

"You asked me a question yesterday, and I want to give you my answer."

It saddened her to watch the shell fall into place over his eyes. His arms hardened around her. "You haven't had enough time to think."

"I have. And my answer is yes."

He scrutinized her face as though looking for any sign of doubt. "You're sure? You don't have to. I'll find another way—"

She placed a finger on his lips. "I'm positive. To show you I'm fully on board, Randolph Meryon, will you be my husband?"

His eyes widened, and he looked away. "I never..." He grunted. "I never expected to be on the receiving end of a Tallavan woman's marriage proposal."

"Don't you want to marry me?"

"I do." He flicked his gaze to hers and away again. "I can't explain it, but those words, when you asked, I had this visceral feeling that I should run. Far. And fast."

"Then I take it back."

"No." He snapped into eye contact with her again, his fingers tightening their hold. "I swore I'd never become a subservient Tallavan husband, cede power in a relationship to a woman. But that's not what's happening. I asked you. You asked me. We enter this marriage as equals. Yes, I'll marry you, Jen O'Malley."

Warm, muscular man covered her, kissing her to seal the commitment. Before she could be pulled under by his sexual allure, she spoke against his roving lips. "Sex isn't a panacea."

Lifted onto his elbows, he frowned at her. "Of course it isn't."

"We'll have to work at this…this marriage. It won't be easy."

"It won't, but if we remember to talk to one another, be honest with each other, we'll get through any rough patches."

"I hope so."

He nipped at her mouth while speaking. "Honesty…and lots…of sex." He leered at her. "It couldn't hurt."

The giggle had barely escaped her when he transitioned into full-bore plundering mode. What the man could do with his lips and teeth was utterly depraved. Every inch of her skin ached to receive his ministrations, to feel the sting of being bitten, especially her nipples, which were still tender.

Her body arched, pressing her breasts higher. At almost the same moment when he bit the dip in her waist, someone pounded on their door.

Randolph's head popped up. "What the fuck?"

Communicating through the thick slab of oak was impossible. Jen held her breath, hoping that whoever it was would go away. At a second round of pounding, Randolph rose and slipped on a pair of slacks. Jen pulled the sheet to her neck.

The conversation was indistinct, but she knew it was serious when Randolph turned with a look of concern on his face. "Sophie's missing."

Without a word Jen threw the sheet back, scrambled from the bed, and searched for her nightgown. When she found it, she pulled it on and dashed for the door. Randolph grabbed her arm. "They're searching the castle, but there's a lot of ground to cover. We'll start with the family rooms."

Jen's brow was wrinkled, and she was biting her lip. "All right. I think we should search the hidden passageway from the nursery. Sophie knows about it."

"Good idea. I'll start with the rooms on this corridor."

"You don't really believe she'd have left Briarcliff, do you?"

Randolph grimaced and lifted his shoulders. "Not a clue where she would go or why she would leave. We'll worry about whether she's gone outside after we look for her inside."

"Right." Jen went at a half run through the doorway of Randolph's room to the nursery and Sophie's bedroom. The secret entrance was shut. Upon pulling the concealed door open, the passage's interior loomed in darkness. *Damn. I need a hand light.*

She looked for the one in Sophie's bedside table, grabbed it, and stepped into the passage, shining the light along the shorter path where the remaining two children's bedrooms were. It was empty. Focusing the beam the other direction, she peered to the limits of its glow. Surely if Sophie were here, she'd have called out. But what if she'd been hurt and couldn't? Jen's stomach churned. *No. That's ridiculous. Stop thinking crazy.*

Working her way along the passageway, Jen stopped to look through each of the peepholes. None of them revealed the little girl. The remaining two rooms belonged to Penny and Claire. It took an extra tug to lift the panel covering the peephole to Penny's room. Relief flooded her when she saw Randolph sitting on the bed next to Sophie, who was curled up asleep. He was staring at her, his face working with emotion as though he were fighting back tears.

Jen slipped through the room's concealed door. His head came up, and she could see that, whatever he had been struggling with, a glint of determination ignited his eyes.

"She's sleeping," he whispered.

"Let's take her to her own room."

Sophie woke while he was slipping an arm beneath her shoulders. She rubbed her eyes. "Uncle Rand?"

"It's me, pumpkin. We were worried when we couldn't find you this morning in your bed."

In a burst of movement Sophie threw herself onto his lap, burrowing her head on his chest. "Oh! Uncle Rand. There was a ghost."

"A ghost?"

"In my room." Her body heaved halfway between a sob and a hiccup, and then the tears came. "In my room. In the dark. Granny Meryon's mad at me."

Jen sat beside them, easing her sore bottom down slowly while Randolph held Sophie tight, stroking her back. "There's no such things as ghosts. And Granny Meryon would never be mad at you."

"She is. That's why she came to my room. To scare me."

He glanced at Jen and lifted Sophie, sitting her sideways on his lap. "If Granny Meryon were a ghost, she'd love you every bit as much as everyone at Briarcliff does. Her ghost is just a story we tell to give ourselves the shivers. There is no ghost."

"But I saw her. A lady ghost. She was floating all over my room until she saw I was awake. I was so scared. I didn't move or anything. And then she left. Right out the door."

"You mean she floated through the door?"

Sophie made a face. "No. She opened it, went out, and shut it."

"Well, there you go." Randolph tugged a strand of her hair. "A ghost would have gone straight through. It was probably a maid checking on you."

Did Genevieve Kavan get in the house again? Staff were being extra careful to lock the doors, so it didn't seem likely.

Sophie's lower lip trembled. "It really looked like a ghost."

"I'm sure it did," Randolph said. "How did you end up in your mother's room?"

"I couldn't stay in mine. What if Granny Meryon came back? So I ran to Mommy's. I thought maybe she'd come back as a ghost and make Granny Meryon leave me alone."

"That was a sensible idea." Randolph's expression grew stern. "But you scared us all this morning when we couldn't find you."

"I'm sorry."

"Well, now you know there are no ghosts. Next time you get frightened at night, you come find me or Miss Jen in my room. Okay."

"Okay." Sophie glanced between Randolph and Jen before addressing her. "Are you going to ask Uncle Rand to marry you?"

"Do you think I should?"

"Cook and Mrs. Polgrey think you should."

Jen chuckled. "Do they? Well, you're the first we've told. Yes. We're getting married."

"That's good. Uncle Rand needs someone to make him happy. And now he'll stay at Briarcliff forever," Sophie said with an owlish expression.

The look on Randolph's face wasn't encouraging. His lips pressed together as though he were about to grimace. When Jen touched his hand, he refused to make eye contact with her.

Claire burst into the room. Her voice was full of emotion. "You found her. Oh, thank heaven!" She rushed to the bed and knelt beside Randolph, reaching for Sophie, who slid into her arms. "*Alanna*, you worried us so. We didn't know where you were." Claire kissed Sophie's forehead and admonished the little girl. "You must never leave your room at night without telling someone."

Face buried against her grandmother, Sophie began to cry.

"Don't cry, *alanna*." Claire petted Sophie. "I'm going to take her and put her back to bed. I think we both could use some cuddle time." Claire rose and took Sophie by the hand.

"I'm sorry. I should have been in the nursery…" Jen bit her lip.

Claire looked at Randolph, her gaze searching. "I can have a maid move into the nursery. Mary seemed to enjoy it before. But you'll still be responsible for Sophie during the day."

"Good idea, Mother." Randolph caught Jen's hand. "I plan to visit the priest and see about arrangements."

Sophie's chin lifted. "They're getting married, Grandma. I was the first to know."

A broad smile broke across Claire's face. "Wonderful news. We'll have to help with wedding plans." She led Sophie, chattering about pretty dresses and flowers, from the room.

Jen followed Randolph back to his bedroom. *I suppose it will be our bedroom now.* Her body seemed to have grown heavy, starting with her stomach. *Probably the effect of the adrenaline rush wearing off. Still...* Was she doing the right thing? When she'd decided, it had all seemed so clear, so obvious. Randolph had almost scowled when Sophie said he'd stay at Briarcliff forever. That wasn't his plan, and she should keep that in mind. This wasn't a love match. But it did involve a child, one whom she would essentially be parenting. Had she truly taken the time to consider such a life-changing decision? Some might say she hadn't. Certainly her mother would oppose the step she was taking. In the end Sophie needed her, and she needed Sophie. Someone to love unconditionally. It wasn't any different than if she'd discovered she was pregnant. A surprise, but one she would welcome and make the most of. She'd deal with life as Sophie's adoptive mother no matter what it brought. As for Randolph, if he was part of that life, then she'd handle that too. It would be his choice, because as things stood, she wanted him to want her for more than a play partner.

THE PARSONAGE WAS SET back to the right of the Briarcliff chapel. A covered walkway connected it to the church, a side entry that allowed the priest access to the sacristy. Father James swung the door open, gave Randolph a welcoming smile, and continued drying his hands on the dish towel he was holding.

"Please come in. I was tidying up after lunch." He motioned for Randolph to enter. "My study is this way."

Randolph remembered the parsonage well. When he was a boy, he'd spent hours being tutored by Father Wilson in the faith. The elderly priest had been thin and ascetic, like a dried leaf ready to crumble. His lessons hadn't been any livelier. Randolph followed Father James, who was a heartier man, watching as the priest removed the white kitchen apron he'd been wearing.

At the door to the study Father James gestured and said, "Have a seat. Would you like tea or coffee? Your mother pampers me with real coffee beans."

"Coffee would be fine. Black."

"Right. Back in a jiff."

Two large, comfortable chairs occupied one end of the room, a small walnut table separating them. Randolph settled into the nearest one. The study he remembered had been transformed into a much more relaxed space, the icons of a suffering Christ and martyred saints that had scared him when he was young replaced by pastoral scenes and a picture of Jesus as the Good Shepherd.

Father James returned, carrying two blue-flowered ceramic mugs. He set one on a coaster and slid it toward Randolph before easing into the other chair. After both men had had the opportunity to drink and appreciate the hot brew, Father James said, "I'm glad you took the time to drop in. I'm sure you've been puzzled by the changes in Penny, especially since I heard you've been named Sophie's guardian in Penny's will."

The mug he held warmed Randolph's fingers. Funny how little things could be so soothing. And yet his stomach roiled, and his mind was in turmoil. Perhaps it was the fact he hadn't been to confession since... It had been decades. Here he sat with a priest, and all the old religious habits of his childhood were clamoring to be brought back from rusty disuse. But he wasn't here to seek absolution. Insight maybe. If anyone might be suited to listen to an outpouring of life's upheavals, it was this man who seemed the personification of tender pastoral care. Certainly Penny had deemed him to be a trustworthy advisor.

"I would like to talk about Penny, but first I need to ask you if you'd be willing to conduct a wedding today. Miss O'Malley has proposed, and I have accepted."

The priest's eyebrows rose. "Congratulations. I would be delighted to marry you. Is Miss O'Malley Reformed Catholic?"

One finger tapping against his mug, Randolph said, "Thank you. No, Jen is not Reformed Catholic. She was raised in the Mother Goddess tradition."

"Not a problem. The civil service is lovely. May I assume you'll have the proper documentation?"

Randolph pressed his lips together before responding. "Already taken care of before I came by."

Brow furrowed, Father James took a sip from his mug. "If I may, you don't seem at ease with your nuptials. I gather you're marrying to provide a mother for Sophie."

"Yes." Randolph ran a hand through his hair. "As you said, Penny made me Sophie's guardian in her will."

"That's a big responsibility."

"It is. But I've decided it's my duty to do so. It will mean spending time on Tallav, which I haven't done for years. My business is on Beta Tau, but it's grown so large, I'm not as hands-on in the day-to-day operation as I used to be." A week every quarter away from the Whip Hand was doable. If he expanded, opened the new venue he'd been considering, he'd need to hand off much of what he did anyway. Selina's business encompassed everything this side of the Sympallan Drift, yet she was home most of the time.

"Change is always difficult."

"Hmm."

Both men sat silently drinking coffee for several moments before Father James said, "Penny came home to Briarcliff for Sophie's sake. They had lived in Cahernamon or visiting other estates until Penny had an epiphany. Sophie wanted to know why she didn't have a father like other children. Her birthday was coming, and she asked for one as a present."

Randolph smiled softly. "That sounds like Sophie."

Father James chuckled and nodded his head. "Yes. Long story short, Penny decided she'd stolen Sophie's family from her, and she set about making that right. She moved home and eventually began reconsidering her reactions and opinions about past events."

"It's hard to imagine Penny sharing all this with you. She was a dyed-in-the-wool atheist."

"Oh my, was she ever." The priest laughed and took another swallow from his mug. "I'm not really sure how it came about, but we became sparring buddies. She'd visit me, and I'd do my best to refute the fallacies in her positions, religious and political. Eventually we got onto more personal subjects, and along the way she had a change of heart. Her matriarchal beliefs were the first to go. But one day she told me she wanted to return to the Reformed Catholic faith."

"You're probably the only man ever to change her mind."

"Oh, I don't believe I was responsible for that. I presented facts, and she changed her own mind. Your sister was an intellectual of superior ability who came to realize that the heart played an equally relevant part in the life well lived."

"I see."

"Her plan was to reunite your family. You. Your father and mother. To bring you together so that Sophie could experience the kind of childhood you and she had at Briarcliff. She would be pleased that you have agreed to become Sophie's guardian. And that you are marrying and perhaps settling down." The priest gave Randolph a querying expression.

Randolph narrowed his eyebrows. "It's the settling down that I question. I enjoy being here with Sophie, my mother, and Jen. Briarcliff is every bit as nostalgic for me as it was for Penny. But I must return to Beta Tau, and I fear the pull to return to Tallav will wane the longer I stay away." And that was the crux of the matter. He'd never been a one-woman man, taking pleasure from the club subs and the groupies who claimed to be auditioning for a role at the Whip Hand. Would he grow tired of Jen? How would that affect the family unit he was forming?

"I understand your concern. By marrying today, you'll be making a considerable commitment. I assumed this was not a love match but one of expediency. If you are both honest about your expectations for the future, you can work through the changes together. Many marriages of convenience turn into love matches, especially if the pair is sexually compatible."

Randolph smiled thoughtfully. "There's no problem with that. If I'd ever taken the time to consider marrying, Jen is the epitome of the woman I would choose." That was the gods' honest truth. "The difficulty rests entirely with me. It's damn embarrassing for me to vacillate the way I have over this. I'm normally decisive. Make up my mind and that's that."

"It's been a matter of days. I wavered for two years before finally entering seminary." Father James set his cup down and shifted in his chair to face Randolph directly. "You seem to be as thoughtful as your sister. Doing right by Sophie and your new wife will require sacrifice, but I think you'll be up to whatever is needed of you."

"I hope so. I'll do my best."

"Now, let's discuss the particulars of the ceremony."

THIS WAS IT. She, Jen O'Malley, was marrying Randolph Meryon, the owner and sadist-in-chief of the most famous kink club in the sector and a pariah on his home planet, Tallav. What would Evaline Braddock say after all her warnings? Nothing Jen needed to hear. If you took the BDSM out of the equation, Randolph was no worse and, in many ways, better than the average Tallavan aristocrat looking for a wife to support them in a life of leisure.

She supposed she was blessed to be impoverished. That type of man didn't come near her. Marriage hadn't been in her future. The O'Malleys would have paid for her artificial insemination with medically verified female-gene-carrying sperm. But she wanted her child to have a father. One who wanted a family as much as she did.

Therein lay the crux of any unease she felt about Randolph. She had no doubt he would support her, even promising to make her financially secure if they divorced in a few years. With those funds she could set herself up and find someone who shared her interests. Other than sado-masochism, Jen wasn't sure what else she had in common with Randolph.

Sophie. They both loved Sophie. It wasn't hard to love the little straw-berry blonde with her bright personality. Jen wouldn't abandon the child. Divorce wasn't an option. If she were to have children anytime soon, Randolph would be the father. They probably should have discussed this, but it was too late now. For good or bad she was marrying the man in... She checked her internal clock. Five minutes.

Her reflection in the mirror stared back at her. Somehow Claire had found the perfect pale blue silk dress. The sleeves were sheer with tiny flowers embroidered in silver and navy. The fitted bodice ended at her natural waist over a flared skirt, all overlaid with the same fabric of the sleeves. Claire's personal maid had curled, pinned, and poofed her hair into a sculptured work of art and applied her makeup. She was like Cinderella, except that she'd already caught the handsome prince's atten-tion and was on her way to wed him.

Claire popped her head in the door. "It's time. Are you ready?"

"I am." Jen smiled at her reflection.

Sunlight filtered through mullioned panes on the main stairs, dimming as they followed the dark-paneled central hall where it reappeared in a late afternoon glow from the tall windows of the conservatory. Randolph stood, enigmatic in a navy evening suit. His gaze pierced her, but it was impossible to tell what he was thinking. He held his hand out to her, so she slipped her fingers across his palm. The gentle squeeze he gave them bolstered her.

His mother stopped before stepping through the door to the terrace beyond. "Smile, you two. This is a happy occasion."

Jen couldn't help but grin, although Randolph's smile seemed forced. He pulled her to face him. "Last chance. You don't have to do this. You don't have to take on my family's problems. Your standing in society will be harmed by associating yourself with me. I'll understand if you've changed your mind."

"I haven't." She pressed his hand tight. "I know what I'm doing and what I'm taking on. But there are benefits to this match. I become a permanent part of an adorable little girl's life. I gain a new family who will be far more loyal than my own. And I have you to warm my bed whenever you come to Briarcliff. The gains exceed the drawbacks. Besides, I don't give a fig about society." She snapped her fingers.

Randolph grinned at her. This time a fully authentic expression. "Me either. Let's go create a scandal." He took her hand, placed it in the crook of his elbow, and led her out the conservatory door to her new life.

14

The sun had set, and lanterns spread a warm glow across the large cobbled courtyard. After a sumptuous wedding feast, the family and the few guests that had been invited left the newlywed couple to enjoy the evening on the terrace alone. Together they sat on one of the many settees arranged under an overhanging balcony. Trellises overloaded with an entire growing season's worth of flowering vines perfumed the night air.

The ceremony had been conducted in front of the large plinth of stone that bore a relief carving of the Meryon coat of arms. It was comprised of a shield with three birds walking up an angled stripe. Tigers supported either side, and it was topped by a flowering vine and a helmet with a peacock tail for a crest.

Jen wondered how much of a stretch it had been to claim it. Without a doubt it was an historical ancient Irish coat of arms. But most of the first families on Tallav could not prove they were of Irish ancestry. Some had even changed their names, placing themselves into the lineage of famous Irish women. Her own family had assumed the name O'Malley in veneration of the infamous Irish pirate queen Grace O'Malley.

So much tradition, but beyond the scandal of an O'Malley marrying a brute like Randolph Meryon, this wedding had flouted many other Tallavan traditions. Although there was a Reformed Catholic priest conducting the ceremony, he had performed the common Federation civil joining service. Rather than the man joining the woman's family, as was customary on Tallav, she had become a Meryon. They'd walked together down the aisle instead of the usual presentation of the groom for the bride's acceptance. Jen couldn't imagine Randolph kneeling and requesting that she take him to wed and promising to serve her all his days. She turned her gaze to study his face. Not the Randolph she knew and was growing to care about. He was rubbing his chin with one finger, frowning slightly.

She brushed her fingers down his shirtsleeve, glad he'd removed his coat and she could feel the muscles in his arm. "What is it?"

"Hmmm?" He dropped his hand into his lap and looked at her.

"Is something wrong? You were frowning."

"Oh. Nothing's wrong. I was wondering why there was a lump in this cushion."

Jen ran her hand behind him to see if she could discover the problem. "Scoot forward." When he did, she tested the seat. "There is a lump. I wonder what it is."

Randolph lifted the edge of cushion. "Stand up." With Jen out of the way, he raised it farther. "It's a book." He picked it up and leafed through several pages. "It's Penny's diary." Clasping the book to his chest, he reached out and shook Jen's shoulder. "We've found the missing diary. I've been wanting to read this…" He pulled her into a hug and then kissed her.

"I can't believe it's been out here all this time."

His expression fell. "She must have left it here when the boy came to tell her about the lamb. Shoved it under the cushion and never came back."

"Rand." Jen stroked his cheek. "Let's not think about that now. This day is about beginnings."

He pulled her tight and pressed his lips to her forehead. "You're right. There's plenty of time for this tomorrow. Tonight is for you and me." His mouth traced a path down to her ear. "Shall we go to bed? I understand it's traditional to consummate a marriage. That's one convention I don't intend to flout."

The instant she nodded her agreement, he grabbed her hand and rushed her across the terrace and through the conservatory door. "Why are we running?"

He leered over his shoulder. "I find I'm eager to teach you more of the joys of sadomasochism."

Out of breath by the time they arrived in their room, Jen allowed Randolph to strip her from her clothes. When she was fully undressed, he clasped her torso between his hands, lifted her, and tossed her into the center of the bed. He pulled his shoes off and removed his shirt, all the while staring at her with eyes that seemed lit with an inner flame.

A shiver ran through her. How had this intoxicating man become hers? It couldn't be the Mother Goddess bestowing a blessing on her. Randolph Meryon was a minion of darkness. The blessed Mother would never send her daughter to such a fiend. But he wasn't a fiend. If he were finally set free, healed from all the pain that beset him, how would that change him? And what would that mean for their relationship?

Having discovered she had a masochist hidden inside herself, she'd prefer Randolph retain his sadistic urges. Urges he was about to unleash on her. He climbed onto the bed on his hands and knees and prowled his way forward like a sleek cat ready to pounce on her. Panther? Mountain lion? When he sank his teeth into the spot where her neck met her shoulder, the type of cat didn't matter. He was hers, and he would bring her pain and pleasure in equal measure, claiming her as his own.

His breath caressed her earlobe, and his voice held a hint of a growl. "I'm going to bury myself balls-deep in you tonight and fuck you until you melt."

A moan, coiling inside her, spun up and past her lips. "Please do."

He nibbled and bit his way down her body, finding new erogenous spots that had never existed until this man took control of her pleasure. His chest brushed across her nipples, sending tiny zings to her clit that became bright sparks when he applied his teeth to each aroused bud. Two fistfuls of his hair clenched tight in her hands, she arched into him.

He stroked his tongue along the bottom of her breast and muttered, "So fucking perfect." He brought his head up and gazed at her with molten chocolate eyes. "I want you to scream for me."

Jen tensed. *What's he going to do?* The thought had no more than flashed through her mind when an avid, hungry smile lit his face. The next moment he took hold of her elbows, rubbing his thumb on the inside of the joint, and brought his lips back to her nipple. She'd been expecting him to do something painful to her breasts, but he merely sucked the tip into his mouth, working it until she was pushing into him again. And then he dug his thumbs into the bends of her arms. The pain was instant and intense. She cried out.

"You can do better than that."

The reapplied pressure struck the already angry nerve endings, and this time she did scream, a wailing shriek. Her body shook when he released her and lifted himself above her on his knees. His fingers flew as he unbuckled his belt, opened his slacks, and slid them down his hips. He wasn't wearing underwear, so his erection popped out, long and thick.

"You make me so fucking hard. Feel that." He thumped his penis on her stomach. "That's because of you. Take it."

He grabbed her hand and placed it on his cock, moving it with his, stroking his length. "This is the prize you win if you please me. Do you know how to please me?"

Through the haze of arousal she managed a response. "Scream?"

"That's one way." He leered at her. "Don't hold back. Let me know what you feel. I want to share your pain."

Something shifted inside her. Up to this point she'd been passive, aiming to satisfy him. His challenge had stirred the aggressive part of her that she kept under lock and key. She showed him her teeth, not so much in a smile but a feral expression of agreement. "All right." She flexed her fingers. "Bring it on. But if it isn't your A game, you can expect me to communicate that as well."

His gaze heated. "Damn straight." He stood from the bed and shed his pants. One hand stroking his cock, he stared at her.

"Spread your legs."

A few moments passed while he continued to focus his penetrating gaze on her.

"Pull your knees to your chest."

She smirked at him. "Like what you see?"

"Touch yourself."

"Here?" She teased a nipple, staring at his eyes, which were locked on to her breast.

"Pussy too."

His gaze dropped to where she stroked her clit with the fingers of her other hand. Pre-cum leaked from the tip of his swollen cock. He gritted his teeth in a fierce expression of hunger. Slowly he crept up the bed until, on hands and knees, his face was poised over her.

He yanked her hand away and brought his mouth to her sex. He lapped at her, his tongue vibrating from his rumbling groan. "You taste like heaven." Two of his fingers plunged inside her vagina, setting a brutal yet exquisite pace. She arched to meet him. Every part of her was fully focused on the upward spiral he was goading her along. He teased her nub, stroking, tapping, and sucking until her legs were shaking with the need to orgasm.

"Now. Come for me now." His fingers curled with each stroke, hitting her in the perfect spot. Then he bit her clit. The intense explosion that followed was like a giant firework, zooming up and up until it burst in a brilliant multicolor blossom that continued to rain sparkles down as his tongue milked every last drop from her release.

He crawled up her, lavishing the nerve endings in her skin with the touch of hot-blooded, sensuous male. He Interlaced his fingers with hers, pushing her hands into the bed. The hard length of him was trapped between their thighs. He lifted, repositioning himself, and surged home.

"Yes." The word was little more than a hiss as it slipped between her lips. Nothing in the world compared to the sensation of being filled by Randolph Meryon. The frenzied pace of thrust and retreat he set forced her to latch on to him with her legs, locking her ankles behind his flexing buttocks. At this moment she was the center of his universe, with the power to make his whole body shudder with voracious erotic need. She smiled her triumph, free to drown in his carnal rampage.

His voice was guttural in its intensity. "I want you to come on my cock." And she discovered that his wish was quite literally her command. Release hit her, the muscles of her legs tightening around him, her pussy spasming around an erection that had grown so hard it seemed to slice through her.

Rand jerked, spilling inside her in repeated spasms. When he fell still, she was a puddle beneath him. He'd said he would melt her, and he had.

It had been thirty-seven hours since the wedding. Randolph had woken the day after to a flurry of activity, preparations for the trip to the city and the guardianship hearing. Discussion of strategy with his mother and their lawyers had taken most of the time on the shuttle trip to Cahernamon. After they arrived in the city, Selena offered Randolph the use of her communications suite at the House of Shirley, the headquarters for her fashion empire. He'd gladly accepted and spent the last half of the afternoon vid conferencing with various members of his staff on Beta Tau and negotiating a lease on property where he hoped to open a new venue. The terms were still not to his liking, but they were getting closer to a workable solution. When he sat down to supper, he'd had a headache and gone to bed early, brusquely rejecting Jen's attempt to snuggle.

The throbbing in his temples had never eased completely. This morning when he dragged himself from bed, it had reasserted itself. He rubbed at the spot where the pain pulsed and glanced at Jen, who was seated next to him at the breakfast table.

She held her hand out to him, a round tablet on her palm. "Take this. You look like you need it."

Randolph grunted and took the med. "Thanks, I do."

"Is everything okay on Beta Tau?" his mother asked. "You never said last night."

"Yeah. Everything's fine. I've had this headache since then." He popped the pill into his mouth and washed it down with a swallow of *aguya* juice, the tart flavor making his salivary glands kick in.

Claire pursed her lips and gave him an assessing look. "It's probably tension. I'm feeling it myself."

"Maybe." The telltale for an incoming urgent comm signaled via his EBC. He winced; the internal beep did nothing for the ache in his skull. "Pardon me. I need to take this message."

His mother's brow had furrowed. "I have one too."

After listening to it, he waited for his mother to finish with hers. When she brought her gaze to his, he asked, "I assume you received the same information I just did?"

"Yes. That was Edward. But I don't think this will change anything."

"How can it not."

"What's happened?" Jen shifted her gaze between Claire and Randolph, finally settling it on him.

Gritting his teeth, he clenched his fist. He shoved back from the table, stood, and began pacing. His mother watched him, her fingers clutching the string of pearls around her neck. She darted a look at Jen before returning her gaze to her son. "There's been a change in today's hearing. A new judge will be taking over the case."

"Severine O'Malley." He glared at Jen.

She gasped and brought her hand to her mouth. O'Malleys were generously sprinkled throughout the government, but Severine was known in her own right as a severe conservative matriarchist. Although they were some kind of second cousins, Jen had never had to deal with her one-on-one.

Claire rapped the table with a knuckle. "It changes nothing. All parties have signed off on the agreement. Judges rarely, if ever, go against the recommendations of the caseworker and Child Protective Services."

The pounding in his head had grown worse despite the pill he'd taken. He shoved his chair in and headed toward the door.

"Rand, sit down and finish your breakfast," his mother said.

"I'm not hungry. I'm going to grab my jacket and walk to the courthouse. I'll see you there."

Jen rose and said, "I'll come with you."

He barked his response. "No."

Her eyes widened, and she rocked back.

It took effort to soften his voice. "No. I need some time alone, to think."

The tremulous smile that lifted her lips made his throat feel thick. He averted his gaze and left, ignoring when his mother called his name again.

The jacket he'd planned to wear today was hanging from the clothes butler. He slipped into it, rolling his shoulders. Long strides carried him out of the apartment and onto the street. He glowered at the beautiful autumn day that met him. Brilliant blue sky and the splendor of the mixed greens, yellows, and oranges of the trees lining the parkway did little to brighten his mood.

Fuck! At every critical juncture of his life a woman had wrenched happiness from him. Why did it surprise him that yet again his future was to be determined by a female? He'd left Tallav to get away from this very thing, and still he'd allowed his mother to suck him into this fool's charade.

A right turn placed him on the avenue that led to Judicial Square. Even from this distance he could see the governmental buildings devoted to adjudicating the laws of Tallav. Other squares followed it, each dedicated to some aspect of the official Tallavan state. When he'd been a child, he'd gone on tours of the capitol's historic sites. The judicial buildings had stood like hulking guardians surrounding a tall pink marble statue of Lady Justice, the focal point of the formally landscaped courtyard at the center of the square.

He had thought Lady Justice looked pretty and kind and absorbed the lesson that in the past it was believed she should be blindfolded, to show she held no favorites in her decision making. But on Tallav, she had no blindfold because her vision was always clear and able to see to the heart of any matter, making her capable of wise and proper decisions.

Justice wasn't blind on Tallav, nor was it wise unless wisdom meant following the dictates of the majority's political beliefs. He stopped in his tracks. *I'd better tell Shane and Maon not to bother coming.* Character witnesses were pointless. He moved to one side of the pavement and opened a comm link with his EBC to Shane.

When Shane accepted the comm, Randolph said, "Hey. It's me."

"Yeah. I'm on my way. Adrianna can't make it. Doctor told her no more long-distance travel, so she's stuck at Gleann Milis until after the baby arrives."

"No big deal. I was calling to tell you not to worry about coming. They swapped judges. The hearing is in front of Severine O'Malley."

"Fuck."

"Yeah. So don't bother. I'm not sure she'd listen to the Mother Goddess if she showed up on my behalf."

"I'll be there anyway. Maon and Selina will too. If things hit the shitter, you can create a bigger stink with a couple of decorated Tallavan marshals and a celebrity like Selina at your back."

Randolph straightened his shoulders. "You're right. I shouldn't let this get to me. Mother says the lawyers have this thing sewed up tight. O'Malley would be going against the advice of everyone who has any input on this case. She tries that, and we'll hit her with a reclamation pool of crappy publicity."

"Fucking straight!"

"See you there. And thanks."

THE LAYOUT of every governmental office in Cahernamon was familiar to Jen. She'd spent the last several legislative sessions running errands for Lavinia O'Malley. Claire had been eager to find Randolph, so she had accepted Jen's offer to take Sophie to the children's waiting room. The child advocate assigned to Sophie had already been there and promised to stay with Sophie throughout the proceedings, including if the judge wished to speak with Sophie in private. It was what Jen had expected, but the confirmation was reassuring. The woman got on well with Sophie and seemed firm in her commitment to making the process easier on the little girl. The idea of Sophie being quizzed by Severine O'Malley was chilling. Very few people would be comfortable encountering Severine face-to-face, much less alone.

She was just in time to join Randolph and Claire before the courtroom doors were opened for the morning session. Maon Shirley, Selina Shirley, and Shane Tiernan had joined them. Both marshals were in dress uniforms. Jen slid her hand into Randolph's, easing up beside him.

"Thanks for coming. I really appreciate it," said Randolph.

Shane and Maon, arms crossed over their chests and eyebrows pulled down, nodded. Selina was rubbing Randolph's shoulder. As one their gazes focused on Jen, and Selina said, "This must be your new wife."

Randolph slipped his hand from Jen's and put an arm around her. "This is Jen. Formerly O'Malley. Now Meryon. Jen, these are my best friends, minus one who is home expecting a baby." He gestured to each.

"Maon and Selina Shirley. Shane Tiernan. His wife Adrianna is on their estate, what, seven and a half months pregnant?"

Shane stretched his hand out, a warm smile on his face. "Yeah, she looks ready to pop, but she's still got some time. Nice to meet you, Jen."

When he released her, she was swept into a hug by Maon, followed by another less effusive hug from Selina. "If you ever need anything, comm us. We're happy to help."

The greeting left her a little breathless. She wasn't accustomed to first family heirs and their spouses taking notice of her, let alone making her welcome into their inner circle. "Thank you." She edged closer to Randolph, relieved when the conversation returned to discussion of the hearing.

The two lawyers who would oversee their case today arrived and greeted them. "We're first on the docket," said Stephen.

"I don't expect this to take long," Edward said. "It should be open and shut. All the paperwork has been filed and all the participants in determining the appropriateness of placing guardianship of Sophie with Randolph and his wife"—he dipped his head at Jen—"have signed off on the agreement. The judge just has to put her stamp of approval on it."

"But will she?" Randolph's voice sounded grim.

"There's every reason to believe she will. If Child Protective Services have found you suitable, the judge would need to show justification for deciding against them. To do otherwise would give you a good chance of overturning her decision on appeal." He rubbed his hands together. "We're about to find out." He gestured toward the courtroom. "Shall we?"

Randolph led Jen to the section of seating reserved for petitioners and interested parties. Their group filled two rows. Others filed into the rows behind them.

A young woman entered the room from a door at the back and called those assembled to order. At her directive for all to rise, Jen stood. The judge was announced, and Severine O'Malley entered, climbed the steps to the judge's seat, and settled herself before scanning the ranks of those who were facing her.

Severine O'Malley was a petite woman, slightly plump, with ash-blonde hair cut in a wavy bob. Her black judicial robe was complemented by a white lace collar and a glimmering strand of the finest pearls. Her appearance made it hard to imagine she was the terror of the Tallavan judiciary. But she was known for sifting people for all their faults with her penetrating gaze. Her questioning had been compared to mental vivisection.

The bailiff called them forward, and they took their places at the petitioners' table, Edward and Steven positioned as bookends. When the bailiff finished reading the petition, Edward rose to address the bench.

Severine glared at him. "I don't need to hear from you. Sit down." Then she focused her attention on Randolph. Her scrutiny didn't seem to affect him. He met her gaze with his own, and Jen was certain the hard chocolate shell hid any emotions he was feeling. Severine sniffed and brought her fierce inspection to Jen. The urge to look away was strong. Beneath the table, Randolph took her hand and squeezed. *Damnation. This bitch isn't going to screw with my head.* Grabbing hold of her newfound confidence, she turned her own gaze to assessing the judge. Severine O'Malley was the same self-important, emotionally sterile termagant as every high-ranking O'Malley she'd ever had the displeasure to meet, each trapped in a worldview based on animosity. True happiness was lost to them.

"Ms. O'Malley, it is your intention to marry the petitioner Randolph Meryon and become guardian to Sophie Meryon?"

"Yes, your honor. Mr. Meryon and I were married two days ago."

Severine pursed her lips and drummed her fingers on the desk before her. "It's a good thing I was asked by the head of the O'Malley family to look into this case. They were concerned that your interests were not being addressed adequately since they were not allowed access to petition files." She glared at Edward and then Stephen before returning her piercing gaze to Jen.

"Mr. Meryon's lawyers have created a loophole in the agreement. A clause that would allow Mr. Meryon an uncontested divorce after three years of marriage, voiding your guardianship of the child."

She turned her basilisk expression on Randolph. "Mr. Meryon, it is the responsibility of this court to assure that whoever becomes Sophie Meryon's guardian, they are upstanding, moral citizens. You fail that requirement. However, in deference to your sister's wishes, a co-guardianship has been negotiated. It is not my inclination to side against a first family's requests. I cannot understand why your mother isn't the petitioner before me, but since she is not, I must ameliorate your influence on the child.

"Ms. O'Malley, I commend you for stepping forward to oversee the raising of Sophie Meryon. Her mother was the voice of the matriarchal party for many years, and dear to our hearts. The beliefs she espoused must play a primary role in the child's education. That you have managed to insinuate yourself into that role is an accomplishment your family will not forget. But it cannot be a temporary task. As I'm sure you understand, you will need to be a part of the child's life until she is of age."

Her next statements were addressed to the court clerk. "To that end I'm amending the agreement. Strike the divorce clause. Add the following: Primary guardianship is granted to Jen O'Malley with Randolph—"

The clerk interrupted. "Jen Meryon."

The judge raised an eyebrow.

"Her name is now Jen Meryon."

Severine squinted at Jen and then returned her gaze to the clerk. "Jen Meryon with Randolph Meryon as secondary guardian. Physical custody is to remain with the primary guardian at all times. In the event of a divorce, the secondary guardian will be removed from guardianship and full guardianship granted to the primary guardian."

When she brought her gaze back to Jen, there was a glimmer of the much-feared curiosity in her eyes. "Congratulations, Ms. Meryon. You have taken on a tremendous responsibility. This court will follow your progress with avid interest." She rapped her gavel on the desk. "Next."

To say she was stunned would be an understatement. While it was true she planned to remain in Sophie's life as long as Randolph allowed it, she had never thought to take the power of planning her future from him. Beside her, Edward was speaking with Randolph, but their words made no sense to her. Her ears were buzzing.

"Are you all right?" Stephen asked, placing a hand on her shoulder.

"I'm...fine. A little dazed. Is there no way we can change the decree? I'm not supposed to be primary guardian. If anyone should—"

Randolph took her other arm in a tight grip and levered her out of her seat. "Come on. Let's get out of here." He briskly forced her to walk to where the others were rising to accompany them from the courtroom and then out the solid oak door to the passageway beyond.

A quick glance at Randolph's expression told Jen all she needed to know. The hard chocolate candy shell she'd seen before had transformed to a steel barrier. He had locked his thoughts down and was blocking anyone from gaining access to his emotions. Damnation. He didn't believe she'd infiltrated his family to take Sophie from them. He couldn't. But inside an empty hollow formed in her stomach. He could and would, adding her to the list of women who had turned on him. Then he would leave for Beta Tau and never return. Somehow she had to stop him from fleeing. The explosion that resulted would be terrifying, but for all their sakes, she had to break the cycle of betrayal.

15

Outside the hearing room Randolph's family and friends clustered together discussing the proceedings. Maon thumped Randolph on the back. "Congratulations. You're now officially Sophie's guardian."

Randolph grimaced. "Secondary guardian. It's Tallav. Women never release the reins of power."

"Now dear." Claire hugged Randolph and pressed a kiss to his cheek. "It's not quite what we hoped for, but in practice it will be just the same."

"How do you know that? Jen could take Sophie out of this courthouse today, and we'd never see her again. That's the control that vile bitch gave our dear nanny. We were set up, Mother. Or can't you grasp that?"

To his left Jen gasped. Her eyes went wide, and her face drained of color. What did she expect? That he'd be jumping for joy that she'd insinuated—that was the word Severine O'Malley had used—herself into his family and manipulated him into marrying her. On the surface it had all looked proper. But underneath it was corrupt. He'd been prepared for Jen, as his wife, to hold authority over him on Tallav. But that wasn't supposed to include Sophie. At least his business and money were all off world.

"Language!" Claire frowned at him. "I know you're upset, but once you calm down, you'll realize that everything is fine."

Just like his mother to want to paper over the truth with false harmony. The indifference he'd always worn as a suit of armor against emotional attacks settled back into place. He'd been discarding it piece by piece since returning to Tallav, but that had been a mistake, leaving him vulnerable. The pain slamming through him was the inevitable result. Once again he was betrayed by a woman, and his own mother wanted him to acquiesce to the deed. "Thank you for your support, Mother. I have business to conduct before we leave the city. I'll meet you at the shuttle." With that he strode down the hall, gesturing with his head for his friends to follow him.

When Shane caught up to him, he said, "Not so fast. You're making Selina run in three-inch heels."

Randolph turned and stepped into an alcove to wait for the others. "Sorry, Selina."

"If I could change anything about myself, I'd add nine inches. I can't compete with long-legged men." She laughed. Maon caressed her arm, his devotion writ large across his features.

A burning sensation took up residence in Randolph's chest. To think he'd been sucked into imagining he might form a relationship with Jen like the one Selina and Maon shared. *I'm a damn fool.*

"What are you going to do?" asked Shane.

Here was a true friend. Shane didn't mess around with platitudes or expressions of sympathy. No, he got right to the point. Randolph looked at the tall, dark-haired marshal with the piercing blue eyes, a man fully prepared to help in whatever way he could. A man. Reliable.

"I've already instructed Edward to work on overthrowing the decree and granting full guardianship to my mother. That's what we should have done from the beginning. None of this would have happened if we'd stuck to the logical, Tallavan thing to do."

His friends acknowledged his statement, and Selina said, "I can ask my personal lawyer, Belinda Stacey, to assist Edward. Belinda has done a lot of pro bono work on behalf of men's rights. She's on the board of Equality for All, the group that made it possible for Edward to practice law. Even though it would be a difficult case for a male lawyer to win, she could help him restore the agreement to its original conditions."

"Thanks. The time for that has passed. I let myself get sucked into my mother and sister's fantasy. It was a mistake."

Selina had been pressing forward, ready to interrupt him; instead she settled back on her heals, looking pained. She and Shane's wife, Adrianna, were the exceptions that proved the rule. Women were not to be trusted. He was grateful his friends had found such staunch, atypical females, but such was not to be his lot. Better he accepted what he'd always known to be true and get back to spending life as he had intended.

Maon broke the silence that had fallen over the group. "Audrina and I are planning on taking the kids to Gleann Milis tomorrow."

Selina quirked a smile and leaned into Maon when he slipped his arm around her waist. "My mom wants to mother Adrianna."

"We'd be happy to take Sophie with us. You could leave her here now," Maon said.

That might be a good idea, but fuck, he'd have to ask for Jen's approval. Sophie was supposed to be in Jen's custody at all times, but that couldn't mean Sophie couldn't visit friends. "How long?"

One hand rubbing the top of his head, Maon said, "One or two weeks. Not really sure. It depends on how long it takes for my rowdy brood to get the boot."

Randolph grimaced at a fresh stab of pain and looked down the corridor, gritting his teeth, then returned his gaze to Maon. "I expect we'll need to return to Briarcliff first. We didn't pack for a long trip."

"We can pick Sophie up tomorrow."

"All right. I'll clear it with Jen." His lip curled.

Maon's brow wrinkled. "It'll give you time to set things straight with her."

"Oh, I intend to."

The glances that ricocheted between his friends weren't lost on Randolph. "Don't worry. I have no intention of harming her. I'm not going to leave myself open to a charge of battery. But I do need to get a whip." Jen was going to discover his skill with a whip went far beyond the ability to crack it.

Shane crossed his arms over his chest. "Don't do anything stupid."

Stone-faced, Randolph scowled at Shane. "I don't do stupid anymore."

"Good. I don't want to have to bail you out of jail." He reached out and tapped Randolph's arm. "We got your back no matter what."

The tightness in Randolph's chest eased. He dropped his gaze to the floor and then brought it up to focus on each of his friends individually before he said, "Thanks."

RANDOLPH HAD TRIED to spend the shuttle ride from Cahernamon to Briarcliff reading Penny's diary. He'd kept his nose in the book to avoid his mother engaging him in conversation. Early in the trip she'd done her best to enumerate why the guardianship decree was exactly what was needed. Finally he'd huffed his desire to drop the topic, and she'd sat back in her seat with a hurt expression.

Despite the shuttle seat adapting to his body, each time he shifted, it didn't take long for the new position to grow uncomfortable. The itch to pace was fingering down his spine. Jen had secreted herself in the back of the shuttle with Sophie. They'd been playing a game, Sophie crowing in triumph when she won. He'd chosen a spot facing them, taking every opportunity to focus a baleful stare on Jen. From the lip biting and the way she fiddled with a button on her blouse, it was disturbing her. *Good. Once we reach Briarcliff, I'll get to the bottom of her machinations.*

Briarcliff's shuttle pad came in sight. The landing was smooth and efficient, and soon they were in the car heading to the castle. "Maon and Audrina will arrive tomorrow morning. If you're agreeable, that is, to Sophie spending a week or two at Gleann Milis?" He directed the frigid question to Jen.

Jen's brow furrowed. Her response was subdued. "Of course. I'll make sure her things are packed tonight."

"No, Mother can assign a maid to see to that." He looked at his mother. "Won't you, Mother? My wife and I need to spend some time together, alone."

Claire frowned. "I'll deal with Sophie. The sooner you two discuss today's events, the sooner life will return to an even keel. You're being petulant, Randolph. Jen, don't let him browbeat you. None of this was your fault."

His voice harsh with anger, Randolph said, "Thank you, you've made your opinion abundantly clear already."

The car deposited them at Briarcliff's front door. The gothic hulk of gray stone towered over him, outlined against the purples and midnight blues of twilight. He'd never been so glad of the medieval affectation his ancestors had insisted on when building the castle. Inside was a dungeon he intended to make full use of, probably for the first time in the castle's history.

He glared at Jen. "Come with me."

Her gaze flicked from him to Claire to the briefcase he carried and back to his eyes. "All right."

She'd find out soon enough what the case contained.

Sophie's voice rang out. "Why is Uncle Rand so mad?"

Let his mother deal with that. He led Jen through dark-paneled corridors to the back stairs that descended to the basement. Lights automatically turned on, revealing efficient, modern storerooms. Dank vaults were less than ideal for long-term storage, and when the staff opposed the sheer creepiness of the medieval style of the original, it had been renovated. Except for the solid, iron-bound, blackened oak door that stood at the far end of the main corridor.

No replica Irish castle would be complete without a dungeon, and so one had been dug below the basement level. No attempt to keep seeping water, spiders, or other vermin out of it had been made. It was the nasty hole that one would expect. Great-Uncle Axton had taken a keen interest in it and had it expanded. Once past that intimidating door, visitors found themselves in a labyrinth of cells and rooms devoted to interrogation and punishment. The gloom was poorly dispelled by widely spaced fake torches that cast long shadows on the rough-hewn walls. Axton had insisted on installing various replicas of torture devices as well as macabre decorations of skeletons and lifelike mannequins stuffed in the iron maiden or crumpled in a heap in a hanging cage.

In childhood Penny had brought Randolph down and given him the full tour, threatening to put him on the rack if he didn't sneak her a cookie every night at bedtime. She'd been eleven years old and he seven. Although he hadn't quite believed she'd follow through on her threat, he had slipped her a cookie for a month before she told him he didn't have to any more.

The atmosphere, working shackles, and the whip he'd purchased were all he would need to break Jen and discover the truth of her involvement in the O'Malley's plan to assume the guardianship of Sophie. The door to the dungeon opened with the grating *scree* of abused hinges. Jen faltered at the first step, so he grabbed her by the wrist and compelled her to follow him. One torch was no longer functioning, making the descent harder and forcing him to slow. Halfway down, the dank air of the dungeon assaulted his nose with an underlying scent of rot, overlaid with years of undisturbed dust. Behind him Jen sneezed.

At the foot of the stairs the sound of small scuttling feet reached them, and one large sable rat darted into a pool of light, stopped, and stared up at them. A shiver ran along Randolph's spine. Stomping his boot, he yelled, "Git." The rat rushed off into the dark.

"I don't like it down here. Please, let's go." The quaver in Jen's voice proved she was frightened. And to be honest, the dungeon was creeping him out too. Perhaps this was a mistake. Had he allowed his anger to push him past his own boundaries? Yes, he was a sadist, but not the kind that lived on fear. A good mind fuck only went so far. Bringing Jen here was skittering right along the edge. Then the broken torch flickered to life, illuminating a mannequin that Randolph remembered as positioned on its knees, hands clasped before it, begging. Now it was on its side, the arms and legs missing. He cracked off a piece from an armhole and showed it to Jen.

"It's all fake. There's nothing down here that will hurt you. The rats won't bother us. If you want to prove you didn't set us up, you'll do this for me."

"I didn't." The glare she aimed at him, full of fire and flash, almost convinced him she was telling the truth. Almost. Pain welled in his chest. He had to determine whether she was a consummate actor or he was a complete bastard. If he had a choice, he'd take being the bastard. Then Jen would be the person he'd believed she was. But he couldn't take a chance on a feeling.

"I need proof."

"What kind of proof are you going to find down here?"

He flipped the briefcase open, pulling out the whip, and brandished it at her. "This will show me everything. No one under my whip lies to me for long."

A thunderstorm roiled in Jen's eyes. She stood, hands fisted at her sides, lips pinched together. "All right. I'll go with you, but if I use my safe word, you have to stop."

"Red. Your safe word is red, but if you use it and force me to stop before I'm finished, it will be the same as saying you're a liar. Understand?"

"If you've prejudged me, what's the point of this?"

His jaw clenched, he brought his hand to her cheek, brushing his thumb over the soft skin. "I haven't. I prefer you to be innocent."

Eyes shining with unshed tears, her reply was quiet, compliant. "Okay."

The ache in his chest sharpened. Fuck. He wound past doorways that opened onto hidden glimpses of torture scenes, made more frightening by the deep shadows that shrouded them. At last he found the room he'd remembered, large enough to swing his whip and lined with shackles high on the wall for stringing up prisoners. He walked to a pair centered on the far side where they glinted in the torchlight. Jen remained beside the doorway, arms clasped around herself, studying the walls.

"Strip and leave your clothes by the door."

She frowned. "Do I have to take off everything?"

His eyes narrowed and lips pursed, he considered her request. "No, just your shirt and bra."

He wasn't certain, but her fingers appeared to tremble while she complied, folding both articles of clothing and placing them next to the exit. "Come here."

If she'd been shaking, she wasn't now. She approached him on steady feet, stood against the wall, and lifted her hands over her head, all the while focusing her gaze on him as though she were daring him to read the truth in her eyes.

"Face the wall." He locked the shackles around her wrists with perfunctory grace, slipping the key into his pocket. "The whip is new. I'm going to crack it a bit before we begin. Get to know it. I'll tell you when I'm ready."

Jen shifted from foot to foot. *Good. I won't need to spend time building tension. She'll be primed and ready.* He hefted the whip in his hand. It was well-made but stiff from being new. He brought it to his nose and breathed in the rich scent of leather. His cock stirred in reaction to a smell he associated with sex.

A series of forward cracks had the sound reverberating off the walls. While he worked it, he observed her reactions. She squealed at the first pop but managed to remain silent thereafter, jumping straight up at every snap. That would change. He transitioned to overhead cracks, making the snap of the whip louder. Squeaks accompanied her startle reflex. She was tough. Most of the women new to a bullwhip, even the ones who begged him to use it on them, would be shaking, some already in tears. All the niceness she'd demonstrated was probably a cover for the typical hard-ass O'Malley female. He clenched his jaw. It shouldn't take long to bring out the bitchy matriarch she was hiding.

"Your turn." With the ease of years of practice, he cracked the whip next to her right hip. Her immediate reaction was to shift left and screech.

"I trusted you, Jen."

The whip popped to her left.

"As much as I trust any woman, which isn't much."

Another to her left.

"Women are born betrayers. But I thought you were one of the better ones."

A crack to her right. Still no tears. Although she was shaking.

"I dropped my guard. Let your sympathy cloud my vision."

Two pops in a row to her right.

"How did you know my mother was looking for a nanny?"

Jen replied, but he couldn't hear her.

"Louder."

"Evaline Braddock told me."

"Another matriarchal bitch."

"No, she's not. My mother met her in school. They were friends. That's all. It was a favor to my mom."

"But you ran back to your O'Malley kin and told them. Helped them plot a way to get control of Sophie. Couldn't stand to let the daughter of a matriarchal hero be raised by a perverted sadist."

"No."

He cracked the whip overhead. "Don't lie to me. I haven't touched that pretty skin of yours, but I will if you keep lying."

"I'm not lying. I needed the job because I was kicked out of the family.

No one would hire me. I was tainted goods to both the matriarchists and anyone else. I wasn't to be trusted."

Randolph chuckled bitterly. "And yet we did. Hired you as a nanny even though that position is usually reserved for serving-class women."

"I'm credentialed. I love working with children."

"Uh-huh." The whip snapped to her right.

Her body shaking, Jen stamped her foot. "I do. I love Sophie. I'd never do anything to hurt her."

"That isn't the point. Why would the O'Malley's turn on their own? Don't tell me sweet, compliant Jen O'Malley did something heinous enough for the O'Malley's to boot her from the family gravy train."

"They thought it was."

Randolph waved his hand in the air. "Spin your story."

"You won't believe me anyway. Why should I even try?"

He gritted his teeth, pacing the width of the room, and turned with a jerk. "Because I fucking told you to." Her spine straightened, and he knew without a doubt if he did nothing to stop her, she would use her safe word. "Don't say it. Don't say your safe word. I want to hear what happened. I do. Please tell me."

The ensuing silence pressed in on him, broken into infinitesimal moments by the thudding beat of his heart.

"It will seem like nothing to you, but in my family it was treason. O'Malley men have no rights. They are kept in the country away from nonfamily until a marriage is arranged for them. If a suitable marriage that will benefit the family is not found for them, they live their lives out in servitude." She jostled her shackles and turned her head, trying to see him over her shoulder. "Can you take these off?"

"Not yet."

"I understand. You need the control."

He cracked the whip over his head. "Don't analyze me. This is about you. So the O'Malley men are treated like a male harem. This is not news. All of Tallav know what the O'Malley bitches do to their sons. Sons, mind you. Not random men, but their own flesh and blood."

Jen shuddered, dropping her head to rest against the stone wall. "Exact-ly." She straightened and tried to look at him again. "Could you please look me in the face? I...I want you to see I'm not lying."

From the catch in her voice, Randolph could tell her nerves were fraying. The same spot in his chest that had ached at her perceived betrayal twinged in response to the sound. *What the fuck is wrong with me?* It had seemed like the ideal plan. Countless times he'd done this with other women, and everything had flowed perfectly. He was known for his implacable ability to strike terror in the hearts of his play partners. So why the hell was he hesitating now? *Crack the whip and tell her to get on with it.* Instead he ignored his own advice and went to lean against the wall where Jen was chained.

"Go on."

Her eyebrows furrowed in a tight frown, she swallowed. "I helped my cousin escape."

Randolph straightened. "You what?"

"My cousin, Nicholas, was his mother's pet. She let him read whatever he wished, take trips to Cahernamon, and do things the other male cousins could never do. He wanted to study architecture off world, and he believed his mother would make it possible. Until the day she told him that our head of family, Cordelia O'Malley, had arranged for him to be married to an eighty-year-old woman. He was being sold off by the family to be the woman's boy toy. His mother told him she was sorry, but she had to abide by Cordelia's wishes."

"Gods. Hard lesson to learn that you can't trust any woman, even your own mother." *That bitter truth was driven home when I was fourteen.*

Jen glared at him. "We're not all like that. Some of us are honorable."

Randolph grunted and raised an eyebrow. "So you helped him?"

She scowled. "Of course I did. It was simple. No one paid attention to me. I was always running errands for somebody, so it wasn't unusual to find me nearly anywhere on the estate. His mother brought Nicholas to Lavinia's several days before the wedding. He was despondent. I think they were worried he might do himself harm, so Lavinia told me to stay with him. They never imagined he would run away. Where would he go? He couldn't drive. I bought him a ticket off world and drove him straight from the estate to the spaceport. We waited to leave until after everyone went to bed, knowing we wouldn't be missed for hours."

Randolph's attention was raptly focused on Jen's story. That independent streak that stood in stark contrast to her normally meek manner must have been a shock to the O'Malleys. "Were you caught?"

Lips pressed in a thin line, Jen lowered her lashes. She hesitated and then said, "No. When I returned to the estate, everyone was in an uproar. Nicholas had been discovered missing from his room, and since I was nowhere to be found, it was determined that I had absconded with him. I don't think it occurred to them that he would leave Tallav. A deputation of cousins greeted me at the garage and ushered me into Lavinia's office. Nicholas was safely gone. I saw no point in lying, so I confessed what I'd done. Lavinia locked me in my room until my mother could arrive and my punishment could be settled on. They cut me off completely. No job. No stipend. My mother wasn't allowed to take me in for more than three weeks. That's how I ended up on the doorstep of your mother's apartment in Cahernamon through the offices of Evaline Braddock."

Could it be possible? Is she telling the truth? Or am I allowing myself to be deceived again? "Were you offered a return into their good graces if you set my mother and I up? Did they ask you to come and make yourself indispensable to us?" He slapped the wall with his palm, causing Jen to jump. "How did they learn that my mother wanted me to become Sophie's guardian? I want answers, because in court it sure sounded like we'd been tricked."

Her head thrown back, Jen let loose a guttural sound that was half scream, half bellow while rattling the chains shackling her to the wall. "You misogynistic prick. I'm a woman, so I'm guilty until proven innocent. Which can't happen because I'm a woman, and no woman is ever good enough for you. No, I'm the fool that sympathized with how your family treated you, how your mother didn't stand up for you, how your sister turned on you. I'm the idiot that expects a little compassion in return when I tell you my family turned on me, and my mother didn't stand up for me. But that's fucking impossible for you because you...hate...women." By the end of her tirade she was fighting against the shackles with all her might, making them clank together and grate on the stone. "Get me out of these!"

What the fuck is she saying. I don't hate women. Despite their betrayal, he loved his mother and his sister. *Misogynist* was the label he'd been branded with on Tallav, but he'd brushed that aside as the bigoted ranting of narrow-minded people who didn't understand kink. He was a sadist who was attracted to women, so naturally his play partners were women. But every single encounter had been consensual, and he'd always addressed the needs of anyone who accepted his invitation to join him, even those who used their safe word when the going became too intense for them.

He didn't hate women, but damned if she wasn't right that he did set them apart as lesser than men. That had been his acknowledged attitude, but for the first time he was seeing it from a woman's perspective. It came like a punch to his gut. He'd deeply wounded Jen, and in return she had blasted great chunks from the facade he'd so carefully crafted in his mind as well as showed to others.

He fumbled, his fingers no longer deft and assured, to release her. When he had, he brought his hands to her shoulders, intending to massage away the stiffness in her muscles.

She shrugged him off. "Don't. Touch. Me." With a stride that was equal parts resolution and anger, she went to where her shirt and bra lay on the floor and snatched them up, carrying them with her as she stalked through the door.

Randolph stood still, disoriented. The core of his being had been hit by an icy blast. He was adrift, unable to determine his next course of action, his mind a fuzzy mess of incoherence. When he staggered back, the rough stone of the wall jarred him and his knees buckled, sending him sliding to the floor. The truth that Jen had forced him to see was hammering at him.

The second time he'd played with her, he'd demanded she trust him, had even questioned why she would. Her response should have humbled him, but he'd accepted it as his due. He was kind, protective, and respectful of others. But those attributes paled when held up against his recent actions.

He was the betrayer, taking her trust and pronouncing her false. She was the innocent one, and he had turned on her, judging her guilty and offering her bitter accusations and the threat of his whip if she didn't admit her transgressions or prove she was telling the truth. Jen, the woman he'd grown to like and for whom he'd fostered an unacknowledged hope that she might be the one he could claim as his own. A woman who was the exact opposite of what he'd accused her of being.

It was no wonder he found it impossible to establish a long-term loving relationship. He'd always blamed the women in his life, but the fault was his. What woman would want to be with a man who would never truly trust her, believe in her goodness or her desire to always do right by him? Shouldn't she expect the same from him? But that had never been something he'd been willing to give. He shook his head. What was he doing, sitting here focusing on himself instead of begging Jen's forgiveness?

He staggered to his feet and strode purposefully to the door. He would make this right. Ahead in the flickering shadows of the dimly lit labyrinth that was the dungeon, he heard a woman shriek.

"Fuck. You are such a bastard."

16

W*ho the heck does he think he is?* Jen swiped at a tear trickling down her cheek and stomped forward into the gloom, trying to remember the path back to the stairs through the maze of turnings in the dungeon. *Self-absorbed asshole.* Despite the damp chill, she was sweating. *Which is the right way? Left? Isn't that the same caged skeleton we saw?*

Without Randolph by her side, the atmosphere of the dungeon had grown even more sinister. She wanted to leave as quickly as possible but didn't want to be spotted half-nude by any staff when she exited. With her hands shaking, she struggled to clasp her bra around her waist. *Crap!* After two failed attempts it was clear she'd have to stop walking and focus on getting dressed. Under the light of a torch, she managed to wrestle the bra into submission.

Why does putting on a bra make you feel more secure? She gave a snort and straightened out her shirt. No sounds came from behind her. Randolph hadn't followed her. *Good. I don't care if I ever see that bastard again.* She blew out a jittery breath and shut her eyes in an attempt to ignore her surroundings.

While she was struggling to find an armhole in her shirt, something skittered past her feet, brushing against her shoe. *Oh gods. A rat. That was a rat.* She turned and moved the opposite direction and ran headlong into a corpse. Her heart rate spiked, and her arms spread wide as she flung herself away from it. The instant before she screamed, her brain processed the scene before her. *It's just a dummy. Get a grip on yourself.* And then a terrible thought struck her. *I don't remember this room.*

Somewhere in the obscurity surrounding her, she had to find her shirt. It had flown from her fingers when the mannequin scared her. Should she look for it? Leave and try to get to her room without anyone seeing her in her bra? *Don't be a ninny. Find your damn shirt and then get out of here.*

But doing that was harder than she imagined. She must have stumbled into a storage room. Her hands outstretched and her eyes opened wide, she searched for her top. *I will not break down.* Piles of dummies rose out of the dark. Her fingers brushed against metal and wooden objects, and... *Ugh!* That pellet had to be a rat turd. *Enough. I don't need my shirt.*

The meandering path she'd taken through the junk made finding the door a challenge. Her heart hammering and knees weak, Jen inched forward, searching for an escape route. When she came to an opening and entered a passageway, tears welled once more in her eyes. Roughly brushing them away with a knuckle, she rushed ahead. This would get her back to the staircase.

She peered into the shadowy rooms she passed, and her scalp prickled. Nothing about this part of the dungeon seemed familiar. This corridor was too long, too straight. When she reached the far end, it was a solid stone wall. And she didn't know which of the many doors that lined it behind her led back to the storage room. She was lost.

Her nails biting into her palms, she stared into the gloom. How many rooms had she passed? More than three? The fourth door opened on a roomful of cobwebs. She shuddered. The sixth doorway appeared promising when she stuck her head inside. Something loomed in the darkness. Piles of discarded props? *Maybe.* If she followed the wall, she should come to the other door where she'd made the wrong turn. Instead she fell, catching herself on her hands, barely saving her face from smashing into the floor. At the same moment that she was hurtling to the ground, a heavy thwack sounded and something bounced. A severed head rolled toward her, stopping to stare straight into her eyes with its own horrific gaze.

Jen screamed, scuttling backward on her hands and knees toward the door, her feet getting tangled in the cord that had originally tripped her. Outside in the corridor she huddled against the wall, her arms wrapped tightly around her knees. It was too much. Sobs racked her until her ribs ached. She would never find her way out of this dreadful place. Not without Randolph's help.

How did I let this happen? Why do I have to be such a damn doormat? Evaline warned me, but no, I have to get involved with a gods-damned misogynistic sadist. Real bright, Jen. Snot running from her nose dripped onto her lip. She wiped a hand over her face and smeared the mucus onto her pants. To her right she heard rustling and then a hiss, followed by the chittering of more than one rodent. A loud thump sounded, sending her scooting farther along the corridor to once again weep in a huddled mess, her face buried in her lap. She began to keen, trying to drown out any sounds the rats might make.

Something touched her shoulder, and a primal scream flowed from her core, impossible to restrain.

"Jen. It's me. You're safe."

She looked up to find Randolph reaching out to her with a tentative expression as though he were afraid he'd crossed a boundary. His face was haggard, smudged with grime, fake cobweb clinging to the top of his head. She wanted to extend her hand to him, have him take her in his arms to comfort her, protect her. But how could she? He would never accept her for who she was. He'd always see her as the O'Malley who tricked him into marrying him despite the number of facts that proved him wrong. *I can't trust him.*

Gut-wrenching sobs overtook her again. She dropped her head to her knees, glad he was there to rescue her but unable to look at him. He slid to the floor beside her.

"I'm sorry. I'm such a jerk."

The regret in his voice made her turn to peer at him through the strands of her hair. Tears trickled, but she stopped sobbing, although her shoulders continued to jerk from the hitches that always followed a crying jag.

Rand was sitting with his forearms resting on his knees, his fingers fidgeting, and his head slumped so his chin nearly met his chest. "I accused you of betraying me when I'm the one who betrayed you. I see that now. I demanded your trust without offering mine in return. I'm...I don't know what to do to make it up to you, but I'm going to try." He ran a hand through his hair, finding the cobweb and picking it out, rolling it in a ball and flinging it away, and then casting a sideway gaze her direction.

Jen shivered and wrapped her arms more tightly around her knees.

"Oh, fuck. You're freezing." He shed his shirt and held it out to her. "Put this on."

Her hand shaking, she took it from him. "Thanks." *Damn. Why does my voice have to quaver? I should be tearing into him. Let him know I'm not some inconsequential little nobody he can treat that way.* She pulled a sleeve up her arm. *Who am I kidding? That's exactly what I am.* With the collar buttoned tight at her neck, the scent that was pure Randolph filled her nose. Her body ached, subverting her intentions to have nothing more to do with him. Somewhere deep inside, she still wanted him. She was that pathetic. When she lifted her head, Randolph's gaze locked with hers.

His lips pressed together, and his eyebrows narrowed. "I've been ignorantly blind most of my life. When you called me a misogynist, it wasn't like all the other times I'd been slapped with that label because of my sexual sadism. You confronted me with a truth I wouldn't have believed if the evidence wasn't right before my eyes. That was a fucking courageous thing to do. Tied up. Completely at my mercy, you flung reality at me, razor-sharp, slicing me to the core, making me bleed from the honesty of your insight into who I am."

Jen sniffled and brushed her hair aside. "I'm glad. Someone needed to set you straight. But I'm not brave. I just lost it."

His gaze locked on hers. "You're one of the bravest people I've ever known, and I have a couple of friends who are marshals."

"You really hurt me."

"I know." He ducked his head down. "I hope you'll forgive me someday."

"Give me some time." She tilted her chin up. "I have to make some changes too. I have to stop making myself a doormat in every situation."

"I've never thought of you that way. Kind. Considerate. Tenderhearted. But not a doormat. You're too strong for that."

"Don't try to flatter me. I'm still furious with you."

"You should be." He rose to his feet and offered her a hand. "Let's get out of here. You can get cleaned up in our room and then get some rest. I promise I won't bother you."

She stared into his eyes. His gaze was steady. He'd said *our room*. Did he think they would continue on as though nothing had happened? She'd have to disabuse him of that notion, but first she wanted to get warm and clean. "Okay." She lifted her hand, and he clasped it, pulling her to her feet.

∽

AFTER GATHERING FRESH CLOTHES, Randolph left Jen in their bedroom. He showered in a guest room and pulled on faded jeans and a brown sweater. Unable to sleep, he wandered down to the library, poured himself a glass of whiskey, and settled on a dark leather sofa to think.

He'd blown his one chance at a family. The ideal of mother, father, and children all loving each another had never been likely, but he might have forged a relationship with Jen based on mutual respect. That possibility was shattered by his own mistaken beliefs.

Why hadn't he ever considered his attitude toward women for what it was? No one had ever called him on it because he'd hidden that nasty little side of himself from everyone. He'd been the perfect sexual sadist. Appropriately terrifying during a scene, but always careful and considerate of his play partners. No one had ever claimed they'd been mistreated by him. Women loved him. Fell all over themselves to get beneath his whip. And when the action became too much for them, he always respected their safe word and took care of them afterward. Hell, he was sure some women partnered with him just for the aftercare.

His misogyny was a brutal truth he'd never allowed to penetrate his conscious mind. He'd always justified his distrust of women on the basis that he was the victim. He was protecting himself from the emotional pain that was inevitable when you let a woman get too close to you. That fact of life he'd learned early. A young teenage boy, he'd been shuttled off to boarding school to come to terms by himself with what had happened in the barn that long-ago night. At school he'd formed deep attachments to the boys, now men, who would become his lifelong friends. And steeped himself in anger toward the mother and sister who had betrayed him.

Could that one event have scarred him so deeply that he'd transferred his anger and mistrust to all women? Apparently it had, and he'd built on that ever since.

Gods, is that why I'm a sadist?

No, it can't be.

Both men and women had found their way under his whip. Predicament bondage, his other specialty, had been applied on any willing body. But scoring the backside of a man didn't arouse him like the sight of red marks on a curvy female ass. *Is that because I'm attracted to women? Or do I get off on women being hurt?*

He dropped his face into his hands. How the hell could he know? Somehow it was all wrapped up in events from twenty-one years ago. He'd been in the loft, checking on a litter of kittens, when Andy had entered the barn with a man from the village. Andy, full name Andromeda, had been the star of his wet dreams. She was curvy in all the best places and had the sexiest little pout to her lips. Never having had sex with anyone beyond his own hand, he could only imagine what being with her would be like. That night she'd been wearing a dress with killer black boots.

On the verge of calling out, he'd checked himself and laid flat in the straw littering the loft floor, snaking his way to the edge where he could peer down and see everything happening below.

Andy had ordered the man to take off his clothes. She had pulled off her dress, and Rand had nearly swallowed his tongue. Underneath it she'd worn a lacy black corset with a tiny pair of matching panties. Her hips had swayed as she strutted to where tack was organized on one wall. After selecting a riding crop and a length of rope, she had approached the man, who had stripped nude and stood waiting for her. With a snap of her crop to his thigh, she had demanded he present his hands.

Rand had watched, mesmerized, as she bound them together and then lifted his arms to secure the rope between his wrists over a hook above his head. She had taunted him, humiliating him verbally while she snapped the crop on his nipples and his engorged cock. Despite his moans and cries, it was obvious he enjoyed the pain. When he had begged for release, Andy had whacked his dripping erection and then grabbed it roughly with one hand, stroking it from base to tip at a vicious pace. She stepped out of the way of the arcs of semen that spurted in long streams into the straw when the man came.

His own cock rock-hard, Rand had nearly come in his pants. He had wanted to relieve the ache in his groin but feared they would catch him spying on them. Andy had untied the man, kissed him fervently, and then told him the price was going up. They had argued while he dressed, but he had finally agreed and left.

Heart pounding, Rand had inched back from the edge of the loft to wait for Andy to leave. His stomach had dropped when he heard her call his name and order him to come down. In expectation of a lecture for eavesdropping and a threat to tell his parents, he'd climbed down, trying to figure out what to say.

Instead she had gone all slinky and sexy and asked if he wanted to have a little fun too. He'd stood frozen, unable to think much less speak. She'd picked up the rope, and before he'd known what was happening, he was tied with his hands over his head. Face flushed and cock hard, he had desperately wanted what she was offering, but at the same time he had the urge to escape, to run away as fast as he could. She had palmed his erection through his pants, and he had stiffened, afraid he would make a mess of himself. She yanked the pants down his skinny adolescent butt to his knees. He had shaken uncontrollably until pain sliced through him, and he screamed. One hand clamped over his mouth, she had continued to whack his deflated penis with sharp blows until he was gibbering.

She had given one final slap to his face and warned him never to spy on her again. Free from the rope, he had fallen at her feet. She had laughed, telling him how she loved having a first family male whimpering before her. Her back turned to him, she'd sauntered to where her dress had been hung on a post. She hadn't heard him rise, pull his pants up, and charge toward her until it was too late.

He had shoved her to the ground, snatched the crop from the straw where it had fallen when he struck her, and laid into her with it. He had hit her again and again, his screams of fury mingling with hers of pain. His blows had rained down on her head and every other part of her body he could reach, and a string of vile curses had flown from his lips.

Like a berserker from the ancient tales, he had thrashed her until another voice bellowing for him to stop finally made it through the red haze that filled his mind. Penny had heard him beating Andy and had entered the barn. When he had looked at her, hand still tightly clasping the crop, sweat pouring from him, Penny's eyes were cold, and she'd asked, "What are you doing?"

She'd left him there, staring down at Andy, who was sobbing and trying to slither away from him. His father had appeared, taken in the scene, and ordered him to his room. It had been hours before his father came to speak to him to announce that it had been decided to send him to boarding school a year early. For his own good. Randolph didn't learn until years later that Andy had been fired. To avoid scandal, she'd been compensated and made to sign a nondisclosure agreement. Maybe if he'd told them she'd sexually assaulted him, she'd have been charged for molesting a minor, but he'd been too humiliated. When, years later, he'd finally told his mother the whole truth, it had been too late.

The day after the assault Penny had disowned him as her brother, calling him a disgusting, filthy male. Two days later he was at boarding school.

Yes, he'd been wronged. He'd been the victim of a sexual predator. The women in his life who should have defended him hadn't, one even turning on him. But that didn't make all women guilty. Intellectually he could accept that, but if he were going to become a better man, a better person, he would have to root out the prejudice that was buried inside him.

He couldn't stay at Briarcliff. It was a refuge for Jen, and he couldn't deny her that. He would leave Tallav. Return to Beta Tau. Jen and his mother would raise Sophie. Jen didn't need him there, a constant reminder of the pain he had caused her. They would never grow closer now. He'd obliterated her trust in him.

The castle had been quiet when he'd walked its hallways. His mother wasn't in her office or anywhere else he'd checked. She was probably in bed herself. Tomorrow he'd break the news to her. He'd be leaving Tallav for good.

17

R andolph blinked and rubbed his eyes. Sometime after his third glass of whiskey, he'd fallen asleep on the sofa. He had no idea how long he'd slept with the heavy curtains closed. His EBC said it was six. The huge hollow that had opened in his chest yesterday radiated an ache that drained all his energy.

He rose, his body railing against him, urging him to slump back onto the sofa while a little voice inside admonished him to drink another glass of whiskey and let the fucking women do as they pleased. He closed his eyes and balled his fists, mentally roaring his response. *Shut up!* How the hell was he going to break his lifelong prejudice against women if his inner voice subverted his effort?

Maon would be here this morning with his kids. His friend had always used Randolph as a sounding board. Time to reverse that, to admit finally that he didn't have life perfectly figured out. First he needed a shower and some food to resist the jumble of emotions that were battering him.

On his way upstairs he met Mrs. Polgrey coming down. She was clutching the locket she always wore, her lips pinched. "Mr. Rand! There you are! Lt. Sanders from the garda has commed. There's been a…a death."

Randolph's heart rate sped up. He grasped the housekeeper by the upper arms. "Who?"

"I've just spoken with your mother; it's Genevieve Kavan. Lt. Sanders didn't give me any details but asked that everyone remain at Briarcliff until she can speak with you and your mother."

"A good idea." He patted the housekeeper's arm before releasing her. "We should go about our day as usual. Please pass word on to the servants that they should remain at the castle until further notice."

"Yes, sir. And I'll see about a nice hot breakfast."

"That's an excellent plan."

She nodded and continued down the stairs. Randolph gazed up at the next landing. Should he speak to his mother first? No doubt his mother was even now dressing. They could discuss matters over breakfast after he commed Lt. Sanders and tried to extract more information from her. He needed to shower and change from the rumpled clothes he'd slept in. But he didn't want to wake Jen. She had to be physically and emotionally exhausted. Until he knew what was happening, he wouldn't rouse her.

Jen lay on her side, covers pulled up to her chin. Her brow was smooth, her lashes feathered against her cheek. She was the picture of peaceful repose. For a moment Randolph couldn't breathe. She didn't stir when he slipped into his closet to gather a shirt, pants, and clean underthings. Rather than going casual, he chose classic tailored items, adding a jacket as a second thought. If and when he met Lt. Sanders face-to-face, he wanted to exude authority. He carefully closed the door after one last glance at Jen.

By the time he arrived in the dining room, his mother was already drinking a cup of coffee and playing with a slice of toast. "Good morning, Mother." He bent to kiss her cheek.

"Good morning, dear." She eyed him with a questioning look, but he had no intention of discussing what happened between him and Jen last night.

He helped himself to coffee and a large stack of pancakes slathered in butter and syrup. Seated, fork in hand, he glanced at her. "I've spoken with Lt. Sanders. She didn't tell me much, but she did say that Genevieve was found at the dolmen."

Her expression pinched. "That foolish woman. She's was probably conducting one of those rituals of hers. What happened? Did she inhale the wrong fumes?"

"No. Someone bashed her head in."

Hand flying to her chest, his mother's mouth dropped open. "Oh, my. She was murdered." The last word was uttered with distaste.

Randolph grimaced. "I'm sorry, that was rather blunt of me." He closed his eyes for a moment. "I'm certain it has to do with Penny's death."

His mother blinked rapidly, dropping her hand to her lap. "But why?"

"Genevieve saw something…somebody the night Penny died. She fooled around with notions that it was supernatural. When she finally decided it had been a real person, the police refused to listen to her. But if there was someone on that cliff that night and foul play was involved in Penny's fall, then Genevieve must have said something that made that person fear discovery."

"You don't seriously think someone murdered Penny. It was an accident, Rand." His mother stared at him, wide-eyed.

"I'm sorry, Mother, but I'm coming to believe that's exactly what happened. We'll have to wait to see what the police investigation discovers."

"It's impossible." She shook her head. "Everyone at Briarcliff thought only the best of Penny. No one would want to harm her."

"For your sake I hope you're right." He took a deep breath. "Mother, I have something else…"

"Grandma! Uncle Rand! They're not here yet. How soon till they get here?" Sophie burst into the dining room, bouncing to hug each of them.

His mother smiled tolerantly at Sophie. "*Alanna*, it's only half six. I don't expect they'll arrive until ten at the earliest. Now sit down and have some breakfast."

Sophie climbed onto a chair. "Mary said I shouldn't pack more than two dolls, but I really want to take Milly, my ballerina, and Bunnzy. Why can't I take all three?"

Randolph sighed. He'd have to wait to tell his mother he was leaving, to escape the turmoil that never seemed to offer him a break and find time to recover his balance. On Beta Tau he could forget about familial duties and return to the life he'd established for himself. A life where women fell in line… *Gods. I'm doing it again.* He brushed a hand through his hair. How could he trust his own decisions now? Perhaps he should reconsider. Especially if it was his inner misogynist advising him to cut and run.

If Penny and Genevieve had been murdered, I shouldn't leave Mother to deal with that on her own. What kind of son abandons his mother? He eyed the stack of pancakes before him, picked up his fork, and took a bite. The sweetness that had been so tempting was cloying now. He pushed away from the table. "I guess I'm not as hungry as I thought I was. I'll be upstairs in Penny's office. Maybe I can get some work done before our visitors arrive or Lt. Sanders comes to speak with us."

A BEAUTIFUL FALL morning was on panoramic display from the window where Randolph stood staring outside while his mind struggled to make sense of all that had happened since his sister's death. A car pulled into the circle that fronted Briarcliff. Before the driver could exit, a stream of children came pouring out of the sliding side door, followed by Maon.

Randolph paused on the landing of the stairs, watching the commotion below, at the castle's front entrance. Devon, Annie, Petey, and Trina were milling about gawking while Sophie was attempting to drag one of her bags out the door. Rand's mother was greeting the children as Audrina, Maon's mother-in-law, introduced them. Petey was considering the bottom steps as though he were about to climb them to discover what lay above when he caught sight of Randolph and edged back toward his brother and sisters.

"Sophie!" Rand raised his voice to be heard above the clamor. "Take your friends up to your playroom. You're not leaving immediately."

After a quick glance over her shoulder, Sophie continued her efforts to get her belongings out the door.

"You heard me, Sophie."

Her shoulders slumped, but then her attitude brightened. "Come on. I'll show you all my stuff."

The younger three came charging after her, past him up the stairs. Devon followed at a more leisurely pace that spoke of his nine-year-old maturity. Randolph descended and gave Maon a thump on the back.

"My dear, I haven't seen you in such a long time," Claire Meryon said to Audrina.

"I do tend to flit about for the House of Shirley. Now that I'm not designing anymore, I get to play with the logistical side of things. I'm having a ball." Audrina waved a hand and laughed.

"Why don't we have tea in my sitting room?" Claire suggested to everyone.

"That would be lovely. I adore my grandchildren, but they are a rowdy lot to be penned up with in a shuttle. Tea is the perfect remedy to soothe my nerves," Audrina said.

"Mother, I'd like to speak with Maon in private about..." He tipped his head to the side.

"Oh, of course, dear." His mother nodded. "That's an excellent idea."

Ushering Audrina from the foyer, Claire said, "Come this way. I was supposed to be shuttling to Cahernamon today for tasting trials. I'm selecting the chef who will compete against local cooks during the Apple Festival, but we've been banned from leaving Briarcliff by the local garda."

Audrina's response was lost as the ladies turned a corner.

"Why have you been ordered to remain at Briarcliff?" Maon peered at Randolph, his forehead furrowed.

"That's what I want to talk to you about. One of the things. It's a long story." Randolph filled Maon in on all the details from Penny's death to Genevieve's murder while they climbed the stairs and went to Penny's office.

Seated in an armchair while Randolph sat behind the desk, Maon tapped a finger against his lips. "I agree. When you add all these facts together, your sister's death sounds suspicious. Someone needs to take another look at the scan's done for Penny's autopsy. Genevieve Kavan's autopsy should be conducted by someone with greater forensic knowledge than the local doctor."

"Yes. Lt. Sanders from the garda is supposed to come and speak with us soon. I'd like you to be there for that meeting."

"Absolutely. She won't get her knickers in a twist if I get involved, will she?"

"I don't think so. She's quite professional. Nothing of the parochial village constable about her."

Maon nodded. "I'll send Audrina on to Gleann Millis with the kids, but I'm staying. I'm glad we'd already planned to take Sophie with us. This is no time for a child to be about."

"Oh fuck." Randolph slapped a hand to his forehead. "I forgot about Darrin." Maon's expression was puzzled. "He's my half-brother. Genevieve Kavan's son. He's fourteen. Just a minute. I need to comm Lt. Sanders."

The call was brief. "She'll be here in twenty minutes." Randolph stood. "Let's get Audrina and the kids on their way."

Maon accompanied Randolph to the nursery to find the usual tumult created by the Shirley children. Petey was battling an invisible foe with Sophie's wooden sword. Devon was throwing a ball against the wall and catching it. All three girls were busy oohing, aahing, and rearranging furniture in the dollhouse.

"Time to go," Maon bellowed. Five heads popped up. The ball and dollhouse were forgotten, although Petey gripped the sword tight and marched determinedly toward his father. "Leave the sword."

"I want to play with it."

"I understand. It's not yours. Put it down."

Petey's face rumpled. "But I—"

"Now."

Petey let the sword slide from his hand and glumly followed his siblings and Sophie out the door.

In the hall Randolph said, "I'll leave herding them to you and go find my mother and Audrina."

"Coward." Maon slapped Randolph on the back.

Randolph grinned. He'd discovered he could handle children one at a time, but more than that and it was the better part of valor to run for the hills.

When he entered his mother's sitting room, Claire and Audrina were nattering away. It was the first time since his return that he had seen his mother enjoying the company of someone outside their family circle. Did she isolate herself at Briarcliff, managing the estate on her own? If the Whip Hand were to close, the employees would find other work, but the people on Rathlin would be in trouble if his mother ever decided to quit promoting the island's products. The well-being of the entire island was a weighty responsibility.

Both ladies turned smiling faces to him. "Maon is rounding up the children and getting them into the car."

Audrina said, "That's my cue." She and his mother rose and gave one another hugs. "We simply have to get to together more frequently. You're such fun to gossip with." She batted her eyelashes at Randolph. "And you, handsome man. Were your ears burning?" She laughed gayly and embraced him in a tight hug. "You're all three married now, and Shane is having a baby. You're next." She patted his shoulder, her eyes twinkling.

He had to admit, it was nice to get a hug from Audrina, but the talk about babies was unsettling. He grunted noncommittally and escorted the ladies out.

On the drive Maon had all five children in the car and was finishing strapping Drina into her car seat. He informed Audrina that he would be staying at Briarcliff for a couple of days but follow them to Gleann Millis soon. After another round of hugs, Audrina climbed into the vehicle. The adults left behind waved until it cleared the circle and headed down the lane.

~

NOT LONG AFTER Audrina and the children left, Lt. Sanders was ushered into the sitting room where she was awaited by Claire, Randolph, and Maon. After introducing Maon to the lieutenant and explaining his arrival earlier in the morning, Randolph said, "Can you tell us more about what happened to Genevieve?"

"First, I need to ask you and Ms. Meryon where you were from ten to midnight last night." Sanders directed her gaze at Claire.

Claire's eyebrows knit together. "Are we suspects?"

"No, ma'am. Since the murder occurred on Briarcliff grounds, I'll be asking everyone who lives here the same question."

Her chin lifted higher, Claire said, "One would have to be outside on the top turret of Briarcliff to see the dolmen from here. I don't imagine anyone at Briarcliff will be of help to your investigation. I was in my bedroom packing for a trip to Cahernamon today. If I'm not allowed to leave soon, I will have to reschedule some important Harvest Festival meetings."

"Thank you, ma'am. I have one more question." Sanders didn't visibly react to his mother's aloof tone of voice. All to the good.

Randolph would prefer a pugnacious investigator to someone who bowed and scraped to an aristocrat. Sanders walked a middle road between the two.

His mother didn't relent in her attitude. "Certainly."

"Do you know of any reason someone might want Genevieve Kavan dead?"

Claire's eyebrows lifted. "Good heavens no. The woman was eccentric and could be a nuisance, but no one held true ill will toward her."

The lieutenant nodded and added a note to the tablet she held in her lap. "Thank you. If you think of anything that might further our investigation, please let me know. You're free to go to the city, but please make yourself available if I have more questions."

"Of course. If you don't mind"—Claire rose to her feet—"I'll excuse myself and let you talk to my son and the marshal."

Sanders stood with Randolph and Maon. "Thank you for your time."

When Claire was gone and they'd resettled in their chairs, the lieutenant looked at Randolph, her gaze piercing. "And you, sir. Where were you late last night?"

"I was in the library here at Briarcliff."

"Alone?"

He gave her a tight nod. "Yes, but one of the staff did ask if I needed anything at about eleven. My wife went to bed early, and I didn't wish to disturb her. I ended up falling asleep on the sofa."

It was impossible to discern the lieutenant's thoughts from her lack of reaction to his response. After each question she asked, she added a note on her tablet and then returned her impassive gaze to her subject, moving implacably on to her next query. "I'll need to speak with your wife as well as the staff."

Randolph stiffened slightly and then purposefully relaxed the tension in the muscles of his core. "My wife is still in bed. I'd prefer you not intrude on her yet. I can vouch that she was at Briarcliff the entire night."

"Very well. But I'll need to speak with her eventually. She can come to the garda station later."

He reciprocated the questioning, his gaze locked on the lieutenant. "Can you tell us more about what happened?"

Her expression went pensive. She reached a decision. "Yes, but please do not discuss this with others. I'll be holding a press conference this afternoon to release what details I consider the public requires."

Settling back in his chair, he exhaled quietly. "I've asked Marshal Shirley to take an interest in this investigation. Please accord him the courtesy of accepting his assistance."

Sanders nodded and focused on Maon. "I'd appreciate whatever help you can give me, Marshal. Ms. Kavan was struck multiple times on the back of the head by a blunt object, most likely a statuette of the goddess we found near the body. It doesn't appear she tried to defend herself, but the autopsy will provide the proof of that. Either she knew and trusted the person who killed her, or someone snuck up behind her while she was involved in her ritual."

"Anyone could have done that," Randolph said.

The lieutenant switched her gaze to Randolph. "Exactly. Which is why we're asking everyone within walking distance of the dolmen where they were last night."

In a tone of consternation Randolph said, "That includes the whole village."

Sanders blew out a breath. "Yes. It does, but until the crime scene techs get us some DNA evidence, we have to spread our net wide."

"What are you looking at as possible motive?" Maon asked.

"I'm sure Mr. Meryon has shared his theory about his sister's death with you." Sanders laid her tablet aside. "Ms. Kavan believed she'd seen someone out on the cliff the night Penny Meryon died. She wasn't a reliable witness, so we discounted it as the workings of a susceptible mind." The lieutenant grimaced. "But now, I'm starting to think Mr. Meryon was on to something. There seems to be no other reason why someone would kill the woman. This wasn't a crime of passion. Kavan was struck enough times to ensure her death but no more."

She pursed her lips and said, "I've spoken with her son, Darrin. He claims she went to the dolmen every week on the same night to pray and offer sacrifices to the goddess for the well-being of the Meryon family and all who lived on Rathlin. She's been doing it for years."

"I'll bet most people knew that," Maon said.

"I'm sure they did," she responded, her voice dry.

Maon leaned forward. "I'd like to come and look at all the evidence from Penny's death and the latest crime. When would be a good time to do that?"

Mirroring Maon's posture, Randolph said, "And I want to take Darrin into my family's custody. He is my half-brother."

Sanders eyed Randolph. "You're admitting that now."

After taking a moment to control the tone of his voice, Randolph said, "I've never denied it. My parents may have felt differently, but the boy needs someone. My mother will rise to the occasion."

The lieutenant rose to her feet and let her gaze move from Randolph to Maon and back to Randolph. "Why don't you both follow me to the station. We can go over things there, Marshal, and you can look into offering emergency fostering for Darrin, Mr. Meryon."

Randolph restrained his smile. *At last someone is going to take my doubts about Penny's death seriously, and I'll have an inside man on the investigation.* "All right." To Maon he said, "Give me a moment to check in on Jen, and then we can leave. We'll use one of the cars in the back lot." Randolph tapped into his inner comm and requested a staff member show Maon to the parking area.

On his way up the stairs to his bedroom, it came to him that the pressure that had been bearing down on his chest had eased. But as he turned the door handle, the weight dropped on him again. He still had the mess he'd made with Jen to deal with. How was she going to treat him this morning? Would she give him his marching papers? That would make leaving Tallav a simpler proposition, but he was no longer certain he wanted to do that. Not yet, anyway.

Jen was sitting up in bed, eating brunch from a tray. She stared at him, chewing and swallowing a bite of food before she said, "Are you coming in, or just planning to poke your head in?"

Randolph cleared his throat. "Coming in, if you'll let me."

"It's your room." Her voice was a monotone.

"I wanted to make sure you're okay."

"Peachy."

He ducked his head and then brought his gaze back to hers. "I have to go into the village. Something has happened. Genevieve Kavan was murdered, and I need collect Darrin."

Her eyes widened and her mouth dropped open. "What?" After setting the tray aside, she threw her legs over the side of the bed. "Do you want me to come with you? I can be ready in a few minutes."

"No. You stay here. Sophie's already left with the Shirley clan, although Maon stayed behind. He's going to help with the investigation. You could prepare one of the nursery bedrooms for Darrin or a regular bedroom. I can't remember how old I was when I escaped the nursery. Mrs. Polgrey will know. I'd like him to feel welcome. He's just lost his mother, after all."

"Absolutely." She stood, pulling off her nightgown as she strode to the closet. "We'll have something ready when you return."

The sight of her soft, sensual curves, rosy nipples, and dark curls at the juncture of her thighs made him ache with a longing that didn't seem sexual even though his groin tightened. Fuck. If only he could hold her, show her how sorry he truly was, maybe she'd look at him again with the heated desire of the past instead of frosty indifference. It was so like her to jump to help someone in trouble, pushing her own troubles aside. How could he have doubted this sweetly giving woman? "Jen?"

She turned to gaze over her shoulder at him.

"We need to talk. Soon."

The frozen mask dropped over her face again. "We do. When things settle down."

She faced the closet again, and he recognized his dismissal. It would take time and effort to heal the rift he'd created between them. He sighed and left.

18

The village garda station crew comprised Lt. Sanders, a desk sergeant, and three constables. The station itself was small and utilitarian. What crime existed was usually minor. First-degree murder was a rarity that had last occurred sixty-two years previously. It was no surprise that the desk sergeant, in whose hands Lt. Sanders had placed Randolph when they arrived, was feeling the power of her sudden elevation in importance.

"He's in an interview room," the middle-aged woman said.

A flush of heat ran through Randolph. He crossed his arms to hide his clenched fists in his armpits. In an even, controlled voice he said, "You have him in an interrogation room? He's fourteen."

Despite Randolph's attempt to mask his anger, the woman bridled. "He's a suspect."

Idiot female. Randolph gritted his teeth both at the sergeant's truculence and his own automatic addition of her gender to his mental disparagement of her. "Have you questioned him? Without an adult present?"

The sergeant tugged on the waistband of her pants. "Only the same as we've done to everyone."

He locked his gaze with the woman's. "Does he know his mother has died?"

She glanced to the side. "Not in so many words." Then she brought her gaze up to meet his and scowled. "But he knows something is wrong."

Incredible. Randolph bit his response out. "Take me to him."

The sergeant drew herself up. "Not possible. He's being remanded to the care of the state."

"What does that mean?"

She puffed out her chest. "Child Protective Services is sending someone to collect him."

Randolph narrowed his eyes. "That won't be necessary. He's my brother. I'll take custody of him."

A slight smirk hovered on the sergeant's lips. "I'd need proof of kinship before I could do that."

Lt. Sanders, who had taken Maon down the hall to her office, must have overheard the conversation. She stuck her head out of her door. "Release the boy into Mr. Meryon's custody."

The sergeant hooked her thumbs in her belt loops, shrugged, and straightened her shoulders. "Anything you say, Lieutenant." She scowled at Randolph. "Follow me."

Darrin was sitting slumped in a chair, his chin on his chest, his hair falling into his face, and his legs sprawled out in front of him. He didn't react when Randolph and the sergeant entered the small room.

Her voice sarcastic, the sergeant said, "Your brother's here for you."

The statement struck the boy like a zap from a shock gun. His head popped up, and he sat erect. "I can go?" His gaze rapidly swiveled from the sergeant to Randolph.

"Yes. I'm getting you out of here." He picked up the jacket draped over the back of Darrin's chair and handed it to him.

Darrin scrambled to his feet. "You don't have to tell me twice." He gave the sergeant a malicious smile as he passed her. "Sorry I couldn't stay longer."

In the hall Darrin asked, "What's my mother done? Has she been arrested? They wouldn't tell me."

Randolph gripped Darrin by the upper arm. "Not here. We'll talk outside."

When they entered the lobby, Lanny Conyer was leaning on the front counter talking to Jemmy, the constable Randolph had seen her with previously. She moved toward them, arms outstretched as though she would hug Darrin. "I'm so sorry to hear about your mother. If there's anything I—"

"Thank you. I'm taking care of matters." He rushed Darrin past her, praying the woman wouldn't blurt out the truth. "Let's head over to your house to talk," he said to Darrin.

The Kavan home was almost exactly as it had been when Randolph had last visited, was it five days ago? It seemed weeks had passed between then and now, but the cottage hadn't changed except for the divination sticks were no longer strewn on the desk. Otherwise the same odor of incense and burned herbs hung in the air, and the shelves held the same clutter.

The sun made the back room cheery as it streamed through the leaves of the potted plants lining the windows. Dust motes drifted, and the worn furnishings added to the shabby hominess

"You want something to eat or drink?" Darrin asked.

"No." How the hell did he tell this fourteen-year-old his mother wasn't just dead, she'd been murdered? "Sit down, Darrin. I have something to tell you." He ignored the flashing white dot at the lower left corner of his vision. Whoever was comming would have to wait.

His voice raised, Darrin said, "I know my mom has done something. And it must be illegal if the garda are involved."

"Sit."

For a moment Darrin resisted the suggestion, scowling. "All right." Then he launched himself onto the far end of the sofa from Randolph.

"There's no easy way to say this." Lips pressed together, Randolph braced himself for whatever followed.

His expression now gone wary, Darrin said nothing.

"I'm so sorry. Your mother was killed last night."

His eyes widened. Darrin lost his usual bravado. "What?" Before Randolph could explain, Darrin shot out a rapid-fire response. "That's not possible. She walks to the dolmen every week. She's done it for years. How could she be killed? Did someone hit her with a car?"

Randolph dropped his gaze to his hands, rubbing the heart bead knotted at his wrist. "She was murdered, Darrin. Someone struck her on the back of the head and killed her." He glanced up at his brother.

Darrin stared at him, dazed, not speaking. He turned to face away from Randolph, shaking his head. Then he spun about and yelled, "You're lying. It's not true. Why are you lying? Do you hate us that much?" He raised his fists, and for an instant Randolph thought the boy might strike out at him. Instead he punched the back of the sofa.

His throat aching, Randolph struggled for the right words, resisting the additional slam of pain as the memory of his mother telling him Penny had died rose like a mental apparition. "I wish I was lying. I wish I could say it was an awful joke. But it's not. And I'm going to make sure we find out who did this to her and why. I promise you. One of my marshal friends arrived at Briarcliff today, and he's already on the case."

Tears were streaming down Darrin's face. "I don't believe it. There's been a mistake. It wasn't her they found. It was someone else."

Randolph sprang forward and caught Darrin in his arms as he collapsed, sobbing.

"It can't be her. It can't. You don't know what I said to her. I said terrible things. I told her I wished I had been born to someone else. That she could die and my life would be better. But I didn't really mean it. I was mad. I take it all back. Please tell me she isn't dead." Darrin shoulders shook. "I cursed her. My own mother. And now she's dead. It's my fault. I killed her."

"You did no such thing." Randolph tightened his embrace. "There's only one person responsible for her death and that's whoever struck her. Whoever that person is, they didn't do it because you were angry with your mother and said some nasty things to her. Every son has moments when he wishes he had different parents. I did. You don't have some super ability to slay people with your words. Good gods, nobody in their right mind would give that kind of power to a fourteen-year-old."

When Darrin pulled his head from Randolph's shoulder, his face was a blotchy, wet mess, his gaze a glassy stare. "What am I going to do now?"

Randolph gripped both Darrin's shoulders in his hands. "You're going to come live at Briarcliff. We'll pack some of your things. We're going to deal with whatever happens together. Understand me? You're not alone."

His chest hitched, and another sob broke free, but Darrin nodded his head.

Darrin's bedroom was far neater than Randolph had expected. His bed was made, topped by a handmade quilt in primary colors that looked more appropriate for a five-year-old boy than a young teen. Sports equipment was piled into a bin in one corner. A desk held an ancient vidscreen and a scuffed tablet. The defining attribute of the room was the drawings that covered all the available wall space. "You're an artist." He studied a rendering of the village's main street. Several ladies were gossiping while their children milled around them. Vibrant life filled the drawing. "This is amazing."

At the closet Darrin was filling a backpack with the clothes neatly stacked on the shelves. There weren't many. He shoved socks and underwear in on top. He acknowledged Randolph with a grunt. "I like to draw." He scanned the room for anything else he might pack.

"We'll get the rest of your things later," Randolph said. It was obvious they'd be doing some shopping for the boy. He'd need something new for the funeral. Randolph ran a hand down his face. *This is so fucked up.*

Before he left, Darrin snatched his tablet from the desk. "Okay. I'm ready."

"Let's go find my friend, Maon. He's the marshal I was telling you about."

The walk back to the garda station was quiet. The few people they met on the way nodded toward them with sympathetic expressions. Randolph was certain his own face intimidated them, keeping them from approaching and making more effusive demonstrations of condolence. Darrin needed time to process before he had to deal with others, whether they be kind or merely curious.

Maon was waiting for them outside the garda station. Leave it to the man to understand that Randolph wouldn't want to bring Darrin back inside. After a brief introduction, to which Darrin responded with a bare nod, his hands buried in his pants pockets, the three climbed into the car and set out for Briarcliff.

THERE HAD BEEN little to do once Jen notified Mrs. Polgrey that Darrin Kavan would be coming to live at Briarcliff. The bedroom next to

Randolph's was selected. Jen agreed with the choice. It would be close by and was designed with masculine tastes in mind. Blues and grays with streaks of silver added color to the minimalist dark furnishings.

With nothing more to do, she returned to her bedroom. Penny's diary was lying on top of the chest of drawers next to the closet. Randolph had been reading it on the shuttle ride from Cahernamon, trying to make sense of his sister's last year of life. Why had Penny hidden the data cube with her new book on it in the secret cave? Surely she wouldn't have just one copy. She could have sent the manuscript to any number of people for safe keeping. Who was she hiding it from? The answers wouldn't be at the beginning of the diary but in its last pages.

Jen snatched it from the dresser and sat on the end of the bed to read. Riffling through the pages, she found the entry Penny had written the night she died.

Our Mothers is complete. I have yet to find a publisher on Tallav I feel I can trust to maintain absolute secrecy about the true content of the book. I cannot give the matriarchists time to create defensive spin before the book releases. I'll never have another opportunity for a surprise attack. I intend to make the most of it to cause as much damage to their political party as possible.

Tomorrow I'll begin the hunt for a Federation-wide publisher. The book will be a guaranteed seller on Tallav and could do well off Tallav if marketed as a salacious tell-all. Release on Tallav first, and then Fed wide. If I can find a publisher willing to adhere to my pre-release marketing. That's the real question. Most will want to market it for what it truly is from the get-go.

Lanny has been nagging me to let her read it. I've told her it's not finished, and I don't want anyone reading it until I feel it's ready. I've sent her on another hunt for an obscure image. I think she's catching on that her research now is busy work. She's accomplished my purpose for her. Every tidbit I've let slip has made its way into the gossip mill. I can't let her discover the true nature of Our Mothers. I know she's searched my file storage, but all my work is on a data cube that I kept with me at all times while I was writing. Now that the manuscript is complete, I've hidden it where Lanny can never find it. I'll retrieve it when I'm ready to send it to a publisher.

In some ways I pity Lanny. This job was to be her step up, to give her standing within the party and assure her a bright future. Once the book is released, she'll never be trusted again. They'll see her as either a fool or a traitor. I believed that Lanny's venomous misandry was at least partially a pose, a way to suck up to the powerful hags that controlled the matriarchists. I know now it's not. She truly hates men with a touch of crazy that even in the past would have made me dismiss her. It's made her the perfect tool. Still I'm not sure what she would do if she discovered what I'm up to.

Jen dropped the diary in her lap. Had Lanny found out? Did she murder Penny? And then Genevieve Kavan to hide what she'd done? That amounted to more than a touch of crazy. But Lanny had been intent on finding both the diary and the data cube. She'd even tried to gain Jen as an ally in her search, ostensibly to assure that Penny's last masterpiece was published, but what if her true aim was to destroy it. She must have known Penny kept only one copy.

She placed her hand on the diary. Randolph must not have read these pages yet. If he had…

This is evidence. I should get it to him right away. A glance out the window showed a storm brewing. The wind had picked up, streaming through tree leaves. The sky was the shade it turned when rain was imminent. She grabbed a jacket and stocking hat, hurrying to put them on as she strode along the corridor. No one was about, so she helped herself to the key for the little red runabout. On her way out the door that led to the car park, she commed Randolph to tell him she was coming to meet him.

There were fancier, more expensive cars in the lot, but something about this tiny apple-red car appealed to Jen. She'd flashed the key and was climbing into the driver's seat when something bumped her in the lower back. Startled, she turned to find Lanny Conyer smiling at her.

"Hi, Jen." Lanny's expression became solemn. "I heard about Genevieve Kavan. Isn't it dreadful? Her poor son. I saw Randolph escorting him from the garda station. Surely they don't think he killed his mother. That would be awful."

Jen clasped Penny's diary to her chest. "I'm sure they don't. Darrin is Randolph's half-brother. Randolph went to the station to bring him to Briarcliff."

"Oh, I know the whole sordid story. Penny told me all about the affair her father had with that woman. Genevieve Kavan was a strange one." Lanny's gaze latched on to the diary. She looked for all the world like a cat ready to pounce on a mouse. "What do you have there? That's Penny's diary. You found it."

"Yes. I-I've started reading it. Penny was a fascinating woman. We're hoping the diary will explain why she wanted Randolph to be Sophie's guardian." Jen glanced into the car, putting one foot inside. "I need to get going."

Lanny latched her hand on Jen's elbow. "What about the data cube with Penny's book? Have you found that too?"

"Umm. Still looking." Jen knew her cheeks had pinked. *I'm such a terrible liar.* "I-I'll talk to you again soon. Let you know about…things."

Her expression feral, Lanny said, "I think you're lying, Jen."

"Wh-why would I lie to you?"

"You know what's on the data cube. It's not the paean to the founding mothers that Penny led everyone to believe it was. So you know I don't want to make certain it's published. I want to destroy it. Isn't that right?"

"I…I don't know what you're talking about."

"Where is the data cube?" Lanny pulled a gun from behind her back and snatched the diary from Jen's fingers, cramming it in her pocket. Both hands on the grip of the weapon, she aimed it at Jen. "I don't want to hurt you. But I need it. Where is it?"

Her heart racing and limbs shaking, Jen was stunned into silence.

Lanny pushed the pistol closer to Jen's chest. "Take me to it."

"I…" *Oh gods! What am I going to do? I can't give her the data cube.* An image of it lying next to the diary on the dresser in Randolph's bedroom flashed in her head. "Randolph has it. He carries it with him."

"Damn." Lanny's eyes lost focus.

Trapped between the car and Lanny, Jen could envision only one way to escape: shove Lanny, climb in the car, and drive away fast enough to avoid getting shot. *If I'm going to be killed anyway, it might as well be as I'm trying to get away.* She was on the verge of acting when Lanny broke out of her reverie and waved the gun at Jen.

"Get in the car. You're going to drive us to the chapel. And don't try anything. I'll have this gun on you the whole time. I've been practicing with it, and I'm not afraid to use it."

Her body trembling, Jen sat in the driver's seat and waited for Lanny to climb in the passenger side. *Okay. Okay. Do what she says. The woman is nuts.*

Wait for a better chance. Once the vehicle started, she pulled out of the parking slot and headed for the chapel. Intermittent drops of rain splattered on the windshield. It was a short drive. Lanny directed her to park by the entrance.

"We're going inside. Don't make any funny moves. I'll let you go once I have the data cube."

Jen recognized that for the lie it was. The gun was no longer visible when she exited the vehicle at the same time Lanny did, but Jen could tell it was still trained on her from under the front of the jacket where Lanny's hand rested. Rain fell in earnest, soaking through Jen's coat in the few moments it took to reach the chapel's crimson front door.

At this hour the chapel was empty. Lanny pushed Jen through the vestibule and up the center aisle. Water dripped down Jen's forehead. The soles of her shoes squeaked on the stone floor. Holding the gun in the open once again, Lanny waved the tip at the first pew on the left. "Pull the kneeler down and get on your knees."

The kneeler slipped from Jen's fingers and banged against the floor. She managed to get herself onto it, but her legs were shaking so badly, she was forced to rest her rear on the edge of the seat. A hint of incense lingered in the air. The statue of Mary stood, arms outstretched, her expression placid. *If you're real, please ask your son to save me. I don't want to die.*

Lanny snatched Jen's attention back with a harsh command. "Comm Randolph Meryon. Tell him you need him to come to the chapel and bring the data cube or you'll be killed. Don't mention my name. He's to tell no one where he's going or why. You got that?"

"Y-yes." Jen tried to reach Randolph. "He di-didn't answer."

Visibly bristling, Lanny moved a step closer to Jen. "Keep trying. He has to answer you sometime."

"I c-can leave a message."

"No messages. I want to know when he's coming. Try again."

For fifteen minutes in which Lanny paced and cursed, Jen's attempts were unsuccessful. The chapel wasn't well heated. The damp from her rain-soaked clothes was causing her to shiver. When she finally got through to Randolph, Jen nearly broke down in tears. She delivered Lanny's message, trying to add a sense of urgency to her tone.

Randolph's heated response made her jump. "What the fuck is going on, Jen? Is someone holding you captive?"

Unable to explain, Jen repeated her statement.

A note of panic tinged Randolph's voice. "Jen, who is it? Who's threatening you?"

"I can't tell you that. Please come quickly. She's getting very angry."

Lanny tersely ordered her to end the comm.

"I did. I did."

Lanny backhanded Jen across her face. "You useless slut! You told him I'm female. I would shoot you right now if I didn't need you alive. I'm so tired of trying to curry favor with you inbred aristocrats. I've never been good enough because I wasn't born to the right woman. You've had it good your entire life. O'Malley bitch."

A coppery taste filled Jen's mouth. One hand held to her cheek, she wanted to scream how ridiculously wrong Lanny was to think Jen had breezed through life, but discretion and pain restrained her.

Not that she could get a word in edgewise. Lanny was ranting now. "Me. I'm the daughter of a service-class woman, raped by the pampered son of the aristos she worked for. They let her keep me. Didn't want to punish the child, they claimed. Ha! When I was fourteen, my drunken bastard of a father went after me. He'd have raped me too if my mother hadn't found us and jumped on him, pounding and screaming that I was his daughter."

Jen stared at Lanny, aghast at the revelation. Nearly raped by her own father. No wonder the woman hated men. Lanny enumerated all the things she'd accomplished despite her low birth. Jen didn't pay attention, letting the ravings of the mad woman fall on deaf ears until she finally came around to recent events.

"I deserve a high-level position in the Matriarchist Party. They owe me. I'm saving them. Penny's book would devastate them. She twisted every historical fact to suit her own agenda. Facts she got from my research. She used me, but I didn't let her get away with it. No, that bitch didn't know what hit her. I just needed a little more time to find the data cube and the diary. And—"

"And what, Lanny?" Randolph's voice sounded from the vestibule. Jen wanted to turn, to fill her eyes with the pure masculine strength of him, but she was afraid of attracting Lanny's attention, which was now riveted on Randolph.

"You better have the data cube, or your wife is dead." The way Lanny twisted the word *wife* on her lips, Jen was certain Lanny would shoot her whether he had brought it or not.

19

Once they got to Briarcliff and settled Darrin into his new home, he'd have a long chat with Maon about...hell, about everything. For now, even in the rain that was falling in sheets, he was steering a vehicle that drove like a dream. Operating a mega-horsepower machine was a rush unavailable to Randolph on Beta Tau. But he'd gladly forgo ever driving again if it meant not having to deal with the crap that had happened in the last couple of days. Admittedly a sizable chunk was his own fault. But not today's appalling revelation. *It's a good thing Sophie is at Gleann Milis.*

Maon had ceded the front passenger seat of the car to Darrin. The boy had spent the drive staring out the window in an attempt to hide the tears that were inching down his cheeks. No. He couldn't desert his brother. Someone needed to protect the boy, keep the skewed mores of the Tallavan aristocracy from messing with his mind.

A tiny white dot denoting an incoming comm call flashed in his vision. Randolph had to give the caller credit for persistence. They'd been comming him repeatedly. They were approaching the castle, so it seemed to Randolph like the best time to deal with whatever they wanted. Once they reached Briarcliff, he would be too busy.

He answered the comm. "Hello."

Jen's shaky voice blurted out. "I need you to come to the chapel. Bring the data cube with Penny's book. Come quick, or I'll be killed. Don't tell anyone else."

The reaction to her words was swift. His stomach dropped, and he jammed on the brakes, sending his passengers sharply forward. "What the fuck is going on, Jen? Is someone holding you captive?"

Her response was to repeat what she'd just said. The hair along his arms and the back of his nape lifted. The weight in his gut hardened to a solid mass. "Jen, who is it? Who's threatening you?"

"I can't tell you that. Please come quickly. She's getting very angry."

The comm ended, and Jen was gone. He pounded the steering wheel. "Fuck!" Wide-eyed, Darrin flinched, pressing himself into the door.

A hand dropped onto Randolph's shoulder. "What's happened?"

Thank the gods Maon's here. "Someone…a woman has Jen and is threatening to kill her if I don't bring the data cube with Penny's last book on it." The cube was back in his room. He pushed the throttle pedal with his foot and sent the car hurtling down the narrow lane toward the castle car park. "I have to go get it."

Maon's grip fell away for a moment, but it returned, a reassurance Randolph badly needed. Maon's voice was crisp, full of the authority of a Tallavan marshal. "This is what we're going to do. Randolph, you'll get the data cube. Can I assume you've made copies?"

"I have."

"Good. Darrin, you're staying at the castle. I want you to comm Lt. Sanders and tell her what is happening. Ask her to come to the chapel. No sirens. You think you can do that?"

"Yes." Darrin's voice was shaky, but he had a determined look in his eyes.

"Tell me about the chapel. How many entrances?"

His response terse, Randolph said, "Main door and a side door from the rectory."

They rolled into the car park, and Randolph brought the vehicle to a skidding halt by the staff entrance and bailed out. Maon followed him with Darrin bringing up the rear.

Maon hollered at Randolph's retreating form. "I'm getting my service weapon. Don't leave without me." Mrs. Polgrey, the cook, and several other staff members appeared along the corridor to stare at the commotion.

With a face full of consternation Mrs. Polgrey asked, "What's happening?"

Over his shoulder Randolph said, "Do whatever the marshal says."

He heard Maon speak to her. "No time, ma'am. This young man will fill you in on the details. But first he needs to make a comm call. Please assist him."

Mrs. Polgrey would come through. Randolph didn't doubt that. He flew up the stairs to the second floor and along the darkly paneled corridors that seemed to stretch for miles. The data cube was right where he'd left it. He snatched it and shoved it into his pocket. Then he pelted through the bedroom door.

He met Maon, running full tilt toward the stairs. "Back to the car."

Randolph didn't respond. He was breathing hard, and their destination was obvious. Outside the rain had finally slowed. Maon blocked Randolph from climbing in the driver's seat.

"I'm driving."

With a snarl Randolph latched on to Maon's shirt to throw him aside.

But Maon was bigger and stood his ground. "It'll be faster. You can go straight in."

His chest rising and falling as he sucked air into his lungs, Randolph grunted and released him, dashing around and climbing in the passenger seat while Maon put the car into reverse.

Maon glanced at Randolph and then concentrated on his driving.

"Left. Turn left here," Randolph shouted. "Then follow the lane. The chapel's at the far end."

Without removing his gaze from the road they were flying down, Maon said. "You're going in through the main door. Do whatever you can to stall her, keep her talking, anything. I'm going to come in through the rectory. Whoever she is, she's killed twice already. When I get a clear shot, I'm taking her down. Don't get between me and her."

"Right." Up ahead the bright red door of the chapel seemed to pulse as though signaling danger. Randolph found it hard to swallow the sour taste in his mouth. *If only Maon would drive faster.*

Before Maon brought the car to a full stop, Randolph was on his way to the chapel entrance, water from puddles spraying up from his sprinting feet. He flung himself into the vestibule and came to a halt. He heard the voice of a woman seething with rage. "Penny's book would devastate them. She twisted every historical fact to suit her own agenda. Facts she got from my research. She used me, but I didn't let her get away with it. No, that bitch didn't know what hit her. I just needed a little more time to find the data cube and the diary. And—"

Through the holes in the carved screen that separated the vestibule from the nave of the chapel, Randolph caught sight of a head with cropped blonde hair. Lanny Conyer. Pounding filled his ears. Every muscle in his body seemed to grow stronger, and a consuming desire to crush the evil hag who had killed his sister and was threatening to do the same to Jen flooded his soul.

"And what, Lanny?" He pulled open the door and stood inside, taking in the scene before him. His heart constricted at the sight of Jen hunched in the first pew her head bowed as though in prayer.

A gleam of insanity flickered in Lanny's eyes when she turned to face him. "You better have the data cube, or your wife is dead." She lifted the weapon she'd been holding against her thigh up, training it in a double-handed grip on Jen.

He pulled the cube from his pocket and waved it in the air. "I brought it. But you have to let Jen go to get it."

Lanny cackled. "You really expect me to do that. I'm not a fool. Get down here and kneel in the pew beside her."

If he followed Lanny's instructions, she might see Maon when he entered the chapel. Better to walk down the left-side aisle and keep Lanny's gaze away from the archway that led to the sacristy and door to the rectory. Randolph held his hands out from his sides, the data cube visible in his right hand, and moved along the back row of pews. "I want to know why? You've killed two people and are threatening another. What is worth all those lives?"

The sneer that scrunched her face was as ugly as the words that spewed from her mouth. "I owe no man an explanation. You're scum. I should shoot you and eliminate your pustulant filth from the world."

With a gasp Jen swayed forward.

Lanny shifted to stand in front of her, dropping her gaze to where Jen knelt. "You're as bad as Penny. No, worse. She was a traitor, but you're an O'Malley. O'Malley's don't take the side of evil, misogynistic bastards like him." She waved the gun in Randolph's direction.

He continued treading slowly to the front of the chapel. The pace was excruciating, but he had to give Maon time to get in position.

Lanny continued ranting. "He beats women until they bleed, and then he licks their blood. Probably would bathe in it if he could get away with it."

Fucking matriarchal bitch. "Would you like me to show you what I do to women? I'd enjoy shackling you to the wall of my dungeon and carving strips of skin from your body. You'd be begging, pleading for your life, for a chance that you never gave Penny or Genevieve. How did you do it? Did you set Penny up and then push her over the side of the cliff? And Genevieve. Did you creep behind her and bash her head in? You even invaded my niece's bedroom, didn't you?" He rounded the front pew and took several steps toward Lanny.

She turned to face him. "Stop. Right there. Don't take another step." She aimed the pistol at Randolph's chest. "I'll drop you in a heartbeat. Put the cube on the floor and kneel in the pew behind the one your adoring wife is in." The gun must be growing heavy because it was wavering slightly.

Slowly Randolph dropped to a crouch, but before he was halfway to the ground, he surged forward. Three things happened simultaneously. The pistol fired. Jen shoved Lanny. And Maon slammed open the rectory door, barreled through the archway, and shouted, "Freeze."

Randolph slumped to the ground, landing on his knees. Lanny, her face a violent snarl, raised the gun, preparing to shoot him again. Jen scrambled along the pew to get to him. And Maon fired his weapon. The sound of his shot wasn't as loud as Lanny's, but the destruction it wrecked was five times worse.

This time it was Lanny's turn to hit the floor. The force of the bullet spun her around. She fell to her back, but unlike Randolph she didn't move. Her chest was a mass of blood and torn tissue, the white tip of a broken rib gleaming at an odd angle. From where Randolph knelt on the stone floor, it looked like her gaze was locked onto the face of Mary, staring at unseeing stone eyes with eyes blinded in death.

And Jen was by his side, reaching out to touch him and then pulling her hands back as though she was afraid to hurt him further.

"She shot you." Her voice was clogged with emotion.

His attempt at a weak smile failed. "Flesh wound."

Jen sobbed and turned her face toward Maon. "He needs help."

Maon was busy doing something, but everything was fuzzy like it was happening far, far away. Dizziness struck Randolph as well as an overpowering urge to shut his eyes. But the burning pain that speared through him kept him partially aware of his circumstances.

He was pretty sure Jen was patting his cheek, but it was hard to hear what she was saying. *Am I dying? I must be. She's crying.* His voice wouldn't work. He needed to tell her he was sorry one more time. He gave a last surge of effort. "M sorr..."

The black that had been creeping ever closer to filling his vision, swept his sight away, but he heard her say, "I know. I am too." Before he sank into unconsciousness, he felt himself falling sideways and wished he could sense her arms around him.

THE INSTANT JEN had registered Randolph's surge forward, she'd been absolutely certain that Lanny would murder him right before her eyes, that he would die. Something inside her twisted and broke. Pain like molten lava boiled over, and she reacted without a thought for the consequences, leaping from her kneeler to shove Lanny, to keep the weapon that was already discharging from striking Randolph. Someone shouted *freeze*, but there was no stopping her.

Time stretched, making each increment of a second vivid and distinct. Randolph fell to his knees, his eyes wide and his mouth open as though he couldn't believe that his attempt to tackle Lanny hadn't worked. That evil bitch, now out of Jen's reach, was taking aim at him again. The sound of another gunshot reverberated through the room. Jen caught herself on the pew rail, squeezing her eyelids shut. Her throat constricted around a scream, turning it to a gurgling squeak. A thud echoed. Steeling herself, Jen peered through narrowed eyes. Lanny was on the floor, and Maon was striding forward.

Jen flew left along the length of the pew and rushed to Randolph's side. Her fingers had gone cold. She lifted her hands, wanting to find out how badly he was injured, but she twitched back, not knowing what to do and not wanting to hurt him. Maon was behind her, dealing with Lanny, making sure she couldn't shoot anyone again. His face blotchy, Randolph held himself perfectly still.

Her throat tight, Jen said, "She shot you."

His response was accompanied by a thin smile. "Flesh wound."

Damn the idiot man! It was impossible to hold back the sobs now. She flung a cry to Maon over her shoulder. "He needs help."

What little color remained in Randolph's face slowly drained until he was ashen, his body swaying forward and back in abbreviated motions. She brought her hand to his cheek, patting it. "Stay with me. Don't close your eyes."

The words that fell from his lips in a mumbled rasp broke her heart. Even now when he was dying in front of her, he was begging for her forgiveness. Sorrow punched her in the gut. "I know. I am too." His eyes rolled back in his head, and he teetered an instant before slumping sideways. She caught him before he struck the stone floor, shifting so she could cradle him in her arms.

Maon knelt before them. "Here, let me lay him down and check him over."

When Maon lifted Randolph from her, Jen's hand was damp. One look revealed what she feared. Blood covered her palm and the sleeve of her shirt. She went icy cold, her heartbeat thumping in her ears like a slow death knell.

"Hold pressure here." Maon pointed to a spot on Randolph's chest where a small smear of blood soiled the fabric of his shirt. "I need to find the exit wound."

Maon ripped off the bottom of his cotton shirt and made a pad, placing it over the entrance wound. "Keep firm pressure."

"Okay." Her hands trembled when she spread her palm over the wad of cloth. She held her breath a moment and then exhaled slowly, fighting to steady her racing mind and calm her pounding heart. She would not be useless in the effort to save Randolph.

It took all her strength to keep the pad from slipping while Maon rolled

Randolph to his side.

"Fuck all." Without further comment Maon pulled the rest of his shirt off and made a larger pad from it. Holding it in place on Randolph's back, he eased his friend down. "Where the hell is the garda? They should be here by now."

No sooner had he snapped the words out than Lt. Sanders was banging through the door from the vestibule, followed by all the village constables, emergency med techs, and Father James.

When one of the med techs bent to examine Lanny, Maon barked at her. "She's dead. He needs your help." Then he rose and allowed the techs access to Randolph, helping Jen to her feet after one of the two women took over applying pressure to Randolph's wound. Jen's whole body trembled as Maon, his arms wrapped around her, relayed details of Randolph's condition. Without looking at Maon, the techs acknowledged the information, their hands flying as they fought to save Randolph's life.

Over her head, Maon filled Lt. Sander's in on what happened. Jen was praying to any god who would listen. She raised her gaze to the stature of Mary. *Please ask your son to let him live. I'll do anything. Convert. If you'll just save him.*

More med techs arrived, guiding a gurney toward them, its gravity field quietly humming. A constable was on one knee beside Lanny's body, but he rose to make room for the stretcher. The well-trained emergency crew had Randolph on the gurney, his arm encased in a portable medical analysis unit, in minutes. Then they guided the unit toward the exit.

Jen attempted to shrug out of Maon's embrace, but he resisted. "I want to go with him."

"I understand. But they'll separate you the moment you arrive at the hospital. Let them do their work. He's in good hands. They'll stabilize him, put him in stasis, and send him to the medical center in Cahernamon. We need to comm his mother and talk to the staff. And someone needs to be there for Darrin. He was with us when you called."

She slumped, the desire to stand vigil over Randolph aching inside her. Then she straightened her shoulders. He was correct. Darrin had just lost his mother. She couldn't be certain how he would react to learning his brother had been shot and was fighting for his life, but it was bound to be messy. "You're right. We have things to do." The burden of responsibility settled on Jen. She'd always wondered what it would be like to be the head of family. She wasn't truly, but she was standing in Claire's shoes for now.

Lt. Sander's rose from where she'd been examining Lanny Conyer's body and stepped toward them, holding Penny's diary. "I'll need statements from both of you. I'll also need your weapon, Marshal."

Maon nodded and produced his gun, handing it to the lieutenant. "Can we do this quickly? Ms. Meryon needs to attend to family matters."

The lieutenant turned her gaze on Jen. "Could you come to the rear of the chapel with me, Ms. Meryon."

Jen blinked. It was odd being called Ms. Meryon. She would have to adjust to it and all that it entailed. In this community at least, she had power. "Of course. I'm not how sure of the details I can be. There were moments when I must admit I was praying more than I was paying attention."

"That's understandable." The lieutenant gestured for her to precede her down the left aisle away from the body lying on the floor and the pool of blood where Randolph had fallen.

"You may sit if you'd like."

"No." Jen shook her head. "I'd prefer to stand."

"I'm recording your statement for official purposes. Do you understand that lying during a police inquiry is a criminal act and may be prosecuted under Tallavan law?"

Jen's brow furrowed. "I do."

"Tell me in your own words what happened today."

With her arms wrapped around herself, Jen related the events that had led to the shootings in the chapel. The lieutenant interrupted her three times to clarify specific points but, on the whole, allowed Jen to relate the timeline from the moment she was accosted by Lanny in the castle car park to when Maon shot Lanny.

Jen dropped her head and then raised it again to gaze bleakly at the lieutenant. "The instant I realized Lanny was going to shoot Randolph is still crystal clear in my mind. Every part of me screamed *no*. I reacted without thinking. Before I knew it, I was shoving Lanny." Her fist pressed to her mouth, Jen tried to hold back the tears that were threatening to overtake her. "But it was no use."

In a soothing tone the lieutenant said, "You probably did save him. One of the med techs said that the shot that hit Mr. Meryon went far right of center, missing his heart. We may seem like a backwater here on Rathlin, but the hospital by the port is top-notch. They treat more gunshot wounds than you might think."

"Thank you. I'm sure Mr. Meryon is getting excellent care. May I leave now?"

"First I'd like you to identify this." The lieutenant held up Penny's diary. "Is this the diary that was taken from you by Lanny Conyer today?"

"Yes, it is."

The lieutenant nodded and then glanced at Maon. "I'll need to speak with Marshal Shirley before he can accompany you."

"Not a problem." Jen straightened her spine. "I'm walking to Briarcliff. I'm to shaken to drive. Maybe it will help to clear my head. Has Mr. Mery-on's mother been notified by the garda of her son's shooting?"

A pained expression crossed the officer's face. "No. I can come to the castle as soon as I finish here."

Jen reached out to touch the lieutenant's arm but pulled her hand back before her fingers contacted the woman's sleeve. "She's not there. Once you freed us to leave Briarcliff, she shuttled into Cahernamon for some business meetings."

Lips pursed, the lieutenant nodded. "I'll contact my superiors, and they'll send someone to visit her there."

"Fine." Jen heaved a sigh. "Thank you for handling this... this mess with discretion. I'm sure Claire, Ms. Meryon, will make a statement in the near future. If you need anything else, I'll be in Cahernamon, at the hospital."

"Thank you, ma'am. I'm sorry we didn't stop Ms. Conyer from hurting your family again."

"Thank you." Jen let her forced smile fade from her lips. She slipped into the vestibule. She'd forgotten that Father James had accompanied the garda as they rushed into the nave of the chapel. He was here now, his face a wash of sadness and concern when he turned to her.

"How may I be of service?"

It struck her that this was a man who took his religion seriously. He was a believer, and that motivated him to care for the members of this community. By dint of her marriage to a Meryon, she had become one of that group. There was no manipulation she could detect in his offer. Either he was what he seemed, a shepherd to his sheep, or he was a skilled liar. But that was the way O'Malley's thought, and she was no longer a member of that family.

"Your prayers would be welcome."

"You have them already, but…I don't wish to overstep, but perhaps I can handle arrangements for Genevieve Kavan. I understand Darrin will live at Briarcliff, and I'd like to spend time with him."

Jen glanced to the side, a frown forming on her face. The priest held up his hand. "A friend of mine, a druidess priestess, will handle the sacred aspects. I won't encroach on the deceased's beliefs."

With her hand pressed to her stomach, Jen let gratitude wash through her. She'd spent her life walking the crooked path that delineated the distinction between what was said and what was meant. This man seemed honest, straightforward, and capable of guarding the sensibilities of all involved. A rare gift.

"That would be appreciated. Claire and I will be in Cahernamon with Randolph, but I'm sure she'd be grateful to leave Genevieve's funeral in your hands. It's probably best if Darrin remain at Briarcliff. Mrs. Polgrey and the other staff will take good care of him, but he will need grief counseling. This is more than a fourteen-year-old should handle on his own."

"I agree. If Darrin is not comfortable talking with me, I can arrange for someone else to see him."

Jen nodded. "Thank you. I need to get going. There's several things that must be done before I can shuttle to Cahernamon."

The priest opened the chapel door and said, "Allow me to accompany you. There are members of the church on staff at Briarcliff."

"Of course." They set out. The clouds that had brought the rain had been swept out to sea. Puddles marked the road; avoiding them was the easier route since the more direct footpath was too muddy. The sun had drifted lower, but its rays still warmed, casting the greens and golds of turning leaves in sharp relief against a cerulean sky. It was glorious. Jen clasped the sight to her heart, an omen that life would once again be filled with light and beauty.

20

Randolph couldn't move. He was half-awake but equally half-asleep. His eyelids remained unresponsive to his commands that they lift. His hearing worked. That voice was his mother's and someone else. Another woman. He knew her. But then the equation tilted, and he drifted back to sleep.

A clatter woke him. This time he opened his eyes to see the very curvaceous backside of Jen. His mind could appreciate the view, but his body was operating in a different reality.

She brandished the spoon she'd dropped as she turned to face him. "Oh. Sorry. I didn't mean to wake you."

"How…" He cleared his throat. "How long have I been out?"

Her ponytail was askew, dark circles rimmed her eyes, and her voice was subdued. "It's been about a half hour since you were brought out of recovery."

"Recovery?" The details of the room he was in shifted into perspective. He was in a hospital bed, his arm wrapped by an analysis and infusion unit. His shoulder and chest were swathed in bandages.

She scrunched her eyebrows together. "Do you remember being shot?"

It took a moment to sort through his memories. "I do."

Lips pressed tight, she nodded. "The EMTs took you to the port hospital on Rathlin and from there you were shuttled to the medical center in Cahernamon. They said you woke up on the trip here."

"I don't remember that."

"You were given some pretty hefty pain meds."

Must still be. I can't feel a thing. The muzzy sensation was both disturbing and seductive. He preferred to be in control of himself, but if the alternative was racking pain, he didn't mind life being out of focus. "How long—"

His mother swept into the room in full head-of-family mode down to the pearls around her neck. "Rand, you're awake. They said it would take an hour, but naturally you would prove them wrong." She took his hand and smiled at him. Deeper circles than Jen's darkened the skin beneath her eyes, and new wrinkles were etched in her face. He squeezed her fingers. She was a Meryon through and through, masking her turmoil and taking charge. But the signs of the upheaval in their lives were there to read.

Lanny Conyer had done more to his family than murder and attempted murder. She'd emotionally ravaged his mother, his niece, and flicking a glance at her, Jen too. His brother's face popped into his mind. *And my brother. I'd like to squeeze the life out of that evil murdering witch.* "Where's Lanny? I assume she's in jail."

Both of the women at his bedside shared a look before his mother responded. "She's dead, dear. Maon shot her."

His breath caught. "What?"

"She was going to shoot you again." The horror of the moment flared in Jen's eyes.

The monitor next to him registered the increase in his pulse. An urge to bellow his satisfaction welled inside him. Instead he spoke one word with savage intensity. "Good."

"Don't think about that, dear. You focus on recovering." His mother smoothed the sheet that covered him.

He knew now without any of the doubt that at the age of fourteen had played havoc on him that his mother loved him. Maybe it had been a mistake for her to send him away, but everyone made errors in judgment. Wasn't he the gods-awful spokesman for that. How could he leave his mother to face the consequences of the brutal events they had just lived through? Wasn't returning to his own self-imposed exile the reaction the old Randolph would support. He couldn't leave. But how could he stay in the same household as the woman he'd crushed with his own pitiless version of cynicism?

Jen was seated in the chair on his left side. He couldn't even lift that hand to reach out to her. Instead he turned his head, focusing his gaze on her. "How are you?"

She glanced up at him and then dropped her gaze back to her lap where she was clasping and unclasping her hands. "I'm fine."

His mother leaned down and kissed his forehead. "I need to go make some comms. So many people are waiting to hear how you're doing. It'll take me at least an hour."

"Thanks, Mom."

The smile he directed at her must have looked exceptionally sappy because she patted his cheek. "Dear sweet boy. Everything is going to be all right."

Alone with Jen, Rand was hit by the inability to formulate a coherent thought. What could he say? Other than he was sorry. Maybe that's all he should say. "Jen—"

"I forgive you."

The words were blurted out so rapidly it took him a moment to process them, and then it was as though all the tension that had been constricting his heart dissolved. Tightly bandaged though it was, his chest felt like it expanded. His gaze steady on her, he said, "Thank you."

She nodded and returned to staring at her hands.

Gods. He needed to touch her, to show her he could be tender. But he was as good as pinned to this bed like a bug in an exhibit. He gritted his teeth and attempted to sit. *Whoa. Bad idea.* The surge of pain grayed his vision. He took long breaths, slowing relaxing back into the mattress as the discomfort subsided. Then he looked at her again. She was still studying her fingers as though they held some important truth. "Come here."

Her head lifted. She stared at him.

"Please."

The wide-eyed expression didn't leave her face, but she did stand and move closer to him. He reached up with his right hand, wanting to caress her cheek, but she was too far away. "Take my hand."

When she did, her warmth transferred to him. He ignored the ache in his chest. "Can we start fresh? I can't leave. My mother, Sophie, Darrin… they all need me. And…I need to be here. For myself. If you want…if you think it's possible…"

She covered his lips with her fingers. "Hush. I'm willing to try. But this time, no sex. It gives you an unfair advantage." She quirked a tiny smile at him.

Warmth filled him. He pressed his mouth to her hand in a quick kiss. "You don't give yourself enough credit. But I agree. Let's get to know each other better first."

Pain sliced through his chest and shoulder when he lifted his head. He squeezed his eyes shut. "Fuck."

"Lie still. There's a pain med feed here." She placed a plastic tube in his hand. "Squeeze the button on top, and you'll get another dose. It won't give you more than you're allowed."

He pressed it. The relief was almost instantaneous, but so was a feeling of lethargy. He battled to keep his eyelids from falling.

Her palm brushed his brow. "Go to sleep. Everything is going to be fine."

I hope so.

⌇

THE COSSETING from his mother was driving him crazy, but you didn't command your mother to do or not do anything. Not if you loved her. Jen was only a little better. Between the two women, they'd settled him into the library on one end of a sofa, a cushion behind his back, a cup of nasty, healthy tea concoction on the side table next to him, and his slipper-encased feet on a hassock. The fact that he allowed it showed how tired the journey from the hospital in Cahernamon had made him.

Penny's diary lay open on his lap. He was rereading the pages that explained Penny's theory for how Genevieve Kavan had become pregnant with Darrin. Genevieve had been a patient at the Mother and Child Clinic on North Island almost forty weeks to the day before Darrin was born. Her appointment was three days after the close of the Apple Festival on Rath-lin. Penny believed that Genevieve had slipped something into Conlin Meryon's drink at the Apple Barn Ball that ended every festival, some kind of rape drug. It would have been easy to do. Apple wine, apple punch, and applejack flowed freely. Randolph couldn't remember a Barn Ball that his father hadn't ended up drunk.

When Genevieve had accused him of fathering Darrin, his father had been adamant that he hadn't touched her that night, not even for the dance that any woman could claim with the husband of the Meryon head of family. He's said that he'd felt ill and left the main barn, intent on making his way to Briarcliff, but he hadn't made it that far. Instead, hours later he awoke to find himself flat on his back on one of the piles of hay bales strategically scattered as trysting spots for lovers. The party had been dying down, so he went and found his wife.

Randolph's mother remembered Conlin had told her that night about not feeling well and falling asleep on the hay bales, but the DNA evidence stood in stark contradiction of his claims that he hadn't had sex with Genevieve. Her claim that Conlin had been drunk and raped her only added fuel to the blazing anger that had sparked to life in Claire Meryon at the suggestion her husband would be unfaithful to her.

If she had been raped, why then did she go to a fertility clinic three days later and wait to come forward with her story until her pregnancy was showing? The fertility clinic had one mission, helping women conceive. Penny believed that Genevieve had drugged their father to obtain a sperm sample from him. And Randolph agreed.

He looked across at Jen, who sat at a library table working at a vidscreen. Her elbow planted on the table and her chin resting in the palm of her hand, she was frowning at the screen. "What's wrong?"

"Nothing." She didn't move her focus from whatever she was reading.

"Nothing?"

A slight turn of her head brought her gaze to his. "It's my mother. She wants to speak with me."

"I see."

"The newsies have been full of what happened. She's been leaving me comm messages for days. I don't think I can talk to her. Not yet." She returned her gaze to the vidscreen.

Randolph fiddled with the handle of the tea cup, on the verge of picking it up to take a sip before remembering it wasn't proper tea. "Are you afraid she'll chastise you for marrying me and getting involved in a huge scandal?"

Her voice rose in challenge. "Of course I am."

In a calm, gentle tone, he responded, "You don't think that because she loves you, she's worried about you? You were kidnapped and held at gunpoint."

She sat back, her shoulders slumping. "Probably. I should call her."

Claire Meryon chose that moment to enter the library with a plate of freshly baked sugar cookies wafting sweet vanilla goodness. "Cook made you cookies, dear. Said they would speed your healing process."

He grinned and plucked one from the plate when his mother held it before him. "And she is absolutely correct."

Jen gave a rueful shake of her head and declined when Claire offered her a cookie. "No, thank you. I need to comm my mother." She rose and left the room, her expression distracted.

"I'm glad she's finally responding to her mother. I know I'd be frantic with worry." Claire set the plate next to Randolph's teacup.

"Yes."

"Is there anything else you need?"

He patted the sofa cushion beside him. "Sit. I have something to discuss with you."

Her eyebrows raised, she sat. "This sounds serious."

"It is." He took in a deep breath, aware that his pain at broaching this topic was clearly written on his face. "Did Penny ever share her theory about how Genevieve Kavan conceived Darrin?"

His mother stiffened and pulled back from him. "As far as I know, she always believed your father lied about his liaison with Genevieve."

"She changed her mind."

Fingers tightly gripping the arm of the sofa, Claire asked, "Why?"

"Three days after the Barn Ball that year, Genevieve had an appointment at the Mother and Child Clinic."

Claire's jaw dropped. "But that would mean…"

Keeping the heat of his own anger banked, he responded with careful control. "She used artificial means to conceive Darrin. She gave Dad a drink laced with something that put him out. Then she collected semen from him."

"She lied. She raped him, not the reverse as she claimed." Claire pounded a fist on the sofa arm, her gaze turned inward. "Damn her. She took Conlin from me. He begged me to believe him, but I couldn't. I wouldn't."

When his mother swiveled to look at him, her face was a mask of pain and fury. "Why would she do that? Why did I ever believe her?"

Randolph held his arm out to her. "Come here." He pulled her tight against his side, his hand firm on her shoulder. "I don't know why. We'll probably never know. She was always a little off in the head."

"Harmless. That's what we called her. But she wasn't. She destroyed my marriage and then lived off my charity." Claire clenched the fist on her lap. "Gods, I could kill her myself if she weren't already dead."

"From what Darrin has told me, she suffered a great deal of guilt."

"Good. She deserved to."

"What will you do now?"

"I'm going to apologize to your father and beg his forgiveness. I pray he will. It's been a long time. He's surely moved on with his life, found someone else. But I can at least set things straight between us. I should have believed him. I was such a fool."

Randolph rubbed her arm. "We all make mistakes. And you had more justification than most. I didn't believe him either, so I'll be asking his pardon myself. This is what Penny would want. For us to try to restore the family as best we can."

"Yes. It is what she wanted." She kissed Randolph's cheek. "I love you. Thank you for coming home."

"I'm grateful you asked me." Life took such unexpected turns. Maybe it was the prayers of his mother and eventually his sister that had made the difference. Penny dying a Reformed Catholic in good standing was a possibility he could never have imagined, and yet it had happened. How ironic that for him, a self-deceiving misogynist, women would be the catalyst for the transformation he was still trying to achieve. He was determined to be a better man, a better son, and with Jen's help, a better husband.

He clearly saw what he'd been oblivious to before, his own need for forgiveness. From now on he would own his mistakes and strive to be slow to place blame and quick to offer grace. What was that phrase his grand-mother used to say? Anytime she was told of the wrongdoing of others, she'd clasp a hand to her bosom, lift her eyes to the heavens, and say, "But for the grace of God." At the age of thirty-five, he finally understood what that meant.

21

It had been two weeks since Randolph had returned home from the hospital, and his stamina was at last returning. He had been lucky; unlike the blast that had torn away Maon's side a decade ago, the shooting had done comparatively little damage to Randolph's body.

The mystery of where Lanny had found a gun had been solved on examination of her weapon. It was one of the pieces from the Meryon armory, a replica C96 Mauser like those used in the early twentieth century Irish Revolution. The ammunition and instructions on how to load and fire the pistol had all been handy to anyone who had the access code to the safe where those items were kept for all the guns on display. Lanny had managed to obtain them, although no one would confess to providing her the information.

The weight of the weapon had kept Lanny from rapidly firing multiple times, and the caliber of the bullet meant it had the penetrating power to drill a hole through Randolph without rendering extensive tissue damage.

So here he was, feeling almost one hundred percent except for twinges when he raised his arm over his head, holding hands with Jen as they strolled through the craft booths that lined the village green for the Apple Festival.

They had been taking their courtship slow. Jen had returned to sleeping in the nursery, but every evening Randolph, Jen, Sophie, Darrin and Claire would gather in the library for several hours, talking, playing board games, or reading. Jen had suggested Randolph read aloud to Sophie and Darrin, so they were working their way through a translated version of *Swiss Family Robinson*, a favorite of Randolph's as a boy.

"Look." Jen pulled his hand, leading him toward a booth dedicated to woolens. "These scarves are gorgeous." She plucked a bright kelly-green one from the display and held it under her chin. "What do you think?"

The woman manning the booth said, "You have a good eye, ma'am. The shade of that scarf is perfect for your coloring. Shall I wrap it, or would you prefer to wear it now?" Not waiting for a response, she knotted it around Jen's neck and stepped back. "Lovely. Wear it with pride, ma'am. It's entirely Rathlin made from the shearing of the sheep to the weaving. I'd be blessed to have you accept it with my best wishes."

Jen brought her fingers up to the soft woolen cloth draped across her chest. "No, no. Let me pay for it."

The woman raised a hand in protest. "Oh no, ma'am. It's a wedding gift along with my wish that you have a happy marriage and many children."

Jen smiled. "Thank you. It's so lovely. How may I reach you if I want to buy more of your beautiful work?"

Her cheek's rosy, the woman stood a little taller. "Bless you, ma'am. The dress shop in the village stocks a few of my pieces, but my main shop is down at the port on the high street. Or you can comm me, Maura O'Jones, Rathlin Port."

Her hands clasped before her and her face wreathed in a pleased smile, the woman watched as Jen and Randolph strolled away. He brought his lips to her ear and whispered, "She'll probably sell out with that advertisement around your neck."

The sugar-cookie fragrance that was essential Jen filled his senses. He'd have gladly turned her to him and kissed her senseless, but they weren't to that stage yet. Now that he was feeling better, a different kind of ache was harassing him. He wanted her. So much so that he had trouble keeping his cock from embarrassing him at inappropriate moments, made worse by his decision not to ease that condition with his own hand. He could and would wait until she was ready to be his. But with her scent overpowering him, he couldn't resist. He placed a gentle kiss on her ear, slipping his tongue out for a brief taste before retreating.

She didn't admonish him. Instead she sent him a heated look accompanied by an enigmatic smile. That was progress. Courtship was a completely new dance for him. Although it had elements of orgasm denial, the point was different. They were getting to know one another better. That was a good thing even though he wasn't certain, as he'd always been in the past when seducing a woman, when to take the next step. It was like he was backtracking, learning what he'd skipped as a young man.

They continued to stroll, Randolph pointing out things he remembered from past festivals. At noon they met Claire, Darrin, and Sophie for lunch under a large tent staked out in the center of the green. On this last day of the festival, the chefs Claire had brought to Rathlin for the Apple Cook-off and three local cooks were competing for the Apple Chef crown. They'd spent the morning preparing three dishes each, a salad, a soup or entrée, and a dessert all made with Rathlin apples. The tent had been roped off. Only those who paid thirty credits could enter, but once inside they could sample all the dishes that had been prepared. Eight privacy voting booths had been set up opposite the serving line where tasters could rank each dish.

Randolph followed his mother, Sophie, Darrin, and Jen through the line, grinning at the banter each contestant aimed at Claire. She was back in form, making them all laugh at her witty comments. Darrin was having a hard time with the extra attention directed at their group. He kept his hands tucked behind his elbows until Sophie shoved a plate at him. The extent to which Darrin allowed her to boss him about amazed Randolph. Sophie giggled when one chef flirted with her, telling her she was the prettiest girl he'd seen all week. The moment was perfect, making his heart swell, and then Jen turned to look at him over her shoulder. She smiled softly at him. Later he could never fully describe the flood of emotions and sensations that overwhelmed him. He'd just say he'd been empty and Jen had filled him. He must have gasped because she wrinkled her brow. It was soon replaced by a broad grin that matched the one that had burst onto his face. At that moment he was absolutely certain that he and Jen would be all right and that his life had just taken an unexpected turn. He was in love for the first time.

Later that evening at the final round of the Applejack Competition, the emcee toasted Rand and Jen's marriage. The crowd broke out in applause and cheers. A chant started. "Kiss. Kiss." So he bent her in a dramatic swoop and kissed her thoroughly, to the delight of his audience.

~

RANDOLPH PAUSED from reading the proofs for Penny's last book. Although the newsies had carried the story of Penny's murder and the attack on Jen and himself, they hadn't been told the reasons behind Lanny's murderous turn. For weeks they had been speculating, wildly in some cases. The publisher had ridden the backbone of publicity that provided, playing up the mystery angle by not revealing the subtitle. The book was simply *Our Mothers*. Preorders assured it would be a bestseller.

Bedtime had arrived for Sophie, so Jen had taken her to say her good nights to the staff. His mother had left for Cahernamon earlier in the day. Darrin had been invited to spend the night with one of his friends in the village. Tonight it would be Jen and Randolph alone.

Randolph had set aside evenings as family time and didn't normally allow interruptions. Whip Hand business was off-limits as were most comm messages or calls. But this incoming comm came with a pink tag from Shane. The baby had arrived. Early. He listened to Shane's voice and could almost see the awe on his friend's face. Katrina Estelle Tiernan was born at half past seven, weighing 3.9 kg, and in lusty good health. Labor and delivery had gone smoothly, and Adrianna was doing well. That was the gist of the message when all the superlatives and statements of astonishment were filtered out.

Ten minutes later when Jen returned and sat in the chair where she had been winding yarn skeins into balls, the bemused expression hadn't left Randolph's face.

"What's got you smiling? Something in Penny's book?"

He'd been sitting with his cheek resting against his fist, but at Jen's question he raised his head and said, "Shane and Adrianna had their baby. Katrina Estelle Tiernan. Let me forward the comm message to you. Shane is overjoyed."

Jen's eyes sparkled while she listened to the message. At its end, she focused her gaze on him and grinned. "He is very excited."

"As he should be. A new life made with the woman you love. Shane would tell you it's a miracle, something he never expected to experience." Randolph patted the sofa cushion beside him. "Come over here, please. I have something to tell you."

When Jen settled next to him, Randolph took her hand and looked into the swirling gray of her eyes. "We've never discussed this, but I assume you want children."

She bit her lip, her expression serious. "Yes. I do."

"Would it surprise you that I've always longed to be a father?" Her eyes widened. "Like Shane, I never thought it would be possible." He pulled her hand to his lips and kissed her knuckles. "I never expected to find a woman who would want to be the mother of my children or be the kind of person I would want in that role."

Jen sat still as though she were holding her breath. His heart ached from looking at her, his sweet, resilient Jen. "If you'll have me, I want to be the husband you deserved from the start and the father to as many babies as you desire. Will you be my wife? I love you."

Now it was his turn to wait. The somberness hadn't left her face. His hands trembled. *She's decided to keep things purely platonic. She can't love me, not in that way after all I've done to her.*

Her response slipped past her lips, gentle and unassuming. "I will."

She will what? What does she mean? What was the question I asked her?

She smiled softly and appended her statement. "I will be your wife. I love you too. And I want to make babies with you."

For a moment he sagged, and then giddiness overtook him. He pulled her onto his lap, wrapped a hand around the back of her head, and kissed her, slowly, thoroughly, leaving no doubt that he wanted to begin that effort as soon as possible. Her scent and taste gave him a heady sense of his own power to make their marriage blossom or to destroy it absolutely. But breaking her heart would mean ripping his own to shreds because that's what would happen if he ever hurt her again.

"Let's go upstairs."

A glint of heat appeared in her eyes. "Yes." She slipped from his lap, clasped his hand as he rose beside her, and pulled him toward the library door. At the bottom of the main stairway Randolph tugged her against his chest, wrapped her tight in his arms, and claimed her mouth in a kiss that seared him down to his toes. Everything about Jen had grown more delectable in the intervening respite from sex they'd taken. It was as though he'd forgotten the fire she produced in him, but it wasn't that. This intensity was different. He would think about that later. Right now he would indulge in this fantasy become reality and savor his wife.

They mounted the stairs hand in hand. When they reached the bedroom, they slowed as though by mutual agreement. He had rarely ever rushed through sex, but this wasn't sex. Still he would take his time. It was new ground, and he intended to learn the cues that would make it the sublime experience he'd been told making love with the right woman could be.

Both of her hands in his, he gazed deep into her eyes. "I love you. I will never purposely hurt you again. I promise to cherish you all my life. You're it for me. I'm yours for as long as you'll have me."

She savored his words, taking a slow breath. "You're everything I've always wanted in a husband. You care deeply, protect those you love, and strive to do the right thing. Those are all marvelous qualities, but the thing I love you for most of all... You're not perfect. If you were, you wouldn't need me. And I need you to need me as much as I do you. I know you'll try with everything you have to keep your promises, but if you fail, I'll still be here to put things back together with you. I love you."

His breath caught. His world narrowed to this woman who stood opposite him, the pressure of their fingers their only contact. When the spell broke, he pulled her to him. "You are so fucking tenacious."

Kisses followed. Clothing fell away piece by piece until at last they lay naked side by side. He skimmed her shoulder and along her arm with his fingertips, reveling in the smoothness of her skin. She shivered and stroked his skin down to his hip. When he dipped his head to kiss her, she met him, entangling herself in his gentle exploration.

The urge to bite her lower lip struck him. He hammered his sadistic nature back into submission. He was determined to prove to himself that he could be as sweet as the most vanilla lover and as good at it as he was with kink.

His erection lay hard, trapped against her thigh. Arousal spiraled higher inside him with each movement of her body as she arched her pelvis into him. He reached between them, slipping his fingers between her folds. Wet. Ready. He rolled her to her back, positioned his cock at her entrance, and slipped into her. Her groan echoed his. Her head cradled in his hands, he feathered kisses slow and easy across her eyelids, over her forehead, and along her jawline, whispering, "I love you." He set a languid pace with his thrusts, watching her responses and altering his movements to bring her the most pleasure.

Need, physical and emotional, pulsed through him. He slipped an arm beneath her and pulled her tight, pressing his face into her neck, treasuring her with every stroke he sank inside her welcoming heat. The ache in his heart grew more acute, filling him with a heady delight. He loved this woman. "With my body I thee worship."

The phrase had flashed into his mind, and now he understood its meaning. The civil service Father James had used to marry them hadn't included these traditional Reformed Catholic words, but Randolph said them now as a pledge. He would sacrifice who he was to assure her happiness. He would give until he had nothing more to give.

When she drew her legs up, wrapping them around his backside, pulling him into her body, her response shattered him. "Me too."

His heart exploded with joy and then release hit him, surging through him bright and hot. Her name sprang from deep inside him. "Jen." She shuddered beneath him, sealing herself to him as she came on his cock. He held her in a fierce hug, not wanting to set her free, wishing they could remain as closely connected as this forever. When she stirred, he eased up, dragging his thumb through the tear that slipped down her cheek to her lips, which she'd lifted in a radiant smile.

"You're mine. Truly mine."

The firm pressure of her palm moved up his spine, and she hooked her arm over his shoulder, sinking her fingertips into his skin. "Always."

22

J en knelt in front of the sofa where Sophie held Katrina Estelle Tiernan, Shane and Adrianna's first daughter. Sophie sat stiff with the awkwardness of a young child who had been handed a treasure easily broken. The baby lay peacefully in her arms, wrapped in a white blanket with pink rosebuds.

"You'll make a wonderful big sister when the time comes."

Sophie nodded her head and agreed, although she didn't fully grasp what Jen had said. She was too absorbed in staring into a pair of blue-gray eyes, telling Katrina how pretty she was.

Adrianna, however, had registered the subtext of Jen's statement. Her face alight, she asked, "You and Randolph plan to have children?"

"We do. Sophie needs a brother or sister or two."

Before Adrianna could follow with more questions, the baby let out a distinctive newborn wail, signaling that life had taken a turn for the worse as far as she was concerned. Sophie's eyes grew wide. She looked to Adrianna for help. "What did I do?"

"Nothing, darling. She's hungry. That's the way it is with babies. One minute everything is perfect, and the next they're hungry or wet or just need Mommy." She bent over Sophie and took the infant into her arms. "This time I think she's ready to nurse. I'll feed her, but then I'm putting her down for her nap. Why don't you go find Padraig now? He'll take you to see the horses. Pansy has missed you since you went home to Briarcliff."

Sophie bounced to her feet. "I missed her too." To Jen she asked, "May I?"

"Yes." Jen laughed. The little girl was already on her way out the door.

Adrianna settled into the sofa, flinching when the baby latched on to her nipple and began greedily sucking. "I hope the soreness goes away soon."

"What was it like? Being pregnant, labor, delivery..." Jen was spellbound by the picture of Adrianna nursing her child, a living example of the classic image of the Mother Goddess. There was something of the divine in the tableau. She could understand how worship of the female side of nature would appeal to many people. But it had become too one-sided for Jen, elevating a single aspect of the godhead over all others. She wasn't sure if the Reformed Catholic beliefs of the Meryons were any better. Their god was male, but they did have a mother figure in Mary. Then too, they always described God as Father, Son, and Holy Ghost. It was all a muddle to her.

"It was an incredible experience. There were highs and lows. Discomfort." Adrianna smiled ruefully. "But also a profound sense that Shane and I had created someone unique, who would have her own impact on the universe. And we were waiting to meet her."

Jen slipped onto the corner of the sofa and smiled to herself, relishing that delight that bubbled inside her when she thought about Randolph. "We'll be starting our family soon. We want to spend more time getting to know one another first and allow Sophie to adjust to having an aunt and uncle in her life."

"I don't think I've ever seen Randolph as happy as he is right now. I've always worried that he'd never find the perfect woman. I don't know how you managed it, especially after that court hearing in Cahernamon. He was livid."

The memory of that dreadful day made Jen shiver. "Working that out was...hairy. I never want to go through anything like it again."

Her brows knit together, Adrianna asked, "Did he hurt you?"

"Physically, no." Jen dropped her gaze to her hands. "He broke my heart, but I think that had to happen if he was ever going to change."

When she looked back up, Adrianna was rubbing Katrina's leg and frowning.

"I'm sorry. But what do you mean? He needed to change? I've always thought he was very self-possessed, knowing who he was and what he wanted in life. What did I miss?"

He is so good at making people see what he wants them to see. "You're right. That describes him to a *t*, but…how much do you know about Randolph's past?"

"Shane has shared some with me. They were best friends, Shane, Randolph, and Maon from their days in boarding school. I know that something happened right before they met, not the details, but that it affected Randolph deeply. He struggled with anger issues, keeping his temper under control. I haven't known him long. The only time I saw him furious was with you. He didn't seem like he was about to go berserk."

"No, he didn't go berserk." Her chest aching, Jen hesitated before continuing. "What he did was almost as bad. He was cracking his whip and telling me if he didn't like what I had to say, we were through. He accused me of lying and manipulation, and even though I had valid answers for every question he spewed at me, he refused to believe me."

Adrianna's mouth fell open, and her eyes went wide. "Oh my gods! He interrogated you with his whip?"

"Yes. In the dungeon at Briarcliff with fake corpses on display and rats scurrying in the shadows." Jen winced when Adrianna straightened and her eyes opened farther. It was impossible to tell what had happened without making Randolph look like an ogre.

"He didn't?" Her voice grew stern. "Someone needs to have a word with him." When the baby, sensing her mother's distress, cried, Adrianna patted her bottom.

Jen waved a hand. "No need." When Adrianna didn't appear convinced, Jen said, "No, really. I've already taken care of that. It occurred to me at last, with the things he was saying and how he was behaving toward me, that he had a real problem with women. I called him a misogynist. Not because of his sexual sadism, even though many people think that makes him one. No. He believed all women were untrustworthy, that a man would be a fool to rely on them."

"But—"

"I know." Jen nodded her head. "It wasn't something overt. He was always considerate of women, but he couldn't form a personal bond because it meant opening himself up to eventual betrayal. Every woman he had loved had let him down or turned on him."

Adrianna's expression was a mixture of puzzlement and concern. "How is it I never felt this from him? I'm an empath. Surely I would have noticed something wasn't quite right."

Her hand stretched out to touch Adrianna's arm. "He didn't know it himself. It shocked him to his core. He's not the same man he was before. He's openly affectionate now, not as reserved."

Adrianna nodded. "Reserved. That's a good description of the emotional read I always got on him. And you're right. Now that I think about it, although I still feel that layer of self-control, there's something else there, beyond the happiness that radiates from him."

Jen leaned forward. "So he seems happy to you? I've been worried that I may have broken him."

"Broken him?"

Her cheeks heated. She'd never discussed her sexual tendencies with someone other than Randolph, but Adrianna had graduated from a sex school and established a Dominant/submissive relationship with her husband. If anyone would understand and not judge what Jen was about to share, it would be this woman. "Until a week ago we hadn't been inti-mate since the shooting. It was"—she pressed her lips together for a moment—"the first time he ever truly made love to me."

Her expression soft, Adrianna said, "That's wonderful."

Jen's throat tightened. "It is, but he hasn't pinched, bitten, or spanked me since then. Randolph helped me discover I'm a masochist. I want my sadist back."

"Ah." Adrianna looked thoughtful. "Give him some time. He's prob-ably sorting things out for himself. I doubt you broke him. If he doesn't come around soon, talk to him. You seem to get him better than anyone else ever has."

"You think so?"

"Yep." She focused her gaze on the baby at her breast. "Someone has gone to sleep. Let me put her down for her nap, and then we can see what our men have been up to without us."

~

"Let's go to the hideaway. My dad and I have been celebrating Katrina's birth with a bottle of 100-year-old scotch." Shane led Randolph along the corridor and opened an oak paneled door.

Before stepping inside Randolph said, "This is like a rite of passage. Entry into the hideaway."

Shane chuckled. "That's right. You haven't been to Gleann Millis since you were old enough to be allowed in."

The room was obviously a dedicated masculine space, complete with chesterfield sofa, a matching set of Eames lounge chairs, and a large trophy case displaying the racing cups won by horses from the Tiernan stables. A variety of liquor bottles stood along the back edge of a small bar. Shane opened the one on the end and poured a finger each into NEAT whiskey glasses.

Randolph settled into a chair and accepted the drink from Shane. Once they were both seated, Randolph held up his glass. "To fatherhood. And your beautiful daughter."

His own glass lifted in the air, Shane's face went soft, his smile distant and unfocused. "To fatherhood."

They both sipped and sat in silence, relaxed and at ease. Finally Shane spoke. "You remember Maon's wedding? We were sitting by the pool and talking about how we would never get trapped into marriage? What happened?"

Randolph grunted. "We came to our senses."

"I suppose we did. Maon figured it out before we did." Shane rubbed his chin.

"No. He found the right woman quicker than we did."

"So Jen's the right woman? What changed your mind? You were ready to burn her at the stake as an O'Malley witch. The next thing I hear, she was kidnapped, and you were shot. Sorry I didn't get to Cahernamon to visit you in the hospital. Maon kept us fully briefed."

"Adrianna needed you to hold her hand more than I did." Randolph took another sip of his scotch. "The court date seems like ancient history." He filled Shane in on events since then, concluding by asking, "Was it like that for you? Did you suddenly know that you loved Adrianna?"

"Hmm. Yeah, I did. She was on the Benefactor's ship, and I was jumping rope and realized I'd do anything to get her back and keep her in my life."

"Nothing like life and death to focus the mind," Randolph mused.

"That's it. My heart already knew what it wanted, but my brain was too cluttered to see the truth until it was brutally clarified. So that begs the question. How are you going to handle the Whip Hand? Sophie and Jen are here. You planning to commute?"

Randolph shook his head. "Gods, no. That would never work. I've taken a back seat in daily operations for some time now. Tom will make a reliable general manager. I've already got managers in place in the restaurant and public venue, but I'll need to hire someone for the private club."

"Do you have anyone in mind?"

"No, not yet."

After taking a sip, Shane asked, "What about Trey Johannsen? Adrianna's mentor at the Opio Institute. He's got the skills and knowledge you'd want. He's meticulous, ethical, and has the demeanor to control any situations that might occur."

Randolph furrowed his brow. "You think he'd agree to do it?"

"If you pay him enough. He's given hints to Adrianna that he's not entirely happy at the Opio."

"I'll look into that." Randolph finished his drink and set the glass aside, rubbing a finger along the wooden edge of his chair. "I don't know any other way to ask this, so I'm going to be blunt." He fisted his hand and stared at it. "Do you think I became a sexual sadist because I hated women?"

"What?" Shane rose to one hip and glared at Randolph. "Where the fuck is that coming from? You haven't sucked up the O'Malley drivel, have you?"

Randolph splayed the fingers of the hand he had clenched. "No. Nothing like that. Jen helped me realize that I've had this underlying distrust of all women since I was fourteen. You know what happened then."

"Yeah. Being wary of women is understandable after that. And that doesn't make you a misogynist."

Randolph winced. "Yeah, it does. I've been prejudiced against women my whole life. I didn't hate them. And I treated them fairly as long as my relationship with them remained impersonal. But I never let any woman get truly close to me. Except my mother, and that's a whole nother thing." He waved his hand. "But whether I'm a misogynist isn't the question. Do you think my sexual sadism is a way for me to act out my animus toward women? Would I be what I am today if those events of twenty-one years ago had never happened?" Randolph flicked a glance at Shane to see his friend's face was thoughtful, his eyes dark and serious.

Shane eased back into his chair and hesitated before speaking. "The things that happen to us always impact who we are. At this point it would be impossible to tease out all the reasons behind why you're a sexual sadist. It's a part of who you are. But why now? Why are you worried about what caused you to become a sadist?"

Randolph sighed and dragged a hand down his face. "Because I made such a hash of things with Jen, we agreed after the shooting to start again, but without the sex."

"That must have been rough."

Randolph grimaced. "I'd been shot, so not so much. But eventually, yeah. The night we got the news about the baby was the first time we made love. It was mind-blowing. Totally vanilla but incredible. Since then I've kept my sadistic side bottled up. But it wants to come out and play. I'm afraid if I let go, I'll fall back into my old pattern of thinking. You don't know how hard it's been to change my assumptions. They pop into my brain all the time. And I don't want that mind-set to mess with what I've got going with Jen."

"So you've played with her in the past?"

"Yeah." He smirked. "I gave her a full dose of my proclivities before I'd let her marry me."

"And?"

Randolph fingered the edge of the chair. "It was good. Really good. Part of the reason I thought I could work things out with her." He narrowed his eyes at Shane when his friend snorted.

"This is something you need to discuss with Jen, not me. If she's a masochist, she's going to want more too. It doesn't have to be all or nothing you know. When the moment is right for vanilla, it can be perfect."

"Mmm." Randolph sighed. "Maybe so. I don't want to screw this up."

"If I've learned one thing about marriage, it's that lack of communication is at the heart of most problems." Shane stood and tipped his glass at Randolph. "You want another?"

"Sure. We're celebrating after all. Love, marriage, and babies." Randolph handed Shane his glass.

"You ready for that last one?"

Randolph smiled softly. "You know. I think I am." *Once I straighten out how kink plays into my love life.*

It had taken days for Randolph to come to a decision and then arrive at a plan for reintroducing kink into his relationship with Jen. A change of venue was an important element. He didn't want any part of what had happened in the dungeon at Briarcliff to interfere. A trip to Beta Tau was the perfect solution. He had a lease negotiation to finalize that was best done in person as well as all the arrangements for taking a step back from the day-to-day operations of the Whip Hand. And he had his private playroom.

They'd arrived at the club late in the afternoon. Randolph had told Tom they were not to be disturbed, that he'd deal with business the next morning. Jen was unpacking her suitcases, rearranging closet and dresser storage to create room amid his clothes. Once the luggage was stored, she placed her hands on her hips and looked at him. "Do I get a tour now or later?"

Randolph patted the coverlet next to him. He'd slipped off his shoes and laid down, observing her while she worked. "Come here." She crawled up beside him from the foot of the bed and nestled into his side, resting her head on his shoulder. Her familiar scent had a dual effect of soothing and arousing him. The term *comfort food* had taken on a whole new level of meaning where sugar cookies were concerned. But his sweet vanilla-scented girl had a tart filling you only discovered when you bit into her. He pulled her in tight and kissed her head.

"I'll show you around tomorrow. Tonight we need to discuss a topic we've been ignoring. If it goes well, I've got something planned for my private playroom."

She stroked his chest with her palm. "I think it's time."

He chuckled and ruffled her hair. "Good." His heart rate kicked up a notch. She surely felt it through her hand. "Why did you let me chain you in the dungeon at Briarcliff and threaten you with my whip? I know it wasn't misplaced meek compliance. But I don't know why, with the things I was saying and as menacing as I must have been, you let me place you in such a risky position."

"I've thought about that myself. For one thing, I'm one of those people that doggedly move forward even though turning around would be the obvious response. Call it a character flaw, an insane level of perseverance."

Randolph grunted.

She toyed with the button on his shirt. "Your granddad said something at Penny's internment that stuck with me. You were so angry at Genevieve Kavan, but you never lashed out at her. You let Father James deal with her."

"What did Granddad say?"

"That you'd learned to control your temper."

Randolph put his hand atop Jen's. "To a degree."

She pulled her hand free and rubbed his knuckles. "You never actually struck me with the whip. Intimidated me? Yeah, big time. But I didn't think you'd physically harm me, and...I wanted to prove to you I wasn't lying. I thought if I let you do it your way, the whole mess could be straightened out."

Randolph swallowed hard around the lump in his throat. "It didn't turn out that way though."

"No. But I had to do something."

"Why?" No matter how much he worked to unravel Jen's motivations, the reasons she'd endured his mistreatment eluded him.

Her voice was soft, almost a whisper. "Because I had already fallen in love with you, and I couldn't let you destroy our relationship before it had barely begun."

Pain filled his chest as though his ribs were squeezing inward. He had hurt her beyond anything his whip could inflict, but then the ache dissolved as a sense of lightness overflowed him. That step too far hadn't been taken. Narrowly avoided because her love had met his inability to trust and had proven itself.

"I am so grateful for your love." He buried his face in the top of her head. "Whenever I got in trouble for fighting with my sister, Grandma Meryon used to say love covers a multitude of sins. She'd always insist that when forgiveness was requested, forgiveness should be given. And she didn't put up with continued animosity. Not that she papered over transgressions. She'd tell me never to mess with my sister's art supplies again, but she'd also tell my sister to keep them locked up better." He huffed a laugh. "I was a serial offender. But we weren't to use another's forgiven offense to justify our own mean-spiritedness." He squeezed her in a hug. "You, being the sweet-spirited woman you are, didn't wait for me to discover the error of my ways, but loved me even while I was treating you reprehensibly. I'm so sorry I put you through that."

She slipped her hand up his shirt and into the collar to caress his neck. "You don't have to keep telling me you're sorry. That's past and done."

"I know, but I still feel awful about my actions."

The touch of her fingers soothed him. "Is that why you've kept your sadistic side hidden from me?"

"No. Not exactly." He searched for the words to explain. "I've been trying to decide if my sadism results from my misogynistic thinking or if I would have become one if the events when I was fourteen had never happened." She buried her face in his neck.

"And?" The warmth of her breath accompanied the whisper softness of her voice.

He resisted the urge to get up and pace, squeezing her to him. "I don't know. And at this point in my life I think it's impossible to know. I'm a sexual sadist. Thoughts of causing you pain still arouse me. As much as I enjoy the vanilla side of our relationship, which a year ago I would never have believed you'd hear me say"—he gripped her shoulder—"I want to restart the kinky side of our sex life."

"Me too."

She rose on her elbow and gazed into his eyes. "You're the person who brought my inner masochist to light. I'd never have discovered her if it weren't for you. Offering you my pain turns me on. Especially since I know you'll never harm me, by which I mean you'd never do something I don't want or won't like. I'm free to explore my nature with you, knowing you'll catch me if I fall."

He pulled her to him with a hand around her nape and kissed her, brushing her cheek with his fingers. When the kiss ended, he asked, "Are you afraid of my whip?"

"Sure."

He winced.

"But not any more than I would be of nipple clamps." She cocked her head slightly. "No, more than clamps. It's the not knowing when you're going to strike. Although"—she chuckled—"as I said, you haven't ever touched me with the thing."

He flipped them so she was beneath him, his body pressed into her softness. "Would you like that? To be touched by my whip?"

"Yes, Sir. Very much."

Happy Mr. Evil came roaring back. "We'll have to do something about that." His cock sprang to attention

In the past when he played with subs, he would withhold his kisses, saving them for aftercare. He discovered that he didn't want to play that way anymore. Kissing Jen wasn't a duty but a pleasure. One he wouldn't deny himself. But neither would he be gentle. He took her mouth with all the ferocity he'd been holding back. And she met him, equally fervent in a heady clash of tongues and lips. He pulled her lower lip with his teeth and broke the kiss.

He rolled off her and stood, staring at her and unbuttoning his shirt. Her eyes were awash in the turbulent gray of stormy skies. She brought her hand up, running her fingers into the mass of her ebony hair splayed out on the pillow. A smile flickered on her lips while she watched his hand move from button to button. When his shirt was off and flung on the bed, she gazed at his belt buckle and bit her lip.

He held out his hand. "Come."

Rather than surge from the bed, she rose to sit on the side with languid movements and lifted her hand to take his like a princess accepting her due. She enthralled him even as she tested his restraint. When her fingers settled over his, he tugged her up and straight into his arms. He nuzzled his lips at her ear. "You'll pay for that." She shivered.

Although it wrenched his whole being, he pulled away and took her hand. Side by side they sedately walked to the playroom, not speaking or smiling but occasionally glancing at each other, her eyes full of avid intensity. At the entrance he swung the door open and gestured for her to enter.

CURIOSITY HAD BEEN BUILDING in Jen since she'd learned Randolph had a private playroom. She'd imagined a space big enough for him to use a whip. Lots of leather in red or black. Chains hanging from the ceiling. She wasn't prepared for what he revealed.

The room was spacious, a large square with a smooth deep brown floor and off-white walls with built-in cupboards and hideaways. In the center on a circular raised platform, a cream-colored leather bench stood. It wasn't in the least intimidating. If she didn't know the room's purpose, she'd have said it wasn't at all kinky, but she'd spotted the cuffs attached to one end of the bench. She swallowed, greedy for the play to begin.

He waited for her to absorb what she saw, holding her hand, saying nothing. When she at last turned her gaze back to him, it struck her. This man didn't need a room built with the intent to alarm those he brought here. The menacing danger came with him.

This room showcased the man who stood next to her, his eyes full of such wicked possibilities it took her breath away. He was like his whip, functionally beautiful, quiescent seeming, but with the ability to strike out with speed in the hands of a master. And he was the master of his own body, his muscles coiled and waiting. Energy pulsed from him even while he stood motionless.

Passion, already blossoming inside her, exploded in ravenous need. She wanted to slide her fingers over his taut skin, to pluck at a nipple, and then follow her ministrations with her tongue, teasing and tasting. But she wasn't free to indulge her erotic impulses. He was in charge, and he'd promised to gratify her hunger for pain. How long would he wait?

Her answer came the next instant when he released her hand. "Take your clothes off."

She complied, removing her clothing at the same leisurely pace they had already established, dropping each item to the floor, allowing the tension to build. When she finished, she faced him, arms at her side, her fingers tingling. He cupped her breast, and she sighed. *Pinch my nipple.* And he did, twisting it hard. She bounced with a squeak and grinned.

His voice husky, he said, "Tonight will be intimate. You, me, and the whip." He fondled her other breast. The wait for him to assault its nipple was excruciating. "I have plenty of other means to torture you, but we agreed to get to know one another. That extends to our kinky sides, too. My whip and I are going to learn your body." Then he tweaked instead of squeezing hard, keeping her off-balance.

He led her up the platform to the bench. "Kneel at this end and lie facedown."

She complied, the leather cool against her torso and the floor hard against her knees. Coaxing was not required. He'd sharpened her appetite. She wanted this with her whole being, wanted him taking her in whatever way stirred his sadistic side to arise, to torment her until she was mindless with suffering for his pleasure. And when he'd had his fill, the ache in her pussy would be satisfied just as he'd quenched the pain in her heart with his love. She'd never been enough for anyone, but for him she was more than enough.

"Grasp the rods by the cuffs." The metal bands clicked into place around her wrists. His hand, warm and solid, stroked down her spine, caressing her bottom. He placed a tender kiss on her shoulder. A shiver ran through her. If he didn't move faster, she'd be begging soon.

He knelt beside her, swiping a strand of hair out of her eyes and behind her ear. "You are so beautiful, bound, stretched before me. The most arousing sight I've ever seen because it's you, my love, awaiting the kiss and sting of my whip. We'll take it slow. I don't know if you'll like the whip. You may hate it, but I do know you'll be fucking erotic writhing each time it strikes. Are you ready?"

"Yes, Sir."

"Call me master in this place."

"Yes, Master."

"What's your safe word?"

"Red."

He stood and walked from her line of sight. A cupboard opened and shut. Her heart was hammering. Would his whip feel like being snapped by a towel? It had to be worse because physics dictated it must be. The crack of the whip happened because it was moving faster than the speed of sound. It was going to hurt. She couldn't wait.

Her reverie was interrupted by an explosive *snap* sounding to the right of the bench. She jumped as far as the cuffs allowed her to and then fell back, her eyes squeezed tight. She pressed her lips together at his chuckle. Him and his mind fucks.

The next crack struck her dead center on her right ass cheek while she was still fuming. And it hurt. More than a towel snap. But the deliciously twisted side of her reveled in it. A zing had gone straight to her clit. Her body's reaction had been completely out of her control. Her leg had jerked up and twisted to escape the source of the stinging pain. At the same time her nipples loved being dragged on the leather bench. One kiss from his whip and she was panting, wanting more.

His voice seemed to thunder in the room. "If you want another, get back in position."

Say no more. He didn't have to tell her twice. Gripping the handholds tight, she was determined to stay still with the next hit. The strike to her left cheek resulted in the same futile thrashing of her leg, but her arousal ratcheted up a notch. She quickly scrambled into place. He followed with two more snaps to each cheek.

"I can't wait to chain your arms overhead and make you dance. The way you're swinging your ass is delectable."

Then he cracked the whip to the left of the bench, and her body responded as though she'd felt it hit her, writhing to escape. His evil laughter floated over her. She curtailed her leg spasm when he popped a strike to the right of her head. Instead she flinched left and then growled and spit a curse at him. "Bastard."

"You're welcome."

The heat of his hand on her bottom was a balm, at the same time more sparks rocketed to her clit when he slid across the tender spots he'd created. "Had enough? I don't want to wear you out. You're getting quite a workout." He knelt beside her, his face expressing he was in full-on Happy Mr. Evil mode.

"Can't wait to fuck me, can you?" She smirked at him.

"Oh, kitten." He wiped at tears she hadn't been aware were trickling down her cheek. "You didn't just challenge me, did you?"

"Do you feel challenged?"

"Gods, I love you! A few more then." The devious intensity of his smile thrilled her.

By the time he'd finished his few more, she was limp, her head floating in subspace and her body wrapped in a haze of pain and arousal. And then he was behind her, his hands firmly locked on her hips and his cock penetrating her in one deep thrust. "Oh gods!"

"No, Master."

The giggle that bubbled inside her was obliterated by the feeling of his erection plunging back to her core. His fingers were clamped with bruising force on her as he moved in and out at a frenzied pace, slapping against her tender bottom. Her breathing was as ragged as his. A pinpoint, brilliant and enticing, was just out of reach. Every muscle in her body was taut, straining.

He slid a hand between her and the bench, slipping it down until he found her clit, and then he pinched it. Pleasure burst inside her zipping along every nerve ending until she was quivering from its force. Then he pinched her again, and another spasm of delight, not as strong but still heavenly, slipped through her.

He ground against her once, twice more. "Fuck!" His body pressed against her, pinning her beneath his weight, and his cock slammed home, filling her with the hot, sticky liquid of his release. He lay over her for a minute or more before finally slipping out of her and lifting onto his knees. She sucked in a deep breath and then melted into the bench. She was his now, his in every way.

His hands stroked her hips and back. His lips brushed whispering strokes over the marks he'd made on her bottom. All the while he murmured words of love and appreciation.

At last he stood and pulled her up, lifting her in his arms. The trip to the bathroom was quick. Warm water rained down on her from multiple showerheads positioned in one corner of the room. A variety of handholds and a seat with a very interesting design made it clear that kinky sex was a definite possibility here as well. She tipped her head back, allowing him to shampoo her hair, not sure whether he ever used soap or continued using shampoo, smoothing silky foam over her breasts and between her legs. She absorbed the indulgence.

Once she was rinsed, he turned her in his arms and kissed her thoroughly, the heat building between them again. He broke away and rested his forehead to hers.

"What would I do without you? I didn't think I'd ever feel for someone like I do for you." He pulled back and took her face between his hands, gazing deeply into her eyes. "You are everything I need. Never doubt that. I love you as my wife, as the masochist to my sadist, and as the woman who saved me from myself. I didn't realize that our shared kink would elevate what we have. What just happened between us is like nothing I've ever experienced. There was a connection, different and amazing."

She smiled. "That's love. It's going to take us places we only hoped existed before. You're it for me too."

"I love you, Jen Meryon," he said and then scooped her up and headed for the bedroom.

"Wait, we're still wet."

"No time. I need you now."

His cock, tapping against her bottom as he carried her, was a testament to that. She laughed in delight, weightless in his arms and giddy knowing that she was a new woman. No longer an O'Malley, she was a Meryon. She was his. And best of all, the most infamous sadist on Tallav was hers.

Discover more of Cailin's sci-fi romance on her website at
https://cailinbriste.com
Subscribe to her newsletters for monthly updates on her releases, sales, and events.
https://cailinbriste.com/cailins-newsletter-sign-up/

Read on for an excerpt from *Trey: Son of Tallav* book #4 in this series.

TREY: SON OF TALLAV EXCERPT

It hadn't occurred to Trey that LS *Quantum* and Beta Tau were two sides of the same coin. Sure, LS *Quantum* was a spaceship, and Beta Tau was a planet. But he'd read the LS *Quantum's* brochures, and in every other respect they were the same large, climate-controlled settings designed to provide trendsetting pleasure venues to paying customers and entertainment for all ages and palates, including his own kinky tastes.

The insight came when a middle-aged woman eased alongside him, brushing her shoulder against his and asking if he was headed to the LS *Quantum* and if so, where his cabin was located on the ship. Her skimpy halter, skintight slacks, and the bright pink hair she was sporting did nothing to enhance her appeal.

This was Beta Tau all over. The glare he aimed at her didn't force her to step back. *Good gods! I'd be at* Quantum's *shuttle service gate if Patsy O'Shaughnessy hadn't insisted on meeting me here.* He scanned the customers of the bland space station lounge. *No. Still on my own.*

An expert at fending off tourists on Beta Tau, he'd offer to take them to the club, tie them up, and use a bullwhip on them. Most scurried away. He handed anyone who accepted his proposition over to staff at the club.

Bondage was part of his personal kink, but he preferred to use a flogger. The whip was the specialty of the Whip Hand's owner, Randolph Meryon, Trey's boss.

The neon-haired tourist ran a finger down his upper arm. "Maybe we could get together on board? I've heard bald men are really good in bed."

He dropped his gaze to where she'd touched him.

The woman tittered.

Eyes narrowed, he leveled his full focus on her. "Sure. If you're into knife play, I might be able accommodate you. I'd have to ask my girlfriend. She's the one who does the cutting." He followed his words with a feral grin.

The tourist turned pale. "No thanks." She scuttled back to her friends who'd been watching the exchange. Wide-eyed, they left the lounge, several looking back over their shoulders to get another glance at him.

He settled in to wait with a grimace that ought to fend off other flirtatious females.

This wasn't a vacation, and he wasn't a tourist.

Nor was he on his way to *Quantum*, away from his normal haunts on Beta Tau, to indulge in BDSM.

No, he had undertaken this two-week-long trek in his capacity as the Whip Hand's private club manager. Rand had hired a young woman to open and run a new venue on Beta Tau based on the Cosmic Cabaret, one of the famous attractions on LS *Quantum*. After getting firsthand experience of the cabaret's shows, Trey was to provide his BDSM expertise to tailor O'Shaughnessy's plans.

Crazy idea. At least I didn't have to travel economy class and spend my nights in a sleep tube. Rand had paid for a cabin that, although small, had allowed Trey to escape most human interaction for the two weeks he'd been aboard the space liner, sleeping, reading, meditating, and sleeping some more. Perhaps his reintroduction into the hum and clatter of humanity after his break had him on edge.

No perhaps about it. He was ready to bellow at the entire spaceport to shut up. Life would be so much better if half the population were fitted with ball gags.

Here he was, per Ms. O'Shaughnessy's request, and she was not to be found.

He eyeballed the entrance, considering whether he should head over to the gate to wait for his shuttle, when a shock of color came flying into the lounge. The slender woman, dressed in a bright, grass-green sleeveless blouse and short skirt, skidded to a halt. Splashed across her face was a wide grin as brilliant as the lime green that tipped the ends of her copper hair. She was looking straight at him. This must be Patsy O'Shaughnessy. Waving, she headed for him.

"Hi. Sorry I'm late. Ya wouldn't believe the crush of folks leavin' *Quantum* today. I'm Patsy. Trey Johansson. Right? Mr. Meryon sent your picture, so I recognized ya. Although I don't expect there's many men that look quite like ya."

Trey inserted a few words into her verbal onslaught when she paused for breath. "Yes. I am."

"I'm excited to meet ya. And to work with ya. I have so many plans I can't wait to share. Our shuttle back to *Q*—that's LS *Quantum* for short— boards in about fifteen minutes. We have time for a quick drink if ya'd like, or we could head to the gate. I could use a drink. Dashin' around." She waved her hand in the air. "I'm so thirsty now. I'm gettin' an orange fizzy. What would ya like?"

Pleasant expression on her face, Patsy waited for a response.

"Oh, uh. Sure, I'll have what you're having."

"Be right back." She twirled and headed toward the bar.

Wow. That accent sounded Irish. And not Tallavan faux Irish. Light complexion, freckles, copper hair, wearing green...stereotype, sure, but damn, if she wasn't Irish, he'd eat a whole pan of fried blood pudding. Something he hadn't tasted in a long time. Fried eggs, tomatoes, white-and-black pudding. A full Irish breakfast like his mother made better than any other cook on Tallav. He missed his folks and his mother's cooking, but Tallav would never be his home. Even if he'd been a member of the aristocracy, he would have left the Tallavan matriarchy in the dust as he had the moment he was of age.

"Here ya go." Patsy handed him a large disposable cup and took a long drink from her own. "Ah. That was what I needed. I had cobwebs in my throat."

Trey tipped his cup back and swallowed three gulps of the sweet orange liquid and remembered why he never drank fizzies. The carbonation bubbled up his nose. He pinched his nostrils, squinched his eyes shut, and waited for the burn to abate.

"Got fizz up your nose, did ya? Ya should drink more slowly if ya can't handle the sparkly. I never have a problem. My whole system's plumbed with synthsteel."

Was this slip of a girl offering him advice as though he were some— "My delicate feckin' nose thanks ya for the interest in its well-bein'."

Blue eyes aglow, she leaned toward him. "Think nothin' of it. *An féidir leat labhairt le haon Gealic chun dul leis sin blas na hÉireann?*"

Sarcasm was lost on Patsy O'Shaughnessy. "It's not an Irish accent. I'm from Tallav, which was infected with a fanatic love of all things from the Emerald Isle when the planet was founded. I never had the time to learn Gaelic, but many Tallavans do."

"Standard it is then. We have somethin' in common. I'm proper Irish. *Erin go Bragh.* 'Tis a pity ya don't speak Gaelic. I don't get to speak it this far from home. Oh, goodness. We need to head over to the gate. Our shuttle will be boardin' soon."

On the way out of the lounge, Trey dumped his fizzie in the trash receptacle. Patsy was ahead of him by a couple of strides, so he had a full view of the subtle twitch her ass made while she walked. *Nice.* From her employment records he had gleaned that she was thirty years old, although she looked younger. That fell within his range, five years either side of his own age, for women he would date. But Patsy O'Shaughnessy was off-limits despite her engaging effervescence. This was a business relationship. For the next two-and-a-half weeks, they'd be working together. Besides, whether or not she'd kissed the Blarney Stone, the woman could talk. By the end of a day spent with her, he'd need to escape to his own room. Plus he didn't do vanilla. Patsy wasn't bland, but neither did she scream kinky despite her association with Cosmic Cabaret and now Randolph and the Whip Hand.

Still, he could look. He'd never been drawn to big-busted women, but a tight bottom was a delight to behold. And touch. Squeeze. Slap. He heaved a sigh. Too bad. He'd already plastered a don't-touch sign across her miniskirted bum.

～

Trey Johansson was every bit as good-looking and well-built as Patsy expected. But she hadn't been prepared for the sheer size of the man. He towered over her. And muscles! Her fingers wouldn't reach around his biceps.

She'd researched Randolph Meryon's home planet, Tallav, to prepare for her job interview. It was a surprise to learn that Trey, or Master Trey as he was called at the Whip Hand, was also from Tallav. He was a BDSM master. A tingle flittered the length of her spine. He'd been sent to gain firsthand knowledge of the Cosmic Cabaret to help her with reinterpreting it for a BDSM venue.

The name hadn't been chosen yet. Her preference was to include *cabaret*. Beyond that she hadn't come up with anything catchy if Rand asked for her advice. Trey's other task ought to assist with that. He was to teach her about BDSM. How he would approach that was the big question. Would he want to initiate her into the BDSM lifestyle or only explain the different aspects of kink and fetish? How far should she let him go if he wanted to make his lessons more real?

A quick glance over her shoulder assured her every inch of the giant with piercing deep brown eyes was following her to the shuttle gate. *Oh my gosh, he's checking out my ass.* Her cheeks heated. Why oh why did she have to have pale skin that showed even the slightest blush? Why couldn't she have been born with dark amber skin like the delectable man behind her? *Pull it together, girl. It's a guy thing. Their eyes are naturally drawn to tits and ass.*

An announcement stated boarding for their shuttle flight would commence in five minutes. Inside the gate seating area, Patsy turned to face Trey. "We have a few more minutes. Shall we sit, and ya can double-check that your bags have been loaded."

Trey pulled a hand-comm from his pants pocket, held it to his ear, and made the call to the automated baggage handling system. After assuring the comm was off, he put it away.

"Ya use a hand-comm? Ya don't see many people that do. I'd probably lose one, so my internal comm is a true blessin'. I don't know how people lived in the past without an EBC. All my data is there at the tip of my thoughts. I was told everyone received nanite injections to build their internal server when they were infants."

"I'm not a fan of tech. I like to keep things simple."

Trey Johansson was even more intriguing than she'd imagined. "So ya don't have an EBC. Where do ya store information? How do ya know when someone is tryin' to contact ya? Goodness. How do ya exist without bein' able to connect with governmental systems? Bankin' systems? Will there be a problem boardin'?" *Why hadn't he or Mr. Meryon told her this?*

"Stop." Trey narrowed his eyes and raised his hand. "Stop. Let me answer one question at a time." In the pause that followed, Trey raised an eyebrow.

Oh, he wants me to acknowledge him. "Yes. Understood."

A flush of pleasure went through her when he smiled. "Good girl. I have an EBC. Every child on Tallav receives one. I use it when necessary. My work-related data is kept on servers like most of yours is. You access it through your EBC. I use a vidscreen." He patted his pocket. "My hand-comm signals me when I have a message. It tracks callers, just like your internal comm. I don't like cluttering my mind. It destroys inner peace."

He dropped his chin and looked at her as though he were expecting her to say something. But for a change she kept quiet. Her thoughts were bustling with everything she had learned about this man. That *good girl* was patronizing but so very BDSM master–like, especially coming from a hunk of handsome with a voice like smooth dark chocolate. She'd liked it. File that away for future reference on female reactions to Doms.

Into the lapse in conversation Trey said, "My luggage is loaded."

"Oh, good. We're all set then."

Silence dropped between them again. Patsy was relieved when the gate announcer gave them the go-ahead to board. Behind her, Trey placed his palm on her lower back, guiding her through the other passengers who were standing and collecting their carry-on bags. The instant his hand spanned her back, its warmth and size made the hairs on her arms rise. *Please let the feckin' man offer me hands-on BDSM lessons.* She'd kill to see him naked, but it had to be his idea, his suggestion. This job was the break she'd been waiting on, and she wouldn't botch it by coming on to a fellow employee.

On board, they found their seats and were settling in when a group of ladies, one with neon-pink hair, passed them. Each one stared at Trey and then Patsy as they hugged the far side of the aisle as closely as possible and scooted by. The woman in back nudged her companion to hurry when Patsy smiled politely at them.

Trey grunted. Patsy turned to look at him. He had a pleased smirk on his face.

"Do ya know them? They looked like they'd seen a ghost and were runnin' for water."

"No."

He continued to grin, but Patsy didn't see what was funny. His next statement didn't clear things up.

"They must not favor green."

"Afraid of green. That's not after bein' a real phobia."

"It is. Prasinophobia. Fear of the color green."

"That's a funny thing to know. You're not afraid of green, are ya?"

"Would I be sitting here if I were?" He pointedly trailed his gaze over her. "One class at the Opio Institute where I worked covered the use of fear by sadists. You can make someone fear any color if you condition them to it."

The Opio Institute. That was the sex school where he'd trained dominants and submissives. "Doesn't sound like fun to me."

Trey chuckled. "I didn't figure you for a sadist."

"Er." The man had a way of throwing her off stride.

"It wouldn't be fun for me either. But fear of color can be used by a sexual sadist to get a satisfying response from his play partner."

"Remind me to stay away from sexual sadists."

Another chuckle. "It's going to be difficult avoiding your new boss."

Patsy blushed and furrowed her brow. "I forgot he's one of those."

Trey's expression became enigmatic. "Don't worry. You'd have to play with him to experience that side of his personality."

Sweet mother Mary. I'll not head that direction. "I'll be dead and my ashes scattered before that happens."

Heated intensity bloomed in Trey's gaze. "Good."

Oh Lord, I'm in for it now.

Purchase Trey: Son of Tallav, Book #4
https://books2read.com/trey

ALSO BY CAILIN

A Thief in Love Suspense Romance Series

It Takes a Cat Burglar

How to Steal the Pharaoh's Jewels

A Touch of Greed

Sons of Tallav

Shane: Marshal of Tallav

Maon: Marshal of Tallav

Rand: Son of Tallav

Trey: Son of Tallav

ABOUT CAILIN BRISTE

Cailin Briste is a USA Today Bestselling author who writes erotic, science fiction, suspense, and fantasy romance. She and her husband are vagabonds, living in an RV named Floyd pulled by a beautiful monster of a truck, Fiona.

Her Sons of Tallav series is set in a sector of Federation space far off the beaten path. The Tallavan marshals are tasked with keeping the peace while coming to terms with the matriarchal system of their home planet, Tallav. Tricky because each is heavily involved in the BDSM lifestyle.

A Thief in Love Suspense Romance series, begins with a cat burglar who steals priceless art and antiquities from other thieves. Sebastian is a Robin Hood character whose Maid Marion is his equal on the rooftops of their futuristic city. Each book in the series focuses on a member of his crew.

The Guardians of the Vale series, starting with *A Prince of Her Own*, will be published sometime in the future.

Subscribe to her newsletter at http://cailinbriste.com/cailins-newsletter-sign-up/ for information about her latest releases, exclusive giveaways, and special prices.